In Good Conscience

Cat Gardiner

The Conscience Series, Book 3

Editor: Kristi Rawley, Periplus Editing
Cover Design: Jane Dixon

Series "Operation" References

Denial of Conscience
Operation Samba: Yungas Valley, Bolivia
Operation Virginia Reel: Virginia, USA
Operation Mambo: Cuba
Operation Kazatsky: Russia
Operation Cancan: Monte Carlo, Seville, Marrakesh

Without a Conscience
Operation Macarena: Peru, Paris, Moscow
Operation Viennese Waltz: Sierra Leone, Austria
Operation Two-Step: Texas, USA
Operation Shag: South Carolina, USA

In Good Conscience
Operation Gombey: Bermuda
Operation Merengue: Dominican Republic
Operation Zeybek: Turkey
Off-book Operation Black Ice: Panama, Bolivia, Peru, Paraguay, Cadiz, Venice, Prague

"Revenge should have no bounds."
~*Hamlet*, William Shakespeare

Prologue

July 22
Virginia

A t three in the morning, under the cover of wicked winds and torrential rain, the sniper had climbed over the fifteen-foot centuries-old perimeter wall, slipped past the guards, and avoided the security trail cameras within the thick forest. Like a deadly Diamondback, he'd advanced in a modified, measured Army crawl using his tight abdomen in conjunction with his moving knees and feet, modeled after the silent stalking of a lethal pit viper as it sized-up its prey before striking.

Each push and pull of his body moved him along the muddy ground covered by decayed leaves afforded precious moments in selecting his hide high above. Using specially designed spiked shoes he had made for tree climbing, he had silently scaled 50 feet up a massive oak with his rifle slung below the leaf and bark-covered ghillie camo covering his body. His hands and feet acted as claws until he settled on a sturdy branch. In all, it had taken him four hours from wall to hide site.

Taking minute movements over thirty minutes, he slowly made sure the rifle's bipod legs were firm upon the bark, ready to take his first shot when appropriate.

That was 40 hours ago, two long, wet days spent watching and waiting for the perfect moment to execute his kill shots, but his specific target was never alone in the house, which was a requirement to this hired-gun mission; his on-again, off-again employer had paid him well for following instructions. The woman must be alone; it was part of the plan.

Loyalty was paid in spades, as was betrayal or defiance. He knew his employer's bent toward evil, having freelanced for him in South America, Italy, and Pakistan through contacts in the rogue element of the CIA as well as the gun-for-hire classifieds site on the dark web. Failure was never an option with this guy. If a mission went to hell, he knew there was another contract-killer right behind to take *him* out. All for a price, all without a conscience. He also knew he was expendable but also held onto his credo that fidelity was as negotiable as the compensation for it. For the right price, he could change his loyalty on a dime.

Although glad to be back in the United States after a long mission, the current conditions were too much like an Amazon rainforest— which proved to be both a boon and a curse. A boon because the sentries guarding the perimeter of this estate had been handicapped by the ferocity of weather, and a curse because it made for a water-slogged camo suit that weighed him down like a wet, smelly blanket.

Today, Sunday, at zero six hundred hours, a much-needed break to his situation came with dawn: sunrise in a cloudless sky. Stilled in his hidden perch, his dark brown eye continued to focus through the rifle scope's crosshair. The rising sun infused shades of russet and gold through the abundant green leaves surrounding him. The weather had cooled from the hurricane-like storm to an eerie fog that clung to the grazing fields beyond the tree-line. He was sure that since the weather cleared, his target's husband would bolt. No man worth his balls—especially one who had an isolated career—could withstand that amount of couple-togetherness without wanting to blow his brains out, even if the sex was awesome.

His mind traveled to some of the more advantageous aspects of this assignment: namely, the perfection of his hide, which possessed a clear view of the entire estate grounds *and* his target through the canopy. His target?—a smokin' hot brunette with long legs and curves that could make any man go insane. Her peaches and cream perfection had been exposed for his lustful libido through his rifle optic fixed toward the back of the house. From his bird's-eye view, he could see everything that happened within the bedroom, the kitchen, the bath, and the sunroom on the first floor. The two occupants passed the rainy days going at it hot and heavy, which was another boon to this op. She was a wild ride in the sack; watching her was an absolute turn-on and made the last, miserable 40 hours nearly tolerable. But damn, he could do nothing to alleviate his predicament, frozen on his stomach as he was.

His image-intensifying night scope came in handy, particularly since the woman's ivory visage was exaggerated in the green low-light when her lover—a stone-cold killer he knew by reputation alone—seduced her, again. Surprisingly, the old dude could go for a hell of a lot longer than he could and she'd responded with equal appetite. The intense eroticism was enough to make any interloper green with jealousy, then red with desire.

Yeah, sure it was a damn shame the woman had to die in the overblown manner devised for her, but—coming full circle in his thoughts—he'd promised loyalty in executing this mission. That's what contract killers did until the job was done. He and another—a girl, he heard—were specifically chosen as the harbingers of war and destruction in his employer's plot: the physical, emotional, and mental obliteration of his enemy. This pseudo-psychological warfare revenge crap was payback and meant to unleash all unholy hell. He, with his sharpshooting specialty rifle rounds, and she, with her bomb-making expertise.

He had a better suggestion—though he'd not voice it: kill the enemy outright with one bullet to the brain, take the target, and alleviate his own physically pressing need. But no, his contract boss got off on the credo: "Revenge was a dish best served cold." The maniacal fucker had been very patient in the knowledge that ice thaws in time. A peaceful hiatus was known to lull a man into a false sense of security, as proven once already with this challenging nemesis. Fury also made a man weak. Blinded by rage and revenge, the enemy would act carelessly until finally facing his own death. The woman's death was meant to torment him. Whatever. Surely, this bad ass son of a bitch wouldn't be affected by any woman's death. Rumor had it he was cold and ferocious.

A flash of brilliant red passed before the scope, landing only a foot from where he lay. A cardinal's tiny scarlet and black head turned in the sunlight, then hopped onto the camouflaged barrel, which looked to be part of the branch. The bird's annoying chirping was like Chinese water torture. But he could not react. Instead, he imagined just reaching out and crushing it within his hand.

Below him, a guard's heavy boots squished the water-slogged leaves on the forest bed. Apart from his holstered side arm and the rifle slung over his shoulder, he wore tactical gear, a bullet-proof vest, and a black baseball cap. Over the last two days, he'd observed about a half-dozen more like him: hard-boiled, idealistic "white hats" all cut from the same mold: American military contractors, just like he was. For a short time, he was once Army, until his BCD (bad conduct discharge.) No worries, he took his skills and sold them to the highest bidder (that had always been the plan.) At only 23 years old, he prided himself on having become sought after. Very few hired guns, could snipe—on the fly—with a mega rifle like a .50 caliber and a handful of specially made High Explosive Incendiary bullets with such successful accuracy at a target range outside 2,000 meters. This assignment would be cake. The forest was only 150 meters from his objective.

"All clear on the southern perimeter," the dude spoke into his comms. "Copy. Is he taking the Spider? ... Right. So, she's staying? ... Copy. Let Dixon know and have the Hummer ready. Send Lennox back here to cover. Over."

The guard made a brief sweep of the canopy, but the sniper was well-hidden, undetectable to even the best of the best. He then proceeded to the tree line and across the pasture toward the horse stable.

Technically, he could pick them off one at a time from his perch: the guard below him, the rifleman on the guard house roof, the sentry in the west field, the ranch hand at the stable. But where was the fun in that? He liked when things unexpectedly exploded into a million flaming pieces.

Just as he'd figured—after getting sexed up, the target's lover was making his getaway. His legendary reputation as one callous, bad-ass, mo-fo was confirmed by that very act of love-'em-and-leave-'em once he had his fill and the weather cleared.

As for him, it was back to waiting and watching for the red Ferrari within his view to leave with only one passenger. In the interim, he'd spend the rest of the morning imagining how his target could feel below him before all hell burned down around her.

***

"Good morning, sleepy head," Fitzwilliam Darcy whispered into his wife's ear. He almost hated to wake her, but he'd not leave the house without doing so. Just a single kiss to Liz's temple could never suffice.

"Hmm ... is it that time, already?"

He sat beside her on the rumpled bed. "Yeah. I won't be gone too long."

Rolling to her back, she looked so ravishing in the diffused early light. Her long hair was splayed across the pillow in an alluring mess. She stretched, raising her hand through the tangles, baring her porcelain décolletage when the bed linen shifted. "Oh, I slept sooo good ... when we finally fell back to sleep. What an incredible night."

"It was. Great meal, good movie, *fabulous* wine, and the company wasn't too shabby either."

"That's not what I meant, and you know it, wise guy. It's what you and your *Chironius carinatus* did with said company that was so great. All the rest was very effective foreplay."

"Yeah ... that was all right, too," he dispassionately teased, with a shrug.

"(Snort) Bulldinkey."

She was right; it was *quite* a night, and this morning he felt like he could conquer the world. The rain had finally stopped, his libido was satiated, and his heart was bursting from looking at her, just from recalling their emotional lovemaking. What more could a man ask for? Well, truth be told, a few things, but those were dark thoughts and had no place at Pemberley on this incredible morning.

Liz chuckled then reached up, tugging his polo shirt to bring his lips down to meet hers. "Don't be long, honey," she whispered before kissing him. Her pliable, soft mouth against his was the perfect sensation in which to begin a day.

"What will you do while I'm gone this morning?"

"I'll probably sit in the greenhouse and check on my new addition. But first I think I'll hit the punching bag before breakfast. I remarkably have a ton of energy humming through my body this morning."

"I wonder why."

She yawned and stretched again. "Has it stopped raining?"

"It has."

Distracted with seduction in mind, her fingers brushed over the tribal armband tattoo around his bicep. "Maybe ... you can be late? Rick will understand."

"I'm sorry, babe. As much as I'd love a repeat of last night, I gotta go. I'm already running late, and you know how annoyingly fastidious Rick is about schedules."

Of course, he'd like nothing better than to stay, but he'd made an unbreakable commitment to his cousin. Coffee and conversation at their usual haunt: Tryst café, inside the Beltway. Rick had something important to discuss, and he was assuming it had to do with unfinished Obsidian "business." Given that he and Liz were enjoying their secluded summer of baby-making while planning a four-week-long vacation in celebration of their first wedding anniversary, he freely admitted that he'd been dragging his feet about leaving Leesburg to going after Sanchez-Morales, otherwise known to them as Diablo. No doubt, his cousin was going to put the pressure on him, give him an earful about going soft. The man presumed that after two and a half months, the Iceman was a melted puddle. Hardly. Just because he wasn't "actively" going after Diablo—didn't mean that he hadn't been busy making plans.

AC/DC was back on his playlist and, physically, he was as buff as the Iceman of old. Daily rifle practicing and teaching Liz Fairbairn's gutter fighting, as well as knife throwing, had consumed them both. His kill-shot was as accurate as ever and he now added pistol acumen to his skill-set. Pre-dawn laps on par with his SEAL training were part of his daily regimen. Further, as almost a necessity, apart from his demonstrative romantic side, which only his wife was witness to, he was back to being one grumpy bastard and damn proud of it!

"I didn't mean you should be late so we can have sex, Fitzwilliam. Sheesh. I meant, stay for breakfast with me," she corrected with an index finger poke to the snake tat on his forearm.

"Breakfast, sex—same thing."

He lifted her fingers to his lips followed by a kiss to each knuckle in tiny pecks. "We'll have lunch together … I promise. Then you and I will go at it on the mats for a real work out, followed by a bike ride."

"Sounds perfect!" Her excited grin reached her hazel eyes.

"Liz, if you need anything, call Dixon; he's in the guardhouse this morning. And before you command me … yes, Higgins is coming with me."

"I'll be fine, Fitzwilliam." Sitting up, she stretched again, dragging the back of her hand up her neck.

Still, he was worried—he always worried—had never stopped silently worrying about Lakmé's safety since Operation Macarena wrapped up in Moscow in late April. He couldn't be her bodyguard every minute of the day. But until he was ready to go after Morales, he'd damned-well make sure that someone would have her back in his absence. Their head of security, Dixon, a 58 year-old crusty Marine— and a deadly son of a bitch when he needed to be—had eyes in the back of his head. Apart from the entire lethal team at Obsidian, he was one of only a few he'd entrust Liz's personal protection to. And, of course, it had to be from a distance or she'd go ballistic on them all. Sure, she could handle herself, but she had a long way to go before being on-par with Caroline's skills. Further, smothering her was something he fought hard against following their dangerous trip to Paris and Moscow and her admonishment of him. Covert protection was tantamount in keeping his marriage conflict-free. He'd learned at least *that* much.

Standing over her, he brushed his finger down her cheek. "Just let Dixon know where you'll be. Please … for me."

"Yes, darling," she placated with a hint of sarcasm, clearly feeling the loss of absolute freedom.

"I know it seems like I'm smothering you, but I'd feel better if you kept him in the loop since the Reynoldses are in Texas for the month."

Smiling, which he knew was fake, she said, "Whatever you think is best."

He knew she was lying, too, but bent, giving her a peck on the lips. "Then I think a Metallica playlist for your workout on the speed bag is best."

"Pfft. Heavy metal? Totally not gonna happen. I think a Haydn allegro is best, thankyouverymuch."

In a flash, she threw back the blankets and rose, promptly snaking her arms around his neck and gifting him with the most provocative kiss. Of course, he couldn't help gliding his hand down her nude form, from soft back to supple bottom.

"Have a good time with Rick, sexy," she said with a pat to his cheek. "Give him my love," she added, sliding her hand down his torso.

"You are a tease."

"Yup!"

In typical Liz fashion, she sauntered to the bathroom with a playful exaggerated sway to her backside, that little heart tattoo tempting him, as if her kiss hadn't been enough to entice him.

"Love you!" she called after him.

"Ditto. Hey, Liz?"

She stopped and turned to him with a sweet smile.

"It's not gonna be like this forever," he said.

"No? Not this happy?"

"Not that … it's not gonna be as confining, ya' know. We'll have our freedom back soon."

"I trust you, and if I ever have any doubt I just think of my hero on the day you tackled me to the ground at my sham wedding. I didn't trust you then—but you proved me wrong. I trust you implicitly."

"I don't know about hero."

"Sure you do … don't you remember how the news nicknamed you 'Hero of the Bride?' "

"You don't need any bullshit newscast to affirm to you that I'd die for you, and I don't need to remind myself that if I did get killed then you'd be free of this mess."

She laughed uneasily turning from him to enter the bathroom with a joke. "Let's hope it doesn't come to that because that-so called freedom means I'd have to enter the dating rat race again."

"That's it? That's all I mean to you? Savage woman."

Her head peeked out from around the door frame. "No, babe. You also make a mean omelet. That's why I wanted you to join me for breakfast."

He laughed.

Ten minutes later, sliding his new driving gloves on, he walked to the Ferrari then took a deep breath of the fresh morning air. Salaam, Mallika, Kalendar Prince, and Elektra played in the west field and the University of Virginia's ponies grazed in the east field. The rising sun kissed the vibrant green grass, breaking through the rising haze of thick mist and odd chill in the air for a mid-summer morning.

Invigorating. Perfect. Sublime. All fitted how he felt this morning. Liz's good humor had fueled the air with a freshness despite the fact that they'd been ostensibly living like they were under house arrest. Her smile made everything right.

Behind him, Nick Higgins, another battlefield warrior he trusted Liz with, sat waiting in the H2. Not that he needed a security detail to accompany him wherever he went, but it did make *Liz* happy until this whole nightmare could be put behind them once and for all. And Higgins was one talented marksman, not to mention an intimidating presence at 6' 4" of brawn. The man had come to be his right-hand these last three months.

He gave Higgins a wave, turned the key to the Spider, then tapped his favorite album designated for when he was in the mood for maximum overdrive. Just so she could hear it through closed windows, he raised the volume of Metallica's "Enter Sandman" as the sportscar burned rubber down the long drive.

As a precaution, when he reached Pemberley's gate, he called Dixon.

"Good mornin', Mr. D," the older guy cheerfully greeted.

"Good morning. I bet you're glad for some sun."

"We sure are. Me and the boys were feelin' a bit hog tied, but we managed to keep those drones in the air despite the wind. What we couldn't cover with them, we covered on foot even in the rain."

"I never doubted that you guys would remain diligent."

"How can I help ya', sir?"

"I'm not sure if Liz will call you, but she plans on working out this morning. I don't think she'll go riding on the estate, but she may spend some time in the greenhouse until I get home. I just want—"

"I understand, no need to explain and ya' have my word not to tell her you called me."

"You know her well."

"It's my job to anticipate her … um … spontaneity."

"You mean impulsiveness. It's okay, you can say it."

The guy just chuckled.

"Thanks, Dixon. Thanks for all you do for her, for me."

"Always, Mr. Darcy. Mrs. D is my number one priority in and outside of Pemberley."

"I know, and that's all I ask. The key word is always … even if something were to happen to me."

"No worries there, sir."

He clicked off the phone then raised the volume to the next song. Yes, today was gonna be a fabulous day!

***

Tick, tock …

The sniper watched the Ferrari peel out, heavy metal music blasting out the windows. Personally, he preferred kick-ass country, true country boy that he was. His eye remained focused through the rifle scope on the receding tail lights as it gunned toward the entrance gate, followed by a custom—hot off the assembly line—Hummer H2. Iceman had finally left the woman. All the horses grazed, which was good because he liked horses. He'd wait until Darcy was far enough away to not know what hit him in his absence.

Then he saw her pass through the sunroom—hair pulled into a ponytail, workout leggings and a snug-fitting white tank top—before disappearing from his view.

There was no rush; he had the time or perhaps, he was just giving her time that she didn't have on her side. Call it mercy for having the greatest tits he'd ever laid eyes on.

After fifteen minutes, he heard a faint sound, like a chopper, growing louder as it came toward him, and his eye blinked in the scope spotting one of the sentries bolt from the tree line along the west field, running at a clip. Another burst from the area of the green house, heading toward the mansion; a third flew out of the guard house, also barreling full tilt to where the woman was. Had he been made?

The noise from the chopper blades filled the air around him, and he slowly shifted his gaze to the left. Facing him dead-on through the leaves was a UAC quadrotor aerial drone, stilled eye-to-eye with him. Damn. He'd been made.

As if the tree had come to life, he laughed, raising an arm and flipping the bird to the person manning the recon helicopter from most likely the guardhouse. He had zero worries of his face being made. Apart from the slits in his mask, he was completely covered, right down to the high tech colored contact lenses he wore.

Two heavily-armed goons ran across the field toward him. The sharp shooter, located on the barracks roof, tried to pick him off with a measly .22 caliber rifle, but to no avail. To even the most observant eye, he was part of the tree, covered in leaves.

He braced himself behind the .50 cal when gunfire rained down on the forest from every direction, hitting the ground and the trees, hoping to make contact with him. Hundreds of rounds pummeled around his hide site.

"You'll never make it to her or me, suckers. It's time to kick some rich ass," he said before taking a deep breath, willing his heart rate to lower, and then exhaling. He pulled the trigger. With one of the fastest fingers in the business, he quickly fired off three rounds packed with C-4 and zirconium explosives from the semi-automatic demi-god.

The first round bulleted through the trees, over the field, and into the horse stables.

Boom!

The wood detonated into a fiery geyser at least one-hundred feet into the air, as the hay caught fire.

Boom!

The next burst the greenhouse into flames; glass and wood incinerated on contact.

Boom!

Finally, the security guardhouse blew with a fireball explosion, immediately dropping the drone to the ground.

He'd saved the two best and most powerful incendiary thermite rounds for last. These were not easy to extinguish. He fired into the not-entirely hidden gas line attached to the brick exterior of the house, followed by one to the propane tank in the outside kitchen.

BOOM!

The ground shook when the multi-million-dollar mansion exploded into a towering inferno of red and orange, blowing brick and stone into smithereens like an atomic blast. No one could have possibly survived. Pity.

In under six seconds, the entire estate named Pemberley had been leveled—set aflame.

Billowing black smoke and raging fire rose in the air from each building.

And so it began … Diablo's hell had cometh to the Iceman.

Fire versus Ice.

1

Girl Power

July 31
Bermuda

Jane Bennet adjusted the pink bubble sunglasses she wore as they snapped photographs of Charlie's dangling legs one-hundred feet above her. An index finger swipe over the lens zoomed in on his backside, squeezed by the harness and beautifully back dropped by the rainbow-colored parasail canopy above him. It was the best way she knew to kill time. Right now, she needed speed and was growing impatient sitting behind the wheel of a boat creeping northeast along the Bermuda coastline at a pitiful 10 mph. It was sheer torture. Like her sister, she was meant for going fast.

Sure, the aquamarine water and the pink sandy beaches were stunning, and the hot sun felt incredible against her tanned body, but she hoped she'd be doing more than catching rays on this scouting mission for Operation Gombey. Certainly more than just driving, monitoring the tow line, or taking "tourist" photographs of watercraft and the shoreline to her left.

Boooring.

Where was the fun? Where were the bad guys and the chance to use some of those gadgets she had lifted from her job at the spy museum or, better yet, her new "skills?" She surmised that part-time employment with Obsidian meant part-time investment in ops.

She would like to at least learn how to work the miniature drone Charlie was maneuvering from up there. From his elevation, and the high-tech bat drone's distance threshold, he was able to see the entire "suspected" Sanchez-Morales compound in detail. Nicknamed "Batman," the Army's small prototype drone for covert surveillance and grenade bombing was silent and with wings instead of propellers; it was the perfect ruse. Not that Charlie actually needed to be up in the air, but he had an itch to go parasailing and stated it could give him a bird's eye view.

From her position on the boat, she couldn't see the vast estate hidden behind a twenty-foot wall covered by lush green foliage, but that little gadget and its aerial view was sending vital information back lickety-split to Rick in DC.

As the boat slowly pulled the cloud hopper, the water's rhythmic lapping against the hull caused her thoughts to drift to her sister, then her internal chastisement over desiring sun and fun of the dangerous kind. What did Lizzy have? Nothing. Her blood boiled, and she fought back the tears that always came when she gave thought to what happened in Leesburg ten days ago.

I want revenge! It's been two days of recon. Where the hell are these La Muerta Mundial cartel drug trafficking a-holes?! That's it! No more sweet Jane Bennet. Vengeance for her sister was paramount—and speed—but mostly retaliatory vengeance.

Tapping her iPhone, she located one of her favorite contemporary pop songs, which evoked happy memories of growing up at Longbourn and how they would put on dance shows to early Britney Spears for their parents. Her sister had zero hip-hop rhythm even as a child, but that never mattered. They still had fun. In fact, those were the times worth remembering—when their mother was still around, enjoying motherhood and her daughters. Music was a happy distraction, filling the house and drowning out Frances's rantings to a husband who wasn't listening anyway.

"This one's for you, sissy. In memory of good times, let's 'Shake It Off,'" she almost blubbered when the song began. Taylor Swift took over her body and her bare feet shuffle danced in the cockpit, executing her best spin moves and running man slides—bouncing the boat and ignoring that Charlie and his tow line were also feeling the crazy beat.

Now, she was having fun. Yeah, Lizzy would be laughing at her and then say something about how she and Iceman's tango could beat her club dance moves in a dance-off. She glanced up at Charlie. *He* had moves! His hip hop rocked almost as awesome as his hip thrusts!

From the corner of her eye, a sleek, black cruiser headed toward them; the red and orange flames painted on the bow seemed to burn as the powerboat skated across the green water, lifting above the waves. It was the second time this afternoon that she'd seen it going in the opposite direction from before, but this time it was closer. The boat passed, creating a choppy upsurge that pitched their little ski boat. "*Infierno*," she whispered, repeating the name on the hull. Instantly, she stopped her hip thrusts and quickly took a few piccies of the stern, making sure to zoom in on the name and the men within. One of the guys on board turned around and waved at her, barely catching her in the act, not that he would have known her sunglasses were a spy gadget! What was a girl to do, acting as a tourist, but truthfully an undercover agent for a government-sanctioned assassin organization? What would Caroline do? She would flash a million-watt smile—and Jane did exactly that.

The cruiser turned around to come about starboard side.

"Shit." Her pulse raced as the two occupants drew closer. Again, she glanced up to Charlie—her happy feet suddenly feeling not so eager to dance but the music continued to blare.

Baring leering smiles, the two men pulled beside the boat. Definitely sexy—and definitely armed. The shorter, slenderer of the two, hot as he was, had a creepy smile and wore a shoulder-holstered pistol below his armpit, and the other looked so hard that she could see his six pack below his tropical wet suit. He wore his black hair pulled into a ponytail and his smile was devastatingly seductive. Leaning onto the transom, Hardbody spoke with an accent. "Are you having fun, *señorita?*"

Before looking up to Charlie she touched the temple arm of her sunglasses again, replying in a trademark flirty voice. "Oh yes! And as soon as he's done hogging the parasail, I'll be up there. But I won't be going this slow; you can bet on that!" Of course, she giggled. She could hear Caroline's advice in the back of her mind. *"When faced with a lusting foe—male or female—work what you have. Your femininity and your assets are your greatest weapons. Your sister learned that in Paris."* She didn't know if they were enemies, but the lusting part was there—like super creepily, too. Further, the connection was too great to ignore: One was clearly Hispanic, and she and Charlie were here in Paget to scout a South American drug lord's compound at the coastline from where they were. Was that too much of a stretch? Were these guys patrolling the shoreline close to the estate's perimeter or securing the cartel's drug trafficking to and from the island?

Two sets of eyes raked down her trim form, desire noticeably settling on her new boobs spilling from the neon pink bikini top she wore. Before going in for surgery, she considered that D cups would be the perfect weapon. Looks like she was correct. Arching her back slightly, in a shameless move, she made good use of her career investment, keeping the guys' attention occupied away from Crash as he drifted behind and above them with the remote control.

The engines chugged as the two boats slowly split the water side-by-side. Jane pointed and remarked with a playful hint of innuendo to the black combat shotgun lying across the seat between them. "That's a mighty big gun you have there." *Hmm, a twenty-round magazine.*

"It is for fishing."

"Wow. I don't think they'll be much left of any fish after that shoots them." *In fact, that Russian Saiga Taktika is so damned bad ass, it's used by most private security companies in Russia.* Charlie had taught her that last month.

"Are you two handsome guys Bermudian police?"

They looked at each other and laughed.

"So, you won't report us for not using a proper parasail boat, right?" She leaned forward, striking a pleading—yet teasing—pose: one hand grasping the railing, the other taking a few more photos with her sunglasses. "It's just, ya' know, for us tourists, $150.00 for thirty minutes in the air is a total rip off."

"We won't say a word."

As expected, dark eyes, again, locked onto her chest when she leaned forward. Hardbody's interest in her was hardly subtle. She wouldn't have been surprised if he jumped into her boat; she just smiled and fanned her neck with her hand, working what she had. "The sun is hot today. You must be dying in that black suit."

As shamelessly as she, he sat upright and unzipped the sleek suit, revealing a firm, hairless chest. Speaking of fish—holy mackerel! A year ago she would have reeled him in ... but now she had to throw him back. Her heart and fidelity lay with Charlie now. Still, her chin unconsciously dropped when the guy shimmied the wetsuit to his waist.

That tattoo on his forearm gave her internal shivers; she had seen images of it in intelligence briefings. The black spider was the mark of Morales's dead Russian lover—the one who had the hots for Lizzy and tried to seduce her with a riding crop. *Holy shit! This guy once worked for Nadya Karakut.*

Pink sunglasses snapped away.

The other guy, she nicknamed Creepy Hottie, lit a joint followed by a deep inhale; the sucking sound snapped her from her fascination with the ink. Almost immediately upon exhale the salt air filled with a cloud of sweet-smelling marijuana.

"I guess that answers my question about you guys being cops," she laughed, promptly shaking her head when he held the cigarette out to her. They obviously didn't care that pot was highly illegal or that the island heavily enforced strict gun control laws. But, if they were cartel thugs then they were above the law. Hell, the law was probably on the take!

"You are very beautiful," Hardbody complimented. "I like American women."

"Thank you!" she gleefully responded fanning her hand through her salt-tangled locks. "Where are you guys from?"

"He is from London. I am from Lima."

Peru! Further confirmation. *That's where Operation Macarena was. That's where they'd kidnapped Rick!*

Thankfully, Charlie's voice came over on the radio. "Yo, Pussy Galore, stop flirting down there and pick up the speed."

The men looked at each other with a smirk when Charlie teased her using the borrowed 007 chic name. It had become a running joke between them.

"That's my cue, fellas. I'm outta here."

"Don't go yet. Leave your friend up there; we want to party, and he will get in the way."

"Sorry, guys when he says 'speed,' I just gotta fly. Thanks anyway."

Hardbody reached out, tightly grabbing her wrist. "I don't think so."

"Aw, shugga, as sexy as you are ..." she whispered, "I have a herpes outbreak right now."

He quickly let go as if she was hot coal.

With a smile, she gazed up to her lover and waved; he motioned down to her to go faster when they changed their location so he could go higher. Man, if only she could be up there with him. But who'd drive the boat and glean all the information she did in this short conversation?

"*Hasta la vista!*" she brightly shouted gunning the throttle, leaving them in her wake. Her blonde hair blew back, and Charlie lifted high above her when the wind caught them both. Behind the ski boat, a trail of foamy white spread on the aquamarine sea as she flew in the direction of Hungry Bay. Finally satisfying her need for high-velocity, she yelled, "This is for you, Lizzy," into the air, turning the throttle even more.

"*Infierno*" blew by them and was gone from sight within seconds, but she knew it wasn't the last they'd see of the patrol boat.

"Okay, hold up here and cut the engine," Charlie shouted over the comms. "Keep a lookout for Batman in a few minutes, then I'm going deep. Pull in the canopy when I'm gone."

She did as he said, feeling euphoric that she might have actual intel to share with him and waited patiently for the drone to finish its recon work.

"Lookout for sharks," she cautioned having seen a few fins earlier and not quite sure if they were porpoise or not.

"Will do!"

It was back to being bored, but she spent the time admiring the mangrove trees that grew along the shoreline, but she didn't need to wait long before the little bat dropped onto the deck.

Looking up again, she shielded her eyes and gave Charlie a thumb up.

"Here comes the remote."

The waterproof drone control and screen slid down the tow line, landing right next to Batman. Charlie gave her a wide wave, placed his portable oxygen respirator into his mouth, slid his goggles down, and a second later released his harness from the canopy. He plunged into the cool Atlantic like a bullet and was gone with hardly a splash.

Never one for manual labor, she sort of resented having to pull in the parasail. Fighting wind, water, and the heavy fabric heavy was bound to break a nail. Oh well, this was what she wished for; she was Obsidian now and had to pull her weight on every assignment. They'd be returning home tomorrow, and she'd be back at the museum until the next op Charlie needed her to come along.

Ten minutes later with aching arms, she leaned back in the pilot's chair, propped her legs up on the dash and resumed waiting behind pink bubble sunglasses. Singing to the music, she wished that Lizzy could be here. These high-tech spy glasses were really hers, hard-earned in Paris. Back home, on the houseboat, she had her store-bought ones that connected to her personal social media photo archive. Shame her father didn't think to capitalize on his invention commercially. He could have made a legit million and not have sold his soul for the dough by treason.

***

Assassinations had never been this Peruvian girl's career goal; she just fell into it when her ex-lover got involved in the drug business.

She liked playing around with guns and was a good shot, but explosives were what gave her a thrill. Not that she had any proper schooling in bomb-making, but that's what online videos were for. One can get anything online, and what she couldn't find on the internet, she could access via the dark web.

Some other *sicarios* and *cruzadors* working for La Muerta Mundial were jealous of her skill-set, which just came naturally. She was a petite woman, and possessed a few things that most of the men lacked: brains, feminine allure, and an inside track to stardom within the cartel. This mission was her turn to shine, sticking it to all those guys back home when she proved successful.

The Dupont area of Washington was busy during the hot summer afternoon, and no one would take notice of her in the tattoo parlor. Her manner of dress was as eclectic as the music and people in this neighborhood. Her cocoa brown skin and the blue streaks in her black hair looked like any other denizen or building's colorful graffiti art. Her style was as funky as her tats and unique as her accent. She fit right in … except *her* phone was a bomb detonator.

"How long will you be visiting the district, Claudia?" the tattoo artist asked, completing the outline of an Incan sun on her ankle.

"I will stay week more, maybe go on tour of government Capitol tomorrow."

"That's cool. So, you're having fun?"

"Yes, there is much to do. I like Washington; the people are very nice."

The alarm clock in her burner phone vibrated from her pocket. "I check my text," she said waiting for the artist to lift the needle from her skin before she removed the phone. "How much longer do you think tattoo takes?"

"Hmm … maybe about another fifteen minutes."

"Good. I have meet-up with friend at 3:00."

"No prob. I'm almost done, just a couple of fill-ins and then cleanup and bandage."

Clients' attention stayed distracted downward on their mobile devices and artists focused on the needles in their hands. Such was the very convenient way of operating out in the open these days. Incan-inspired artistry continued on her calf with pleasant small talk while she set the timer to the rooftop explosive, which she'd beautifully concealed in the air conditioning unit's compressor across the street.

"All done!"

"I like very much. I like that you add red flames," she said thinking of how they were so appropriate now that she was part of Diablo's worldwide family. Internally, she braced herself because in three minutes, the entire block was about to feel the ground shake.

Perfectly timed following a healthy layer of antibacterial ointment and a bandage …

BOOM!

In the chaos, she slipped out the back door with a smile on her face, scattering the wiped-clean pieces of the phone down the alley as she made her way to the street corner for a taxi.

***

"Hey, Sarah, your contact in Bermuda was spot on. The location in Paget is definitely the place," Rick Fitzwilliam said into his secure speaker phone as Batman the drone's images came over Obsidian's private server designed by their IT, Jack-of-all-trades, Quartermaster-esque gadget guru, Thomas Bennet.

"I'll be right down. I have some good news, too."

From behind his desk in the newly installed hidden workspace, he gazed up at the four monitors above him, eyes narrowing in his examination of the details from the intel that Charlie was sending on Operation Gombey's recon mission.

Like most of DC's seedy, interconnected tunnel system that ran below the district, this location was safe from the Five Eyes, other prying international ones, or any domestic letter agency or crime syndicate. Further, it was both away from—and connected to—the Bingley Dance School. Above stairs a respected Italian specialty grocer, Prospect Salumeria, gave Obsidian the cover and protection they sought.

Once a Cazzatto Compagnia Mafia front for racketeering, and other nefarious activities, the grocer concealed a cavernous office behind four subterranean meat lockers. This space became Obsidian's new headquarters, the new epicenter for intel gathering and it was directly accessible through a narrow passage up into the dance studio on the next street over. Here he was safe—and so were Obsidian's operations in what had been most likely a speakeasy during Prohibition. He paid handsomely for the luxury rental, proving that old contacts on the shadier side of contract killing could be beneficial, especially when they shared an enemy. Not every Italian wise-guy liked dealing with South American drug kingpins. It was a matter of power—trafficking vs. support—and the remaining non-Cosa Nostra syndicate bosses still operating in America wanted control of it all. The old-school, old-timers sympathetic to Obsidian's situation also wanted Sanchez-Morales dead—or at the very least out of the American drug trafficking business. Even the Cazzatto Compagnia branch controlling Northern Italy had contracts with La Muerta Mundial, and although their agreements with the late Lord of the Jungle had been amicable, they were not as such with his son—the new kingpin.

This place was perfect. After what happened to him in Peru, and to Darcy and Liz in Moscow, Rick hadn't taken any chances on inadvertently exposing the school should he have been compromised upon his arrival back home. Within days, he'd made arrangements to secure this location. Pemberley's destruction over a week ago proved that Diablo had eyes on the street—on them.

His girlfriend of almost three months entered the chilled room via the hidden door in the plaster and lath leading up to the supply closet in the dance studio. Strains of a cha-cha-cha breached into the room lined with metal desks, television monitors, and several old-fashioned cork peg boards for important visuals that he wanted on hand. He liked everything clean and clutter-free, intel housed digitally, but images staring him down helped to fuel the fire.

Sarah's breath misted in the cool air when she spoke in proper Queen's English. "I don't know how you withstand the temperature," followed by a kiss to his welcoming lips. "You're almost frozen."

"I like it in here. There's a sense of warmth that comes from knowing that this place is hidden, and that no infrared, satellite, or spying eyes can breach the cold steel. Our server and identities within Obsidian are well protected."

"Quite; it also helps when it's 35 Celsius outside," she replied, glancing up at the center monitor. "Wow. The mansion in Bermuda is just as Leonards described. That little drone does a bang-up job."

"Here's the image of the underwater cavern where they're smuggling drugs through narco submersibles. It's the perfect entrance."

"Is that Hungry Bay? How on earth did Charlie get through the mangroves?"

"Yeah, he's pretty amazing. We're lucky to have him on our team." He glanced up to her rosy cheeks bending over him, chilled from the 58-degree temperature. "Just as we're lucky to have you onboard."

"Tell that to your ex-girlfriend. Now I understand why you all refer to her as a spitting cobra. For the one-hundredth time … These feet. Do. Not. Dance."

"I'm sorry about her. It's not about dancing; that's for sure. Hell, I don't even dance, and it's not even about me, per se. It's about her inability to deal with rejection and replacement."

"And so soon, too. I suppose her ego is getting the better of her."

"It is."

"While I didn't expect that we'd get on, I did at least expect her civility."

"I'll talk with her if you'd like. We're a team and, I agree, can't have this discord, especially now."

"I fancy I can handle myself. I survived kidnapping in the Amazon; I'm not afraid of her," she smiled, and he couldn't help gazing into her blueberry-colored eyes filled with humor. Her down-to-earth manner and pretty face coupled with her intelligence and unique wit, not to mention her excellent intel gathering capabilities made her a perfect fit for him and his romance-challenged history.

"I hope she doesn't cause you to re-think our relationship and the arrangement we made."

"Definitely not, no itchy feet on my part. Both Jane and well … Liz … certainly have made up for Caroline's cool welcome. I'm not going anywhere."

Hmm. What about his *welcome?*

Clearing his throat, he broke the awkward tension. "What's your good news?" he asked with a pensive smile.

"We located another home for Morales!"

"You're kidding. Where?"

"An associate at the *London Times*—a ... um ... friend—continued with my exposé on drug trafficking into England. I cautioned him off the investigation, but after Peru, he felt that the story was too hot—too fresh—for him to let go of. His enquiries with a source in the Royal Navy led him to Panama."

"Makes sense. Under Noriega, Panama was a hotbed of trafficking in a cozy relationship with Escobar's Medellin cartel, and now it's a hotbed for money laundering."

"Indeed. We may have a solid lead here. If only Morales can stay in one place long enough to get eyes on him." She walked to the titanium box resting at the edge of his desk and absently ran her hand over the cover, silently pausing with a furrowed brow. It was no secret how upset she was about Leesburg—and Liz. Her gaze fixed on the photograph pegged in the center of one of his information boards. Taken by the drone of the sharpshooter who got away after raining fire down upon their family, it was there to remind him that not just Diablo would meet his death on Operation Gombey. The sniper's masked face and ghillie-suited body was haunting, his cold and blank dark eyes barely visible through the narrow slits of the mask were menacing, but they had to find him first, which right now seemed an impossible endeavor considering that biometric scans had failed in identifying him.

"Thank goodness for the drone's internal memory card," she said. "Any word on the ballistics?"

"Let's just say the locals are either stalling or they're backlogged. I'm guessing forensics stumbled upon military grade thermite—that would explain both their holding back information and the fact that the fire department couldn't extinguish the mansion. Don't worry ... we'll get him and Diablo."

"How ... What's going to happen now? You know ... in Bermuda?"

"Well, Charlie's making the final assessment and arrangements and we'll have a go-plan for Operation Gombey in 72 hours."

"A kill shot, you mean?"

"Thus far, our target is not in residence, but Bermuda is a good place to start—rattle his cage a bit, let him know that Iceman has finally taken his challenge and is coming for him just like he wanted."

"I am surprised that Darcy has waited this long; he was gutted."

"Believe me, it's been a struggle, but surprise and preparation are our best advantage. He's using the time wisely by planning his counterattack. " 'He will win who, prepared himself, waits to take the enemy unprepared'."

"*The Art of War*," she voiced with surprise.

"Yes. In my experience, only a fool would knowingly provoke Darcy's ire and now Morales is entirely unprepared for what the Iceman will unleash. My cousin is assessing the target's package."

"Package?"

"What the enemy values most."

"Hmm. I recall all too well the destruction he and Knightley brought with them into Peru."

"That was child's play, just your run-of-the-mill extraction. However, with that said, if Morales *does* show in Paget—it's the end of the road for him."

"Good. I want him to pay for you, me, Julia Bertram, and Liz." She opened the cover of the box and removed one of the Electro Magnetic Pulse pistols that Bennet had created for them. "Will your cousin need this?"

Chuckling, he rose then removed the Glock from her hand, placing it back in its case. "No. Darcy may be a deadly marksman, but he's going to employ his SEAL training on this one: underwater demolition, and, if necessary, his hands. He's going old school."

"You sound like you feel bad for Morales."

"Not in the least. Make no mistake—I want him to pay as miserably as possible. What he doesn't know is that no man has loved a

27

woman more than my cousin loves Liz. Diablo struck at the wrong man's heart. There are dark places hidden in Darcy's soul, scarring born from traumatic experiences in his youth. Nothing—not the military, his sister, or I could keep him from entering those places. But Liz, that's a different story ... there's no stopping Iceman now. His anger is like a man on fire."

She looked up at him with an odd expression, as if frightened or disbelieving—or was it something else?—perhaps a question of whether he loved her like that. Loved her with every fiber of his being, with every breath, loved her enough to die and kill for her without second thought, only acting on the impulsive thundering of his heart as it ripped from his chest?

Did he love Sarah like that? He'd have to search his heart for that answer. Heck, he wasn't sure if she even had those feelings for him. Sure, he'd die for any man or woman; it was the Marine in him, but would intense love be the reason? He was the best at failed relationships, not everlasting ones. "What is that look?"

"Nothing ... just ... a woman is fortunate to be loved that much by her partner," she shrugged with a thoughtful smile and an uncomfortable few seconds of silence passed between them until the fruit of Jane's bubble sunglasses snapped them from their musings.

They turned to view the images as they flashed onto a screen above them: Jane's suntanned selfie, Charlie's legs, Charlie's backside, the ocean, pink glitter toenail polish.

"It looks like Jane is having a lovely time," Sarah laughed, but he didn't reply.

The next few images were different angles of a boat straight outta hell. "*Infierno*. I'll contact Leonards about the boat," she said.

"Do these guys look familiar?"

"No, but the bloke on the left is quite a bobby dazzler."

He elbowed her before pressing a few keys on his laptop. On two other screens, their faces went through international and domestic facial recognition tracking, examining the smallest details of their face with lightning speed. It would take some time, but hopefully they'd get a hit.

Two additional photos scrolled onto the monitor. "Well, well, well. Look what we have here," Rick said.

"What is it?"

He zoomed in on the guy's forearm. "This spider tat … he must have been one of Nadya Karakurt's *soldados*. More than likely he's working exclusively for Morales since Knightley killed her in Moscow."

"Bloody hell."

"Yeah, what is it with these gangs and cartels?—they give themselves away with their friggin' tattoos."

Heavy metal "I Stand Alone," ringtone rang out and he answered without greeting. "I was just talking about you."

Knightley's usual blasé attitude was replaced by concern. "Hey, we have a huge problem."

"A missed step in the merengue? Or are we talking a blown Achilles?"

"I haven't left for my dance lesson yet. This is a major blowout. Switch on the local news."

He glanced at Sarah. This couldn't be good; the last time he got bad news over the television was witnessing Darcy jump into a hail of bullets to protect the daughter of Operation Virginia Reel's target. Now that was a cluster-fuck.

Replacing the image of *Infierno* on the monitor, the newscast popped up. A blonde reporter stood below the corner street sign of U Street & 12th Street NW, speaking into a microphone. "Witnesses in the tattoo parlor and the pizza shop across the street from the residence say the explosion happened around 2:15 this afternoon. Authorities suspect it may have been a faulty gas line, but the bomb squad is already here given that magnitude of the explosion. Right now, there are no confirmed casualties, but the residence in question has been obliterated. Peter, it's going to take some time before the fire marshal and the Metro police can get in there with bomb sniffing dogs to assess the cause of the explosion."

"Do they suspect home grown terror, something along the lines of the Chelsea bombing in New York City last year?"

"It's too early in the investigation to say what caused the blast but sources have indicated that the FBI will be brought in on this. Witnesses say it shook the ground, and as you can see behind me, the glass in the pizza shop was completely blown out ..."

The camera zoomed out from the reporter to the street view: the fire engines, bomb truck, the pizza shop—the burning remnants of the building in question—a building he knew all too well. Their safehouse.

"Ho ... ly shit," Rick said into the phone, stunned. "Were you there?"

"I was a half a block away. I had just left through the alley after getting my dance gear. Man, thank God I dodged that bullet. The place leveled and I would have been all over U Street."

"Blimey, that's ..." Sarah said, mouth dropping open.

"Yes it is," he replied over his shoulder.

Yeah. This was a double code black situation. Diablo blew the safehouse ... and since when did Mr. Clean give a crap whether he lived or died?

"Effective immediately, we're terminating your lessons in the merengue and switching your syllabus to the gombey."

"I thought you didn't think I was ready for the gombey."

"Well, our semi-retired master instructor had specifically suggested your suitability, but I've just reconsidered my reservations. I think, given your talent, the gombey may be right up your alley."

"I sorta liked the moves of the merengue."

"I understand, but our upcoming dance showcase is going to be an explosive hit and we need all our talented students. I'll contact the instructor and let him know that his program is a go, so please come to the studio tomorrow afternoon at your usual appointment to learn the initial moves."

Tapping off the call, he turned to Sarah. "I'm sorry, Sarah, I have to call Darcy and send him these images from Bermuda and apprise him of what happened in Dupont. Please excuse me."

"Sure. Will you be coming home for supper?"

He smiled. *Home.* "You're a good sport, just going with the flow from the safehouse to my house in Maryland and now, for safety, my aunt's guest house in Virginia, but I promise to make it all up to you, love."

"So, you'll be the chef tonight?"

"Yeah. I'll cook."

She turned to the door and he called after her. "Hey, that friend of yours with the *Times*. I don't need to know what he was to you, but—"

"Don't you trust me?"

His lip twitched as he walked to her. Standing only inches apart, their eyes read the other's. Yes he trusted her. She smiled softly before his lips met hers.

2

Haunted

Late, July 31
North Carolina

Lifting the rocks glass filled with Jack Daniels to his lips, Darcy's stare fixed to the licking flames in the stone fireplace as the wind outside the restored farmhouse howled with ferocity. Such was North Carolina's Black Mountain Range—the nighttime temperature was unpredictable even in the summer. Tonight, felt like fall had come early. Under other circumstances, he might enjoy being back in the home where he had lived with his sister before marrying Liz, but things were different now. Being here was only a matter of necessity.

In the amber-infused darkness, he sat in his much-missed leather club chair, fighting dark thoughts as they drifted down into the abyss of his soul. They'd haunted every second of every hour since July 22. He had died that day and only after seven heart-gutting hours of absolute despair, his heart had begun to beat again. He shuddered at the recollection of what had caused him to cry. No, not cry—sob.

Like every night since, he'd replayed the morning of the explosions over and again in his mind, taunting him, destroying him. The memory of it was part of his blood now—the pain something he held onto as it created a monster straddling love and hate, trapped in perpetual battle as the need for revenge consumed him.

"Stay the course," his cousin had cautioned. "Do not, I repeat, do not go after him yet. We need to be smart about this. I know you're hurting, but leave it to Obsidian to get you solid—clean—intel. I've got both Sarah and Charlie working on it as we speak. So be ready to go when I green light the op."

"To hell with that," was the impulsive, emotional reply the first time Rick told him to stand down on the day after the explosion, but the expert tactician was right. Beating Diablo at his own game was essential: *"He will win who knows when to fight and when not to fight"* was tantamount in the *Art of War*, a warfare stratagem his cousin had recently begun to study. Haste would only cause him to fail, just as they all had in Operation Macarena. If the SEALs had taught him anything it was not to run to his death. Further, his cousin was unbendable in his own planning of the op.

"I want Knightley on this, too," Darcy had insisted

"No. He's on another mission. Charlie has your back as we originally planned."

After today's call from Rick, he was finally given the go order: Bermuda. So tonight, his focus pinpointed like a laser on the diabolical plan formed months ago but was now taken to an entirely new level over the last sleepless ten nights. Like *The Count of Monte Cristo*, he'd planned his revenge right down to the smallest detail. It wouldn't be long now before Diablo was stripped of all he held dear right before his eyes—destroyed one after the other—until meeting his demise.

Silently, he wondered if his "at the ready" sentry was causing him to lose his mind. The only other time he'd functioned and survived on so little sleep was during SEAL training, but he was a decade younger, conditioned for mental and physical depravity. With Obsidian, he routinely endured sleep deprivation for a *few* days at a time, not a dozen. But breaking down was essential to getting to Iceman—the Black Op stone-cold sniper turned assassin. Admittedly, this descent into darkness was a transformation that, like a snake shedding its skin, needed to take place. He was in dire need of a haircut and a shave, but that was for civilized men. He was well on his way to becoming uncivilized.

Each day, he functioned only on two hours of light sleep even though the house near Asheville could not be any more secure. But he'd believed that of Pemberley, too. Only this secluded refuge was entirely structured for under-the-radar/off-the-grid living, perfect for the life of an assassin, and barely inconvenient for any "connected" occupant. Georgiana and Justin vacated it for Southern California after they married; they wanted to live in the world, not isolated from it. Of course, when they learned of his purported "CIA career" they understood why seclusion was necessary for him.

Here there was no footprint in anything: no cable, no trackable mobile phones, no internet access via traditional means, and definitely no social media. "Clouds" were in the sky, and "Smart" was something he needed to be when going after his enemy. All communications were non-GPS satellite fed. Deep in the mountains, the house had every creature comfort needed, including a store house of food and an old root cellar stocked to last well over a year. Water was spring fed into a deep well and an old-fashioned water tower was used for non-potable. Cash was king for anything essential that they didn't have, but the most important part, in his opinion, was that the house was ostensibly invisible from the air. Thanks to the revolutionary mirrored rooftop solar panels that reflected the forest, it still generated enough electricity for 3,000 square feet.

He fought the closing pull of his eyes by taking another deep drink. Maybe this one would erase the film from playing before his mind's eye. With crystal clarity, he could still see himself receiving the phone call on speaker in the Ferrari from Dixon back at Pemberley and the man's cries on the other end. God, how they had filled the car. He'd been unable to say anything beyond, "Get back now! Immediately!"

That command had scared the shit out of him; he had no idea what he'd be coming back to but as the Spider sped closer to Pemberley … he could see the once-blue sky growing black as tar above the tree line in the distance. His heart seized; he left the H2 in the dust, but even 120 mph felt like slow motion in his panic. He fought the fear with each passing mile, through back roads and winding turns. Liz was all he could think about, and he beat himself up for leaving her this morning, for inviting her into his dangerous life that came with deadly baggage in the first place … and lastly, for waiting so long to go after Morales!

Fisting his left hand, he gazed down at the liquor in his right, hypnotically swirling the remnant of melted ice within, and like clockwork, his heart raced when he was unable to stop the horror movie from playing in his mind's eye …

His blood froze when he drove through the open gate to Pemberley. For as far as the eye could see, red flashing emergency vehicle lights cut through the charcoal smoke, which filled the morning air. Night had fallen like his heart into his stomach. At least six ambulances, a dozen police cars, four fire trucks and three county animal control vehicles lined the drive.

"We're sorry, sir, but you can't go in," a deputy sheriff commanded, waving his arms.

"This is my home! I need to get to my wife! I—"

"I'm sorry, it's not safe. You'll have to stay here and let fire and rescue attend to survivors and control the blazes."

He didn't wait to inquire about there being more than one blaze. The blood turned to ice in his veins and he clenched his jaw, not replying, just shifting the Ferrari into gear. He gassed the engine with a sharp turn to the wheel then smashed through the east field horse fence. Wood splintered and soared clearing his way to the green pasture. The UVA horses bolted and ran.

Fast wasn't fast enough across that grassy field. He'd never—ever—been so terrified in his entire life.

"No. Please God. No!" he repeated like a mantra over and again.

And then he saw the horse stable, blazing to the point that nothing would salvage.

Gripping the wheel, his knuckles turned white, his breath labored; he broke into a cold sweat like his blood poured from him. "She's safe. She wasn't in the barn. She wasn't in the house. I know it. I just know it. Please. This can't be happening."

And there it was: a screaming inferno. Pemberley. Hell.

As the car sped closer, his stare riveted on the orange tongues raging from every window. The back of the house was gone, replaced by thick flames. Plumes of furnace-black smoke rolled upward from the missing roof. Scattered on scorched pasture and driveway were remnants of their home— and his childhood: shards of debris and burning wood, which had exploded. Two fire engines attempted to put the blaze out, but it was fruitless; it raged like his panic.

He braked hard, threw the car into park and flung open the door, bolting into a run the second his feet hit the ground. Jumping the horse barricade fence, he screamed "Liiiiz!" before his shoes even touched dirt.

His feet did not stop charging until someone grabbed him from behind. He didn't know who because pain and fear blinded him to anything other than finding her.

"My wife! Where's my wife? Let go of me! … Liz!!" he shouted, strug- gling to break free while his gaze remained fixed on the house. It looked and sounded alive, consuming its sustenance with rage, unaffected by the torrent of two fire hoses.

"It's too late, sir. The house is gone," the guy tried to reason. "They can't control the blaze."

"Get the fuck off me! My wife needs me!" He fought wildly, overcoming the vice grip and turned, cold-clocking the man out in one maniacal punch.

Running to the circular drive, he roared, "Liz!" at the top of his lungs, swallowing the acrid smoke.

Both cops and EMTs charged at him when he attempted to go to the missing front door. Three times he broke from their restraint trying in desperation to enter—three times he failed in despondency—the flames were too hot, too overwhelming. She was in there!

The scorching heat emanating from within felt like a thousand degrees, burning his eyes and flesh just from proximity, but that didn't deter him from bolting below the jet stream to the back of the house, searching for any way in—all reason was lost—just his need to save her remained.

Again, the men fought him, holding him back. "If you go in there, there's no coming out, Mr. Darcy!" one of them shouted. "It's too far gone."

"I don't care about the house! She's in there … my wife is in there! Liiiiz!"

His lungs seared.

It was hopeless.

He was defeated.

Coughing wildly, he dropped to his knees … and cried. "Liz!" He gave into sobs that wracked his body and softly blubbered … "Lakmé … baby …"

Barely coherent himself, Dixon came up behind him. "Mr. Darcy. I'm so sorry."

Blankly, he looked up at the beaten battle-hardened warrior standing beside him with tear tracks down the soot and burns on his face. Darcy could hardly comprehend the next words the man choked out.

"We … I … couldn't get to her in time …"

As though a light bulb went off in his head, he abruptly stood, desperately insisting, "She's in the greenhouse! The greenhouse!"

"That's blown, too, sir." The man's hands grasped his shoulders. "Liz is gone, Mr. Darcy."

Yes. He had died that day. July 22 was his personal Pearl Harbor and 9/11, and the day he declared war on his enemy—not the foolhardy hired-gun who'd blown Pemberley, but the man who did the hiring.

At the end, three good men on their security team had perished in the blasts: one in the guardhouse piloting the drone, the other two entering the house to safeguard Liz. All that remained of their home was burned stone and ash; the stable where his father destroyed their family was scorched to the ground, along with three Harley Davidson motorcycles. His mother and Liz's cherished greenhouse became just a bittersweet memory that horrible day. And Liz …

One hand tightly fisted, his other raised the rocks glass to his lips before he abruptly rose, pushing the images of all the burning effigies of his entire life and his immense guilt over Liz down into the black void, then vacated the master bedroom, glass still in hand.

A nod to Dixon taking a much-needed break from duty in the great room preceded a quick grab of his jacket and he was out the front door. Illuminated by the pale moon, his boots crunched over the gravel driveway leading down the hill as the wind tore at his face. He welcomed the snap of air, hoping it would refresh him even if his nightmare and pistol accompanied him to the small horse stable.

Higgins, just back from a quick trip to West Virginia, emerged from the shadow when he turned the corner toward the dirt path. "Everything okay, Mr. Darcy?"

"Everything's fine. I just needed some air. Did everything go as planned in West Virginia?"

"No problems at all. Money and a good beat down were great motivators. The poor kid nearly shit his pants."

"As much as it kills me in this case, I still believe that everyone deserves a second chance to hit the reset button. Fear is a great motivator."

"Well, he doesn't know where Morales is but he's accepted the conditions as I presented them. I hope for his sake, he takes this chance you gave him."

"And if he doesn't then I'll put a bullet in his head. Thanks for everything. I owe you."

Sure, he should have killed the bastard, but Sun Tzu was right: some enemies could be useful assets down the road—just as some long lost friends could be. If there was one thing he counted on to help him in his battle against Morales, it was that almost everyone owed him in one form or another. The visit Higgins paid to West Virginia was not only for information or for the delivery of mercy and redemption but one to insure he'd have a marker to call upon one day.

And just like that, his trusted confidant faded into the dark, unseen even by any interloper should they arrive.

The silhouette of the barn, backdropped by the starry midnight sky, welcomed him. Here, amidst the hay and the mixed smells of cedar and a crisp night, he found the sanctuary that he'd been seeking since arriving in the mountains after the funerals. He switched the barn light on and walked to Salaam's stall.

"Hey, fella," he said when the stallion came to the gate followed by a nudge of his nose at the window bars. "Yes, I know."

Darcy pulled back the box door and entered. Rubbing the horses neck, he said, "No, buddy. I don't have anything for you."

As he often did when growing up, he rested his head against his warm companion, soaking up the silence, the trust. Salaam asked nothing of him beyond honesty. His pets to the horse's shoulder were greatly appreciated, and they remained like this—both beasts—

corralled and needing something unattainable: their idyllic life with Liz before July 22nd.

"I'll take you out tomorrow. We'll go for a good run. I promise," he mollified with a rub to the horse's face.

"Sure ... promise Salaam, but not me," Liz's saucy voice rang out behind him.

He jumped, startled that the woman of his thoughts had awoken. He'd left her in such a deep sleep beside the fire.

"I'm just as cooped up as the horses," she added.

Dressed in a white satin chemise and draped in a cream-colored blanket, she looked like an angel right down to her bare legs and untied hiking boots. For the thousandth time, he silently thanked God that she wasn't a real heavenly spirit. He'd never even imagined that that fireproof panic room under his office would ever be put to use, but for the first time she'd listened to him, and it had saved her life.

Knitting his brow, he was unable to control the severity of concern in his tone. He didn't mean to sound so harsh, but it came out less than stellar—far less than she deserved to be spoken to. "What are you doing up? And not even dressed warm enough. You'll catch your death."

She snorted, unaffected by his inadvertent censure. God, she knew him and how to break his severity so well.

"You're right, poor choice of words," he said.

A little smile twisted her lips and she opened the big blanket to him, which they both needed. Patting Salaam's neck, he chuckled. "Sorry, pal, but she's a hell of a lot prettier and smells better, too."

"Hi, baby," he moaned stepping into her cozy orb as the wool wrapped around his body. His arms encircled her waist and he drew her into him, kissing her head, feeling so much better just having her body pressed to his. "I'm sorry I woke you."

"It's almost like I sensed that you weren't in the room with me, or that I just simply didn't hear the clink of the ice in your whiskey."

Looking up at him, her cocked eyebrow told him exactly what she thought of his late-night drinking.

He wanted to grunt in protestation, but he knew that sharp tongue of hers would have a passive aggressive retort.

There was no denying it to himself or to her, he was fast becoming the man she never knew—the one who mercilessly killed Lucy Steele in Cuba without a second thought. "Back in Black" was more than a song to him; it represented the dark temperament, unattached, and un-emotional, hard-edged resolve of the stone-cold killer within him. "Jack," his trusted liquid friend, came with the re-emergence of those unsavory attitudes. The drink was his solace and comfort; it took away all the guilt that came when his conscience surfaced, even though it innately guided his actions. In order to bury Morales, he needed to become Morales and was well on his way to doing so.

But he wasn't the only one who had changed since July 22. As he expected after such a trauma, Liz's temerity and petulance died a little that day. It felt like their early days when he'd protected her in Monaco and Spain, and she was relying on him, versus her own intuition and skill. Yet, there was a strength that she'd not had before. It was even more pronounced than when they'd vacationed in Greece.

He smiled softly in admiration of her metamorphosis into "Liz" with her quiet bravado and optimistic grit following Monte Carlo. It was hard for him to fathom that she'd ever been that sheltered "Lizzy" he'd met at the dance school. The woman hadn't even a cell phone and allowed herself to be bullied into marrying a man she didn't love!

The red-hot fire, which had grown in her belly, fueled by con-fidence and freedom, had been only temporarily abated in the burning ash of their future at Pemberley. Her shock and fear would immobilize anyone—and for far longer than ten days. As for him, he'd lived half his life in the circle of hatred and revenge to Wickham, grooming himself in the most life-threatening danger for almost a decade waiting to take the ultimate kill-shot.

Whereas now he acknowledged that Iceman was part of him, Lizzy of Longbourn was long gone. His wife was ready to move forward again.

"I was wondering … can Jane come to visit for a few weeks?" she asked.

"I'm sorry; she can't."

"Well, then, can I go into the little historic town with Dixon or you?"

"I don't know; let me think about it." His heart was breaking for her. Right now, his enemy thought she'd perished in the flames, and here hidden away in the Black Mountains no one knew either of them, but things could change on a dime. She sighed, and he pulled her closer.

"How long do I have to be dead for?"

He didn't answer, and she pulled back.

"Fitzwilliam, how *long* do I have to be *dead* for?" she repeated with emphasis and a set to her lips. Now it was he who pulled back with a drop to his arms before heading back to the stall, to his refuge beside Salaam.

"I don't know, Liz."

"Yes, you do. I'm not blind to what you're doing, what you're becoming. You're getting ready to go after him."

"We talked about this. After what happened at Pemberley and then to the safehouse in DC, I have no choice. Obsidian isn't safe; as far as I know they found you via Rick when he came back, followed him from Peru to U Street then to Georgiana's wedding—I don't know, but I can't take another chance that those I love could be harmed."

He watched her expression change when she considered that Jane was now part of Obsidian—and possibly in danger, too.

"I understand. I really do, but it's just … this is hard to witness. I hardly know you anymore. Alexandre Dumas and Jack Daniels are making you distant; you're cold." She visibly shivered.

"I don't mean to be, not to you."

She walked to him, tightly clasping the blanket with both hands. "I know you don't, and I know that you feel responsible for what happened, but you shouldn't. It was my fault. In Moscow I told you to stop being so overprotective of me. I even made you miss the shot to kill Morales."

"Damn, Liz. You didn't cause this! You are not responsible at all!" He raised his voice—crap—Jack's influence had gone too far. "I'm sorry ... but nothing has changed from before I left for Peru. My past almost got you killed, and they're not going to stop. First Rick, then you, then yesterday ... Obsidian's only safe place is blown to hell. Who's next? My sister? *Your* sister? Who's safe from this damn nightmare?"

"Stop it. We've gone over this fear a hundred times already and everyone is prepared—even Gigi. It's her choice not to come here. For God's sake, she and Justin have at least half-dozen men on their security detail."

"Big deal. They should never have left in the first place; I all but gave the house to them. Do you realize what trauma she's already survived—what would happen if she's, God forbid, kidnapped again!"

"I do. Please, honey, calm down. You need to sleep. You've been on guard for over a week straight and you look terrible. Your thoughts are darker, more pessimistic than I've ever known."

Closing his eyes, he shook his head feeling defeated by her rational calmness. "It's what happens, Liz. My life has come full circle in 14 years."

"I know, but you're scaring me." She enfolded him again in the blanket. "I ... I need your strength; I need the man I fell in love with. He's so far away right now."

Shit. She was about to cry, but he'd not stop her from doing so. She had yet to purge after her entrapment in the burning rubble, but he had.

"Babe, I *am* the man you fell in love with. *This* is me, stronger than ever."

"No it's not you, Fitzwilliam."

Kissing her head, he moaned. "I'm sorry. I'm so sorry."

"I just want my life back. I need to focus on the future."

"And so do I, but I don't want you to fear anything. I vow to you, you will have your life back after Bermuda. Until then, know in your heart that nothing has changed between us; I'm not entirely unfeeling, yet."

"Bullshit. You don't even make love to me anymore."

Yeah … that was a problem. He *was* pulling away, like someone who knew his end was truly near, that going after Diablo would mean he wouldn't come back to her. Maybe psychologically he was readying her for the next reality check: life without him. Or maybe he was afraid of getting her pregnant. All their plans and hopes of bringing a child into their world had died. At this time in their lives, it was the absolute worst thing he could think of.

He couldn't reply and just remained silent to the accurate assessment that he was changing and leaving in a day or two.

"I'm ready to leave here," she said. "As gorgeous as *your* farmhouse is and as lovely as the mountains are in the summer, and I'd normally consider our visit here a welcome retreat—but it doesn't feel like that—not after what happened. Without any freedom to do anything but mope around, I'm lonely, even with you here, and I miss the Potomac and our family. I have to restore normalcy, which includes our relationship, or I'll go insane."

He deserved that. "Yes, it's been a long week and a half, and I understand how you're feeling, but Virginia is unsafe." He solemnly added, "Right now, there's nothing of ours to go back to."

"I don't agree. There's always Longbourn until we can rebuild."

Now *he* cocked an eyebrow. Living with Tom would be the death of one of the three of them, and it wouldn't be him or Liz. Besides, it was too soon for her to show her face in any place or with anyone connected to her. Diablo was still out there.

"Dad won't mind if we move in with him for a short time."

Again, he said nothing about *that*, because it was no secret that Traitor Tom (as he silently referred to him) was his least favorite person. "Not even Longbourn is safe."

"Oh."

His finger lifted her chin after it dropped in disappointment. "Hey, I have an idea. How about we go for a ride down to North Fork Valley along the reservoir tomorrow? Maybe we can pretend it's June and you can find that Fitzwilliam guy you love so much."

"I know where he is." She tapped his chest with her index finger. "He's trapped in here."

"Hmm ... maybe. We'll leave the security team at the farmhouse and it'll be just us—"

"And your Beretta."

"*And* your Hibben knives."

Like a burst of sunlight through the dark clouds, she grinned, enthusiastically asking, "I can practice?"

"Sure," he laughed lightly, bent and then whispered in her ear. "And I know the perfect place to seduce you."

"You do? And where is that?"

"At an abandoned hunter's cabin I bought a few years ago following Cuba when I considered becoming a hermit."

"Oh dear. It was that bad?"

He smiled wryly. "Steele's betrayal was one thing, but my total disregard of principles in killing her tormented me. One-shot, one-kill without so much a consideration shouldn't apply to someone you supposedly care for. The line was not blurred when I crossed it that day."

"I can see how it would upset you; you chose your profession to help change the world for the better. I believe that everything you do is in good conscience, but you're human, not superhuman, and that day her duplicity blinded you."

"It blinded my conscience when a simple left hook and a toss off the boat would have sufficed … so, I restored a log cabin to hide my demons away in."

"Yet you changed your mind."

"Yeah. Before I left for Cuba, life was very different for Georgiana, having just moved out of my aunt's house and in with me. I had assumed that we needed time together, but quickly realized she didn't have any interest in reacquainting with me—not that we didn't get along, but she spent most of her time down with Asheville's bohemian hippies, chasing guys, and protesting one thing or another. So, after a few months of licking my wounds after Operation Mambo by working up a sweat making the cabin livable, I finally decided to go back to Obsidian instead of hiding away in some one-room rustic cabin. My anger toward Wickham had grown in transference from Lucy."

He patted the horse's neck, then smoothed it. "I should have listened to my instinct and remained in that damn cabin by myself," he regretfully voiced.

"Stop it." Dropping the blanket, she cupped his face with both hands, locking her eyes to his. "You are the best of men, Fitzwilliam Darcy, but I'm afraid of you losing yourself like you did back then. You have my absolute support to make that bastard Diablo pay for what he did. Those guys who were determined to protect me deserve justice—*your* kind of justice. But you don't have my support in destroying your soul to bring it."

Taking her hands in his, he held them against his chest, his heart full of absolute contrition and tender love. "Liz, you're my salvation and so long as you love me … so long as I have you to come home to, that won't happen. I promise you, and my word is my bond."

3
Freedom

August 2

S tanding at the kitchen sink, Liz admired the wildflowers climbing up the dilapidated fence beyond the open casement window. Colorful Morning Glories entwined with overgrown Mountain Mint made such a pretty picture. The distinct scent of the mint fragranced the air, and the loveliness of the open blossoms and birdsong filled her heart. The sun was bright this late morning but the temperature was mild for this time of the year. For long minutes, she stood there lost in thought as the water trickled from the faucet into her glass, her mind drifting to the beauty and tranquility of Pemberley's greenhouse and her orchids, particularly her recent rare addition. The Lady's Slipper clipping had come anonymously from England and, of course, she assumed it was a gift from Fitzwilliam, but he denied being the sender stating it was highly illegal to even touch the wild plant. Of course, its mysterious arrival added to his justified paranoia; he even went so far as to drive to the Post Office and to ask his friend in the Leesburg police department to fingerprint it! His reply was simply, "Paranoia is the height of awareness." Still, the recollection of the *Cypripedium calceolus* and the disappointment she felt of it never blossoming for her caused her heart to sink at the loss of such a protected beauty no matter who sent it.

Trying to buoy her emotions, she closed her eyes and imagined the beauty within Longbourn's greenhouse; soon she'd be there—her protective cocoon, the sanctuary she cultivated after her mother's sudden departure. Life would return to normal and she and Fitzwilliam would have another greenhouse, other beautiful blossoms and, more importantly, his tortured soul would be at ease once again. The storm would pass, but right now she felt helpless to help him through it. She frowned with worry at the burden and fears (particularly for Gigi and her) he carried with him every day. As for her, every morning since that terrible morning was a struggle, but she'd not let Fitzwilliam know of her own demons. Good Lord, he was a mess as it was. Her memories of being trapped and polarized by fear in the panic room would send him into hyper-overdrive. She needed to be strong for him; she needed to smile through her nightmare and focus on their future—and in order to do so she needed to keep the details of her experience to herself. Some white lies should be kept to oneself and it was in good conscience that she resolved to maintain the charade.

Yes, the delicate white star trumpets of the *Ipomoea lacunose* clinging to the fence were beautiful, perhaps heralding new beginnings.

"Howdy, Mrs. D," Dixon greeted from behind her.

"Oh! Good morning, Dixon. Did you get any sleep last night?"

"Don't you worry about me, ma'am. I was born at night."

"Just like my husband then."

"SEALs or Marines, we boys were made tough."

"Apart from you, the only other Marine I know is Fitzwilliam's cousin. He's sort of an unassuming tough guy behind his expensive suits and agreeable disposition."

"Some of us leathernecks are saltier than others, especially us older guys," he said with a wink before filling a coffee mug from the old-fashioned percolator he swore by. "Mr. D asked me to tell ya' that he'll be back in time for your ride this afternoon. Seein' that the rest of the team went with him, it's just you, me, and Clarice 'til they get back," he said confidently patting the 1911 pistol tucked in its shoulder holster. She'd chuckle at the name of his handgun if she didn't feel so annoyed by the information of her husband's sudden disappearance.

"Gee, I didn't hear them drive away; I just assumed he was down at the stable this morning. Did he say where he was going?"

"Lennox and Bell left at sunrise for Asheville with your husband, and Higgins took the H2 on some special errand to run for him."

Unable to stop her angry reaction, she turned with a huff. Truly, it wasn't Dixon's fault, but after all she and Fitzwilliam discussed the night before and his adamant refusal to let her out of this mountain prison, his going into town screamed a dangerous double standard!

"Asheville? Oh, it better be important. The man took away my mobile. I can't text or call my dad or sister, and he's running into town and not just that rinky-dink podunk one on the outskirts. He's in a city—and not with Nick protecting his back! What the hell?"

"Aw, he'll be fine. Those Army boys have his back—" he stopped his sentence when they heard a familiar sound coming up the drive: the growling rumbles of dual exhaust motorcycles!

She turned from Dixon and eagerly searched out the window. Her heart flipped when two black Harleys rolled over the gravel. Oh Lord—Fitzwilliam looked incredible straddling the bigger of the two bikes, his muscular thighs surrounding the hard leather seat, his gloved hands wrapped around the handlebar grips, boots propped on the foot pegs. He kicked the stand down then removed his helmet, revealing tousled hair and a two-day old dark stubble.

Butterflies fluttered in her stomach at the hard-core biker image he presented: charcoal-colored T-shirt under the worn leather jacket, his black jeans and long hair. She'd frequently seen him like this, but something about this morning stirred her out of any doldrums or ire! His look reminded her of the day she got on the back of his Harley for the first time. That illogical image was imprinted in her memory forever: she, crying, in her white wedding dress, and he, scowling, in his black leather. Stone-cold, bad-to-the-bone, and unforthcoming—he was mysterious and dangerous, and sexy as hell. On that eventful night when she shamefully (and very uncharacteristically, but super effectively) manipulated him by smoothing her hand down the front of his jeans, she was gone—totally, undeniably, gone to the dark side— and probably would have screwed him right there in her hothouse. There was no doubt at the time that he would have dispelled her pre-conceived notions that sex was overrated. One year later, and he still had that passionate effect on her; the only difference being that her attraction to him extended way beyond the physical. Fitzwilliam Darcy had a pure heart and a keen intellect.

"See, nothing to get yourself in a tizzy over. For all Mr. D's occasional saltiness, he's quite a softie when it comes to making you happy, I'd say."

Her grin was probably touching her earlobes when she effused, "Yes he is!" and bolted from the kitchen, flip flops nearly tripping her up on the way.

Exiting the house, she stood on the back porch, hand on hip and her eyes locked to his laughing ones.

"Don't be mad at me," he begged.

"I won't be mad if you tell me that SuperLow that Adam is rubbing—in a very unhealthy manner, by the way—is mine," she teased, making both men laugh.

"Do you forgive me for being such a jerk last night?"

Sauntering to him, she smiled. "There's nothing to forgive, but I will accept your more than generous peace offering."

Her husband rose from the cockpit, lifting his muscular leg over the seat. Those thighs were the ultimate tease for her sex-starved soul and body. His grin was something she hadn't seen in over a week and that, too, fluttered her physical response.

"I'm sorry I left you this morning, but I did promise you we'd go for a ride today, didn't I?"

"More than one," she replied with innuendo, relishing the promise of intimacy he'd made. "Please tell me you were careful in town."

"I was careful in town."

"Was he careful in town, Adam?"

"Yes, ma'am," he replied with a grin.

Walking to her, her hot husband smiled then glanced over at Adam squatting beside the bike. The man's freckled-face smile confirmed that he coveted the Harley as much as she did.

"Close your eyes, Bell, I'm gonna kiss my wife."

The man barely glanced up from his inspection of the SuperLow's rear shock.

"I don't think he cares," she said as Fitzwilliam swept her up into his arms.

"I brought you something," he said when their lips parted.

"More than the bike and that kiss?"

He removed a black plastic bag from the motorcycle's saddlebag then held it out to her. "Well, something to replace what was lost at Pemberley. You can't ride if you're not dressed appropriately. The Black Mountains are a whole hell of a lot more treacherous than the hills around Leesburg."

Glancing into the bag, she spied leather pants and jacket. "I don't mean to sound ungrateful, but I think leather may be too hot today."

"But it's safer than those denim shorts you have on."

"But, *darling*, riding pants are much more difficult and time consuming to peel from my body."

"Then we better not waste precious minutes. I'd like to be on the road within the next 15."

Ignoring his command, made with a raised eyebrow and his need to play warden on their planned escape from prison, she recognized that the mere allowance of this break-out was huge—for both of them. Instead, she focused on the naughty smirk playing on his lips. As his nature, he didn't need to voice his amorous intentions or what was on his mind. His expression essentially conveyed that nothing, not even leather pants, would get in the way of his hands against her skin on a steamy summer afternoon. For that, she'd overlook his due diligence.

"Fifteen minutes? My, my, you're excited."

"Yes, I am," he teased with a swat to her backside when she turned from him.

"Don't get too attached to that bike, Adam. I'll be out in *five* minutes," she called out with a laugh and a skip to her step as she entered the house.

Her dark thoughts of earlier were easily replaced with excitement for the day ahead. For one, her husband had significantly dialed down his dark aura, having escaped the confines of the farmhouse and the purchase of a new Harley, which meant he laid down some serious cash. Perhaps, like the purchase of the SuperLow, his attitude was for her benefit, but the man did love fast toys and this newest beast he rode in on looked top of the line. She'd not bring it to his attention, but in the light of a new day, there was a glimmer of her Fitzwilliam before the explosion and not so much the Iceman of this past week. Maybe her own happiness had to do with his eased brow brought on by the baring of his heart and mind the night before and the sound rest that followed for them both. Or maybe she felt giddy because it was just the promise of a certain type of freedom she so enjoyed: that of two fast-spinning wheels under her body, satisfying her need for speed. And, of course, there was always the base reality that her excitement was just horniness at the prospect of *finally* having wild sex with the bad boy who owned her heart and knew how to masterfully employ his delicious inches.

For all her husband's protestation and compulsion to keep her safe from danger, he could relate to what she was feeling, but he had his thoroughbreds to ride at breakneck speed through the fields. Not yet a skilled horsewoman, she had nothing but Georgiana's *Sex in the City* and Fitzwilliam's (she assumed) *Sons of Anarchy* DVDs.

"We're going out, Dixon!" she excitedly called to where he sat in the kitchen.

"You'll be fine; you're in the best hands, Mrs. D. Go and have yourselves a real good time. Your Hibbens are in Mr. D's office where you left them."

Plastic bag in hand, she stood at the threshold, "What will you guys do while we're riding?"

"You know, the usual. The horses need tending, and I'm hopin' to stoke up that old forge out back and work on those throwers I promised to make ya'."

"You should definitely take a break now that Hank and Adam are back. I feel bad that you've been stuck up here with me day and night. I guess Nick will be back soon, too?"

He shrugged and then took a bite of the microwavable breakfast burrito.

These poor guys were tied to surveilling this lonely place, particularly Dixon—her constant shadow—guilt ridden as he felt. She wondered if they all felt as stir crazy as she did. A master bladesmith like Dixon must miss his solitude when metalworking. And Nick must miss his daughters up north terribly. "Fitzwilliam says it won't be long until this is all over."

"Makes no difference to me. You're stuck with me, ma'am, and that's my choice. And, one day, when little 'uns are running around, they'll be stuck with me, too. And when they get older, I might not be able to keep up with them, but I'll always have my eyes on them. I won't let you down again."

She smiled wistfully. Children. Today, she'd try to think more optimistically about the future. "You've never let me down. Ya' know, I know you have your own family, but I'd like to think you are part of ours too after these few months. *Uncle* Dixon."

"Aw, I don't have much kin, at least not many worth sending Christmas cards to. Like I said, I'm salty but if y'all want to adopt me as a surrogate uncle, I won't object. I'd be honored." He smiled back baring his yellowed teeth beneath the beard.

"So would we, and for the record, I don't think you're salty. You've always been sweet to me."

"Go on with ya'." He looked away and brought the coffee mug to his lips telling her that she hit that soft spot he hid so well.

***

Once again, Fitzwilliam had proven his assessment correct—she needed the leather for the ride, but not now. Although cooler in the mountains where the Darcy compound was, as they descended into the valley toward the reservoir, it grew warmer. She was sweating her butt off!

He was also right about the danger. The winding turns down into the valley made her uneasy, having been off a motorcycle for a few weeks. She'd only been riding for a year, whereas it was second nature for her husband. The man was born for the bike, just as he was for horse riding; he mounted things very well. She may have been born to be wild like her sister claimed, but she had to be honest with herself: she lacked the absolute confidence that came only with advanced skill and experience.

No longer so petulant in fighting his biking instructions, she loved following his lead, secretly mimicking his manner of turning, how his body dipped, how he throttled or down shifted—oh, yes, and the dreaded counter steering. Not to mention, she loved looking ahead at his jean-clad backside.

The Black Mountains were breathtaking. Lush and picturesque, she could see why he had chosen to move here after leaving the Navy. Clearly, he had planned to stay, and privately dreamed of his eventual return to horses given that the old barn at the bottom of the hill had been ready for the arrival of their four.

With Vivaldi's "Four Seasons" filling her ears, she followed Fitzwilliam down a winding road bordered by green pastures and forestry. It really was a beautiful ride filled with challenges and a few hair-pin switchbacks to keep her adrenaline happy (even if unnerved) but she prevailed through the danger. Finally, he turned down a nameless tree-lined by-way, slowing the Harley on the red hard-packed dirt and gravel. His deep voice halted the music when he spoke to her through the headset comms. "This access road leads northeast to Big Cove, near the cabin. How are you feeling?"

"Good. I like the new model; it rides a lot smoother and is significantly lighter than my other."

"That's not what I meant."

She laughed. "I feel great! Reborn! Tomorrow I can ride all the way back to Longbourn Plantation."

Of course, he didn't reply—that would mean he had to say no to her twice in as many days, and he hated that. For all his controlling nature, still a work in progress, he never denied her anything.

"Try to ride in the shallow so that you're not messed up by the gravel so much. You don't have off-roading tires. Not that this is off-roading or a mountain path, but you're maneuvering 800 pounds over dirt, not street."

"Okay. 'Cause there's less traction, right?"

"Yeah, but give the bike the reigns to do what it's gonna do, just keep your head up and focus. Don't panic when the front wheel jiggles a little. It's natural."

"Right."

"And when in doubt, throttle out if you find yourself losing traction; it'll help you get control and keep the bike upright."

"Yes, dear. Can I go back to listening to Vivaldi now?"

He lightly laughed. "Yes. We'll be on this and a few other small roads for about another thirty minutes. I just wanted to give you a few pearls of experience."

"Thank you."

The music came back on and she lowered the volume of "Summer," suddenly feeling a little insecure about the gravel pathway and his instructions. Like he said, it wasn't off-roading, but she had only sorta-mastered pavement—and tarmac. "Babe?" she asked with a slight tremor to her voice.

"Are you all right, Lakmé?"

"Yeah. Just a little nervous."

"Hey, hon, you got this; just loosen your grip and enjoy the experience. I'm not always going to be here to advise you, so listen to the bike and your intuition. Both Al and I taught you well and you proved your skill in Moscow."

"What do you mean—not going to be here?"

"Nothing … I just meant we're not going to live forever. Do you want to stop and take a break?"

"No. I can do this. So, you're assuming you'll die before me?"

"Haven't you ever heard of actuarial life tables? Forget what I said and get back to concentrating on the road."

Her front tire slipped a little and she followed his directions, just letting the bike right itself without her braking. She tapped the music controls on the dash; Vivaldi wasn't nearly as relaxing as her husband's warm caramel voice. It didn't matter what he would say while her nerves frayed, just so long as she could hear him in her head.

"Keep talking to me," she said. "And not about either of us dying."

His chuckle sounded like a baritone Aria to her. "What do you want to hear?"

"Anything."

"How about the story of how I almost didn't survive SEAL basic training."

"Um … that sounds death related."

"But I did survive …"

"I find it hard to believe that you didn't fly through training."

He laughed. "Let's just say, at first I thought I was in over my head, but I was a fighter. Only about 20% of the candidates make it out of BUD/S, and while I didn't ring out, there was one situation that nearly took me out."

"Bulldinkey."

"I'm serious. In the first week, I nearly drowned swimming 50 meters under frigid water."

"But you're a great swimmer. You can hold your breath for, like, ever."

"Not when I have the flu."

"Oh shit. What happened?"

"My muscles and lungs were giving out, but I thought of Georgiana, Wickham, my parents, and what washing out would do to me after all I'd come through … and then I fought harder, pushing my limitations … Actually, I'm glad it happened. Neither the Navy nor my demons could break my determination, and BUD/S broke my anger in a way that Naval training couldn't. I was able to become the warrior they needed, and that I needed to become."

"But what about the flu? Did they give you time to recover?"

"It doesn't work that way. I continued on and a couple of weeks later I survived Hell Week on only four hours of sleep. Man, Knightley and I had one hell of a good time learning how to blow shit up underwater even though our broken down bodies were barely alive."

"Wow. You never told me any of this. And then what happened?"

"I learned that I couldn't do it alone. As much as the Navy tried to mold me, it was the SEALs that created me. Somewhere between my discharge and Operation Virginia Reel, I lost my way."

"I hate Lucy Steele."

He just laughed then continued telling her stories from his qualification training and "frogman" days, as he referred to them, something he had seldom ever spoken of, not for her lack of asking but because he resisted the sharing of his military life. She never prodded. It was as if Obsidian had consumed them—and him. It saddened her that Obsidian had directed him on another path (as honorable in a way as it was.) The SEALs had made him more focused, responsible to his unit and brothers, and stripped him of his anger. But desire for revenge ran through his veins, and Obsidian knew it. Obsidian made him Iceman, and she didn't think she could ever forgive what it did to that noble Special Ops warrior she knew he was.

In his fascinating tales, the road beneath her wheels, the dense tree-line flanking them, and the ninety-degree weather were all but forgotten.

Now that he seemed willing to discuss his experiences, she had hundreds of questions. But she decided to just listen for now; she had a lifetime ahead to ask them.

Fitzwilliam stopped his bike in front of a tin-roofed cabin, just visible about fifty feet in from the "road." "This is it. We'll walk the bikes from here."

After placing the stand down, she stretched her back, thankful for their arrival. They'd been riding for an hour and her bottom was sore, her back stiff, and beads of perspiration were trickling between her breasts as the sun beat down on her. "Please tell me there is air conditioning."

He just laughed.

"Hey, it looks like you had a recent visitor."

"Why do you say that?"

"These tire tracks look new."

"Probably someone with an ATV, cutting through the woods. This trail isn't even on a map," he said dismissively, which was stinkin' odd given how if even a branch was out of place at the farmhouse he could tell.

"No, these are truck tires."

He finally looked to where she pointed. "Just a Forest Ranger."

Following behind him, she pushed the SuperLow through the trees until they reached the overgrown bramble surrounding the rustic house. Its once-quaint porch was covered in leaves and debris, and a fallen branch had bent the porch roof eave causing it to list on one side.

They parked under a small portico, promptly removing their helmets, and Fitzwilliam met her gaze with a beaming smile. "You did great back there. I'm proud of you."

"Thanks, Frogman. I was a little afraid, but you helped to calm me down."

It had been years since he'd been here, yet his first and foremost concern was her—not the storm damage done to his wilderness sanctuary. He came to her then removed the helmet from her hands, placing it on the bike's seat.

"Look, babe, you're a strong rider, so don't give into the falsehood of fear. In fact, you're stronger than I am in so many ways. Hell, what you've come through without even a complaint or a tear proves it."

He thought her silence on that issue was strength—good. She fooled him well then. "You promised that we wouldn't discuss anything upsetting."

"You're right." Glancing around him, he asked, "What would you like to do first—clean the cabin, practice knife throwing, or go for a refreshing skinny dip in the swimming hole out back?" Smiling, he waggled his eyebrows and her reply was an unzip to the jacket he'd bought her, revealing a pink tank top.

"I did *not* come all this way to clean an abandoned log house."

"Point taken. Let's at least do a walkthrough. It's been over two years since I came down here and the last few winters haven't been kind."

Liz was certainly curious about the place, but how could she tell him that she really didn't want to go from one secluded hideaway to another. Walls were the last thing she wanted, and there was no danger of discovery deep in the mountain range. He led her to believe that they'd be *visiting* the reservoir, maybe taking out a canoe or something, not hiding in a cobweb-riddled shack.

Taking her hand, he led the way to said shack but abruptly stopped. "What's the matter?"

"Nothing."

The man was getting adept at raising his eyebrow when questioning her, and he was smart enough to know that when his wife replied, "nothing" it was definitely "something." True to form, he furrowed his brow, silently assessing her. He understood her message, and his response was not to reply with words but action. He turned on his heel and led her into the woods, their heavy boots crunching the leaves and fallen branches as they drew closer to the sound of rushing water. Her heart leapt at the thought of a secluded waterfall, something the mountains surrounding Asheville were touted for. She'd yet to see one since their arrival but did see the small pond at the bottom of the hill leading up to her prison.

"I purchased this land because of its proximity to a natural water resource and on a hot day like today it's the perfect place to just get lost with you. If you don't mind, I'd like to go for a swim and clean off all the road dust."

"Mind? ..." they entered the clearing where three rock plateaus of fanning waterfalls fell into a clear swimming hole surrounded by bedrock. "I so do not mind," she said with a light laugh.

Hand-in-hand they stood in silent awe of the tranquil falls, enjoying the sound of nature and the absence of civilization. The sweet fragrance of wild honeysuckle and pine filled her lungs with each deep breath.

Fitzwilliam broke the silence, but his gaze remained lost on the sunshine dancing upon the rippling pool at their feet. "I love you, Liz," he softly said.

"I know."

"And I'm sorry about last night. I didn't mean to frighten you."

"I know that, too."

"I'll not elaborate, but I hope you know that because of my love for you and my professional experiences, I may do things without explanation. You just need to trust me, no matter what. Right now, our life is not a normal one, but it will be after I set it right. I promise you. I … just ask that you—as you always do—continue to use lateral thinking in all things."

"Of course." She hadn't time to expand on the conversation when he turned to face her with a wistful smile, brushed his finger down her face then embraced her cheeks with the palms of his hands. His reverent kiss was the same one that told her that everything was going to be all right. She'd come to rely on the way his lips caressed her as a hidden message just for her, one that repeated "Trust me." But today it quickly changed, searing in hunger and desperate need as though this opportunity would never come again.

His impassioned hands pushed back her jacket, dropping it to the ground. Hers did the same to his. Their lips parted for only a second when he pulled his T-shirt over his head; she did the same with her tank top before she was back in his strong arms, their skin touching for the first time in almost two weeks. His mouth consumed hers with a fire she hadn't felt since the day of the explosion when she emerged from the rubble, and she responded to its intensity with a throaty purr.

She felt the already rock-hard size of his desire against her hip; it had been too long a separation and their bodies responded of their own immediate need for satiation. Her womanhood fluttered and clenched at the stiffness pressed between them.

Quickly responding, her nimble fingers unbuttoned his jeans, releasing him into her hand; her husband's moans of rapture filled the air when he dipped his head back.

With a two-finger snap at her bra's front closure, her breasts spilled into his ready hands, surrounding them, thumbs brushing her taught peaks. She arched her back, inviting more of his dizzying pleasuring, lost to each caress of her skin.

"Let's get out of these clothes ... (kiss) ... and go for a swim," he whispered.

"Yes. Oh, yes."

Disrobing as fast as they could, they kept glancing up at each other, and while she would have enjoyed him slowly peeling the leather from her, every second not touching his throbbing body was an unwelcome delay.

Backdropped by the cascading fall, Fitzwilliam stood at the edge of the pool, nude and proud with his weight shifted onto his left hip, his right leg out slightly from his muscular body. Like a god of the forest, his tall, commanding physique was harder and more muscular than she'd ever seen, making his impressive manhood appear even more powerful. Dark eyes filled with desire drank in her own bare presentation, and he held out his hand to her.

Wantonly exposed to the flora and fauna, she took his hand; they were Adam and Eve, devoid of shame in their nakedness, eager to become one in flesh, and uncaring should they be discovered.

In one effortless scoop, he lifted her into his arms, carrying her deep into the cool water. The tickle of him brushing against her backside teased her and when he secured his footing at the bottom of the pool, he let go of her legs.

"It's cold," she said.

"I'll warm you up." His arms encircled her waist and his legs wrapped around hers.

"I can't wait," she breathed, gliding both hands up his chest and over his shoulders to comb through the wet locks on his neck.

"I promise, I'll never shut you out like that again. I don't think we've ever been physically apart this long since we got married."

"I *need* it fast, but I want it slow. I need you to give it to me hard, but I want to go all afternoon. God, I've missed the feel of you inside me," she whispered into his ear as if verboten to admit her desires aloud.

"Lizzy …" He breathed with a seductive lift to the corner of his mouth.

Anytime he called her "Lizzy" she knew he couldn't hold back from giving her what they both needed.

"Follow me," he softly said, taking her hand in his underwater.

He led her to a submerged rock ledge smoothed by the centuries of gently flowing water. He sat on the stone, and her breath caught at the way the cascade hit his back and hair, rolling down his muscular chest. His engorged tip breached the surface, bidding her to ride with unadulterated desire.

Grasping his bicep, she straddled his thighs, her lips hovering over his, her breath labored with passionate eagerness. Why did she feel nervous? This was her husband after all—but their emotions had been laid raw these days.

So caught in the intensity of their locked eyes and the touch of his hand against her backside and the pressure of his arousal against her pubis, she couldn't speak, only breathe—his anticipatory smolder was the match to their explosive coupling.

He was beautiful: strength and honor, a calm and a storm, love and lust—and he was hers forever.

His powerful hands grasped her waist, lifting her face to the stream of water as he lowered her onto his erection.

They cried out in their rapturous connection, and he captured her mouth with his. Hungry lip suckles accompanied his upward, filling thrusts as she rode hard with the water showering upon them.

They loved each other furiously with satisfied moans and total abandon. Deep and delicious, he touched her core, sending her soaring time and again.

She didn't think of anything beyond what he made her feel: desperate for all of him because it might be the last time.

4
Making a
Memory

W e're not going to run into any hikers or hunters, are we?" Liz asked with the most alluring embarrassed flush to her cheeks.

Darcy chortled. "Five minutes ago you were buck naked lounging beside a waterfall and didn't seem to care."

She gasped. "You didn't say there was a possibility of getting caught!"

"Can you blame me? I had other things on my mind. Besides, it's unlikely that anyone comes back here. The shell corporation I formed owns the farmhouse as well as 50 acres around this cabin, which—technically—includes the waterfall. It's private, posted land," he replied looking down at her as he held her hand through the forest. She posed quite an image, should they be happened upon: sheer bra and skimpy panties—and clunky boots.

Looking up at him, she squeezed his hand tighter so that she wouldn't lose her footing. "I'd be mortified if anyone saw us like this. Are you sure it was just a Forest Ranger?"

"Don't worry. I don't think he'd care if he found me in my briefs, but you on the other hand …" he playfully smiled. His heart felt so light he could fly. Loving her twice in an hour had set him free from his anger—even if it only a temporary fix. That's the thing about their connection—he might not always find the exact words in his heart, but he damn-straight knew how to tell her what he felt through sex.

Rivulets of water from her slicked-back long hair rolled down her chest, absorbing into the mesh fabric clinging to her bosom. If he didn't have plans for them, he'd head back to the pond—or against a tree. That had always been a secret desire of his: untamed sex in the woods. Emotional release aside, the end to their abstinence had unleashed a teenage horndog.

They neared the back door of the cabin and he dropped their bundled clothes onto the lone Adirondack chair facing out onto the forest. "Well … I hope you like the place," he said turning the knob.

"No key?"

"Not today."

Anxious for her approval, he opened the door inviting her to enter before him as he watched her profile go from wariness to joy-infused when she crossed the threshold.

"Oh. My. God." In wonderment, she glanced over her shoulder to him. "How did you do this?"

"Those tire tracks belonged to Higgins. I sent him down here this morning with explicit instructions. He does have a knack, doesn't he?"

"Oh, Fitzwilliam—it's so beautiful!"

He beamed, elated to see her so happy and that she appreciated the romantic details decorating the clean cabin: fresh flowers, a red rose petal-strewn new quilt, the table set for a romantic luncheon with linen and china. Chilled champagne and a full refrigerator waited for them for lunch.

Bouncing her fingers on her thigh, she bit her lip to keep from crying, but it was useless—her eyes filled with tears. "You're such a romantic mush."

Taking her fidgeting hand in his, he kissed her knuckles. "Only when it comes to you. Do you really like it? You're not just saying that to make me feel good, are you?"

"I was wrong … this place is a magical love nest. It's the perfect getaway!"

"There's just an old turntable, no internet or television. There's just you and me, the sun, and the stars—"

"The waterfall and the swimming hole,"

"And lazy days ahead when all the other crap is behind us."

"I love it."

"If you like, we can build on this log foundation, maybe add a loft in the vaulted ceiling, or a wing for the bedroom. Like I said, we own a lot of land, certainly enough for a stable, and I can expand the meadow just beyond here into a pasture for grazing."

"So, you're saying you don't want to eventually go back home to Virginia?"

"Liz, *you are* my home and I want to go wherever you want." He shrugged. "Geography makes no difference to me. It's a big world and I'm open to the possibilities so long as you're there."

"I feel the same, but I'm a Virginian—always will be, I guess."

"Yes. Seven generations … I know."

"Ha. Ha. You should be just as proud of your Virginian roots."

"You know I am, and I do hope to rebuild, but the land doesn't define me. The legacy of what my family did on that land is what's important to me. That's where your father and I differ."

"I suppose, but this quaint little place is even more secluded than the farmhouse, and well …"

"Okay, then how about we expand this into a getaway house that we design *together*."

She walked around the large rustic room, dragging her fingers across the white tablecloth. He could see the wheels turning in her mind as she considered his suggestion.

"I could build you a beautiful greenhouse, maybe even try to replicate the one you love the most—the one at Longbourn."

Was he trying too hard? He wanted to get today just right—needed to say all the right things for them both to hold onto after tomorrow morning. He wasn't this nervous before his departure for Peru in April, but this was different, way different—different enough that he could lose her forever. Shaking that untenable thought from his mind, he refocused on their future—together.

"Or ... we could just keep it small and special like this, just one room and give it a woman's touch," she said dreamily.

"If that's what you want. Whatever you want, babe."

"Yes. That's what I want."

"I'll build a bathroom though."

Her head snapped up. "What?"

"Yeah ... there's an outhouse back in the woods."

"Oh Lord. You were really going all-out hermit, weren't you? Does anyone other than Nick know where this cabin is?"

"Nope. Not even Gigi." He walked to her standing beside the fireplace and took her hand. "Could you remember how to get here without me?"

"Yes."

"Then don't forget this place when I'm gone, not just for the memories we'll make here today, but if you feel in the least bit of danger, I want you to come here with either Higgins or Dixon. Otherwise ... (kiss) this will remain our secret love shack."

Sliding her hands up his bare chest, she cooed, "I promise, but when you get back I want air conditioning in here, darling."

"Yes, dear. For today, we'll have to settle on that fan, maybe even lunch in our underwear." He couldn't help but to wiggle his eyebrows.

"I like that; underwear only should be our rule whenever we're here. Now what's for lunch? I'm starved!"

"I'm not sure what Higgins was able to find so early in the morning, but so far he hasn't missed a thing."

From the compact refrigerator, he removed bottled water, an antipasto of cheeses and meats—even shrimp! Hummus, olives, and an assortment of other delicacies that Higgins miraculously found. The man must have gone into Asheville before coming down into the valley, and that meant they'd luckily missed him by mere minutes, otherwise it would have ruined the surprise.

Liz set the food out on the coffee table then relocated the dishware and champagne glasses, but not before snapping one of the white daisy stems overflowing from the coffee can vase and sliding it into her hair. This was her day and if she wanted to sit on the sofa to eat, so be it, which was fine with him because he wanted to touch her, not sit across a table from her on a wooden chair.

"Nick outdid himself; you should give him a raise. Who knew that huge hunk had a romantic touch inside him."

"Higgins picking daisies ..." He snorted, "Now, that would have been a photograph to send to his kids."

She kicked off her boots then sat cross-legged on the sofa. The flower in her hair and the way she twisted her neck as she bit into the curved shrimp fascinated him, giving him pause, thumbs braced at the bottom of the champagne cork. There were many imprints made to his mind today, but this one of her toned body glistening from perspiration—in see-through undergarments—as she bit into the pink crustacean, and the rosy hue to her cheeks from their lovemaking, made him nearly pop his own cork.

"What's wrong?" she asked with a full mouth.

"Nothing, you're just ..." Tongue-tied, he shook his head with a smile.

Liz snorted a laugh and went back to eating, snapping him from his admiration. A pop to the cork sent it flying across the room,which he did deliberately just to hear her laugh.

Hopefully the champagne wouldn't knock her on her ass. They only had about four hours before leaving for the farmhouse. As skilled a rider as she had become, she was not ready for navigating the mountains in the dark and definitely not when drunk.

Sitting beside her, he, too, crossed his legs on the deep sofa then poured their champagne.

"What shall we toast to, Lakmé?"

"Hmm … Us, for starters, the tango, opera … children, and happiness. Forever."

"Sounds like a plan."

He kissed her, hoping upon all that was holy that that plan was the one to outlive all the others, no matter what.

The afternoon drifted by with Otis Redding vinyl records spinning on the turntable and languid conversation about their dreams until the last song played "These Arms of Mine." His girl leaned back against the pillow at the armrest, propping her bare feet onto his lap. Their gaze locked on each other and a comfortable silence settled onto their romantic interlude as the lyrics floated around them. She was dissecting him, maybe admiring, definitely thinking of something that amused her evident by the quirk to her lips.

"I love watching you, watching me," he finally said, caressing the top of her foot.

The wiggling of her painted toenails, alerted him to her desire and, of course, he complied, always enjoying how her perfect toes felt in his hands. Sometimes, she'd giggle, most times she moaned in response to his massaging ministrations. Today, she just simply instructed, "Make it good since you're leaving me in the morning."

Startled, he furrowed his brow. "You know?"

"Of course, silly. Why else would you go through all this trouble to make today so special?"

Oh, she was so brave; what a front she had put on today. It was almost as masterful as his own.

"I didn't realize I was that transparent."

"Babe, it's what you *don't* say that usually gives you away."

"That's not entirely true." Sure it is. He'd just admitted it to himself moments before.

Rolling her eyes she said, "For *example*, that first time I met you at the dance school. I felt like such an awkward spaz, technically alone with my two left feet and no dance partner, Jane making moves on everyone in pants, and Bill ignoring me while making googly eyes at his partner. And then you thundered in—my tall, dark and mysterious hero."

"And your point is?"

"That once I was able to ascertain that your menacing scowl didn't represent fault finding, it became clear that you had the hots for me from the moment you saw me through the glass. Further, you were fighting the feeling tooth and nail. When dancing with me, you said absolutely nothing, yet I knew you wanted to rip the blue sundress off my body and screw me right there."

He chuckled. "I don't quite remember it that way."

She dropped a grape into her mouth. "Of course, you don't. That would've made you a perv, and we both know that you're not."

"It was yellow, the dress was lemon yellow … and, in my defense, it was cold in the studio. How could I not look?" He smiled wickedly.

"See—what did I tell ya'? It's your smolder that gives you away … I can give you more examples if you like."

No, he didn't need more examples. He knew them all and redirected the way this conversation was going by tickling the instep of her foot. She broke out into a fit of laughter, wiggling on the sofa.

"Stop. Please. Okay, okay … uncle! No more examples. You're ent … irely mys … terious."

Raising her foot to his mouth, he first kissed her big toe then wrapped his lips around it. Popping it from his mouth, he kissed it again. "Stay right here, just like this, and I'll be right back. I have something for you."

He could feel her amorous gaze peek around the edge of the sofa, eyes burning upon his backside when he strode out the front door to his Harley.

"Hurry back!" she teased with a laugh, and he did as commanded, quickly removing the day's most special gift of all from his saddlebag.

Wrapped in simple brown paper with a red bow, he held the package out to her. "I bought this for you because … well, your last one—not that you used it much anymore, but it was destroyed in the hothouse." Damn; he was stumbling over his words. "It … um, your first one … saw me through that dark time when I came back to Pemberley. It gave me hope, helped me to face my demons."

She sat up, looking adorable with her disheveled hair, dried in a wild mess, and he pulled the fallen daisy from her locks. Untying the ribbon, the paper fell open revealing a new—blank—sketchbook.

"Oh, babe," she softly said, smoothing her hand over the image on the cover: two lovers entwined in a sensual tango. "She's wearing a red dress."

"Like the one I bought you in Seville."

"I love it! Thank you!"

"I thought you might want to take up sketching again. I also found you a professional set of colored pencils, but I left them up at the compound."

Crossing the length of the sofa, she lunged into his arms with a mind-blowing kiss. He felt the wetness from her tears against his cheek and tightened his embrace, heart thundering against his chest wall. How the hell was he going to get through tomorrow? How could he ever leave her?

"See," she whispered when her mouth left his wanting more. "You don't need to say anything at all. I can feel your heart beating against mine, just as steady, just a strong." She took a breath. "I love you so much, Fitzwilliam."

***

"Let's spend the night here," Liz had offered, and Darcy would grant her anything if it meant one more moment with her hidden away from the world and all its ugliness.

He reveled in the feel of her body molded into his, her backside pressed against him on the bed as he held her tightly to him from behind. But then she shifted, breaking from his embrace to roll onto her back.

In the soft glow of the moonlit room, the maple tree's shadow danced upon the cabin wall, but he barely paid attention. He laid there propped on his elbow, listening to her steady breath and watching her eyelashes flutter. The old oscillating fan clicked with each slow pass it made beside the brass bed, and his thoughts drifted to what would be easier on her: leaving her now with her sweet dreams and incredible memories or riding back to the farmhouse together with the sun peeking over the horizon. What would be easier on *him*? Saying good-bye in the light of day or departing without her seeing his own concealed tears? Dawn, he determined, was the enemy sneaking up on them and stealing what was left of their reprieve. This was killing him … but Iceman lay just below the surface, ready to end this nightmare in the best way he knew how. Above all things her safety was paramount.

As she peacefully slumbered, he couldn't help but touch her; he dragged a finger down her collarbone and traced a path to the sensual notch at her neck. His own skin tingled at the feel of her special erogenous zone until he kissed the hollow, mouth lingering on her soft flesh.

This would not do. Why sleep away their last moments together when he could be watching her laugh?

Seeking her response, he kissed Liz's velvety, open mouth, pulling her top lip into his in a tiny suckle. She tasted like champagne. As he hoped, she stirred, involuntarily opening her leg as if to invite him. Yeah, his princess knew him well, but tonight, he wanted a different kind of intimacy.

"Liz," he whispered, slowly gliding his hand up her thigh, lingering on the snake and orchid tattoo on her hip.

He kissed her, again and this time she kissed him back.

"Hmmm. What time is it?" she moaned.

"After three, I think."

"Are you all right?"

"Yeah, I'm fine. Let's dance."

"Fitzwilliam? Are you dreaming?"

"No. Let's go outside and dance in the moonlight."

"You're crazy."

"Maybe, but I don't want this night to end."

She rolled to her side and faced him, tenderly caressing his brow. Like a beacon in the darkness, her beautiful, concern-filled countenance burned his soul.

"Oh, baby ... you're afraid, aren't you? Afraid you won't come back," she whispered.

"Come dance with me."

A little smile of acquiescence formed on Liz's lips, and he rose from bed, walking to the sofa where she had disrobed his gray T-shirt before retiring. Of course, he'd prefer them both au-natural, but there would most likely be a chill in the night air.

"Do you have tango records here?"

"Shhh," he whispered holding the T-shirt and her socks out to her, followed by a kiss.

Once he slid his briefs on and she pulled the second sock up, he took her hand; his other grabbed the secure satellite phone Rick had given him before they departed Virginia.

Liz giggled when they exited the back door, unfazed when her feet crunched the twigs and leaves accumulated around the perimeter of the structure. The moon was high and bright, but its splendor was encumbered by the tree canopy.

"Where are you taking me ... and there better not be bears," she stated with a lightness to her voice that confirmed all the reasons he adored his Lakmé. But as they entered the forest, he didn't answer. Heck, hadn't she said that his silence spoke volumes?

About one-hundred feet to the left of the cabin lay a picturesque meadow he had mentioned earlier, and yeah, he, too, hoped there weren't any bears around.

Feet touched tall grass when they stepped beyond the tree line, and Liz halted in her tracks, mouth agape, eyes widened. "Wow," she breathed.

Above, the near-full moon evaded the scattered clouds, mysteriously illuminating them against the blackness. Mystical and magical, the glow of twinkling stars kissed the earth below by painting hundreds of white oxe-eye daisies a silver-blue tint. The same daisies in the cabin.

He couldn't have asked for a more perfect location in which to spend their last few precious hours together as though the only people in the universe. His breath caught at the sight of her hazel eyes sparkling from the reflection above, a wisp of her hair carrying on the warm breeze, her smile growing in absolute mirth and marvel.

His forest nymph glanced up at him then chuckled. "Transparent," she playfully mouthed.

He thought of all the things he had yet to say but resolved that of the many songs he could think of, the slow ballad he'd chosen combined with his body language—and the steady, powerful cadence of his heartbeat—would have to say it for him because words seemed trite in expressing the depth of his need and love of her.

They stopped in the center of the meadow, and he dropped her hand to locate the music on the phone, but she was oblivious to his actions in that moment. She was lost in the magnificence of the scenery, head tilted to the sky, searching for the North Star (as was her habit.) Van Morrison's piano and percussion brushes filled the silent night. In awe, he watched her stretch her arms out on each side, slowly turning her body in carefree circles as though soaking the moonbeam into her own angelic radiance. The field of pale silver at her feet was her celestial stage; the majestic oaks surrounding her were her stilled audience, and he, her most ardent devotee, was mesmerized.

He thought of a line from *The Count of Monte Cristo*: *"Woman is sacred; the woman one loves is holy."*

"Dance with me," he said coming behind her with a slide of his arm around her slender waist, halting her turns before she got dizzy.

Turning to face him, her smiling lips met his and she clung to him, devoid of a proper dance frame as his body swayed, bringing hers into its rhythm. "Someone Like You" and the moonlight wove their spell. Liz followed his lead of basic dance steps lightly walking through the wildflowers in an improvised, slow fox trot.

Trusting his lead, she mirrored his movements then turned under his arm at his prompt, coming back in his tight embrace. The synergy of their bodies moving as one felt like a dream; he pressed his cheek against hers and slid his hand down her spine to the small of her back. Her heartbeat against his bare chest stirred him and he breathed in the distinct fragrance of Mrs. Elizabeth Darcy—his best half.

The song lyrics in this four-minute moondance resonated deep in his heart:

She made it all worthwhile.

His hard road was about to end forever.

He'd been everywhere on every continent and had been left wanting … until her.

She helped carry his heavy load, changing his life through her light and love.

There was no one like her and there never would be again—their heartbeat was one.

She breathed life into his soul and he knew that the best was yet to come.

"Liz," he breathed into her ear. "Make love to me."

The song came to an end, but their comingled breath continued the ballad as he laid her down among the flowers. After tonight, never, would she ever, have any doubt that he'd move heaven and earth to come back to her—no matter what.

5

Freezer

August 3
Washington, DC.

Fanny Pryce, receptionist at Bingley Dance School, liked bald men, so she tried to say but, like Knightley, she wasn't very good at the dating thing. Whereas he was unlucky and terrified to pursue anything with anyone and still entirely convinced that death was a welcome option to escape guilt, she was just shy—and that had some appeal. Of course, last week's beer following her shift at the studio did not make it a bona fide "date," but there was definitely something in the air between them, an unspoken acceptance of each other and no need to share their back story. And as far as he could tell, her history was scarred. She was restrained, awkward, and trying to fit in. Behind her sad eyes, there was tenderness. Yet, her cheerfulness indicated her determination to rise above whatever happened to her in her past. Was everyone affiliated with this dance school messed up? Other men might easily overlook this low-maintenance, unassuming young woman who wore dresses buttoned to her neck and oftentimes wore her hair pulled back off her face, but in his opinion, it was what he *couldn't* see that was the attraction. She was an heirloom rose hiding in bramble. Make no mistake, though, he'd had his fill of vapid, foreign models and gold diggers (not that he had as much gold as his employer) when working in Monaco. What a life he'd led. Had anyone else had as much empty, meaningless sex as he had?

Despite the explosion on U Street the day before, he had a metaphoric spring in his step. Hell, there might have even been a whistle to go along with it, but he didn't want to appear uncaring that Obsidian's world was getting smaller by the day. It's not that he was unfeeling, but his skin had thickened significantly after accidentally shooting his son.

Exiting the taxicab in front of the dance studio, he considered what might lie ahead for him in Bermuda. This was one mission he wasn't so sure he wanted. First of all, it wasn't government sanctioned—not that he was always a "play by the rules" kinda guy, but still. Secondly, since the sniping failure of Operation Viennese Waltz, the ease of the Merengue was much more suited to his style of assassination. Pistol ready, get in, do the job, get out. But Darcy needed his help and for that he'd go to the ends of the world; that's what they were trained to do. His buddy had been the only—o.n.l.y—one there for him following the death of his son, and he'd never forget that loyalty, that friendship. He'd have his back no matter what.

The security bell chimed when the establishment door opened into an almost-empty studio. Above the dance floor, colorful paper streamers draped from the beamed-rafters to the turning disco ball and a banner spanning the mirrored wall read: "Mambo Italiano Night," which he assumed was in preparation for the monthly dance party the next night.

"Hi, Mr. Knightley," Fanny greeted with a sweet blush to her cheeks. Her light brown hair cascaded down to her shoulder and she wore a little mascara, making her blue eyes look so much more expressive.

"Hey, Fanny. Nice to see you. And you can call me John, ya' know."

"Oh, okay. Are you back in town for long ... *John?*"

"No, I leave this afternoon following a meeting."

She fidgeted behind the desk, took some cash from a newly arrived student then gazed back up at him with a soft smile on her peachy lips. Rushing to words wasn't Fanny's style, but he was patient as she found her confidence. "You know, I've never seen you dance," she finally said.

Looking over his shoulder at Caroline dressed in a white sheath dress and colorful scarf tied at her neck, he chuckled, leaned over the counter, then whispered. "I don't want to show up my boss. Do you get to dance at the monthly parties?"

"I could if I want; I mean ... I'm allowed after I check the guests in, but I have two left feet and ..."

"Maybe when my meeting is over, we can take a spin around the dance floor."

"But the party isn't until tomorrow. I ... um." Fixing the collar of her dress, she swallowed. "Okay."

What on earth was he thinking? Not that he didn't know how, but he hadn't seriously danced since attending the Annual Rose Ball in Monaco as the escort to one of his employer's many lovers who he wanted on hand—but not so near to his wife!

"Well, it's about time, Mr. Clean," Caroline said from behind.

Rubbing his bald head, he winked at Fanny before turning to face the other beast in his life. Flaming red hair pulled into a chignon gave the appearance of a classier side of the vicious woman. A lethal Kunoichi, female Ninja master, former CIA officer would never come to mind unless, of course, one knew her temperament.

"Hey ... you're looking almost like a lady, Caroline."

"As usual, you're an hour late, but I'll forgive you considering yesterday's misstep. Follow me."

As instructed, he languidly trailed her four-inch silver stilettos to the remodeled office. Gone was the window, and in its place was an acoustical soundproof door. In the dead of night, the day after Rick's arrival home from Peru, trusted contractors (who had done this at Pemberley), stripped the office to its studs and re-built it into a secure type of SCIF (Sensitive Compartmented Information Facility). To students, the two new instructors, and Fanny it appeared as an ordinary office. And just like the one that saved Liz's life, it was fireproof.

"Have a seat, and keep your feet off the desk," the co-director of Obsidian commanded with a point to her index finger, like he couldn't see the chair, or this was his first time visiting. Inwardly, he rolled his eyes. Since her break-up from Rick, she'd grown bitchier and harder to deal with, even curtailing her ritualistic fuck-'em and dump-'em casual hookups. Maybe that stint she did (and he heard every ugly bit of it from the van) in Paris at L'Enclave ruined her—or was it Liz's doing by delivering a long overdue set down regarding Darcy? Maybe he had it all wrong … could she have enjoyed that BDSM crap with Karakurt at the zoo and was now batting for the other team? At any rate, she was as gorgeous as ever, but in need of … something, from someone—anyone—just not him.

The door sealed behind them and she sat on the opposite side of the desk. "I'll ask, but only because I must—were you harmed in the blast?"

"Your concern is overwhelming. Sorry to disappoint, but I'm fine."

"Did the Feds arrive on scene? That could be a real problem if your gear and personal belongings were there."

"I didn't hang around long enough, and I've already been debriefed by the Director."

She removed an emery board from the desk's top drawer, then dragged it over her pink thumbnail. "Is there something you need to tell me?"

No. That raised eyebrow of hers was not going to get him to confess about his interest in the school's receptionist.

"Tell you?" He tightened his lips and nodded. "Well … I did hear that they're opening a fetish club near Chinatown. Given your recent Parisian exploits, you might appreciate some dim sum and rubber flogging."

"Very funny. Why don't you tell me all about that fetish club after your visit with Rick?" Although I doubt your virginal friend out at reception gets into bondage." She glanced up at him with an expression that made the skin on his scalp prickle. "Unless, of course, you and—"

He cut her off before her offer. Apparently, her fascination with him hadn't disappeared altogether.

"Listen, as much as I relish our insulting banter, Darcy and Rick are waiting for me."

"Darcy hasn't arrived yet, and don't get your hopes up about Bermuda—Morales has yet to be located."

"Then why am I going?"

"I honestly don't know why Darcy specifically requested you being added to Operation Gombey or why Rick finally acquiesced. Gombey is off book, and as I keep saying to him, we need to stay focused on real business. Operation Merengue's target is a prime directive from the Agency and should be Obsidian's number one objective. The Agency—and Obsidian—are laser-focused on bringing down this organ and human trafficking ratline, and your style of hit is the best way to accomplish this. The number one human rat is protected—by someone. Take him out and the whole house of cards comes down."

"It's that big?"

"Yes. The one in the Caribbean is the smallest of the six trafficking hubs across the globe."

"You are right, pistols are my preference, but I'd rather hook up with Gombey. We're all at risk until Morales meets his end, and I'm all for Darcy's payback. Liz almost died."

She just stared him down, narrowed her eyes, and he silently watched as those red lips curled into a smirk.

"Hmm, yes she did."

He couldn't help but to consider in the silence between them that she might actually have wished that to happen.

"I suppose Operation Merengue will have to wait until Morales is ancient history."

"I'm proceeding. Now that I'm back in the field, I'll be taking over Operation Merengue, utilizing ..." she involuntarily smoothed the hair at her temple, "other means."

He stood and walked to the closet door that led down to the "freezer," then pressed his thumb to the biometric scanner. "Hope you can at least work off some of that frustration you've been holding onto since Paris."

Caroline didn't have time to reply. The door closed behind him and he was thankfully out of ear shot, headed down through the dimly lit labyrinth of musty lathe, broken steps, and hidden doors. A brilliant subterfuge, but "rat" line could just as easily apply to this descent into the freezer. He could hear them through the century-old walls.

***

Seven hours ago, Darcy had left Liz on eastbound I-40. At her insistence, she wanted it that way—and, of course, she assumed she'd be riding alone back to the farmhouse. Yeah, like he'd let that happen. Dixon was waiting in the H2 at her exit as soon as she got off the interstate. A dirty trick, for sure, but he couldn't help smothering her and was also afraid she'd get lost finding the farmhouse. In fact, Dixon would have been annoyed if she returned home alone, which of course, Darcy never would have allowed anyway.

Her song, the "Flower Duet" was playing in their helmets when the exit sign came into sight.

"This is your exit," he said as calmly and reassuringly as he could. "Ride it north to Rambler's Road."

"I remember."

"I love you, Lakmé," he barely voiced.

"I love you, Fitzwilliam. I'll be waiting."

God, he hoped she would be because his plan was going to take a whole hell of a lot longer than a week.

The sun had been up for a good forty minutes and the lavender sky burned bright in the east, beckoning him away from her. "Keep that satellite phone with you at all times and I'll call you when I get to DC."

"Okay ..."

He could hear the tremble in her voice. "Liz, don't worry."

"I'll try not to."

"Babe ... I promise you. I will be back. You can count on it."

And that was it; the last he saw of her in his rear mirrors was her turn off onto the ramp before the comms went dead in the growing distance between them.

After that last communiqué with her, he had shut his emotions down. She was back at the compound now, safe and sound with four men who, he knew, would give their life for her. They'd all gone through hell at Pemberley and had proven their loyalty. She'd always called them by their first names (except Dixon because he insisted); her kindness and respect to each of them made them feel like family. If she knew Dixon's whole sordid story brought about by the drink, she'd more than likely be afraid of him.

Higgins, a former Navy man like himself, was brilliant and loyally trustworthy ... and lethal. As for Hank Lennox and Adam Bell, those young guys had just come from multiple tours of hell in Afghanistan and had nowhere to go; he hired them immediately following an extensive background check. Homelessness should never be the only recourse for any person, especially a vet transitioning back to civilian life. Wherever he and Liz eventually set up home, it would be their home if they wanted to or remain in North Carolina until they could get on their feet.

He and his new beast (a Harley Davidson Softail Breakout nicknamed "Black Ice" for his recaptured persona) rolled into Georgetown with a bellowing growl. At three in the afternoon, on a day hot enough to melt the pavement, the Prospect section was busy and the traffic murderous, making the chip on his shoulder and the scowl on his face all the deadlier.

Nothing had changed since the last time he'd been in this neighborhood for the intel briefing of Operation Virginia Reel a little over a year ago; that mission had restored his life. It seemed prophetic that he was returning to Obsidian's headquarters for another op, knowing full-well that it would also restore his life literally and figuratively.

As instructed, he drove past the Bingley Dance School and turned the corner, driving half a block before stopping in front of an Italian grocery store; its red and green window sign flashed "Prospect Salumeria." He had to admit, the ruse was clever, and he was curious to see what type of set-up Rick had installed and how it connected to the dance school.

Parked in front, he sat there straddling the bike with the exhausts bellowing and boots firmly planted on the asphalt. In 48 hours, he'd never see DC again. This was it—the beginning of the end of this life as he knew it. There would be no turning back. He kicked the stand, cut the engine, then removed his gloves, leaving his helmet on until he entered the shop. There were cameras everywhere.

A bona fide grocery store by all appearances, it was crowded, but Perry Como's Italian song distracted waiting patrons two rows deep at the deli counter.

"*Ciao, Signore*! Take-a da numba and-a we be with you *presto*," an old man wearing a stained butcher's apron greeted, barely visible through the hanging salami above the counter. His bushy eyebrows and short stature was just as Rick described, and as instructed he introduced himself to the former mobster accordingly.

"I'm here from WGL; you called about trouble with your gas meter."

"*Sì, sì*! Yes." He waved his hand to a girl in her late thirties, stocking shelves with cans of tomato sauce. "Rita, *cara*! *Vieni qui*. You-a show da man the gas. *Signore*, my granddaughter will take-a you the way."

She smiled timidly and motioned for him to follow through the stockroom, the meat processing room, the kitchen, and then finally down a narrow staircase into the basement.

"It's back here," she said, walking past several freezer lockers before stopping at a large metal door. Opaque vinyl strips, clouded from age hung at the opening when she pulled the door open to a locker crowded with skinned animal carcasses hanging from tracks along the ceiling. In fact, there were so many, that he wondered if they were real or not. They walked sideways through long rows of cattle and goat until she stopped, slid a row aside with a push of her hand, and then looked up at him with a mischievous grin. They stood at a dead end, facing the back of the cold metal locker: a solid plate of steel. To his astonishment, she wrapped her chunky arms around a side of beef and effortlessly tugged it downward as if it on a bungee cord. The wall popped open on one side and the meat popped back up on the track.

"You might have to duck and hold your helmet in front of you, but go all the way down to the right, and they'll be a door. That's where your friend is."

He peeked his head down the dark hallway.

"Don't worry. You'll fit. If Joey the Meatball could, you certainly can but you're a lot taller. When you're ready to leave just come back up this way and pull this cord."

"Won't the shop be closed?"

"No. My grandfather stays late. He and his goombahs play scopa in another room until my grandmother gets pissed off and makes him kick them out. It's usually around three in the morning when he goes to his apartment upstairs."

She smiled, again, and held out her hand bidding him to enter.

A thought occurred to him and he stopped in his tracks. "What's your grandfather's name?"

"They used to call him *Padrone*, but he's just Vito Cardillo now."

"I'd like to talk with him after I wrap up my meeting here, just a little confidential business I need to see to, and to see if he can store my motorcycle for a while. Can you arrange it, Rita?"

"Sure! Any friend of Mr. Rick's is a friend of his, but he doesn't do business for the Family anymore."

"But he has friends, and I need a respected Family man to help me with a sticky situation in Italy."

"He locks the shop at six. I'll let him know that you'll come to see him."

"Thanks. I appreciate your help."

He entered the alley and the wall closed behind him.

Standing in the unfinished space between meat locker and Obsidian's bunker, he dragged his hand along the plaster wall until touching more steel. *Impressive.* Rick had certainly gone through great lengths to conceal Obsidian's operations, but it was friggin' cold.

He hadn't time to knock when an airtight pocket door automatically slid open, leading him to believe that somewhere in the darkness a security camera was fixed toward the door. Eyes squinted from the bright overhead lights and the rapidly moving data on the monitors against the wall when he entered.

After his eyes adjusted from dark to light, his gaze fell to Knightley's crooked tooth when his friend smiled.

"Dude, you almost had us sending the cavalry out," he said.

"Sorry, guys. Liz and I spent the night …" He shook his head, stopping the irrelevant explanation, the details between him and his wife. "Traffic was a bitch and I had to stop at the bank."

His cousin came to him with an unexpected bear hug, then Knightley gave him a firm handshake. "Good to see you, Darce."

"And you guys, more than you know."

"How's Liz holding up?" Rick asked.

"Safe. She's amazingly tough and sends her love."

"When you speak to her give her my regards." Rick leaned back, assessing Darcy. "Well, you look like hell, cousin."

"Yeah. Yeah. I know, but at least I'm not dressed like I just walked off Savile Row. For Christ sake, you're a Marine, wearing a three-piece suit and wingtips in a subzero meat locker. Is this for Sarah's benefit?"

A quirk to Rick's lips told him all he needed to know—his cousin was falling in love with the British journalist—and the man didn't answer the query.

"And what are you smirking about, Mr. Clean? How's that girl you had your eye on back in April?"

"None of your business."

"Is that it, Knightley? Is that what has you on life support?"

Knightley walked to the monitors, diverting the conversation with a simple. "Maybe. So, this is the estate in Bermuda, huh? Tell me, again, why I'm on this op, 'cause, I gotta say, rifle sniping isn't my strong suit anymore."

Darcy rested the helmet on top the titanium EMP box. "Because I specifically asked for you, knowing how much fun you had during BUD/S. I thought you'd want to jump at the chance to light the place up with me like old times."

Rick changed the image on one of the monitors to the underwater cavity. "This cave is our primary target, accessible through this mangrove swamp canal, which is barely navigable by kayak. The cartel is using it for semi-sub smuggling of narcotics that come in every Sunday. The above sea level cavern is soft limestone and it's situated below the main house on the eastern perimeter of the estate. Charlie's intel indicates that it's patrolled from both land and sea. He spotted two sentries in the grotto itself."

On the monitor, he flashed an image of a speed cruiser painted with flames. "This boat makes a surveillance pass every hour. '*Infierno*'," he snorted. "Another sick reference to Diablo's massive ego. Two of the six patrolling thugs are former Karakut henchmen, most likely absorbed into the cartel after she was killed in Moscow. Sarah's contact says the subs are bringing in thousands of tons of Fentanyl and cocaine a month for distribution in the US and UK. The local authorities turn a blind eye; so basically, the cartel is running that part of the island. I'm sure the police department is filled with foxes on Diablo's payroll."

Darcy turned to face Knightley. "The drugs aren't our focus—per se—but it sure sends a message that I mean business. That's why Bermuda is a three-man op. Charlie and his Army drone will drop enough grenade power to level at least 6,000 square feet of the house; you can set the explosives on the hull of the yacht and the dock, and I'll be detonating the tunnel and cavern."

"Are there sharks?" Knightley asked.

"Since when do you care about sharks?" Darcy replied question for question.

"I don't really, but being chum isn't the way I want to go should I lose the fight. If I wanted to be eaten alive, I would have stayed with my ex."

"What happened to 'go hard or go home?' Man, you grew too soft in Monaco; there was a time when *you* were the predator."

"Damn straight about that!"

He flashed a grin to let him know he was pulling his leg. "Aw, don't worry, Mr. Clean, I'll always have your six should any big bad great whites start circling around that shiny head of yours. I'm not afraid to stand my ground."

"Sheesh, who pissed in your Cheerios, Darcy?"

"Morales, the minute he tried to assassinate Liz."

"Can I continue, boys?" Rick asked breaking up the playful teasing between two old friends. "You two will meet Charlie at 22:00 at Hampton Roads Airport in Chesapeake. He's flying back from Bermuda, refueling, and dropping off Jane. He'll have everything you need for this mission: scuba gear, explosives, and navigation charts."

Opening his desk drawer, he removed two passports and a brick of one-hundred-dollar bills. "Your new identities," he said handing them out.

"Edward Ferrars," Darcy said aloud, opening the forged British passport. "Had to be British, huh?" he joked.

Knightley leaned against the desk, folding his arms across his chest. "So this is a tit-for-tat, Bang and Burn mission. I like it. Then what?"

"Then we bullet out of there, recover from the dive then fly out the next day. I'll be HAHOing over Panama with my Baretta."

"Panama?"

"Morales has a compound up in the mountains there … and I'm going solo at that point."

"*That* I definitely don't like. What if something happens? There'll be no comms, no back up …" Knightley objected, looking to Rick for agreement. "It ain't gonna happen. We work in pairs, a team, Darcy. Or did you miss that in training?"

Incredulous, Knightley looked to Rick for a second time. "Did you approve this? We do not go into battle alone."

"I did not approve it, but Iceman is rather impenetrable in listening to sound reasoning."

"That's right; not on this one, and nothing is going to happen to me. But if there is a fuck up, then I want you to be the one to break it to Liz. I'll rely on both of you to be there for her."

"What? Nothing is going to happen, and I'm definitely not suited for that particular mission. I think Charlie … or her sister?"

He couldn't help it; he rolled his eyes and shook his head. Sweet as his sister-in-law was, that would be one mission he'd rather someone who could relate to heart-wrenching grief. She'd probably crack some nitwit joke about being single.

"No. I'd rather you talk with her." Turning from his friend, he spied the image of the shooter at Pemberley. Many times over the last week, this image and those dark, lifeless eyes crossed his mind—and Higgins'. In fact, after that horrifying day Higgins had become obsessed with settling the score.

"Are you going after him?" Rick asked.

"He's no longer worth Obsidian's focus."

"I disagree. His mission for Morales may not be complete. After all, you *are* still alive."

"I wasn't meant to be the target. Diablo's picking off all of you, one by one, to get my attention. Glancing over his shoulder, he, again, looked at the photograph of the assassin who tried to kill Liz. "I don't think we'll see him again."

Rick bitterly laughed. "Iceman is so confident."

"On this … yes I am. He's just a stupid kid who got charmed by the money that comes with the life of a hired gun. Let it go."

He removed the image from the tack board and handed it to his cousin. "I already deep-sixed this, you should, too."

Ever the director of Obsidian, Rick ignored him and tacked the photo back on the board.

6

Bermuda Triangle

August 4
Paget Parish, Bermuda

Despite the cloudless nautical twilight, a storm was about to hit Bermuda. Over a mile out from Hungry Bay's shoreline, the choppy water told the story: it was going to be a big one. For Knightley, and him, the almost 2000-meter tactical dive to Hungry Bay would be cake—even in these rough surface conditions.

With binoculars in hand and bare feet resting on the transom, he searched for *Infierno*'s third pass and readied his mental outlook for the mission ahead. The boat rocked, tugging the submerged fishing lines hanging over the edge of the boat, but he ignored them, instead visualizing the op strategy for what felt like the millionth time since his secret pre-dawn visit to these exact waters. All his plans had been made, everything in place, now just came the explosive execution, and a bottle of Jack Daniels afterward. Yes, he had intentions of at least a "lost week" bender after this part of the op in Paget.

Absorbed in his revenge, he ignored his heart, pushed down all thoughts of the ramifications of the "real" Operation Gombey—the one he alone strategically planned since even before July 22nd using Obsidian's intel. His only prayer was that nothing would go wrong and "The Count" Edmund Dantes's words resonated in his mind: *"And now...farewell to kindness, humanity and gratitude. I have substituted myself for Providence in rewarding the good; may the God of vengeance now yield me His place to punish the wicked."*

He fought the other line that wouldn't let go of his conscience … as good as it was. *"Hatred is blind; rage carries you away; and he who pours out vengeance runs the risk of tasting a bitter draught."*

Breaking the tension in his body and the dark cloud in his thoughts, beside him, Knightley hogged Charlie's binoculars and, like two warring teenagers, they bickered over who had it longest. The drunken, half-naked female partiers on the sunset cruise catamaran anchored a couple of hundred feet from them were oblivious to the spying by the "avid fisherman and divers."

He shook his head wondering if Charlie, ever the smooth dog, would eventually truly commit to Jane, even though he had dropped the "L" word a few months back. Those two were cut from the same cloth, committed-yet-not-entirely, and he questioned just how monogamous their relationship was. They both seemed to have one foot inching toward straying. Whatever. It wasn't his concern, but it did trouble Liz considerably. He only hoped that whatever happened between his buddy and sister-in-law, it would happen amicably and not affect the dangerous business they were both involved in. The last thing Obsidian needed was another Caroline and Rick … or him and Caroline … or him and Steele. And, if he was truly being honest, now was the time to admit … like him and Liz. How could he regret and, at the same time, not regret the best damn thing that ever happened to him?

"Hey, Charlie, what's the story behind this Army drone?" he finally asked after an hour of silence.

"Hey look who's come back to life."

He just stared him down with what Liz referred to as his "stink eye."

"The thing is righteous! With a few modifications," and here he gave Darcy a poignant look, "made by your father-in-law, it can fly up to 400 feet elevation with a 300x digital zoom lens. He developed a mini-battery so that it can fly over two miles for an extended period. The grenades were my idea. Bennet is one bad-ass tech freak."

Darcy grunted. He hated that Tom the Traitor was still working for Obsidian. But what else was a man to do when technically still on house arrest?—which, in truth, was bullshit because the man figured out how to manipulate the ankle bracelet's GPS tracking.

"What else has he produced for Obsidian?"

"For starters, those satellite phones we're all using now. Caroline let it slip that he's co-opted some outdated, inactive communications satellite flying around out there. Ya' know … something from like the Cold War."

"Interesting …" He stored away that bit of information. Apparently, his father-in-law's career with the Department of Defense could yield more fruit than he even considered, albeit still breaking the law! "So, what you're saying is that it's now an Obsidian satellite?"

"Sorta, but not really. We're just borrowing it without their knowledge."

"Darcy, you gotta see the night vision Ray-Bans he made me. Despite him selling out his country for a mint, the man's got serious talent. He reminds me of Q in a James Bond movie," Knightley added.

"Hmmm. I see he's been busy still working as Quartermaster." *And I doubt Liz knows about it.*

"When was the last time you saw your father-in-law?" Knightley asked.

"Months. I try not to. His recollection of my fist in his face and my recollection of how damn good it felt keeps us apart."

"He's got a girlfriend, I think," Charlie blurted.

"What? Oh, Lord."

"Yeah. I went out to see him last week to pick up the drone before leaving to scout, and I heard a woman's voice coming from the kitchen, then I saw a flash of blonde hair in the window … ya' know I came through the back door. When I asked if he was alone, he lied. Flat out fed me a line of crap. Maybe she was his assistant or his psych nurse—but then, why lie? I don't get it; the geezer is like a four-foot-two computer nerd who can't leave the house. How does a guy like him meet a British bird? It's not like he's some swingin' hip, happy guy."

"Another Brit? Has Obsidian sent out 'Special Relationship' invitations?"

Charlie snorted. "Sure seems that way. She called him 'honeybun'."

That shocked the shit out of him. Liz definitely didn't know about Bennet's girlfriend or she would have said something about that, too.

"Maybe they met online. Those sites are international, you know. I mean … I'm not saying I know anything about or signed up for online dating, but anything is possible about Bennet," Knightley said.

Darcy chortled. If that wasn't transparent he didn't know what was. As Liz would say, "Me thinks thou dost protest too much."

"Ha. Ha. I didn't meet Fanny online."

"What! Whoa. You're dating *my* Fanny? Dance school Fanny? Holy-roller, plain-faced Fanny?"

Uh oh.

Knightley handed back the binoculars and stood in the boat, towering over Charlie with a glare he hadn't seen in a long time. "Don't insult, Fanny. She's a nice girl."

Charlie swallowed. "Yeah, of course she is. I'm just surprised."

"Don't be, and if you call her plain-faced again … well … it won't be pretty."

"Sit down, Knightley," Darcy said.

"I'm sorry, Charlie. I'm just anxious to get this shit underway."

"It's cool. I get it."

Darcy glanced at his wrist chronograph then raised the high-power binoculars again, zooming in on the mangroves. "They'll be passing any minute. We better start putting our gear on."

As they did so, he went through the dive. "Let's go over this one last time. If we've timed this right, when the boat passes, well do this dive to the targets in 34 minutes at a shallow 60-foot depth. The three of us will triangulate from here. Charlie will relocate the fishing boat to the designated coral reef to engage Batman once we arrive at our targets."

"Right. Darce, on recon …" Charlie added, "it took me four minutes to swim through the mangrove canal, and I'm giving you eight to get through the canal, wire your C-4, and get the fuck out of there. At my go, Batman will drop two non-signatory explosives on the far side of the house, 30 seconds later Knightley's detonation will blast the dock and then, Darcy, you'll rock the island in the submarine cave."

"Got it."

"The sub is most likely in there getting loaded—so we're going radio silent on this. Knightley, make sure you're far enough away from those babies when you discharge the remote. The shock wave is gonna be awesome. Remember—center of the hull, and the beginning of the dock. I'll be monitoring everything transmitted from Batman, your head cams, and your individual GPS. All will be relaying real-time back to Rick in DC."

"So, if all goes according to plan, we'll meet before moonrise at the Apollo shipwreck in one hour, and if things go to shit, E and E. We'll meet at the shack in Cox's Bay." Knightley added. "It's 21:17 now, the Cessna leaves at 23:00 hours tomorrow after we've recovered from the dive."

Darcy stood then pulled his wetsuit hood over his head, "Let's do this."

He and Knightley wearing closed-circuit rebreathers on the front of their wetsuits and waterproof rucksacks carrying their gear, explosives, and remote detonators on their backs stepped into the water. With nothing more than dive knives, compasses, and depth gauges leading them to their individual targets, the two Frogmen gave thumbs up, sending them on their course of mass destruction. Black as stone-cold, obsidian lava, they disappeared underwater toward the extinct seamount called Bermuda.

***

Twenty minutes into the dive, the party catamaran and any other boat life had moved on and the dark silhouette of Charlie's boat bobbed against the last remnant of twilight. He pulled up the bait-less fishing rods, readying to disengage the cuddy's GPS lock that kept it "anchored" for "fishing." With Panama hat still in place, he sat at the edge of the cuddy, by all appearances, a relaxed, late-night fisherman about to relocate to better feeding grounds, but his heartbeat said otherwise. As an adrenaline junkie, he was so friggin' on edge—in a good way—he could barely contain himself.

He loved this wild stuff, loved being in the thick of it. But damn!—he didn't want to be one of those guys. Yeah, sure, he enjoyed diving—in the sky, in the Caribbean—but not with pounds of C-4 strapped to his back and only a narrow window of escape before detonation. There was always that thrill of something going wrong and cheating Murphy's Law, but those were two of the hardest SEALs he knew—no prob for them.

Night's falling felt portentous; he listened to the lapping against the hull, the only other sound besides the pulsing beat in his ears like the tick-tock of an old-fashioned clock bomb in a movie.

Glancing at the monitor on the dash, Charlie's gaze switched back and forth on the split screen displaying the soup-like, mysterious world from the guys' head cams: dark coral reefs, waving sea grass, gloved hands, and passing fish. Better them than him—he'd much preferred high altitude free-falling from a plane or body surfing. Deep-water, tactical diving wasn't his thing, but he wasn't above learning with a pair of propulsion jet boots! Now that would make it more interesting and a shit load of fun!

Even in the fading twilight, faint light pierced the surface of the water so that their night vision wasn't necessary. Under the yacht and in the mangrove, it would be a different story, particularly since there will be no moonlight for a couple of hours.

"Who would've thunk it … Fanny and Knightley," he chuckled into the salty air; that thought popping into his head out of nowhere. "I bet Caroline is freakin' out." Shaking his head, he rotated the chair, started the engine and left his position for the reef. In twenty minutes, Batman would be wreaking havoc.

Slowly, he trolled the inky water, watching the fishing sonar/GPS on another screen. Truth be told, he missed Jane's companionship; she was a great navigator when she focused. He'd always been a solo, serious kinda guy when it came to the death business, but having her along certainly made him re-think the solitude. She'd love this, and he loved her; she made everything fun—even the deadly stuff.

He stopped the boat and shut down the engine, locking it above the deep coral reef below. They were three sides of destruction now—one at the north end of the estate, one at the south end and, he, navigating Batman from the west.

He narrowed his eyes at the split screens; Darcy entered the brackish water, thick with tangled mangrove roots covered with silt and sediment from the sea floor. Charlie shuddered, recalling his own difficulty getting through the roots on his recon dive. Even in broad daylight and being unencumbered by the weight of heavy scuba gear, it was a challenge. The tree canopy had blocked the sunlight, but still he had been able to easily locate the clear channel that the ten-foot wide narcosub traveled through. Darcy had only his night goggles and, hopefully, calm focus, because that shit under there could be claustrophobic. A minute passed, and the canal became black as ink on screen until Iceman's gloved thumb rose into the lens of the camera. He'd located the access path, the deepest portion of the canal.

Charlie breathed a sigh of relief.

The image on the other side of the monitor was dark and murky. Knightley must be positioned below the keel. The head cam wasn't picking anything up, just murky floating sediment until the red blinking GPS signal halted, positioned at the sea wall at the dock. Two hands, holding the carefully packaged explosives, passed across the camera lens before vanishing again into the darkness.

A faint light allowed Charlie to observe Darcy's tactical skills when he arrived at the limestone mouth of the cavern ahead of schedule. The Frogman concealed himself within the surrounding mangrove as he steadily rigged the explosives to the entrance. Back on his SEAL game, the man operated methodically, quickly, without hesitation—and completely concealed to the guards he knew were within. When Darcy glanced down to remove his dive knife, Charlie had a glimpse of two white food-grade buckets and a soft beach cooler wedged into the silt.

"What the hell is all that trash? Drug containers?" But he disregarded it, instead switching his attention to Knightley wrapping up at the dock piling.

"Almost time," he said to the inert drone waiting on the floor.

Darcy wiggled from the roots, his GPS signal tracking *forward* into the cavern, not away from.

"No, no—fuck no!" He yelled at the screen when the cam's vision grew brighter and the mangroves disappeared. All he could see were underwater limestone walls and the hull of the submarine when it came into view.

"What are you doing, man? Get the hell out of there!" He shouted into the night air, abruptly standing up.

Foolish or brave? At least he was fast, and in only a matter of seconds, Darcy pressed another explosive device to the propeller, and swam back toward blackness. His GPS showed movement to safe harbor, but Charlie couldn't see a damn thing through the head cam.

A long stream of air released from Charlie's lungs and he noticed that Knightley's GPS and cam were also on the move.

Two minutes passed; both men gave the okay sign.

"Let's rock-n-roll, Batman," he said, directing the drone using the remote control. It lifted into the air and flew off the boat, silently soaring across the darkened sky toward its destination: the mansion was lit up like a Christmas tree just waiting to be bombed the shit out of.

On the hand-held screen he lined up the bat, then pressed the red button, releasing two incendiaries filled with thermite. Sight unseen, they descended in the dark until the explosion lit the sky!

BOOM!

The aerial view in the darkness was a spectacular show.

He re-positioned Batman to over the dock and waited 30 seconds to capture Knightley's handiwork on video.

BOOM!

Water, wood, and fiberglass blew into the air in an extraordinary golden geyser below Batman! *Take that Morales!*

The drone was now on the move to oversee the destruction of thousands of tons of drugs in the mangrove cavern. Hovering over the canal, it waited. Thirty seconds passed. Forty. Forty-five.

Nothing.

"Fuck!"

The red dot of Darcy's GPS was immediately on the move toward the cavern, his cam showing the descent into mangrove blackness once again, and Charlie lost visual. He was going in either to replace the charge or to fix it, maybe he needed a closer range for discharge, but he would have known that from the start—

BOOM! BOOM!

The blast was so powerful, Charlie felt it in the cuddy. It threw him backward with a "Holy Fuck!"

Frantically, he ran to the dash examining the two side-by-side, split-screen monitors.

Only one GPS tracker remained: Knightley's.

Darcy's red tracker was gone from the screen.

Knightley's head cam showed fast movement over hard coral.

Darcy's head cam was out, replaced by static.

Rendered immobile by shock, Charlie's heart squeezed—and then came the text from Rick. "What the fuck just happened?"

He couldn't think—his mind scrambled at the unexpected. He couldn't reply; his palm was frozen to his lips. It was right there in front of him—no GPS, no cam. Darcy didn't make it out in time. There was no way he could have survived the canal in that double blast.

There was no possible way.

7
Pieces

August 11
North Carolina

D arcy hadn't shown at the safehouse in Cox's Bay … or at the Cessna.

In the course of a week, Obsidian's three men had barely uttered a word about Darcy—or their fear of the worst—to one another in their haunting, disturbing search for signs of life. After day four, following the violent storm, all hope was gone, but they continued searching anyway, carefully keeping their distance from the local authority and cartel's investigation above and below sea level.

It destroyed them all when they came to the decision to end the search. Both the preponderance of and the simultaneous lack of physical evidence determined the end of Operation Gombey's search and rescue. Three men, all who had witnessed death on and off the battlefield, came back with the same conclusion: Darcy was dead.

As expected, Rick had taken the news the hardest. Battling his calm, reassuring confidence and the overwrought feeling of hopeless despair, he had hopped on the first flight to Bermuda—arriving eight hours after the destruction of Morales's compound. Faced with the initial findings, the stalwart Marine bit his lip, nodded his head, fought back the tears, and suited up to join the dive in Hungry Bay. He had to see for himself, had to bear witness.

Bingley's trademark affability was gone, and Knightley considered what a fucked up wake-up call Iceman's death was to Bingley's happy-go-lucky attitude. The guy was beside himself and unable to speak, even if he wanted to. While he hadn't thought them the "best of friends," they were "very good friends." Maybe the emotionally stunted Bingley looked up to Darcy for the honorable man he was. Guilt could also be playing mind games on the guy, too. Operation Gombey had been Crash's mission—his scouting, his plan—even if Darcy went off op by laying the second device on the sub.

That last bit would remain between the Obsidian men; they'd never tell Liz that Iceman made a foolish decision by increasing the explosive power. He might have survived. He should have known better—the man was a damned good Frogman!

As for himself, he could no longer proclaim that emotions were best when stored away. They were right there on his suit lapel, represented by the U.S. Navy SEAL Trident pinned to the fabric. He lost a brother that night and it eviscerated him.

In three distinct ways, they'd all lost a brother that night.

And one week later, the three Obsidian men were still the only three who knew that Fitzwilliam Darcy wouldn't be returning to Liz.

With emotions momentarily in check, Knightley sat beside Rick in the rented SUV, driving through the mountainous countryside from Asheville to the Darcy farmhouse. Barely conversational himself, he observed how Rick's jaw clenched, the swollen veins on the man's temple, and his wane complexion as he no doubt, played the horrors of what they'd seen through his mind for the millionth time. Rick's hands tightly grasped the Escalade's steering wheel, and not because of the winding roads. Those two glasses of wine he'd drunk on the short flight were hardly the reason. They were to be the bearers of horrible news, and as brokenhearted as they were, they needed to be strong for her.

"You'll put the obituary in the papers, right?" Knightley broke the silence between them.

"I'll take care of it—maybe say something about a diving accident in Bermuda. The best we can hope for in this situation is that exposing Iceman as the culprit in explosions, Diablo will move on."

"Right. It doesn't seem right, does it? Darcy dead—Morales alive."

Rick sighed. "I'll have Sarah make the funeral arrangements back in Virginia while I'm in California breaking the news to Georgiana."

"We should have called Liz sooner, let her know we were coming, let her know that I'll be staying around for a few days."

"No. It's better that we just show up."

"Man, what the hell are we going to say?"

"Not *we* … you. He wanted *you* to do it. I'll have enough on my hands telling Darcy's sister and their dear friends, the Reynoldses. And I can't guarantee that I wouldn't fall apart when telling her. Shit. That's the last thing *any* of them need to see."

"This is a fucking nightmare," he groaned, resting his head back against the seat. His heart squeezed.

"It's damn real."

"Are you gonna … ya' know … tell Liz the details? She's the kind of woman who'll want the details."

Rick glanced over to him with a horrified expression. "What are you crazy?"

"I'm sorry … I'm not thinking straight. You're right. That's one genie you can't put back in the bottle."

"She doesn't need to know anything other than there's no body to ship back for burial."

"What are you gonna say when she asks why?"

"So then *you* tell her that her Navy SEAL husband was blown to shit and devoured by sharks!" Rick shouted. "That all we found was his mangled rebreather and a half-chewed fin, that there had been enough blown flesh floating in that canal and washed out to sea in the storm to bring two dozen sharks into the bay!"

He heavily breathed. "Fuck. This sucks," he moaned, looking out the window at the passing landscape. His fingers toyed with the pin and he shook his head in despair.

The truck turned up a gravel drive, scraped by the trees lining its perimeter, and instinctively Knightley's pulse increased. This was it.

Suddenly a copper-haired guy, with pistol drawn at eye level stepped out from the trees directly into their path.

"Jesus!" Rick startled, slamming on the brakes.

"Out of the truck," the guard commanded.

As instructed they exited, halted at the open doors, and raised their hands in front of them.

The guy spoke into the walkie-talkie pinned to his tactical jacket.

"We're here to see Mrs. Darcy. I'm Rick Fitzwilliam, Darcy's cousin. Are you Dixon?"

"No." Carefully, he walked to them as another armed guard came down the drive, shotgun slung over his shoulder, and eyes fixed on him. "What's your business with Mrs. Darcy?" red asked patting Rick down then removing his billfold from the inside pocket of his suit. He tossed it to the other "kid" headed toward Knightley.

"We're here with bad news," Rick dourly replied. "About my cousin ..."

"He checks out," the other guy said after looking at the contents of the wallet. "Are you Knightley?"

Darcy must have prepared them well in the event of anything; there was a familiar blankness to both their expressions, as though they'd seen hell and "bad news" was par for the course. "Yup. John Knightley. It's the chrome that gives me away, huh? Are you guys Army?"

"Drive up and park around back. Someone will meet you to take you to Mrs. D," the redhead said with no acknowledgement to being former military.

The farmhouse was huge and for a split-second Knightley considered Darcy one lucky devil, but caught himself.

"Have you been here before?" he asked Rick.

"No. When he came to work for Obsidian, he purchased this place for him and Georgiana. She's in Laguna Beach now, and the Agency kept me pretty busy. I could never get away from the DC area for pleasure, and then there was the whole Caroline issue. I didn't tell him I was dating her—and we were sort of connected at the hip."

"Hmm … Do you think Liz'll continue living here?"

"I don't think so. She'll probably sell it to you if you ask. If I know Liz, she'll head back to her father's estate." Rick parked the truck beside an open barn, which at one point most likely had been an old tobacco barn. The Ferrari and a black Harley were parked within.

Up the drive, the two guys lumbered behind them and a third came out the back door of the farmhouse. The dark mien on his face was frightening.

"Is he dead?" he bluntly asked followed by a blink to his eyes and a subconscious pull-back of his shoulders.

Rick just nodded.

"Bad business. I'm sorry to hear that."

"Are you Higgins?"

"Yes. Mr. Darcy's personal security. I take it you're here to tell his wife?"

Drawing his lips into a thin line, the former Marine nodded again, calling on that inner strength of his.

"She's out back with Dixon. Follow me."

Side-by-side the three men walked through the trees toward the symphony carried in the breeze. With each step, the music grew louder as they drew closer to the source, filling the mountain air with a majestic Aria that only an opera lover could appreciate, but Knightley wasn't one of them. What would be considered a siren song to some, felt ominous to him. All that female shrieking made the hair on his arms stand on end.

On any other day, the image Liz presented to them would have mesmerized him, and he did—once again—consider Darcy a lucky dog. For even with the news they would impart, she would always be Darcy's. Not even death would take him from her. No other man could fill Fitzwilliam Darcy's shoes. His hold on her was too great. At that thought, he wanted to weep for her and, in truth, for his own losses. He had loved Katie, but she didn't have the mettle to overcome the shadow of death and sought to place blame—as justified as it was—in the accident.

Liz stood in the middle of a grassy clearing with the sun beating down on her. Strapped around her thigh, a multi-knife sheath carried several throwers below denim shorts; her shining, brunette waves fell around a floral T-shirt. Her security detail Dixon was overseeing her practice session; the burly guard handed her one of the longer knives displayed on a makeshift table supported by two construction saw horses. A diva's shrill voice emanated from the portable CD player at the edge of the table.

Dixon, of course, spied them watching her but did nothing to break her focus. Yeah, he knew by the expressions on their faces and the suits on their backs, particularly when Rick's lip's tightened and he slowly shook his head.

With utmost concentration, she stared down the paper "man" target tacked to a tree, delicately held the thrower's tang in her hand, rocked it back and forth, and then released it with a measured flick of her wrist. The blade held its velocity and height for 25 feet before making contact in the center of the target's head.

"An Iceman kill shot," Rick softly said, clearly admiring her accuracy after such a short time of instruction. It was bittersweet given that Darcy couldn't witness it. In many ways she'd been his protégé.

"Mighty fine toss, Mrs. D. It's amazing how far you've progressed this summer." She leaned back on her heels and admired her proficiency, arms folded across her full bosom.

She spoke with beaming pride, evident by the tone in her voice. "I know, right? I'm a far cry from that boring kindergarten teacher in my past life."

But Higgins, standing beside Rick, broke the spell by clearing his throat.

As though time had slowed, she turned to face them; in recognition, a broad smile quickly spread on her face and then her mind caught up with her impulsive greeting. The enthusiasm slowly receded in dawning awareness that the two miserable-looking visitors stood before her without the man she was expecting.

Knightley half-smiled, conveying sorrow rather than joy at seeing her.

Her hand flew to her heart and she stepped back taking a panicked, labored breath. She said nothing, but even from their distance he could see her complexion turn white as a ghost. She knew.

Abruptly she turned from them, running balls out into the trees.

Dixon held his hand up to them, halting them from their pursuit and then he was gone—hot on her heels.

The music ominously continued to play. He hated opera.

***

"Mrs. Darcy! Liz!" she heard Dixon yell from behind her as she weaved through the trees, her heart pounding furiously, trying to outrun the news they brought with them.

No! she fought, but her cascading tears knew otherwise. A branch lashed at her face, but she kept running, narrowly missing other low hanging ones. "This … is … not … happening."

Ripping the Velcro knife sheath from her thigh, she ran faster, panting wildly.

"Liz! Stop!"

Unable to catch her own breath, she didn't care that the poor man sounded winded and kept running, hoping to outrun him. Hastily, she glanced over her shoulder to gauge his distance, but it was her downfall; she tripped, falling flat on her face into the leaves.

"No, no ..." she cried, and no longer able to run from her fears she violently wept, balling into the fetal position when the wracks took hold off her and her emotions poured forth. No one needed to tell her what she saw written on their faces. No one needed to tell her what their manner of dress meant.

"No! You promised, Fitzwilliam!"

Had he? He'd known long before he left, sensing his own demise, like all men who lived on the edge. Why else would he have made their last day together so special for her?

Pulling her legs into her curled body she held them close, uncaring about the scrapes and knot forming on her head. Her tears soaked her dirty face and the leaves pressed to her cheek. Tighter still, she buried her forehead against her knees, holding them to her, willing this moment to be only a nightmare, not a reality.

"I'm ... I'm sorry .... Mrs. D," she thought she heard Dixon's heavy panting, hand on the tree trunk beside him as he attempted to catch his breath.

"Tell me I didn't see them? Tell me he was behind them, in the trees, come home to me," she sobbed, tasting the dirt on her legs.

Like the father or brother she desperately needed, Dixon managed to sit her up into his arms, cradling her with shelter in the storm. "He wasn't in the trees. Darcy is gone, Liz. He's gone."

"Noooooooooooo," pulled from her lungs.

The pain shot through her heart with halting truth as it ripped from her chest. Uncontrollably weeping against him, he just let her emotions and tears flow without a word. All she heard was the sound of her shattering sobs pounding from her lips, shaking their one body.

The tears tracked down her cheeks, filling her mouth with the bitter salt of life, love, and death.

"I'm sorry … let it out, darlin'."

She didn't know how long she sat there crying, but this man, this stranger-turned-family, finally stood then scooped her back into his arms, carrying her through the woods to face her husband's brothers.

"He's dead. He can't be dead." She blubbered, resting her head on Dixon's shoulder, letting the tears silently drop onto his solid support through the trees, into the field and back toward the house.

"Do I have to face them?"

"Not if you really don't want to, but Mr. D would want you to be strong."

"I can't … I don't want to hear it. I can't bear it."

"I know, but you must. I'll be right there beside you, and those fellas love you."

They neared the side of the porch and she whispered with a swipe to her cheek. "You can put me down now."

Her legs felt wobbly as she climbed the porch steps to the front door, like they would buckle and collapse under her, but Dixon was right there holding her waist. She felt as though her heart would pound right out of her chest and just stood at the closed screen door, blankly staring at it, but discerning the men within. In her hesitation, the horror came, the fear of *those* words, and then more tears rolled down her cheeks, dropping from her chin. Biting her top lip, she was sure it bled. Her fingers beat against her leg and she looked up, but her eyes were tightly sealed.

He came behind her—not Dixon—but Fitzwilliam, and his ghostly voice whispered into her ear, "You got this, Lakmé. You're stronger than even me."

No. She wasn't, but she'd try to be.

Reaching for the door handle, her fingers trembled until Dixon's hand clasped over hers, opening the door.

Immediately, John and Rick stood from the sofa, and Nick came from the kitchen holding a tall glass of water. Four warriors who represented different parts of her husband's life, all loved him in one way or another struggled with the reality, two had been commissioned to break it to her and two there to keep her from killing herself.

The air felt heavy with a cloud of dark disconsolation. Silent mourning and unspoken grief draped the room in a black veil.

Immobilized, she saw the tears prick Rick's blue eyes, but he, too, stood stoically. Surprisingly, it was John who came to her, wrapping his strong arms around her body in a tight hug, but her own arms hung lifelessly at her sides.

"I'm sorry, Liz," he quietly comforted, and when she felt his body lurch, she knew he was crying. She hugged him back because she knew that, John understood her absolute shock and pain.

When he drew back from her, his tear-filled eyes locked with hers. "There's no easy way to do this but giving it to you straight is the only way. Let's sit down and talk about what happened in Bermuda."

Her cousin held out his hand to her and she took it, taking a seat between both men; although squished, the heat of their bodies felt comforting in light of the chill invading her entire being. Every movement she made seemed heightened, outlined with a clarity of 3D as if she was in a movie—just the understudy, not the headliner to her own life.

She looked over to Dixon seated beside the fireplace, and he smiled thoughtfully, encouragingly.

"It was quick," Rick said, the muscles at his throat flexing. "I promise you, there was no pain whatsoever, Liz."

Mind frozen, she nodded but words failed her; questions were superfluous. She didn't want to know "how it happened" just the "how can we reverse time?" Her tongue felt thick with dryness and she swallowed hard.

"We were diving … I planted the C-4 on a yacht, and he affixed the explosives in and outside an underwater cavern where the cartel hid a narcosub for trafficking through a mangrove swamp. Something went wrong with either Darcy's remote or the explosive device, and when he neared the cave to examine, both blew. We don't know the cause of the delayed discharge, only the heartbreaking result."

Her breath caught at the image in her mind and her strangled words came out. "Did ... did you ... find him?" Again, her breath came short and fast as she sucked in air in the struggle to stay alive.

Rick's cold hand squeezed hers and in what felt like slow motion she looked up at him. He hopelessly shook his head.

"Then ... he could still be alive. He's alive. He ... can hold his breath ... a really long time."

"No, Liz," John solemnly said. "He's not alive."

"I can't believe that." Turning slightly to face John, she begged. "You know him, John. You know what he went through in SEAL training and how he can survive anything." She suddenly remembered all his promises. "He's alive; I'm sure of it! He gave his word that he'd be back and he always keeps his word!"

He shook his head, but she wouldn't believe him, couldn't believe him!

"Rick, you know that Fitzwilliam wouldn't *allow* himself to get killed. He's alive—I know it to be true. This is bullshit!" She pleaded as if she could convince them all, but her cousin just stared with tears in his eyes at her, too upset himself to say anything.

"I wish to all that is holy that was true, but it's not. Liz, what Rick can't say because it's too painful is that ... we *found* him ..." he swallowed hard, "in ... pieces."

Horror-struck, she couldn't speak. The room suddenly swirled around her; her body swayed from left to right. Falling like the black curtain of her consciousness, she fainted onto Rick's lap.

8

Requiem

August 20
Virginia

This wasn't how Liz expected to return home.

Behind huge black sunglasses, her red eyes wanted to cry, but there was nothing left. After a week with Gigi in North Carolina, both lost in abject despair, the tears had bled her dry; she was lifeless now, devoid of will to think, feel, talk, or even move. She just stood there, looking up at the sky. At that moment, all she noticed were the dark storm clouds above the Darcy family cemetery, rolling across the sky; the wind pushed them aside, making room for the darker ones and creating eerie shadows over the headstones. Subconsciously, she searched for a sliver of white cloud, the metaphoric silver lining, and tried with all her might to conjure the memory of the magical sky over their starlit moon dance. Remembering was too difficult; her mind was a foggy, cloudy haze of nothingness.

What she did feel was a sense of disconnection to this feckless charade because it wasn't Fitzwilliam's final resting place. The empty casket housed only red satin while her husband's unrested soul floated around somewhere, released from the torn flesh decaying at the bottom of Hungry Bay or being picked at, like fish bait, in the ocean. Perhaps, he didn't mind. After all, he was a Frogman. That image haunted her *waking* nightmares. The valium took care of her *sleeping* nightmares.

She blinked once, twice. Yes, she was still alive. And like a messenger from the floating soul of her lover, a brightly colored Monarch butterfly came into focus as it swam through the air over the grave. A fragile beauty, it gently floated above the mourners and then fluttered back over the flowers along the mound's perimeter. Finally, it departed for the rose garden flanking the cemetery.

Like slowly reviving from a coma, she became aware of the gathered crowd surrounding the tombstones of Fitzwilliam's parents and grandparents. Had they, too, seen the butterfly or was it a sign just for her? It was free, not troubled by the horrors of its past that even her love could not erase. One day, she'd be buried beside this grave, but he wouldn't be there and she'd still be alone. All but five or six of these 60 or so strangers knew the casket was empty. How does one explain that he was blown to bits? How does one reconcile that even in death they wouldn't rest together? How could they comprehend the cavernous emptiness she felt?

"Father, we commit Fitzwilliam Darcy's body to the earth, from which our bodies were originally created, and we rejoice in the fact that his spirit is even now with You, the Father of spirits," the minister prayed, holding his hands out over the meaningless mound of dirt.

A loud nose blow came from his aunt Katherine, as she stood at the head of the grave beside the holy man. Her big black hat and old-fashioned blusher veil hid her pulled-too-tight facelift. Sandwiched between Rick and Sarah, they comforted the officious woman—and in the process kept her far away. She was in no mood for bullshit.

Starting with dear Gus and Doris Reynolds, her gaze followed the line of mourners, scanning those who loved Fitzwilliam most, finally falling on one of the two women holding her up: her sister-in-law. At her other side Jane, who had been her constant comforting shadow from the minute her plane touched down in Asheville, then back to Virginia. Perhaps Fitzwilliam had been right all along. Her sister was making up for all the mistakes of her past. Further, she felt the grief of losing a brother-in-law and understood there was no place for her bubble-headed levity. Still, Jane was Jane and insisted that a widow should wear a couture black suit and Prada accessories; the cat's-eye glasses and an up-do were the "absolute must for any funeral." But she did draw the line at pearls. Only the snake necklace, having been safely protected in the safety deposit box would do today—and every day thereafter. Otherwise, she was too spaced out to give a crap. She could wear burlap and wouldn't care. In fact, she didn't even care that her shoe heels were sinking into the ground.

She turned her head to examine Gigi; though Liz's vision was impinged by swollen eyelids and dark-tinted lens, she could see Gigi's gut-wrenching pain written in her blue eyes. The minister's rambling words became garbled background noise to her resurrected thought process. Poor Gigi portrayed a woman in control today, but Liz knew otherwise considering the trauma she had experienced as a child. Was Fitzwilliam's accident just another deathly abandonment in the string of many others? The girl had been inconsolable upon hearing the news, and her husband Justin was ill-equipped to deal with such mourning.

Liz knew that the thoughtful, tender smile upon Gigi's lips was no doubt a struggle but one made for her benefit. As her sister-in-law slid her arm around her waist she whispered in her ear, "He loved you so much, Liz. You changed his life."

Finding her voice, it took every ounce of strength left in her to comfort her sister-in-law. "We both changed his life. No two women could have been luckier to be loved by such an admirable man."

A single tear did drop. She must have stored it away for this very moment.

"I don't know what I'll do without him," Gigi said, sniffling.

"You'll go on living, and be proud of what your brother stood for and against."

"And so will you; you'll get through this."

She blankly looked at her. "No. I won't," then turned back to face the minister as he made his closing remarks. Right now, she meant what she said. What was the point of living without him? When he died he took with him her breath and heartbeat. Her half-dead brain inhabited a shell now. For the first time in her life, she had *true empathy*, not just compassion, for her father's depression.

She could now understand the depth of despair he felt when all hope was lost for a loved one to return to your embrace. The overwhelming sadness that you'd never hear "I love you," again, never to joke with or dream beside … never to raise a family or hear a little Fitzwilliam's baby laughter.

Here at the minister's final blessing would have been the moment when she threw herself onto her husband's grave—if he were in it.

"After saying our final farewells, let us remember that his spirit and love carry on in our hearts. Go forth in the certain hope of being reunited with Fitzwilliam Darcy at the end of time. Go forth with God's peace and may the Almighty bless you now and forevermore. Amen."

The funeral ended and both girls flanking her turned to their partners, hugging and openly crying. The ever-watchful Dixon and Nick weren't far behind her as some mourners—like Caroline— lingered feet from the grave with a final good-bye. Most quickly left, but she stood isolated—the unapproachable grieving widow, saying her good-bye—at the end of the grave, looking down at the dirt and the red roses at the head.

Robotically, she held out her arm and released a stem of "their" Longbourn orchid from her fingers. A symbol of pure love, the *Coelogyne ochracea*s hit the grave with a delicate thud.

The pain, the misery of losing her best half, pierced her heart like a knife.

Her legs gave way and she fell to her knees crushing the colorful flowers. Tears broke through her dam, cascading like raindrops down her cheeks and blurring the image of the three stark white orchids. For just this moment, she and her husband's wandering spirit shared an embrace without touch and she begged beneath her breath. "Please. I don't want to wait until the end of time. Find a way, any way ... to come back to me ... or take me with you, babe. I told you in Moscow, I'd rather die together than to live without you."

Closing her eyes, she wept, floating with him above the grave, imagining his face on that blissful night of lovemaking in the moonlight ... until gravity accelerated in free-fall when her father broke her from the spell, assisting her pitiful self up from the ground.

His loving voice was a soothing balm as she struggled to put her emotions back in their box. "Sweetheart, you'll get through this," he gently said handing her his old-fashioned handkerchief.

"I don't know, Dad."

"You will. You're a strong girl."

She couldn't help but to notice that despite his obvious concern, he appeared unusually put-together in a black suit. Clean-shaven and clear-eyed, he looked healthy. Had he gained weight?

She wiped her tears below the glasses and sniffled. "Thank you for being here today."

"You're my kitten. Of course I came." They hugged, and he softly said, "I'm sorry about Fitzwilliam. He was a good man, and I mean that."

"Thanks. I know you two had your differences, so it means a lot that you came. But *how* were you able to come?—that's the question."

"Ah, well, don't tell your CIA friends, but I figured out how to adjust the ankle monitor's GPS tracking system. They think I'm sitting in your greenhouse listening to Chopin."

"Very clever *and* illegal." The smile slipped from her face as quickly as it came because there was very little feeling behind it.

Her father touched the necklace, cradling the snake's head in his fingers. "I recall the first time I saw you wearing this at the airport after my rescue."

"Let's not think of that day."

"You're right. The necklace is a keepsake of your love, I imagine."

"It is. It's very dear to me, but I discovered yesterday when I removed it from the safety deposit box that the clasp is messed up."

"I can fix it for you, if you like—just leave it with me and I'll replace it with something secure."

"Oh! Thank you!"

"You can come pick it up at Longbourn and stay indefinitely. It is still your home, Lizzy; it's where you belong now."

She sighed. "Honestly … I don't know where I belong. I think I might go … I don't know. Fitzwilliam's sister invited me out to California until I decide what to do. I might …" she glanced at Jane talking with Charlie. "Maybe I'll temporarily move into Jane's loft since she spends so much time at Charlie's houseboat."

"I understand. You have a lot of important decisions to make, but if you move home, we can be a real family again."

Were they ever? They hadn't been a family since their mother left, but she wouldn't pour salt in his never-healing wound, especially today. Things were different now, and as sympathetic as she was to his continual disconsolation, she was a different woman. Lost didn't mean she'd be slipping back into doormat behavior out of grief or a need to be needed by someone—anyone.

"I appreciate that, but before I make any decisions, I'm returning to North Carolina. There are things I need to attend to there. The horses, you know. In fact, I'm leaving with the Reynoldses and Gigi and Justin immediately after the luncheon at Aunt Katherine's."

"Of course, and whatever I can do to help, just ask, Lizzy-bear. You can count on me to do the right thing this time."

"I'm sure I can. So, maybe you can ship overnight the necklace to me when it's done? Fitzwilliam has a corporate P.O. box in North Carolina."

"That sounds just fine. May I walk you to the limousine? My shoulder is stronger than I look."

"Of course. It seems like Jane, and our friends have been carrying me this last week, but I don't think I can make it by myself. I feel a little weak."

"You need to eat something."

"What's the point?"

"As you have always supported me, let me be here for you for a change."

He held out the crook of his elbow and she slid her arm through. Side-by-side, they walked in silence toward John waiting for her at the open car door as her father's free hand gently patted the one draped in his arm.

"Liz?" a man called out to her and she turned, recognizing immediately the handsome, once rugged, man stopping two feet from her. Gone was the cowboy hat and blue jeans, replaced by a fine suit.

Dave Wentworth. Oh Lord. "Dave," she said with a pensive smile (a measure of guilt that she had ever considered him eye candy) and a nod, unable to say much more.

"Please accept my condolences," his smooth southern draw offered.

"Thank you. You came all the way from Tennessee just for Fitzwilliam's funeral?"

"I got an email from Crash and, well, I wanted to pay my respects to you in person."

As if his presence alone didn't make her uncomfortable enough, she heard Jane gasp behind her. Immediately, she recalled Jane's description of him: "Wet-worth." The remaining blood in her body drained from her face. She cleared her throat and nervously adjusted her sunglasses.

"I appreciate your thoughtfulness. Oh! Dave, this is my father, Tom. Dad, Dave visited Pemberley with Charlie in April."

The men shook hands with pleasant greeting and condolences, and then the awkward, thick air expanded to near-choking level. Not that anything had happened romantically between Wentworth and her, but it was obvious he had once been interested in hooking up during her husband's mission to rescue Rick. His attendance at the funeral was perplexing, and she wondered if his intentions, in light of her husband's death, were opportunistic. Still, she couldn't be rude given that he traveled so far to pay his respect.

"Will you be joining us back at my aunt's home for a memorial lunch? You're more than welcome, and I'm sure you'd like to catch up with Charlie. He could use a good friend now."

"I sure will. Much obliged."

Jane murmured something to Charlie behind her but she couldn't make it out, and John motioned to get in the limo. In fact, he looked a bit annoyed.

"Um … the limo's waiting. I'll see you later, I guess," she said.

A minute later, she was seated in the limo with John and Dixon in the back seat.

"Do you know that fella well, Mrs. D?"

"Yeah. I was wondering the same thing," John groused. "I didn't like the way he looked at you. It's a funeral for God's sake and he was undressing you with his eyes."

"He wasn't, John. He's not like that."

"It looked disrespectful, ma'am. I think Knightley and I would feel better knowing who he is."

"He's nobody special, just one of Charlie's Army buddies who came to help with security at Pemberley when Fitzwilliam was in Peru."

"Is that all?" John questioned. She wouldn't play into his hand; he was just looking out for her—not questioning her faithfulness to Fitzwilliam. Everyone knew that was unshakable and always would be.

"No, that's not all. He's the one who taught me how to knife throw."

A tap to the window interrupted them and John rolled down the window.

Nick's concerned expression met them. "Who was that guy?"

For the first time in a week, she chuckled. It was as if over-protective Fitzwilliam hadn't left at all.

If she remembered nothing else from today to write in the journal that he gave her, she'd remember this, and sketch the butterfly.

***

Panama

The green season kept the gringos away, but unfortunately Juan Morales-Sanchez wouldn't be staying long to enjoy the visit. He'd be leaving his residence (Casa Luz) on the mountain above Cerro Azul for drier weather in four hours. He'd flown in the night before to see to La Muerta Mundial cartel business by meeting privately with his banker. His ever-growing competitor in South America, El Negro cartel, was hitting his finances hard with this most recent stunt on the Bolivia/Brazil border. The latest tip off to Bolivian national drug authorities had led to the seizure of 1,500 kilos of refined cocaine; he'd feel the financial hit for months to come.

Still angry, he stood at the window of his mountain hacienda gazing out at the lush forest below, lost in perplexing thoughts of El Negro and the millions it has sheltered in Panama.

It had been a frustrating month, but he'd finally had justice for his father's murder.

"I will miss you, *mi querido*," his Panamanian lover of eight months stated. Pilar stood behind him and ran her delicate fingers up his ribcage; his lungs filled with her spicy scent.

He snickered when her full breasts pressed against his back. "You will not. Perhaps you will succeed in seducing Luis to see to your needs while you wait for my return."

"I am insulted you think so little of my affections."

His hand clasped hers draped across his chest and he tugged her around to him. "You are here at my bidding and paid well for it. Do not be so fooled to think that I do not know of your carnal pursuit of Luis. He, too, is paid well—but for his loyalty to me and only me. All along, he has had my permission to see to your lustful needs, but he has not done so out of respect for me."

"It is only to make you jealous, my love. And … I do need the money. Mamma is sick."

"Jealous?" he laughed.

"You do not mind?"

"Why would I? I do not love you." He cruelly kissed her plump lips. "I own you."

She reached up and touched his brow. "You own my heart, but what can I do to own yours?"

Morales turned from her, and her hand dropped from his brow. He walked to his desk, fiddled with his sharp letter opener, and finally looked back up to her. "Pilar, you are a plaything, a diversion when I am away from my home." Gazing at her sensual body below the white, gauzy dress she wore, he drank in her luscious curves, unable to deny his admitted appetite for her. "As lovely and talented in the dungeon as you are, your only purpose is to satisfy those carnal pleasures. It is the way it is. Love is a delusion."

"I do not believe it. What of that spider woman? You loved her."

He stared her down, annoyed that she knew of Nadya, yet humored that she believed he had loved the Russian.

"She is none of your business."

"Juan, what if I want more from you? Do you deny me my heart?"

"Your heart is not what I want from you, just your wet cunt. You would do well to remind yourself that our arrangement is a means to care for your family." He raised an eyebrow. "Is that not why you tease Luis—to add to your purse?"

Pilar recoiled from his words, but he didn't care. He could have a harem at his bidding if he so desired. A fresh crop of men and women were trafficked in from all over the world, but he desired local flavor.

A knock on the door, interrupted her simper.

"Come."

His *secretario* walked into the room. "Señor, I am sorry to interrupt, but I have word from Claudia in Virginia," Luis reported. The man avoided Pilar's stare, and that was rather humorous. Oh, how he loved playing people against each other like chess pieces.

"That is all, Pilar. I will see you in your suite before my departure. Be ready and wearing red."

"Do … you need the camera?"

"Of course. I enjoy examining our dungeon play when we are apart." He sat back in the desk chair and chuckled as she walked to the door. "Sit, Luis."

As instructed, his lieutenant took the seat on the opposite side of the desk then slid a computer tablet across the wood. "Claudia has done well and has sent us these photographs taken at the funeral today. It is confirmed—Iceman's woman is alive."

"Alive? How is this possible?"

"I do not know how she survived the blasts, but she was at the funeral and there is no mistaking that it was her. See, look at the photographs."

With one hand, Morales tapped an open switchblade against his desk blotter as the other swiped through the images; his lips drawn to a taut line. His blood raged at how well Darcy had played him. "*Sí*. It is her."

"But it is over now, *Jefe*, and you have won! Your vengeance for your father's murder is complete. I must commend your plan; Iceman acted rashly—foolishly in his rage to seek justice for his woman."

"Perhaps. Perhaps not. We shall see." Swiping through several more images of the mourners rife with grief, some faces he recognized from the intel provided by Carlos when he tailed Richard Fitzwilliam and the British reporter back to Washington. "Iceman fooled us once with his wife's survival in Virginia; you can understand my need for continuing surveillance now that she has mysteriously materialized."

"Yes, of course. I also received an e-mail from the coroner in Paget. After the sharks and storm cleared, the flesh our men recovered near the cavern, he determined to be human—whose remains we cannot be sure as many died that day. The coroner does not have the facilities for DNA examination or forensic matching."

"La Muerta Mundial lost many good soldiers and my prized yacht! And what of the contracted hitman responsible for the Darcy estate explosion? Where is he?"

"He has disappeared and is not answering our CIA back channel contact or his dark web email."

"Pity, but perhaps it is for the best. Talented as he is, I do not like loose ends. Is there anything else you need to tell me in regard to Iceman?"

Luis placed three newspapers in the center of the desk: Bermuda's *Royal Gazette*, a *Washington Post,* and a *New York Times*. "We can be sure that it was him in Hungry Bay. The obituaries state an untimely death while diving on vacation in Paget on August 4, and our men located an American Navy combat diving knife and strips of wet suit in the limestone rubble near the mangroves."

He swiped through the remaining photographs, stopping on one where the widow knelt, weeping at the grave. "She is as beautiful as I recall her on that motorcycle in Moscow."

"Not as lovely as *Señora* Morales."

"I think ... that no man would willingly leave such a woman he loves by faking death. If he is alive, then Darcy will return to her very soon. These tears this woman expresses look genuine. So, he may be dead, but only time will tell."

"It has already been sixteen days."

"Yes." Handing the tablet back across his desk, he added, "Claudia has done well; instruct her to maintain surveillance on the former Mrs. Darcy for another two weeks. We shall see if he returns, and if not, then we will declare this over. I have my hands full with this El Negro's attempt to take over the cartel's Central American business now that our narcosub is at the bottom of Hungry Bay. If Darcy returns, tell her to kill them all."

"*Sí, Jefe.*"

"This El Negro ..." he shook his head and sighed deeply. "Our men in Tarapoto heard rumors that El Negro will pay handsomely in cryptocurrency for sabotage of the coca."

"But they are loyal to you."

"They are loyal to money. Luis, I want increased security in Bolivia and Peru. Notify our Colombian and Mexican friends that war may be coming and I want additional protection in Paraguay to Brazil."

"It is worse than that, *señor*. Our Italian associates in Venice and the Spaniards in Cadiz have heard the same. There have been threats against the narcotic and weapon shipping containers. Even London is uneasy."

He tightened his fist. "I want the head of El Negro! Who is he?"

"No one knows, but other cartels are on alert, too. After the authorities shut down our convoy near the Brazilian border, many fear the same. We must change our delivery routes and cultivation locations."

Under his calm exterior, Morales' blood boiled; he rose and proceeded to the exit, leaving Luis where he sat. "Have the helicopter ready and ... as much as it may pain you to do so—dispose of Pilar before my return. After one last fuck, I do not think she will be able to please me again."

"Pilar?"

"After you have your fill, of course. You continue to have my permission."

"Thank you, *Señor* Morales. She is quite lovely."

"And willing." *For such an unattractive man as you.* "I will expect your immediate return to the family as planned. The children will be happy to see you for your godson's birthday."

9

Between Here and There

Morning, August 29
Maryland

How long do you think he'll be staying with us?" Jane whispered to Charlie across the galley table over breakfast. Not that Dave could hear them from the shower on the opposite side of the houseboat, but still.

Looking so adorable with his blond locks sticking up on end, he shrugged both shoulders without a glance up from the newspaper spread out on the table. He'd been so serious since Darcy's death and more than one student at the dance school had mentioned it. He was different, but she understood.

"It's ... a bit weird, don't you think?" she continued.

Now he shrugged his left shoulder while shoveling cereal into his mouth with his right hand. "Not that I'm complaining ... because he looks so damned hot in the morning, but it's close quarters in the houseboat, and he is sorta cramping our style—if you know what I mean, babe."

Finally, he dropped the spoon and guzzled his coffee.

"Did he say how long he intends on staying?"

"Jane, I don't know and it's not like I can ask him to leave. If he's so damned hot, why are you complaining?"

"Boy, you're testy lately. Are you jealous?"

"Do you want me to be?"

Now it was she who shrugged and went back to eating her cereal.

"Maybe I *am* jealous. Maybe I don't like the way you lick your lips when he walks into the room."

"They're very chapped," she lied with a mouthful of Lucky Charms, and he just chuckled sardonically.

"Aw, don't be jealous, teddy bear. You're the only one I'm interested in; you know that. It's just that it's been over two weeks since his arrival. Isn't it time to go yet?" she whined, employing her cutesy baby voice while rubbing his privates with her bare foot under the table. "And I miss you ... like tons and *so* not enjoying sex at the dance school just to avoid him hearing us here on the boat," she added massaging him some more.

"Fine. He did say something," he finally admitted, succumbing to her foot rub, just as she knew he would. Persistence always paid off when it came to her man and "Big Chaz."

"He's hanging around for your sister's return from North Carolina so he can ask her to dinner."

She dropped the spoon along with her chin. "No way!"

"Are *you* jealous?" he laughingly asked.

"Of course not ... I mean, under any other dramatically different circumstances I'd think Lizzy scored big time. 'Cause even you can't deny that he is one My. T. Fine bronco-busting, bareback riding cowboy, but Darcy has only been dead for, like, less than a month. I admit, I'm not the sharpest tool in the box, but is he an idiot? Even I know that's wrong on so many levels. You need to talk him out of it.

She's way too raw, totally not ready to enter the dating world." *But maybe he doesn't want to date. Hmm … maybe it's just sexual?*

"Yeah it is still too raw—for all of us," he dourly agreed, rising from the banquette.

"Did he talk to you about her? What did he say? How interested is he? Just a casual hook up or is he wanting more?"

"I don't know. Guys don't talk about that shit, and I'm not gonna ask. If he wants to crash and burn, that's totally his problem. If she wants to burn off some tension, then that's her decision. Don't get involved."

She held the empty cereal bowl out to him and shrugged. "I guess, but it would be good to know what his intentions were. Maybe I should warn her."

"I'm tellin' ya'—don't get involved, Jane.'

"I can't promise that."

"Look, Rick is sending me to Central Asia tomorrow for recon, so … behave while I'm gone."

"You know I will."

He replied with a cock to his eyebrow.

Just then a shirtless Dave came to the galley door. Rivulets of water trickled down from his dark wavy, wet hair to his muscular pecs, eliciting a lip lick and her stare to the single bead clinging to his nipple. Oh, Lord, if Lizzy did hook-up with him then, wowza, she would be one damn lucky girl. Even if she just used him for sex so she could get Darcy out of her mind for a short time. Sex didn't have to accompany feelings, just horniness. A good screw, wearing a cowboy hat, could just be hot and fun without all those messy emotions. That treasure trail of hair was way to appealing for her sister to pass up on.

"Did I hear you say you're headed outta town, Crash?"

"Yeah. I'll be back next Tuesday."

"Then, I better get my things and be on my way, find myself a hotel. It wouldn't be proper, me stayin' here alone with your girl."

"You could stay, Dave!" she blurted a little too forcefully. "I mean … don't leave on my account. I'll go hang out in my Georgetown loft until Liz's return."

"I heard she was comin' back to Washington soon."

"She'll be back home on Friday, which I think will be good for her. Although I haven't heard from her since the funeral, I have no doubt that she's a mess—grieving, you know. She needs a support system, maybe some late-night drunk fests with her sister."

"Her grief is understandable, but some folks heal better on their own."

"I can see that. She loved her husband *soooo* much. But I know Liz—without sisterly intercession, it could be *years* of despair and crying. Trust me, she'll never get over him that way. They were soulmates, you know."

"If you don't mind me sayin', maybe she just needs a little distraction to go on with her life." Dave stated.

His expression darkened like he understood that kind of grief and then walked to the coffee pot. As he poured himself a cup, she admired his rough looking, working hands, and as much as she fought the urge, her appreciation traveled downward over the well-developed sinews of Dave's back to his tight bottom and how his worn blue jeans hung at his hips. Turning, he leaned against the counter; his hairless chest and those vivid blue eyes nearly held her captive, but she forced herself to tear her gaze away and looked at Charlie, her man. Yum. Her tongue took a long swipe over her top lip where it lingered. She'd find it hard to get over *him,* too.

"Well, I guess I agree with you there," she said. "Liz does have her whole life ahead, and Darcy would want her to live it. It's going to take a lot of time though," she admitted. *Hmmm … but perhaps an uncomplicated roll in the hay could be good for her. I'll have to inquire.*

"Were you ever married, Dave?"

From the corner of her eye she saw Charlie's caution with a shake to his head and then a grimace when the man in question answered.

"Never got that far, but close. Any way … you just let me know if you think it best if I move on out to a hotel. I don't want to be a nuisance."

Charlie slapped his friend's back. "Stay here, as long as you like. Jane'll move back down to DC and be there for her sister's arrival. Who knows, maybe she'll pave the way to convincing Liz to move on."

***

Washington, DC

At nine in the morning, Liz waited on the park bench butting the picture window of the Bingley Dance School. Exhausted, she fought the pull of her eyes and fixed them to the city traffic chugging along. While it was a good distraction from nodding off, the noise and the people were too much; she suddenly felt confined, missing life at Pemberley and wishing that she'd ridden the SuperLow back to Washington.

She hadn't been to Bingley Dance School in ages, but following her visit with the Darcy family lawyer she had questions that needed answers. Unbeknownst to anyone other than Dixon (and the lawyer), she'd been in DC for a week staying at a luxury hotel near the National Mall. No one needed to know that she'd come home early because frankly, she couldn't bear to hear the "you should …" "why don't you …" "if I were you …" well-meaning but meaningless suggestions on how to recover from the unrecoverable, how to move on when she didn't want to. Why bother getting back to living, when—without Fitzwilliam—there was no living.

Apart from the hunter's cabin, Black Mountain had only unhappy memories for her. After a week-long cry-fest with her sister-in-law at the farmhouse, she did manage to leave with a measure of peace in that both Hank and Adam would be staying on with the Reynoldses. She and Gigi agreed to wait until both felt strong enough to discuss selling the place. In the interim, Gus would teach the boys the horse trade and everything would go on as before. Nick left for home in New York City and that broke her heart, but his life had been Fitzwilliam's life—sort of a symbiotic relationship that no longer existed. She'd miss him, but his teenage girls were likely overjoyed for his return.

As for Dixon, he'd never left her back, side, or front! But today, she was (finally, technically) on her own, free of his constant shadow as if she were a Hollywood A-Lister. Oh, he insisted on coming along, but even with everything that happened, Obsidian's identity needed to be kept secret, and there was the real possibility that she was under surveillance or danger. On the surface, she won the standoff with Dixon by promising him Maryland crabs and that she'd be extra aware of her surroundings. Yes, she was aware. So aware (as Fitzwilliam had taught her) that she knew Dixon was in the coffee shop across the street watching her and the raven-haired waitress. Poor guy could be living life and not remain tethered to her. Resisting the urge to wave at him, she instead toyed with her snake necklace—which she had received in Asheville the day before she left.

Gone were her blue jeans and leather apparel, replaced by summer sundresses now that she wasn't on the back of the bike and at home. *Home?*

Dropping her hand from her neck, she balled a fist, opening and closing it, just as Fitzwilliam had always done. It proved to be a great stress reliever, so much more effective than tapping her fingers against her thigh. *What is home?* She was just a hopeless drifter now: no home, no purpose. Neither a wife, teacher, nor mother—just a widow—a ridiculously wealthy widow. And here came the inopportune tidal wave of grief, as it sometimes did from just a thought or action. Tears welled. *He was my home! He was my purpose!*

"Liz? Is that you?" Caroline's voice snapped her from her forthcoming breakdown. Her inquiry had almost a pleasing sound to it, like she was happy to see her, which was unexpected. To the best of her recollection, their good-bye following the funeral luncheon had been strained. Glancing up, she admired the woman's shining tresses falling around her shoulders. Backlit by the sun, Caroline was stunning and, for a second, a pang of sorrow pierced her heart. No doubt, Fitzwilliam had once enjoyed those copper locks falling around him. A man like him is had been worthy of such a beautiful, talented woman—certainly not a boring teacher who hadn't a thing going for her. It was uncomfortable and upsetting to think of her husband's former lovers now that he was dead.

Oh, would she ever stop using present tense when words such as "Had been, "former" "had once" were more accurate? Probably not. She'd always think of Fitzwilliam in the here and now because he was with her in spirit.

"Hi Caroline," she sighed, forcing a polite smile.

"I'm surprised to see you. I just assumed you'd be staying on in the mountains."

"No. There's nothing there for me."

Caroline removed the establishment's keys and unlocked the door. "Well, come on in and we'll catch up. Are you doing okay?"

"Not really."

The woman in front of her clearly had to be the spitting cobra's doppelganger, because there was no way that the Caroline she knew could be this kind and inviting in both manner and body language.

After re-locking the door, her perfectly manicured, red talons pressed the key code to turn off the security alarm and then she flipped the lights.

"The studio looks so pretty. It's been a long time since my dance lesson."

"Yes! I recall it was for your wedding first dance."

"Instead, I met Iceman."

Walking to the office, Caroline smiled wistfully. "Lucky girl."

"Yes, very lucky." She tightened a fist. "I ... um ... I'm actually here to talk to Rick. Is he around this morning?"

"Probably. He's been cooped down in his office since the funeral. We hardly even discuss business … apart from him sending up his little Yorkie to relay information and nip at my heels."

"Do you mean Sarah? If so, she's from London, not Yorkshire; the accents are entirely different."

"The inference is there. He sends that Brit up to my studio just to annoy me. Really … tea in Washington? This is a coffee town."

Nope, this was definitely Caroline.

"Lately, I've been enjoying chai, and I always considered The District quite international."

The woman didn't reply, but rotated her head with narrowed eyes and pursed lips. She appeared to be on the verge of a quip, but it died on her mouth before execution. Perhaps widowhood had some benefits.

"The office window is gone."

"Yes, Darcy hooked us up with his construction team and voilà, we now have a fireproof SCIF, just like the one that saved your life."

"I see. I hope you never need to use it. It was a frightening experience that I'll never forget." *That explosion is the reason Fitzwilliam is dead. I sent him to his grave.*

Caroline pressed her thumb to a biometric pad and the door slid open.

"Yes. I imagine being locked within for such a long time as your home burned above you, was less than stellar." She withdrew her phone from her purse, then made a call, speaking low to her as the call rang on the other end. "I'll have Rick come up here. His cave is … chilly."

"Good morning to you, too. You have a visitor…Liz … Obviously she's in DC, not in the mountains … Are you sure? … Okay and, please, I'm in no mood today for your little lap dog. Keep her far from me; I have work to do before my first student at noon."

She tapped the Blackberry and smiled. "He wants you to go down to the freezer."

"The freezer?"

"You'll see," she replied with an eye roll as she walked to the supply closet. "Through this door and down these steps you'll travel a narrow passage. It's dark, so watch your footing for broken steps. It will lead you directly to his office." Caroline slid a cashmere sweater from its hanger and handed it to her. "You will definitely need this."

Unnerved, her pulse increased with the first step and then, when the door closed, the rushing blood in her veins throbbed in her temples. Her heart hammered. She braced her advance with palms pressed against the confining walls and almost immediately broke into a cold sweat. But, taking small steps, she pushed forward. So did her waking nightmares the deeper she descended into the unknown abyss before her. In the darkness of this tunnel, filled with a dim green hue, her mind was back in Pemberley's bunker on July 22nd.

The 1st movement of Haydn's trumpet concerto allegro filled the bunker to the rapid beating of the speed bag.

Suddenly, the walls and ceiling shook around her from what sounded like a sonic boom outside, but she couldn't be sure, continuing to focus like a laser on keeping good time, and connecting fists to bag with a steady cadence. The concerto's exhilarating trumpet pushed her onward.

Again, everything violently shook in accompaniment to an even louder boom. This time there was no mistaking it as an earth-rocking explosion on the estate. The heavy bag dislodged from the ceiling and several standing bags toppled over. Panicked, she watched as a rolling cabinet crashed into the floor mats. Her feet stumbled below her, trying to keep from falling, and she grabbed onto the side of the rifle safe bolted into the steel wall and the concrete foundation.

Cracks were forming and spreading in the ceiling.

Plaster and concrete fell from above her head.

The room was going to cave.

Only seconds, which felt like an eternity, passed and she ran to the exit, but everything suddenly went silent: the lights blacked out, the music stopped, and the biometric scanner locked the door. In the darkness, she furiously panicked, tugging on the metal door—but the security bolts were firmly in place. "Please, God! Start the generator! Start the generator!!" She labored, fruitlessly pulling on a handle in wild terror.

And then she remembered: the steel panic room at the back of the bunker. Fight and flight kicked in and she ran balls out toward the far end of the room, jumping over fallen objects, jelly legs barreling over the workout mat, barely tripping over ceiling debris in her desperation for shelter and survival.

As she pulled the door closed, another explosion blasted in a thunderous roar—this time, she saw the entire bunker burst into a white hot fireball through the remaining last aperture before it slammed shut with her safely sealed inside the pitch black panic room.

She backed away from the door to the far corner where she knew the small air shaft was; it led out to the old unexcavated escape route used during the Civil War. Frozen in the corner below it, she internally shook, taking deep breaths, terrified that the fire would consume her oxygen supply or burn her alive.

Heat! Oh the heat!!

"Liz?" she heard Rick call out to her, his faint voice growing louder as it pulled her from her nightmare. "Liz, are you there?"

Feeling lightheaded and nauseous, she pressed her forehead against the cool plaster wall to keep from passing out. Everything spun but a sudden hand came to her rescue, clasping her bicep to keep her from going down.

"Liz! My God! What happened? Are you okay?"

"I … oh Rick!" She fell into his arms and the dam broke, sobbing for the very first time about that day. Now that Fitzwilliam was gone, it was safe to let the tears and emotions flow out of her.

Both of his arms encircled her, but he said nothing as she bawled. "It's everything. I never told Fitzwilliam about that day at Pemberley. It was bad … really bad, and still haunts me. Now … he's gone. I can't do this without him."

"What can't you do?"

"Life."

He sighed regretfully. "I know it's hard, but I'm here for you; we all are. You can tell me everything, Liz, even about your experience in the bunker. I'll pretend I'm him and I promise, I'll answer just as he would; I'll even growl."

She couldn't help but to chuckle into his chest.

"C'mon, let's go talk about it over an Italian espresso or a cup of joe in my office."

"I hate coffee now."

"Okay. I'll have Sarah get us some tea on her way in."

"Nothing for me, thank you." She sniffled with an embarrassing snort of mucous and wiped his suit lapel. "I'm sorry. That day came back so vividly. I cry all the time."

Rick smoothed the hair from her face and smiled thoughtfully. In barely a whisper he said, "So do I."

She swallowed the knot in her throat. "How selfish of me."

"You're not selfish; you're grieving. Saying good-bye to someone you love is the hardest thing to do. It's only natural to focus on yourself and what was and struggle to think of what will be. Never apologize for self-reflection at this time."

His hand never left hers as he slowly led her down the hall until they stood at a metal door and another fingerprint scanner.

"Where are we?"

"*This* is no man's land. We're between here and there."

"Sort of like me."

"For obvious reasons, we otherwise refer to it as 'the freezer.' " With a press to his finger a pocket door slid open and she was met with a brightly lit space—the snap of cold air hit her face and bare legs, quelling the clammy flush to her chest and cheeks. To the left of the room was a sleek-styled sofa with blankets stacked upon a pillow.

With furrowed brow, she examined the inert monitors affixed where antique-tiled ceiling met wall. It seemed odd that they weren't busy doing something—anything—related to the many ongoing sanctioned Black Ops. Several newspapers lay strewn on his desk, but overall there was no sign of Obsidian business.

Turning to face him, she was finally able to get a good look at her cousin in the light. Dark circles under his eyes and ginger whiskers indicated his uncharacteristic disregard of his normal fastidiousness. "Are you living here, Rick?"

"I guess you can call it that."

"But what about Sarah?"

"She understands *my* being selfish."

"Ah." She nodded, taking a seat on the blue sofa, eyes zeroing in on the filled tack board. "Have the police found the man who tried to kill me?"

Rick cleared his throat and uneasily walked to her. "Unfortunately, it's a dead end. The ballistic evidence, the spent incendiary shells found in the forest, was stolen from the Leesburg police department on the 30th, their servers wiped clean of any reports."

"I see."

"It's most likely the cartel cleaning their footprint."

"And what about the explosion at the safehouse?"

"Nothing. Another dead end. The DC police said it was a faulty air conditioning unit that triggered a gas line explosion."

Again, she scanned the cold interior and wrapped her arms around herself. "Did Fitzwilliam come to this place?"

"He did." Sitting in the chair on the opposite side of the coffee table, Rick clasped his hands between his knees and leaned forward. "We briefed here before the guys left for Bermuda."

"I couldn't tell him about Pemberley," she blurted.

"You should have. He of all people understood trauma—he could have helped you through it."

"I just … I don't know … didn't want to worry him further. He was already wound so tight about protecting me from Diablo that I just knew if I shared my experience in the panic room, he'd not have waited for Bermuda and maybe have done something drastic, probably even foolish without a plan." She flexed her hand again then abruptly stopped, instead rubbing her stomach, which roiled from nervous anxiety. "Ironic isn't it? He was killed anyway, even after waiting and planning."

"In the end he succeeded, Liz. I'm sure his death puts an end to this. All he wanted was your safety, and he rests in peace knowing that now."

"It's a heavy load to carry. How do I not feel guiltier than I already do?"

"I wish I could tell you, but I ask the same question every day. How do I not feel guilty about sending him to his death?"

"I know John feels terrible. We talked at length about grief and how he survived. I can't imagine the guilt he felt after accidentally shooting his son."

"The circumstances were horrible to begin with, but Knightley is a survivor—as are you. It's good that Knightley has gone back to work, taking one of the few ops on Obsidian's docket."

"Is that why I haven't heard from him in the last few days? He'd been texting and calling at least five times a day to check on me, but now … nothing."

"He finally agreed to go out in the field—since you kept blowing him off every time he reached out."

He raised a pointed eyebrow and she felt bad. John had been there for her from the beginning, but she had to get on with her life on her own.

"I'm sorry. I'll give him a call."

"You can't now; he's off the grid in Austria for the next ten days, finishing a job that he started last year in Sierra Leone."

"And I suppose Charlie feels guilty, too?"

"Sure. Operation Gombey was his mission. He skated the edge of losing it when we couldn't find Darcy."

She leaned back and examined Rick's face. "But you did."

"Not the way we would have preferred; the bay was loaded with sharks almost immediately, and that's something that still puzzles me. My only guess is that Morales kept the bay bait-friendly to keep away curious divers and tourists."

"Oh." She couldn't go there and just let the words die in the air as she switched gears. "Is … I mean … do I still need to worry about Morales coming after me? Not that it really matters, but as dear as Dixon is to me, I think I'd rather be alone right now, and I feel bad that he has to hang around."

"There is always a chance of anything—but it's unlikely. I was just reading this morning that authorities in Bolivia are gearing up for a drug war between two cartels. La Muerta Mundial has other things to focus on besides the unnecessary assassination of a grieving widow. Darcy's death is what Morales wanted and that's what he got."

"Right." She stretched her arms out in front of her and said, "I'm, uh, thinking of getting out of here. I really don't want to move in with Jane, so I think to clear my head and maybe find some direction for the future, I'll go to some of the places Fitzwilliam and I dreamed about visiting together."

"I know you're probably feeling liberated, no longer at the end of La Muerta Mundial's barrel, but are you sure that's wise right now?"

She nodded. "Yeah, I do. After I visit my family, I'll be taking off."

"So, you'll let Dixon go?"

"I'm good—it's time for him to have a real life. He has to feel released from his guilt over the explosions at Pemberley."

"I don't think he'll see it that way. The man's devoted to you."

"Please don't make me feel guilty about him, too."

"Sorry … Well, then do you want Darcy's bike for your trip?"

"Black Ice?"

"My Italian friends who own the grocer on the block over have been minding it in their back courtyard until I got up the nerve to tell you it was here."

Wow. She hadn't expected that. *A cross-country bike tour?* "Definitely. The bike he bought me, I left in North Carolina and … I'd really like to ride."

"In addition to the keys, do you want his belongings from Bermuda?"

She looked away from his gaze and a shadow fell on her thoughts. "Not yet, so please keep them for me."

"I will. Now … if you'd like, please tell me about that day at Pemberley. It could help you."

"I'll be okay, really, I will. I've been journaling about it, so maybe that will help. I think the dark confines of the access hall just set me off." She sighed in resignation. "I think it's best if I just put it behind me. All that matters is that I survived it to have more time with him. We made some incredible memories at a very special place outside Asheville, and if I must live on—then I have that and every day before July 22nd. That whole remembering the past as it gives me pleasure thing."

"I think that's wise, but I'm always here for you, Liz. You know that, right?"

"Sure. Same here. We're still cousins." Smoothing her hand over the quilt folded beside her, she asked. "Well, enough about pitiful me. Do *you* want to talk about it?"

He simply chuckled.

"I'm sure you have Sarah's good advice, but I'm a good listener."

"I haven't told her yet, but I'm … I'm gonna shut down Obsidian at the end of the year."

"But why?"

"Because you're all my closest family, and, like Darcy, I now have greater clarity that if something else happens to any of you—even to Caroline—it would destroy me. He was light years ahead of us in his decision to leave, and I couldn't understand it. Falling in love with you showed him the way out. And after his death, it occurred to me that each one of us in this business is broken in a way and existing in isolation, getting empty thrills from the emotive high when we successfully bring down the evil and corrupt. But each of us have lost sight that we're still harbingers of death, no matter how noble the mission. My own neck I have no problem putting on the line, but to direct the others to do so ... I don't want that responsibility any longer. The cost is too great; my cousin's death crushed every one of us."

"And there's Sarah's welfare to consider, isn't there?"

"Very astute, as always."

"Do you love her?"

"Yes."

"I knew you did." She smiled as best she could. "Do the others know about you shutting down?"

"Not yet, but I'll talk with Caroline when the time is right. Given that she thinks this is all one big game and gets off on pain, she'll gladly take over." With a sly smirk, he looked down at his hands. "She'll probably rename it something ridiculous like *bakemonojutsu*. It means, ghost arts."

It was funny, but she didn't laugh. "I'd say I was sorry, but that would be a lie. I feel torn because without Obsidian I never would have met the man of my dreams, but because of the work he did for Obsidian, he's dead. I know you don't need the money, and I'm sure there are a ton of other things you can do to defeat evil."

"There are. Like you, I'm between here and there. So why are you here today? Certainly, not to see me."

"I love you … of course, I want to see you, but you're right. I'm here because I noticed something strange in Fitzwilliam's Geneva bank account and thought you might be able to shed some light on it."

"Sure. I hope I can help."

"I had forgotten all about his Obsidian payment account, and then when I met with the lawyer the other day, he gave me the list of holdings, account numbers, passcodes, etc. Of course, I logged in when I got back to the hotel and a few things struck me as odd. The first being a two million dollar wire transfer on July 30 to a bank in Morgantown, West Virginia."

"I'd say that's odd."

"Then, he liquidated almost all his personal stocks and holdings, purchased a ton of cryptocurrency and the other thing was that he transferred six million dollars to an account in Panama on the day he left for Bermuda. It wasn't his first wire transfer into it."

"Oh?"

"Yeah. About two months ago, he'd liquidated a bunch of stock and transferred about 12 million to that same account. And I'm almost embarrassed to tell you how much he transferred to a bank in England."

"How much?"

"Twenty-two million."

"Whoa. I knew my uncle was extremely wealthy, but … that's a lot of dough."

"Should I be worried? I mean … do you know if he knew someone in Panama City or in England? I know I'm gonna sound paranoid, but you don't think I have anything to worry about do you? I mean, I trust him, but … you hear about these things—people living secret dual lives, another wife and family. Maybe my husband never had intentions of returning to me."

"You listen too much to opera. Real life isn't always *Madama Butterfly*."

"No, it's a friggin' James Bond movie. You know what I meant. It's just that in this miserable fog I'm under, my imagination is running wild. Don't listen to me; I'm not thinking straight."

"Paranoia is the height of awareness," he stated.

"Fitzwilliam once said those very words to me."

"He stole it from me," he joked with a wink. "I assure you, you don't have anything to worry about, Liz. The only dual lives Darcy vacillated between were life and death, nothing more. There was only you. I don't know anything about England or West Virginia, but just before leaving for Bermuda, Sarah had received a tip that Morales had another compound in Panama. It was the plan that Darcy would parachute in following execution in Paget. I agree it's odd and that's a lot of cash, but I suppose he wanted it at ready hand. I don't know; perhaps his last transfer was just in case a sticky situation presented itself—like what he encountered in Peru in needing chopper transport to rescue me."

"Ah. He never mentioned that part of the op." Even still, it didn't assuage her uneasy feeling. Something wasn't right. While they rarely talked money because, frankly, the only thing she brought into their marriage was her love, he'd never said anything about liquidating, moving it around, hiding it for security reasons.

"Did your lawyer give you any information as to the banks in any of these places?"

"He couldn't get any information out of the British, Swiss, or the Panamanians."

"I'm not surprised. That's why so many secretly hoard their money in Switzerland and Panama. Along with the Caymans, they're known safe-havens for money laundering and tax cheats—not that Darcy was one, but in our line of work … well, you know, off-shore is safer." He shrugged. "You'll most likely have to go to Switzerland with the death certificate and the necessary inheritance paperwork to get real answers."

"I don't have a passport anymore; I lost it in Moscow."

"Hmm. Well, was there much money left in Darcy's Geneva account after all the transfers?"

She laughed wryly. "Uh, yeah. Apart from Georgiana's massive inheritance, he'd moved the bulk of his father's liquid assets into it. After all those transfers, there is still ..." She could feel the blush rise to her cheeks. "One hundred and eighty-two million in the account."

"Shit. I didn't realize."

"Neither did I, but there is something else. When I went to the safety deposit box at the bank to get my necklace and the cash Fitzwilliam had placed there in the event of an emergency—I found a bunch of passports. I'm assuming they're from his days with Obsidian?"

She reached into her handbag and withdrew the satellite phone and a rubber-banded stack. "I wasn't sure what to do with all these, and ... here ... I don't need Obsidian's phone any longer, I guess."

Nodding he took everything from her. "Thank you. I'll hand these off to Charlie, since he's our cobbler. Fabricating and legitimizing our cover identities has been a fun hobby for him. Of course, they'll have to be destroyed and removed from the various international government agencies who issue passports as well as custom and visa databases."

"You have access to that?"

He just smiled.

"The top passport is female," she added, tapping her knee. "A pretty brunette."

"Some of these are Steele's passports. She and Darcy coordinated on a lot of jobs, acting as husband and wife."

"Oh." *He did the same with Caroline, too.* She was glad she didn't rummage through the stack. It only would have upset her further.

Rick stood and, as she surmised, he wanted to change the topic to something more lighthearted or end their visit, needing time alone. "Look, I don't think you should leave the way you came. It's too traumatic for you. So, I'll take you out another way, but, I know I don't need to say it … it's classified."

"I understand."

"I'll take you to Darcy's Harley, and we can get something to eat. Although you got this sexy new haircut and look as gorgeous as ever, you can't hide the fact that you haven't been eating much."

"I'm not in the mood to eat anymore, but I can sit with you."

"Oh, you'll change your mind when you see the Italian subs this place makes."

10

Resurrections

Washington, DC

Removing her sunglasses to get a better look, Claudia bent over the wooden bench outside Bingley Dance School then rested one hand on the heavily tinted window attempting to peer inside. Unfortunately, she couldn't see anything; the vertical blinds were still drawn before opening for business. She'd been following the Darcy widow from as soon as she magically reappeared in Washington after the husband's funeral. The woman had one top-notch security team at the cemetery, and, following a memorial lunch at some hoity-toity mansion, vanished in the large crowd. Of course, she'd not told that to *el jefe*. As far as he knew, Mrs. Darcy has been under her radar for the last two weeks, not one.

Imagine her surprise when the woman's phone GPS came back online, and she was able to track her to The St. Regis hotel. So far, nothing appeared unusual in her behavior or contacts. That brute always accompanied her though: to a lawyer, to some bike shop in Alexandria, dinners out. Mostly, though, the grieving widow didn't leave her suite, and there was no sign of the supposed dead husband, but this Iceman had fooled Diablo once already by faking her death. If he were alive, he'd have shown at the hotel and she'd have seen it since she'd installed herself in the room next door only hours after Mrs. Darcy's surprising arrival back in town.

Cash was king and so was a little flirting with the reception clerk. After all, what man could resist a supposed foreign dignitary from Peru, cleaned up and wearing a designer suit that clung to her curves and three crisp one-hundred dollar bills slipped in behind his pocket square?

But today, like the last six, she was back to wearing black shorts and a ball cap. Each day, behind dark aviator sunglasses, she'd kept her distance from the woman and her hired thug, but thankfully, he was nowhere to be found this morning.

"They're closed, Miss," someone said from behind her.

Startled, she looked up into the reflection of the glass at the bearded face of the "hired thug" and his sinister smirk. His beefy stature and towering height was no match for her unarmed five-foot-one frame, so she played innocent. Turning to face him, she definitely felt small and intimidated without a weapon other than her cute looks and disarming accent, and for the first time all her cocky confidence had disappeared.

"I hear that this establishment has good Salsa classes," she lied.

"I heard the same. Did you also hear that the St. Regis has comfy pillows?"

"I do not know what you say."

"Sure, you do. Did you also read about Mr. Fitzwilliam Darcy's funeral in the newspaper?"

"I do not know that person, *señor?*"

"Hmm, and how did you like them blue crabs at Joe's?"

He stepped closer and she dropped her bottom onto the bench, her pulse racing, pounding in the artery at her neck. He bent closer to her ear, but she knew better than to touch or bite him. The cold, hard steel in his voice told her that he'd kill her even with busy traffic behind him. He was very much like Diablo.

"I've been watching you watching us for a week now," he whispered, his muscular body blocking the view from the street of potential witnesses.

"That is not true. You have me confused with someone else. I just want dance lesson."

"Don't they teach you in spy school that tattoos'll give you away? That's a mighty fine looking Incan sun on your calf. You were at the funeral and, coincidentally, enjoy the luxury room beside our suite, and lookee, here you are once again.

"It *is* a coincidence."

"*I* have a lesson for you—you're no match for me or her. Leave. Go back to where you came from little girl."

"I am on holiday." Damn, her voice trembled.

"Sure you are. Now, you're not gonna make me show my Mr. Hyde are you? I like Mr. Hyde, but he hasn't come out to play in a very, very long time. Today might be the day."

"I ... I do not know this man either."

"If you go, I won't kill you. If you stay ..."

Now her hand trembled and the fake smile left her face. "There is nothing you will do," she finally admitted with absolute false bravado because her insides where trembling. "I ... he will kill *you* both when I tell him."

The man laughed mockingly. "*He* failed once already."

As he slid the smartphone from her death grip, he spoke with a measured calmness that only diabolical confidence could convey, "And, he'll have to find us first," then shattered the phone under his boot in a hammering stomp. Laughing again, he took her off guard when, in one swift move, he shoved a large, strong hand onto the base of her throat and squeezed—the other gripped both her flailing hands.

Impaled to the back of the bench, she was unable to move, and the tight choke made her gasp and inhale. The wood slats dug into her boney spinal column.

Those eyes. His evil gaze burned into hers, and his lips curled menacingly.

"What is his name?" he demanded.

She couldn't speak.

"Is it Morales?"

She tried to nod but her neck couldn't move—nor her lips, but the fear in her eyes must have given away the answer.

He smirked then bent again, pretending to kiss her for any curious onlookers and whispered. "Disappear, *señorita,* because if you don't, I will torture you, killing you slowly if you mess with Mrs. D. Do you understand me?"

She nodded.

"Feel this hand …" he taunted, squeezing tighter. "It's my weapon of choice. Hers are knives and she will cut you open without a conscience."

Never—*ever*—had she felt such fear. He laughed and let go of her neck and fists, flashing open his hands with spread fingers.

She peed on the bench.

"I'll be watching you; don't be watching us," he said before crossing the street through on-coming traffic.

Coughing wildly, she thought *I won't be here for you to do so!*

***

Virginia

Thomas always enjoyed Lizzy's greenhouse and today, as he sat within writing computer code on his first-generation laptop, his thoughts meandered to his daughter's diamond and ruby snake necklace. It truly was a stunning piece and he could understand why it had so much meaning to both of them. The tattoo on his son-in-law's forearm had attested to his interest in snakes and, as a little girl, his once-Tomboy had an attraction with reptiles of all kinds. But the necklace was so much more than a fascination for either of them and, truth told, he couldn't help but to admire Darcy's ingenuity—as mad as blazes as he was with him. Now back in her possession, it was a tangible piece of their commitment.

All around him, his little girl's magical touch remained in this hothouse. As green a thumb as he had, he hadn't been able to save all her orchids; she had possessed something special, a patient nurturing that filled this glass abode with life and love. It was a sanctuary. He sure did miss her, and not because she took care of him for all those years after Frances left, but because she was very special. His heart broke for her unnecessary pain.

He gazed up from the digit-covered computer screen and gazed out the small panes of glass. His right hand reached out to the well-loved cassette player beside him. The sentimental lamentations of the cello in Schubert's Serenade (Ständchen) D. 957 lulled him and delighted the flowers, and he sighed … his mind drifting to the second of two near heart attacks in the last five weeks. This one shocked his ticker the day before the funeral.

What a meal! What a night! He thought to himself leaning back in the dining room chair. Why, he hadn't eaten this good in the last year, not since before Jane was caring for him.

"If I didn't tell you earlier, I just love what you did to the old place, Tommy," she cooed.

"Lizzy's husband arranged for everything. It's because of him that the histories of seven generations of Longbourn can continue in these hallowed walls."

"Oh! You didn't say. Did he loan you money?"

"He gave us money by starting a trust fund for the plantation in the girls' names. Quite generous of him. I know it's a little too late to tell him, but for all our disagreements, he was a good man. He sure loved Lizzy, and that's what's important."

"I wish ... I could comfort her, or at least accompany you tomorrow to the gravesite service."

Now was not the time. Some things required easing into. His eyes raked over her petite, rounded figure and his pulse increased slightly. He adored the way she looked, and the way she spoke, that hint of British accent she'd acquired after many years of living in England and those endearing colloquialisms. Her lovely rose scent wafted in the air. And above all, he loved the way she made him feel: alive again and filled with hope, wanting to do everything for her to make her happy and healthy.

Across the table, he took her soft hand. "How do you feel tonight?"

"Better than I've felt in months, thanks to you and Doctor Donaldson."

"Will you let me go with you for your results next week?" She laughed. He loved that, too.

"And what of that ankle bracelet?"

"Ha! If tomorrow goes off without a hitch, then I'll never leave your side as we go through treatment together." Her eyes pooled with tears, and so did his.

He told a funny joke to distract her maudlin thought. Although, the memory of the joke was escaping him—but it had made her laugh, and together their laughter was the dessert to the Beef Wellington, professional chef that she was! The energy within the dining room was filled with happiness and promise now that the cloud of depression had lifted from this place. What a laugh she had! What a sassy, loving, handsome, talented— and forgiving—woman!

"Oh! I meant to tell you—this afternoon, I read a fascinating article about the Lady's Slipper orchid," he said.

"Such a tragedy that it's lost now, but at least Lizzy was safe. That's all that matters, but believe, you me, I had to beg, borrow and—according to the British government—steal to get the clipping. Did she ever figure it out?"

"No. I thought I'd let you tell her when the time was right. They call her Liz now, you know, but she's still Lizzy to me."

"She's a grown married woman now, Tommy. 'Lizzy' is for little girls."

"She's still my little girl."

"Are they not both your little girls?"

"You are right, but Lizzy is more like me—and sweet Janie, in many ways is more like her mother."

"Based on what you've told me, she sounds to have all the shortcomings and none of the attributes, but a golden heart all of her own. Are you sure she can't cook?"

"Ha! I was a skeleton under her care," he laughed. "Ramen noodles and peanut butter and jelly sandwiches were the extent of her proficiency in the kitchen!"

"Well, I'm here now, and you'll be fed like a king."

"And I promise to cook for you, when you can't."

Rising, he pushed the chair back then rubbed his bloated tummy. "I'll get that magazine in my library and meet you out back on the verandah, so we can continue this conversation about Janie and her fella."

"And I'll bring the peach Schnapps, so we can get tipsy when talking over what to do about Lizzy and the late Mr. Darcy. I'm going to need a drink or two for that conversation."

"Yes, you will," he said as he walked from the room.

"How about we change things up with a little Jazz tonight?"

"Change is good."

Her laughter rang out from down the hall. "You sure are a different man, Tommy!"

"I'm working on it."

At the closed office door, he turned the knob, opening it into pitch black. With the heavy draperies drawn, the route to the desk would be un-navigable to most eyes, but each piece of furniture within his private refuge had been in the same exact spot for forty years. He walked the familiar path toward the lamp at the corner of his desk.

"Does Liz know that her mother has returned to Longbourn?"

That voice! Shocked, he abruptly halted, his hand flying to his head, and then a pull to the antique lamp cord clinked the light on.

Darcy.

Leaning back in the swivel chair, the dead-man's feet rested on the corner of Great-grandfather's desk.

"Oh, my. You're alive. What have you done, Fitzwilliam?" Quickly, he ran to the door and closed it, turning on his heel to face his son-in-law. "What have you done?" he repeated in a condemning whisper.

"I'm doing what I should have done following Moscow."

"Do you know what your so-called death has done to her? She's devastated." His blood boiled, and he tightened his fists at his sides. Physically striking a man wasn't his nature but, by God, he'd do so if Darcy stood directly before him and not seated in his favorite chair.

"I do, and I'm broken up by what she must be going through. You think I like causing her pain? You think I want her to feel as I did when I thought I lost her that day in Pemberley? But this decision was my only recourse."

"I don't know or care what you feel. My daughter is my only concern."

"That would be a first. Look, Bennet, have some faith in Liz. She's a brilliant woman and when her head clears, she'll figure it out. When she

does, she'll understand what I had to do to keep her safe. Good God—I left her enough clues."

"You hope she'll understand?! And get your feet off my great-grandfather's desk!"

His son-in-law stood; the man was a mess: overgrown hair, whiskered beard, clothing no better than a street vagrant. He was tired and pained, evident by the deep scowl and dark rings below his eyes. Further, by the tone in his voice, he was hoping—probably praying—that Lizzy would refuse to believe he was dead.

"Don't think me selfish in all this," Darcy thundered. "She—along with everyone else—needed to believe me dead. Do you honestly think that my enemy—the man who runs an international empire of drugs and weapons trafficking—wouldn't consider my death a ruse? Pure emotions don't lie, and Liz wouldn't be able to pull off acting the part of a grieving widow."

"Sit down, Fitzwilliam," he said, walking to the chair nearest the bookshelves. "I have a good mind to punch you in the face."

Darcy snorted a laugh.

"I'm serious. This decision you've made without consulting her will be the end of you both. She's heartbroken. Janie tells me that she's not eating; she cries non-stop, day in and day out. How could you want her to feel such despair? You're supposed to love her! Not abuse her, and certainly not break her heart."

"This coming from the man who made his 'Lizzy-bear' a doormat housekeeper and tried to sell her like chattel into marriage with a gay man just so you could save your precious Bennet heritage. She had dreams of children and you had no qualms about taking that away from her as long as Longbourn could survive."

"I was wrong. I was ill, and I'm going to make it up to her."

"Oh, please, Bennet ... save the bullshit excuses and stop trying to posture yourself as a man of character now—not to me. I know who you are and

what drives your conscience. I've lived the past year healing the wounds you inflicted on my wife's psyche, which did more harm than those exacted by the abandonment of that woman in there."

"And now you have added to them. Is that the mark of a noble character or a loving husband? Those dreams of a child, where are they now?"

"They're in the secure future I'm paving for us." He laughed derisively, shaking his head. "Don't lecture me about how to be a loving husband, you sanctimonious hypocrite. This was the most difficult decision I have ever had to make. To risk losing her forever, just to keep her safe. If I'm dead, she remains alive; it's as simple as that and I don't owe you any further explanation. It's between my wife and me—our private world doesn't include your opinion or censure."

"Tommy?" Frances called from the hallway.

"I'll be right there, sweetie," he called back, walking to the door. "Just sorting through the pile of magazines."

"Okay, honeybun. I'll be outside waiting. Don't be long."

He turned back to face his son-in-law, his brow knit. "Why are you here?"

"Because you have skills that I need—and you owe me."

And there it was. He knew that the two million dollar Longbourn Plantation Trust came with strings. A shrewd man like Fitzwilliam Darcy was calling in his marker.

Holding up a piece of paper, Darcy said, "Since you have continued your relationship with Obsidian and acquired access to a satellite, you're in a unique situation to assist me. You also happen to be the only computer genius and hacker I know. Here is what I need to get this nightmare over and done with in under ten days."

He laughed. "You want my help to keep deceiving my daughter?"

"No. I want your help in keeping her safe, and that comes by getting me vital information of Morales's operation and his transport routes from the dark web."

The sheet of paper crossed hands and he perused the demands. "And if I don't help you?"

"Then Liz and Jane will discover that you've been hiding a houseguest ... for how long?"

"Five weeks."

"Hmm. That won't go over well, I assure you."

"I suppose it'll go as well as finding out her husband is still alive." Take that!

Darcy grunted. "Further, I'll tip off the feds that you're unlawfully violating your sentence by tampering with your GPS. But don't worry, they'll allow conjugal visits in federal prison."

Looking away, he knew Fitzwilliam meant what he said.

"Since you've already used my money to restore your most prized possession, I expect payment in return, which includes your confidentiality."

He felt small and trapped, and returned to the chair, sitting with a thud and the instructions in hand. His fingers raked through his hair as he read the fine penmanship. "Drug ratlines, weapons trading, the cartel's communiqué ... this isn't going to be easy to infiltrate."

"I don't care how you do—just do it."

"You'll need a lot more than what's on this list to pull off your plan. I'll need to establish a back channel to coordinate and share intel with you in a secure chat room. You'll need a satellite phone. This'll take time."

"You have less than two weeks before all hell breaks loose with my target in Panama."

"At the very least, we'll need a Tor—and Onion Router—to remain untraceable."

"Look. You're the computer geek. I have no idea what you're talking about, nor do I care. Just …" he sighed and softened his tone. "Just, please do it."

"And who is this person whose identity you want me to use as a sock puppet?"

"He's the assassin who blew up Pemberley."

"My God! Did you kill him?"

His son-in-law leaned against the desk and folded his arms. "No, but one of my security team paid him a visit and convinced him to permanently leave the business. Let's just say, he gave up names and information networks in exchange for his life and enough money to last a lifetime. It's all there on that piece of paper."

"You paid off the man who destroyed your ancestral estate? Impossible!"

"Again, there's the difference between you and me. Liz is more important than a few buildings. She's more valuable than every penny of the Darcy wealth or lineage."

"How ever did you find him?"

"The Leesburg crime lab. We got to him before they did and now they have no record that he ever existed."

"You're so sure I won't turn you and your hired-thugs in?"

"I'm dead, remember? You're not. And you wouldn't have the guts to face the repercussions of messing with my security team."

He glanced back down at the paper. "What is this El Negro's part in all this?"

"A South American cartel attempting to destroy Morales. They are our scapegoat in the destruction."

So much to take in. How would he keep a straight face tonight when discussing "the late Mr. Darcy" with Frannie?

"And tomorrow is your funeral. What do I say to Lizzy?"

"Be your loving, supportive self … Dad. Oh, and one last thing. More than likely, she'll be wearing the diamond necklace I bought her, but I tampered with the clasp. I'd like for you to fix it and while you're at it, find a way to transmit its comms to the phone you and I will communicate through."

"Acoustic signatures," he said defeated. "It hears and collects sound emitters from microphones and mobile phones, even satellites, all over the world—24/7."

"Good. Because I'll be all over the world over the next week or so and I'll be relying on you to keep me motivated."

"You … you're going to spy on her?"

"No. I'm going to listen to my wife's dulcet voice because I miss her so damn much, and she's the only reason for attempting to pull this off."

"Will you be there tomorrow—at the funeral?"

"Let me be clear—laying low and staying away from her these last two weeks hasn't been easy, but I'll be there, rifle-ready, because Morales's thugs will be there as well, making sure that the grieving widow is, in fact, grieving and that I am, in fact, six feet under."

"Good! Then you'll see what you've done to her. Maybe your conscience will kick in and you'll end this charade."

"My conscience is fine … how is yours, honeybun?" He raised an eyebrow.

A long breath left his mouth and he looked up at the former SEAL. "If I do this, then I want your word that you'll make this right, that you won't let it go on too long. I'm worried about her mental state."

Darcy pulled the curtain back and opened the window before answering. When he turned back around, his face was dark and impenetrable. "The only person I give my word to is my wife, and I gave it to her before I left on this mission. I will be coming home to her, and it's only a matter of days before she realizes every carefully planned action and word I said to her."

The icy edge in his son-in-law's voice frightened him, causing him to stammer. "How ... how will I reach you?"

"The address where to ship the phone is there in the instructions. After tomorrow's service, I'm leaving for Panama and relying on you to get me the information and equipment I need."

"Fitzwilliam, not that it's any of your business, but Frances and I have forgiven each other. She's here because she has cancer and wants to make amends with the girls. I'm going to take care of her while she gets medical care. We've all made mistakes, and well, it's important that she apologizes and explain to them what really happened." This was his opportunity toward redemption; she had no one to turn to in England.

His son-in-law said nothing beyond narrowing his eyes. With one leg out the open window, Darcy's retreating body halted when they heard the knocking upon the door. "Tommy, are you all right?"

"Don't disappoint me, Bennet. And the quicker you tell Liz about her mother, the better it will be for all of you."

"And I'd give you the same advice."

"Keep in touch—or else," Darcy said before disappearing into the night.

The door opened, and Frances stepped into the library. She looked at the open window and noting the blowing curtain turned to face him. "Was someone here? I heard voices?"

"Just a ghost," he replied running his shaking hand through his hair.

In the past, she would have been annoyed by his proclamation, but this matured, dying Frances just threw back her head and laughed. "One of your dead ancestors I presume?"

That was over a week ago, and everything was underway just as Darcy had meticulously planned. Within two days, the updated encrypted satellite telephone as well as other "doo-dads" he thought would be useful had been overnighted to a Mr. John Thornton at a postal address in Panama City, and a second package was on its way.

In truth, these efforts for his son-in-law had kept him from obsessing over how to tell his daughters that Frances had come home; he went right to work the day after Darcy had broken into his library. Just thinking about the expected confrontation between mother and daughters had caused him enough stress that he had to take an anxiety pill!

He had hacked into the cartel's communication network where Diablo's lieutenant instructed the soldiers over the dark web. He didn't need to create a sock puppet in order to circumvent a footprint back to the United States. Instead, through ghost IPs, he employed one of the CIA's hacking software programs that—if explored in depth—would appear as though an Argentine entity had infiltrated their server. This would send La Muerta Mundial on a wild goose chase, distracting them with thoughts of El Negro's impending drug war.

Morales was planning an all-out death match, and as much as Bennet hated deceiving his daughters, he found it entirely intriguing to watch— in real-time!—how the drug lord daily changed his trans-portation routes of narcotic convoys all over the world. Darcy would need to be Superman to keep up with the many trafficking channels. This was phase one. Phase two was to deplete the man's liquid assets right out from under his nose—that required access to the twelve banks where he hid his money all over the world. Slowly, every pound, dollar, euro, bolívar, and peso would find their way, as donations, into worthy NGOs that fought the very crimes he committed. Phase three was the end of the road for this Morales character—if they could find his home base.

He rubbed his hands together, his mind slipping to greedy thoughts of siphoning some—just a little, of course—of the money for himself, for Frances's medical expenses, for living expenses now that restoration on the Plantation had used most of the Trust money. Obsidian money seemed to be drying up following Darcy's death. As quickly as the thought crossed his mind, he banished it, recalling the dirty "easy money" that got him arrested in the first place. He'd hold to his word to turn over a new leaf—one of honor and integrity, one of service, not selfishness. Drug money was as evil as Al-Hanash's terrorist money; accepting any of it was the last stop in perdition. That wasn't the legacy he wanted to leave to his daughters.

Through the glass he watched Frances excitedly walk across the lawn toward the greenhouse. Today was a good day for her; her pain seemed to have lessened and she'd eaten a good breakfast. Her short hair, spiked with a little styling gel, made her look like the hip young girl he fell in love with in the early 80s. With a cheerful smile, she waved to him. "The phone rang, but I didn't answer it," she said.

"Did they leave a message?"

"Yes. It was Lizzy; she's coming by the day after tomorrow! Oh, Tommy—there's so much to do and so little time. I need to go food shopping, arrange lunch, buy her flowers, get my hair done."

"Would you like me to call Janie and invite her, too?"

"Be a dear! Yes! Just like old times. Oooo, I'm so nervous but so excited!"

He smiled from the depth of his soul; he hadn't seen her have this much energy since her arrival. Perhaps they could be a family again.

11

Scorned Woman

Late Afternoon, August 29
Panama

S *eñor* Thornton, you have a letter and a package," alerted the desk clerk at the weekly rental hostel. He spoke to Darcy in Spanish with a knowing smile. A trusted asset from his first visit to Panama four years earlier, the man was one of only two who knew that the former SEAL was visiting the capital city on spurious reasons, but the clerk/informant didn't care. He wasn't paid in cryptocurrency to care—only to provide information and whatever else he needed. He retrieved an envelope from the small slats along the wall, then bent to remove the package from under the counter.

"Thank you, friend," Darcy replied with a well-practiced English accent, tucking the letter into his cargo short pocket.

He gripped the parcel (addressed in Bennet's distinctive handwriting), turned away from the desk clerk, and climbed the stairs two at a time up to his lousy accommodations on the second floor. This hostel was the type of place where no one had an identity. Either that or they wanted no one to remember who they were. Not one guest cared that the rooms were no more than an old bed and nasty bathroom. Here, John Thornton—a cover identity that he used often with Lucy Steele in his early days with Obsidian—was just another strung-out druggie, another criminal in hiding, another homeless drifter, another gambler who'd lost everything. For God's sake, he looked the part right down to his dirty fingernails and month-old scraggly beard.

In his vigilance to remain undetected for a few weeks following his death, this flea bag hotel had hardly become a home away from home, but Panama itself, was an amenable destination in which to spend his time. Just as he recalled, it was an interesting mixture of international business and cosmopolitan nightlife, yet managed to maintain its exotic island-like charm. The food was incredible, and the people were friendly. Liz would have liked it. And in better times, when this part of their life was long behind them, he'd bring her back here.

He opened the door just a crack and peered in before entering. Bone tired from ten consecutive, two-mile winding jogs to the summit of Ancon Hill, he stretched out on the unmade bed; the springs groaned and squeaked under his weight. Liz would cringe if she saw how he was living. Sure, he could have stayed in high priced, classy digs, but that would have been counterproductive, drawing too much attention to himself.

Where is she now? Where is she living? Are the guys taking care of her? He hoped she was staying with Jane—or better yet, that she had decided to remain in Asheville to be near the horses and their little love shack. That would be the safest, best-case scenario, and he grew cold at the thought of her as the desperately lonely widow (something he hated to have done to her), returning to Longbourn to take care of both those selfish assholes! She had enough money to go anywhere her heart desired and, rest assured, he'd find her when this was over. But until then, he would not ask his father-in-law. He ached for news of her, even just a photograph, but resisted using the code Bennet provided to access the necklace comms transmitting 24/7 to the satellite phone. In his heart of hearts (and Bennet had successfully added to the guilt), he knew that would be considered spying on her, invading her privacy. *That* part of his plan—meant to lessen his worry for her—didn't sit well with his conscience. And many nights in this shithole, he lay there, tempted … just to hear her breathing while she slept.

And what the fuck had his death done to Georgiana? Thank God she had Justin. But she'd be safe now that her assassin brother was six feet under, and that was all that mattered.

He pulled the envelope from his pocket and flipped it over in his hands. His mind drifted, as it frequently did, to his trip back to Leesburg nine days ago.

Since the evening of his narrow and well-planned escape from Hungry Bay, time had passed torturously slow. The only satisfying highlight, which had sent him on another bender with Jack, had been observing his wife from three hundred yards across the headstones. The more things changed, the more they'd stayed the same. Never had he imagined that he'd once again admire her beauty, be moved to such emotion through a rifle scope. His heart ached, his guilt rose, but keeping sentry over her that day was necessary. *Maybe I should have told her my plan.* No, she would have insisted on coming with him, and he couldn't successfully do this last mission with her by his side. *His* life was expendable; hers was not. Would she have agreed to stay hidden in North Carolina if he had told her? Again, his gut knew she would not have been safe, not have taken every precaution to remain hidden—no matter what Dixon or Higgins said or did. After a week up there, she had been going stir crazy—wanting to go shopping, wanting her sister to visit. He had the advantage of living a stealth life for many years; she had not. As for faking death and causing her grief … for that he was guilty as charged. But her tears would throw off the enemy; she would not have been able to fool a man such as Morales otherwise.

As it was, the funeral had exposed two unfamiliar faces among the mourners, but he mistrusted the male, believing he had "other" designs on Liz. It was all over that guy's face and it upset him, watching how he watched her through the assembled crowd of mourners.

Suitors immediately coming out of the woodwork for her affections weren't something he'd planned for in his absence. Her grief and the guy's lingering to talk with her at the end of the service was too much to witness and he was thankful to leave for Panama in 36 hours. In time, he'd get up the nerve to ask Bennet who that man was, but he had a sneaking suspicion it was Charlie's friend, Wentworth.

He tightened his fist before sliding the boot knife from its sheath followed by a swipe through the top of the envelope with a quick, smooth tear then slid out the folded piece of paper: *I accept your offer. Panamá Viejo. Bell Tower, Cathedral de Nuestra Señora de la Asunción ruins— 9:45 tonight.*

Since his arrival to Panama, he'd been surveilling a woman who came and went from Morales's gated compound up near Cerro Azul. Always unaccompanied, she got off the bus at the bottom of a winding dirt road where she then walked a mile up to the hacienda at the very top of the mountain. It was this way every day and yesterday, he finally made his move by riding next to her on the over-crowded bus for the hour-long trip from Panama City. Rightly cautious at first—as was he—she finally succumbed to his charm and smooth accent, but then when her satchel fell from the overhead compartment, she became a willing conversationalist following his gentlemanly assistance.

All pre-conceived notions of her being a housekeeper at Diablo's hacienda banished at the curl of her lip when he asked about the wealthy owner of said hacienda: Juan Sanchez-Morales. One thing was for sure, Pilar Montegro—who lived in the unsavory El Chorrio district caring for her mother—was a scorned woman and *that* he could use to his benefit. He had not failed to notice her curled lip when she described the scar that ran from his left temple to his thin lips. He held her missive in his hands and smiled at his success. She would help him.

Tearing open the FedEx box Bennet had overnighted, he removed the two modified burner phones they'd discussed on the dark web chat room his father-in-law created. The genius had programmed this handy device to bounce ghost IP addresses and to Bluesnipe with digital recording capability. It would be the key to discovering where Morales's home base was.

"Bennet, you're well on your way to redemption," he said as he placed the phones back in the box. He walked to the closet, bent to his gear bag on the floor, and removed the false bottom. A brick of fifties—$50,000—were right there. The money was half of the promised reward to get Ms. Montegro settled into a new life after she assisted him with specific intel.

After tomorrow, he could leave for Bolivia—the place where it all began with Operation Samba and the murder of the Lord of the Jungle.

***

The UNESCO World Heritage Site of the Old Panama Ruins wasn't unbreachable after closing hours. Well, at least not to Darcy. Located along the shoreline of Panama Bay, a few stone walls and metal railings couldn't keep him out after dark. At his back, the waves broke onto the beach and above him the gentle sway of trees shifted in the breeze. Somewhere beside the outdoor museum, lively music played and in front of him, set against the rising moon and silver clouds, the ancient church's bell tower stood dark and portentous on the humid tropical night.

Back in black, he blended in the shadow, stealthily making his way to the structure, careful to keep out of the spotlights lining the perimeter of the stone foundation. Surrounding the grounds and church courtyard, remnant stone effigies of the crumbling ancient city ominously stood guard over the once-Spanish capital. Nuestra Señora de la Asuncion Cathedral had survived earthquakes, fires, and invaders—and now it would act as a gateway to destiny: Liz's, Ms. Montegro's, and Morales's.

He silently climbed the steps two at a time, to the zenith 22 meters above the city. "Is that you, *Señor* Thornton," she asked in a whisper when he emerged from the shadow. Her dyed blonde hair shined in the moonlight breaching the arched stone window facing the sea. His gaze immediately fell to the nasty bruise on her cheek.

"It is. How did you get up here after closing?" he asked in Spanish.

She chuckled. "*Mi hermano* is security guard."

"You didn't tell him about our meeting, did you?"

"No. No. But he hates Morales; he would be glad if he knew. Luis, Juan's *secretario*, told me yesterday the plans Juan had for me, but he could not do it because he loves me, so he says. I know that is a lie. It is only my body he loves; he is no different than his boss—but he promises to pay as much as Juan has to use my body."

Caution still ran in his blood and reason, but oddly, his gut trusted her, feeling bad at how she was used by Morales and others. "I think you're right about Luis, and I think you need to leave Panama before he has his fill. The cartel is very loyal to its *jefe*, Pilar, and in the end he will do as instructed."

"*Sí*, and then who will care for my mother? My brother?" She laughed. "He will not. Why do *you* want to kill Diablo so much?"

"Because he tried to kill my wife, and if I don't succeed, then he will."

Was it the pain in his eyes that gave it away when she surmised? "You are from Virginia," she said with a nod to her head.

"Why do you think that?"

"Because there is a *cruzador*—I heard through the door—Claudia is her name and she was at a funeral in Virginia watching the widow. Your widow?"

He was right; the female at the funeral was cartel sent to observe Liz, but he did not answer.

"They were to follow her for another two weeks, but that is now over, I think. There is war coming to the cartel," she informed him.

Yes there was. The Black Ice. I'm the war. "I'm relieved to hear she's out harm's way."

She smiled. "How long are you married, *señor*?"

He couldn't help softly smiling at the thought. "It'll be a year next month."

"Do you have a baby?"

"Not yet."

"Then, I will help you."

"Thank you, Pilar. Can you tell me if your friend Luis is Diablo's lieutenant? *Jefe de Jefes'* number two man?"

"*Sí.* He is and godfather to his children. They are very close; he manages all his affairs and travel."

His lips twitched in thought. "Do you know where Morales' family is? His main residence?"

"No. He never says, but he, hmmm, brings coconut sweet cakes. The box reads from St. Tropez, always these sweets. I think you Americans call them macaroons."

"That's good; it's a start, but *this* will tell us everything we need." From inside the pouch secured under his pant leg, he withdrew one of the phones. "Pilar, I need for you to get this phone within ten feet of Luis's phone. The rest will take care of itself."

"You do not want me to kill him?"

"No, that would be too dangerous for you, and right now, I need him for information. The phones will force pair, sync together and his conversations and digital activity will lead me directly to Morales and his dealings."

"And his family."

"Yes."

"And you promise to kill *el jefe* for me?" Her fingers subconsciously smoothed over her cheek.

"For you and for my wife. He'll not hurt either of you again."

"And then you will go back to her?"

"If she'll have me. I am technically dead."

"I think … you are good man, *Señor* Thornton, but I think she will be very angry with you."

He wanted to thank her for the compliment because, man, he needed to hear that he was a good man.

"I know she will be, but I must avenge her—and protect everyone I love from this madman. He's involved in so much more than the international drug trade."

"*Sí*, he runs guns and makes slaves of men and women."

"I'm sorry. He'll never hurt you again. I promise."

From inside his tactical jacket pocket, he removed the brick of bills; expressing his thanks the best way he knew. "This will help you start a new life. Here's $50,000. You'll get half now, and the remaining 50 grand when you return this same phone back to me tomorrow evening at five o'clock. Tocumen International Airport—Gate C. Be ready to leave the country. You cannot go back to Panama City or Cerro Azul."

"Can my mother join me?"

"Sure. Take your family wherever you want. It's a new beginning."

"I think Argentina would be nice. Maybe I meet a good man there. A man who will protect and love me like you do your wife. Not beat me like the devil."

12
Rock the Boat

August 30
Maryland

Through the rain-streaked windshield of the H2, Dixon craned his head from behind the steering wheel to admire Charlie's houseboat. "Nice place your sister has here," he noted when they pulled into the parking space beside the slip.

"It's her boyfriend Charlie's, but it might as well be hers for all the time she spends here." The man's perfect for her, yet she can't make moving-in 'official'."

"Maybe she likes her personal freedom and independence."

"In a way she does, but it's all a deceptive illusion. She's never been alone, per se. She's sort of a serial dater, which translates to freedom to come and go without commitment—even though they're together 24/7. Don't tell her I said so, but it's just been bothering me lately."

"When she stayed at the farmhouse, she seemed grounded, and looked serious with that fella at the funeral."

"Oh, she is serious with him … kinda. It's hard to tell with her. She gets bored easily, and her frequent way of handling conflict or real emotional stuff is to joke and then just cut and run without a care in the world."

"Yet, she did a right proper job of being there when the chips were down after the guys came to see you."

"You're right; she did. I never said she wasn't a loving sister … just, I don't know … I just want for her what Fitzwilliam and I have. I mean, had. Although she's a romantic dreamer, she's simultaneously commitment phobic."

She didn't mean to share so much about Jane, but it was safe in Dixon's vault. Just as her drunken breakdown the night before when she took the scissors to her long hair in a mad cutting frenzy was safe with him. The man was as tight-lipped as they came, particularly when it came to her personal affairs. Further, she trusted him with her life and when he offered no explanation to his insistence that she get a new phone with a new number, she didn't question. Why had he walked beside her not behind her after her visit to the dance school? He hadn't said—and she hadn't asked, assuming it was nothing more than a change of protocol.

It surprised her when the man of very few words stated, "Ya' know, I knew a woman like that. She had a kind soul, and sure knew how to love a man, but she hated disappointing people. When she had her fill, it was easier to just go than to witness breaking their heart with words and tears."

"Did you date her?"

"Yup."

"Did you marry her?"

"Yup."

"Did she leave you?"

"Yup. And she took my dog with her."

"That doesn't sound very kind or the right way to love a man."

"I didn't say she was an angel, just chicken-shit, and … maybe I deserved it. I wasn't always this happy go lucky, honorable Marine you see."

Happy go lucky? Bwahaha! He made a joke! And she rewarded him with a laugh.

"Well, go on with ya'. You take as much time as you like, and don't be so hard on your sister. Most folks hide their pains and put on masks. I'm gonna stay right here with Clarice and enjoy the rain."

She glanced over at his sympathetic face. Dixon didn't like the rain; it made his knees hurt.

"Let's hope she's here. Thursdays are usually Janie's day off from the museum."

"I told ya' you should've called or at least texted her that you've come home early."

"I thought about it, but then she'd insist that I meet her at her loft, and I really don't want to stay there. And, I guess, like her, I don't want to hurt her feelings."

She opened the door and stepped out into the rain, bolting through the puddles in a mad dash around the side of the boat.

Standing on the deck, she knocked against the cabin entry then glanced out at the choppy water while she waited. A memory popped into her head of the day her sister left Longbourn; those red tail lights headed down the dirt drive had broken her teenage heart, had made her sick to her stomach as the awareness dawned on her: she was all alone. Her father's words echoed in the back of her mind. *"She's just like your mom. It's just us two now, kitten."*

She knocked a second time, disregarding the prophetic recollection but it ushered in the familiar stomach churn filled with nervous anxiety. *Cutting and running. Is it a pattern in my family?* Isn't that what she was about to do herself? But unlike her sister's actions when both she and Dad needed her to stick around, no one needed Lizzy of Longbourn/Liz Darcy of Pemberley/or now, just homeless Liz, least of all Jane. Probably due to her slight hangover, bile rose up her throat and she bolted to the railing, depositing her breakfast (meager as it was) in one massive hurl overboard as the rain beat down upon her.

"Liz? Is that you?" That honeyed accent asked from behind. "Are you okay?"

Wiping her mouth with the back of her hand, she tried to smile, playing off her vomiting with aplomb, which was impossible given that it was obvious.

"C'mon inside and I'll get you something to drink."

"Is Ja … I'm sorry. Hi, Dave."

"Howdy." He put his arm around her shoulders and guided her into the cabin.

Damn he smelled good. Damn his body was warm and supportive. *Damn. Damn. Damn.* Her breath must stink!

"Is Janie here?"

"She went to her apartment in Washington since I'll be hanging my hat here for a couple more days."

"Oh." *Double-damn. I can't be alone with him. Can I?*

He led her inside, making sure to support her in case she was to get sick again, which was sweet but it made her uncomfortable.

"I'm mortified. I don't know what came over me."

"Don't be embarrassed. It took me a couple of days to get used to the boat. As you know, I like my wide-open spaces from the back of a horse or in my pick up. I'm not partial to open water, but I'm mighty grateful Crash and your sister let me stay on here."

Inelegantly, she backed up toward the bathroom, just in case she threw up again. "I'll be right back. Hold that thought," she said, hoping there was a bottle of mouthwash on hand.

What is he doing here? And would it be rude if I left abruptly? I could claim severe illness. I mean … I did just throw up. She stood before the mirror and nervously raised her hand to touch her newly cropped pixie hairstyle, still damp from the rain. *Well, if nothing would alter his good opinion before, this hair will—and the vomit, of course. Oh, why does he have to be so attractive?*

Leave it to Janie to keep mouthwash, Waterpic—and Dave Wentworth—at the ready.

Further embarrassed by the sound of her gargling, she promptly spit out the mouthwash then wiped her lips. She pulled the towel from its bar and ran it over her wet shirt and bare legs—mentally willing her sensitive nipples to stay put. She was deliberately wasting time, afraid to join Dave on the opposite side of the door, recalling all too well their initial attraction. But she couldn't avoid the weird confrontation and exited feeling self-conscious. Honestly, as damned perfect as Wentworth was, there was nothing appealing about her, so there was nothing to worry about.

"Are you feeling better?" he asked, taking a seat at the banquette, placing two mugs at the table.

"I don't know what came over me."

Dave smiled thoughtfully, and his blue eyes softly examined her, his lazy drawl comforting, "I made some tea. It might help with your queasy stomach."

"Thank you. I used to be such a coffee drinker, but after Fitzwilliam's death, I oddly switched to tea. The thought of a latte repulses me."

"I bet you're finding that all your tastes have changed."

"Yes. I don't even watch the same TV shows as we did. Every single nuance of my life has altered. We may have only been together for a year, but never had I felt so in-sync with a person." Her heart stabbed. "Now I'm outta sync."

"I recall feelin' a similar loss when I left the army. Not that I'm implying that life with your husband was regimented, but it's just difficult to change gears so suddenly." He raised the mug to his lips—and they oddly fascinated her.

"I'm real sorry about your husband's passing. Was it sudden?"

Blown to bits. Eaten by sharks like human bait. I'd say so. "Yes. A diving accident."

He pursed his lips and shook his head. "Bad luck."

"Real bad luck. It's a struggle to get up in the morning, but I guess I'll survive." An uncomfortable silence fell between them until she said, "I'm … uh … getting ready to leave town and wanted to say good-bye to Janie. I think she had high hopes that I'd move into her place until I got my bearings, but I just need to get on the bike and go."

"Is that why you cut your hair?"

"Maybe. I don't know. Fitzwilliam loved my long hair, but I think this is easy to maintain and, like I said, everything is different now. I don't care so much about my appearance as I did before," she positioned, subconsciously touching the moist tendril at her temple.

Shrugging, he raised the mug again, sipped, then looked directly in her eyes. "If you don't mind me sayin', I think you're real pretty."

She sipped her tea, thankful for the warmth and the needed break to consider how to handle his compliments. "You're sweet, but I can tell when a man is lying." That wasn't entirely true. The only one she prided on being able to dissect was Fitzwilliam because when it came to her, he wore his heart on his sleeve.

"It's the truth. You're one of the most genuine girls I've met—I told ya' that back in April."

"About that … I'm sorry about how awkward it got."

"What happened wasn't either of our faults; it just happened between us. Sometimes you can't predict or avoid chemistry. It is what it is. Listen, I'll be honest with ya', I stayed in Washington so that I could maybe take you out to dinner or out to a night on the town."

Stunned, she sat back without answering, considering the offer now that his intentions were laid on the table. "Dinner? Oh, Dave. I don't know what to say."

"Say yes. I promise, there won't be any reason to feel guilty afterward, and you'll have a good time."

Guilty? A good time? What is he thinking—a one night stand?!"

Again, she took a long drink then uncomfortably answered. "Gee, I'm flattered. But …I'm not ready for something like that, and I'll be honest with *you* ... I don't know if I'll ever be ready to move on, definitely not like that."

"You misunderstand my intentions. I'm not here to romance ya'. I'm here to offer you a distraction from the pain that's tearin' at your soul." Dave looked away to the rain streaked sliding door leading out to the deck. "I know loss, Liz."

"Those dog tags in your truck?"

"Yeah. Ken was my best bud, and while it devastated me, I saw what it did to his wife. She couldn't hold it together."

"I'm so sorry."

"After I transitioned back to civilian life, I spent some time with her and the kids at their farm. I saw how she lost confidence in how she looked, how she felt about hers and the boys' future. It seemed like the simplest gesture helped her the most. I don't know, I just thought that maybe you goin' out to a movie with a friend—a male friend—could help get your mind off things."

He understood, and she felt like an idiot for possibly misinterpreting his intentions—all based on that innocent silly attraction months ago. Still ... there was a certain gleam in his eyes. "I'm leaving tomorrow after I visit my father, but ... maybe if you give me your mobile number I might call you when I ride through Tennessee after I take on the Tail of the Dragon outside Asheville."

He held out his hand across the table and she took it, enjoying the soothing warmth and the rough calluses. Silently, she wished it was Fitzwilliam's.

"Sounds like a plan," he said with a glorious smile. "I hope you do call."

"Okay then ... no strings, no romance, just a rain check for a barbeque between two friends."

"You're goin' on a death wish ride, aren't ya?"

"Something like that. Fitzwilliam loved that wild motorcycle challenge, and we had talked about doing it together when I was ready ...

but we never got around to it. Anyway, apart from my sister and good friends, there's nothing tethering me to anything."

"I felt that way, too. Just get it out of your system, but don't do anything crazy."

She couldn't promise that but just smiled back.

"Are you ready for a ride like that?"

"God, I studied that map so much over the last week, I think I could do it with my eyes closed." *At least I hope so!* "I had a really good teacher."

***

Panama City

Yeah, Liz would love Panama's cultural flavor, Darcy mused, watching the locals enthusiastically enjoy English soccer on the lone television beside the bar of Café Coca Cola in Panama City. Off the beaten path, the city's oldest restaurant wasn't far from the Colonial ruins where he'd met Pilar the night before.

While enjoying the local fare, he focused on the calling card he'd leave tonight at Morales's compound up in Cerro Azul before departing for his next hit at the exact locale as Operation Samba. The hearty late lunch was meant to tide him over for the next 24 hours until his arrival in La Paz. He felt oddly relaxed wearing a Panama hat and his spirits were high in anticipation of the meet-up with Pilar at the airport to receive the burner phone he'd given to her. Hopefully, she'd been successful in cloning it to Luis's phone. *Traitor Tom* was growing on him.

Unable to stop the ice in his veins from melting, he allowed a genuine smile to form when three local musicians began to play traditional calypso music inside the joint. It was happy and filled with promise and he vowed to take Liz back here when all this crazy shit was over with. Together, they may not live as the Americans Mr. and

Mrs. Fitzwilliam Darcy, but Mr. and Mrs. John Thornton from England did have a nice ring to it.

Placing the fork down beside the bowl of yellow rice, he leaned back in his chair, gazed out the window then took a swig from the glass soda bottle. *What is she doing? Is she okay?* God, he missed her. With no photograph in his wallet, her beautiful countenance filled his mind's eye and for a second he closed his eyes, imagining her expression beside the waterfall and how she'd kissed him.

His heart skipped and then his resolve broke; he removed the phone from his pocket, logged in the special access code, and tapped the Bluetooth earpiece. Her voice immediately filled his head when the necklace's signal routed through the satellite and his heart soared. He clung to her first six words, analyzing and dissecting her tone and inflection to determine her state of mind.

"… my appearance as I did before."

"If you don't mind me sayin', I think you're real pretty."

Who the hell is this southern boy?

"You're sweet, but I can tell when a man is lying."

"It's the truth. You're one of the most genuine girls I've met—I told ya' that back in April."

The heat of anger rose from his neck to his head. *Wentworth!*

"About that … I'm sorry about how awkward it got."

"What happened wasn't either of our faults; it just happened between *us.*

What the hell happened? What the hell happened between them in April!?

"Sometimes, you can't predict or avoid chemistry. It is what it is. Listen, I'll be frank with ya', I stayed in Washington so that I could maybe take you out to dinner or out to a night on the town."

Fisting his hand, his relaxed mood disappeared. *Had Liz cheated in April?*

"Dinner? Oh, Dave. I don't know what to say."

"Say yes. I promise, there won't be any reason to feel guilty afterward, and you'll have a good time."

What the hell kind of good time are you offering my wife? A long pause followed and he was on the edge of his seat in anticipation of her answer. He hadn't even been dead for a month!

"Gee, I'm flattered. …"

He yanked the Bluetooth from his ear, blood roaring through his veins. But then the weight of his own sin crushed him like a ton of bricks: as far as Liz knew, she was a widow, no longer bound to fidelity by marriage, no longer his wife—and it was all of his own making. He'd have to deal with his jealousy for it served him right. Again … it came down to reminding himself that he chose the right way not the easy way.

Crestfallen and angered at himself, he tossed $40 on the table and left the restaurant. Panamanian and Bolivian revenge were only hours away.

13

Fire on the Mountain

Early Morning, August 31
Panama

Morales's private compound, beyond the outskirts of Cerro Azul, was not easy to breach, especially at zero two hundred hours when one was intent on death and destruction. After two weeks of surveillance, he'd not only memorized where ID check points and private security were, but also knew the exact layout of the mansion's grounds (thanks to satellite footage) and the interior, having examined the architectural blueprints Bennet sent him. At 3,000 feet above sea level, accessing the residence by land was doable, but not without back up or a heavy distraction for his plans. Tonight, his method of infiltration was by air.

Dressed in onyx tactical face and body gear, he and the hang glider's sail blended into the eerie sky like a bat outta hell. With fists clutched around the control bar, he ghost-soared above the Chagres National Park rainforest at a clip, approximately 30 mph. The cooler weather at this high-altitude felt refreshing while the repetitive sound of the flapping canopy added to the tranquility of skating on air. There was calm in this moment, but he was the storm about to descend on Morales's home and men. Bermuda's home explosion was revenge for Pemberley; this was payback for U-Street and for Pilar, even if her abusers were not in residence. Retribution for Liz would come at the end of this road with a bullet to Diablo's head—Iceman style.

Much like riding a motorcycle, hang gliding came naturally to him, both employing the same weight shift control and balance. Re-checking the altimeter attached to the right landing wire, he noted: six thousand feet above sea level. Tonight's perfect breeze and rising air from the mountainside kept him aloft with steady precision until he was ready for his descent to Diablo's Casa Luz. The starlit sky married the abyss-like mountainous land below him and in his mind he visualized the op about to go down. Two throwers, two suppressed pistols and his most valuable weapon: his hands, and he'd be a lethal force to reckon with once he landed at the edge of the cliff beyond the heliport.

The flutter of his glider skating on air measured the adrenaline coursing from the thrill of the flight. He should do this more often. No doubt, Liz would love it since "born to be wild" had become her theme song. He'd known from the moment he held her in his tango dance frame at the school that they were two sides of the same coin.

Wentworth, and his slick cowboy act, might give her a temporary sexual respite from her grief, which he'd have to accept, but the guy could never replace what they had, and when he returned from the dead, he'd fight for her and apologize—again and again and again— until he truly took his last breath.

A glance at his wrist to the GPS pre-programmed with the coordinates of his landing site and the mansion's location indicated it was time to start his calculated descent.

Backlit by the moon, the silhouette of two *cruzadors* (security protection) at the edge of the heliport came into view when he flew overhead toward the clearing at the very edge of the cliff beside a steep valley to his left. He held tightly to the control bar with one hand, maintaining balance when he withdrew his Beretta—firing one than the other with dead-on accuracy. Both bodies fell alongside the glider's canopy. His boots touched ground in a running landing, and he quickly released the harness. Leaving the glider ready for departure in seven mikes, he bolted toward the forest edge.

His feet barely disturbed either flora or fauna as he went pistol ready from tree to tree, carefully avoiding the security cameras position in the branches above. The house was dark, he could see through the tree line that at the back door an armed guard stood smoking.

Suddenly, air knocked from his lungs when a boot kick to his back sent him to the ground; the gun dropped to the rocky soil with a thud.

Another kick almost landed on his head, but with lightning response he rotated his body, capturing the foot in his hands before contact and snapped the ankle within his grasp just before his own kick in the enemy's solar plexus sent him flying. As the sentry fell backward, Darcy withdrew the sheathed knife attached to his leg and flung it into his chest before he could make another sound.

"Fuck," he silently groaned, rising from the forest floor and grabbing the Beretta. He stealthily came around the side of the building, surprising the back-door man with an effortless pistol shot then dragged him to the side of the hacienda.

Above him, on the verandah a light switched on and he froze, back pressed against the perimeter wall, careful not to create a shadow in the moonlight. The door opened and someone exited outside; he leaned over the railing.

Positioned at the corner of the building beside climbing roses, Darcy peered around the edge and took his shot—one to the temple; the cartel scum fell three-feet from him, eyes open. He joined the other in a heap of death.

He secured one foot in the rose-cover trellis, disregarding the thorns and brambles on the two story climb.

Ten seconds later, he ducked below the camera at the roof peak and slipped into the verandah's open door, entering the luxurious bedroom. He flipped the light switch off and stealthily made his way to the connecting office where the moon shined through the black security bars covering the outside of the unbreachable window. From his pant pocket he withdrew one of Bennet's new toys and held it near the perimeter walls as he silently moved from shadow to shadow. The electronic device vibrated in his hand when it passed over an 18" deep cigar humidor behind Diablo's desk. Clever.

A press to the button on the side of the device disarmed the cigar humidifier's alarm and hygrometer before he opened the fireproof glass door and slid out six cigar cases one at a time. With the base now empty, a concealed safe was revealed; Bennet's invention opened the safe with the press of a button. Jackpot.

The safe was filled with stacks of envelopes, a couple of notebooks (which he'd painstakingly examine when he got to Bolivia), and bricks of cash, which he'd pay forward to his asset in Peru; he emptied the safe, shoving everything into his backpack. He replaced the cigars and slipped in a little "love letter" then closed the door. Stealing the contents in the safe was simply theater. The fireproof stronghold would live to tell a story: a love letter from El Negro would provide the perfect scapegoat for his actions. Written in Spanish, the letter read:

"We will destroy La Muerta Mundial cartel and take all that you own. Nothing is beyond our reach. El Negro is the new Lord of the Jungle. We bring death to you and the world."

He grabbed a few Cubans for later from the top of the humidor and placed one between his lips. Glancing at his watch, he noted that three minutes remained.

On his way out the door, he pressed enough plastic C-4 against the wall to level half of the mansion. Casa Luz (House of Light) indeed.

Back down the trellis and through the woods, his pistol worked double duty until with two magazines spent, he quickly harnessed, grab bed hold of the hang glider's control bar and ran off the cliff. Soaring with the black mountain at his back, he said "Fire in the hole, fellas," and smirked when the explosion lit up the night.

***

Prague

Morales reached for the vibrating mobile phone on the nightstand beside his bed, and his wife groaned. Although accustomed to being interrupted—by him—she still expressed her displeasure.

"Five in the morning," he said in equal disapproval, grabbing the telephone. "What?" he growled into the phone.

"*Jefe* ..." Luis's voice wavered on the other end.

"Do you dare wake me? This better be good. Have you arrived in Prague yet?"

"No, *señor*. I was called back to Casa Luz early this morning. I will not be able to make my flight until this evening."

He sat up in bed and tightened his fist.

"The hacienda ... It was destroyed. There was an explosion," Luis weakly said.

He gritted his teeth and could feel the burn of anger to his cheeks. "Explosion? What happened?"

"We do not know yet, but security checkpoints at the bottom of the mountain say no one breached, no one had access. The drones and video surveillance show nothing. Defense had been tightened both on the perimeter and the checkpoints as you instructed."

"Then how did it happen!"

"El Negro. Your safe—it was only slightly damaged, and anticipating your instruction, I only opened it to verify that the book on the Panamanian officials was still secure."

Luis grew silent.

"And?!"

"It was empty except for a note. It was the enemy—El Negro."

Diablo threw back the bed linen and rose.

"Juan … come back to bed," Maria groaned.

"Shut up! Where was our security around the mansion?" he barked into the phone.

"Dead, *Jefe*. Twelve men, all dead, including one of our skilled *cruzadors*. They must have come with an army."

Storming from the bedroom, he grabbed the robe hanging at the door. "I want these people gutted like pigs! If you don't find the head of this El Negro and cut it off … then it will be your head! Do you understand me? It will be the piñata at your godson's birthday! And dessert will be your shriveled *cojones*—not macaroons from the local sweet shop!

"*Sí … Sí, señor.*"

***

Bolivia

Bone tired from his midnight op in Panama and having not slept in close to 32 hours, Darcy welcomed the frigid snap of air when he exited El Alto International Airport into "the city that touches the sky," La Paz, the capital of Bolivia.

Surrounded by barren land, he momentarily admired the stunning landscape of the snow-covered Andes Mountains surrounding the airport and took a deep breath, needing the invigorating clean air—as thin as it was.

The 3000-meter altitude barely affected him when he slung his heavy gear bag over a shoulder and searched through the thick, lunchtime traffic for a particular vehicle to transport him to yet another sleazebag hotel—the same one where he stayed during Operation Samba. Located deep in the valley, it was an hour drive both from the airport and to his sniping location within the South Andean Yungas rainforest.

His mood was shit—of course it had been since leaving his Lakmé—but it was worse tonight after listening to another brief, heart-breaking snippet of conversation from the necklace during his flight.

Dixon's muffled voice asked, "Mrs. D, are you all right in there?"

"I'll be okay, I think."

Perhaps she'd removed the necklace from around her neck because her voice sounded far away—and then he heard her retch into the toilet and his heart sunk. *Damn. She's sick. If only I could hold her head and rub her back.*

"Would you like me to make you some tea in that there hotel coffeemaker or I can call up for room service and get some toast. You have to eat, Liz."

"I'm not hungry."

She sobbed then blew her nose.

"Damn you, Fitzwilliam. You weren't supposed to die."

She opened the door and Dixon's voice sounded clearer, caring for her just as he had hoped.

'C'mon, let's rent a movie. It'll take your mind off things. We'll get one of those chick flicks you like and I promise I won't roll my eyes like last night."

"You will." Liz deeply sighed. "Dixon, have you ever felt like you didn't belong anywhere?"

"Sure, lots of times, but you and Mr. D changed that."

"I'm glad. I'm just sick of … everything. I can't wait to get out of town—to just go and not look back."

"Okay. Do you want to go for a drive tonight?"

In her silence, he can see her tapping her thigh, chewing at her lip with her upper tooth, her eyes filling with tears and then her damn sobs came, again, muffled by what he assumed was Dixon's strong chest.

He had done this; the guilt strangled him and he disconnected from the necklace before hearing anything else that would cause him to lose the focus he needed for the next three days. He missed her more than anything and the guilt was eating him up, but he was only just beginning his attrition warfare as a wrecking ball to the constructs of Diablo's life. He needed to remain detached and gelid to keep that lethal edge and not be swayed toward his alter-ego—the man his wife loved.

A beat-up, black Range Rover pulled up and his former MI-6 contact sat at the driver's seat with a smirk.

"Bloody hell, you're late," Frederick Hale—if that was in fact, his real name—greeted.

Opening the door, he climbed in, cold mist exiting his mouth when he replied. "Good to see you, too."

"I hardly recognized you under all that hair."

"The life of a vagabond. Thanks for answering my inquiry."

"Glad to be of service."

Of course he was glad to help. Who wouldn't be on board for a quick $250,000 worth of cryptocurrency? All his worldwide assets tapped for clandestine assistance had been cultivated through many years affiliation with Obsidian and he was calling in the many favors he had tallied over his tenure.

"Where are we headed?" Hale asked.

"The hostel up at Yanacachi."

"Right-o."

The truck fought its way back into traffic, nearly rear-ending a fuel tanker when it slammed on its breaks. The ex-spook swore out the open window with a raised hand and a two finger salute.

"Imagine my surprise, hearing from the Iceman on the darknet's Widows and Orphans portal. It's been at least three years since you Americans dropped into Russia and saved my bum."

He chuckled wryly. "It's the least we could do. You were in quite a situation."

"Indeed, but we're even after this."

"We are. Did you get the payment?" Darcy asked.

"Just as you promised."

He glanced over his shoulder at the tarp-covered mound behind the seats, assuming it all to be the necessary supplies and incendiary weapons for the bang and burn mission ahead.

"The word is you retired from all this excitement."

"I did."

When Hale realized that he wasn't here to socialize, he reached into the glove compartment and removed a map. "Have a look at this. I've marked the intersecting zip lines the workers use to transport the coca from each planting field, and I've arranged for a speed boat to take you to and fro checkpoint on the river and I'll pick you up at the hostel once your mission is complete. I have to say, you couldn't have timed your op any better."

"Why's that?"

"Local forestry and conservation are burning off the overgrown jungle areas up along the *camino de la muerte*. I don't know what you have planned, but based on those incendiary tracer bullets I had to track down, I'd say you're going to have a jolly good time blowing La Muerta Mundial's coca fields."

He said nothing, but Hale continued on. "There is a three-day halt to harvesting, in case you're concerned about civilian casualties."

At least there was that. Despite the flight delay, his exhaustion and his worry over Liz, he'd think optimistically about the mission ahead of him. At least the mobile phone handoff from Pilar in Panama and the destruction of Morales's Casa Luz had gone off without a hitch. Pilar's pledge to be at the ready for his final instruction was also promising. The woman was just as eager to take a match to everything the monster touched and only *she* could deliver the homerun to his idyllic life in Prague.

"This mission could get a bit dodgy if you're not in and out," Hale said. "There is a sudden change of weather coming. A rainstorm is headed up from Patagonia."

"I'll be gone in under 28, but rain is good. It'll cover my tracks," *and temper the fires from getting too out of control.*

"Be forewarned though—the cartel has increased security."

"I'll handle it."

"I forgot about those rumors of you being a cracking good, one-man wrecking ball."

"I started them," he chuckled wryly.

"So, how many hectares do you estimate?"

"Morales's crops total about 35,000 acres of illicit cultivation."

"That's a lot of plume when it blows. I included a respirator to get you out of the thick—just in case that was your plan. The controlled burn-off will stop the blaze from spreading deep into the Amazon, too."

"It's not my plan to decimate it all, just enough to impinge his livelihood. It is an ecosystem, after all."

"If that's your plan, well—you're looking at a war with the cartel. Of course, the ever-growing El Negro Cartel and the local coca farmers will be quite chuffed. Hell, they might even make you a local hero, but Morales will seek revenge."

"Been there—done that. Who do you think terminated his father?"

Hale glanced over to him with a devilish smile. "Well, then you're going to need the bottle of Singani I included in your gear. No extra charge, of course."

"Not on this one, Hale. I have to keep my head, keep my focus."

"Then this must be serious. When did you ever pass up a good drink to unwind after an mission?"

"Since it became personal."

"I may not have personal skin in the game, as you Americans say, but I could use the money."

"What are you saying?"

"I'm saying this drug epidemic is getting out of hand—and if your plan is to bring down Morales, then you might as well go the full monty. I can help."

Never one to make an impulsive decision, he didn't answer at first, analyzing the pros and cons of bringing in someone to do his dirty work. In the end, he considered the advantage of one less destination to flag his passport. Like all his other assets, Hale (in essence) meant nothing to him beyond being another contact in this dark world of contract killing, so his conscience would be clear if shit went sideways. If the Brit wanted to do it, then the consequences where totally on him.

"You want in on this?"

"Aye. Five hundred thousand and then you'll owe *me* one."

"Take it or leave it. I'll owe nothing to anyone. After this, I'll be disappearing with the wind at my back and you'll never hear of Iceman again."

"As you wish."

"I'll give you location, dates, and times of Morales's operation through Bristol. His *comercializador* has set up several companies in West England to launder his narco profits through. Your mission, your glory, your gamble. If you pull this off, they'll Knight you for sure, Hale."

His phone beeped; he glanced down at the encrypted text from Bennet, pressed in the security key code, and watched the symbols turn to words:

Peru is a go tomorrow. Same contact from Op. Macarena ready with transport and necessary munitions. He won't wait past 2200 hours. Wants US dollars.

He texted back: *Make travel arrangements for remainder of trip. Using designated portal on dark web, initiate contact with Italian friends for meeting in Venice 2M in crypto.*

"Good news?" Hale asked.

"The best kind."

Per protocol he deleted the communiqué.

14

Back to the Beginning

September 1
Bolivia

T he soupy fog that blanketed the black Amazon rainforest
concealed Darcy as he hitched onto zip line from zip line just as
the sun rose from slumber giving off an eerie glow. The chatter
of waking parakeets and Spider Monkeys broke through the dawn and
filled the dark canopy, but the treacherous North Yungas Road—aka
Death Road, *Ruta de la Muerta*—far above the luscious green valley was
still silent at this hour. He didn't use a harness, just his powerful grip
on a removable handlebar. His measured, warm breath evaporated into
the moss-colored wool face mask he wore, the moist heat caressing his
lips. With night vision goggles firmly in place and a satellite GPS
strapped to his forearm, he navigated a five-mile route through the
forest toward his destinations; the cables were secured and available
just as Hale had mapped out—and as he recalled. None of this was

new ground for him. He remembered the outlay of this forest well and trusted his instincts.

Dressed in varying shades of green jungle fatigues, he disappeared into the luscious canopy. His mood was black and focused; the frozen blood in his veins kept him detached from the killing and destruction he'd do today. When all was said and done, the Bolivian authorities, CIA, and DEA will all thank him (or rather El Negro) under their breath, and the locals on the take would be released from threat of death or blackmail.

He felt invigorated inside, relishing the rush, the heady thrill of revisiting Operation Samba to destroy part of what the Lord of the Jungle had cultivated for his son's rise to ascension.

In the distance he could see the cartel's sentry patrolling the coca fields' perimeter, and he made note of their position. Like the angel of death flying through the night, he zipped over them on perfectly concealed lines suspended from one side of the valley to the other, through the Cloud Forest to the center of Diablo's coca fields. His blood raced with the speed of the trolley.

At the end of a third cable, he dropped onto a thick branch and then secured his detachable trolley onto another crisscross section of taut wire. He was off again in a flash, careening 25 meters overhead, zipping above lush fields and hanging orchids. At the ready, his Beretta was tucked into its shoulder holster, and his sniping rifle attached to his back.

In a matter of minutes, the sun would be cresting over the horizon of the Andean mountain range, and as Hale indicated, the farmers and state forestry authorities would begin arriving for burn-off. The smoke and flame would be his subterfuge in escaping back over the zip lines.

Below him, his first destination was tucked at the bottom of a ravine: a hut used for coca extraction and processing supplies—further evidenced by the steep decline of the zip line used for the coca leaves delivery. The toxic stench of kerosene and bleach mixing with the pungent jungle flora filled his nostrils. In a breathtaking drop, the cable descended sharply from seventy-five feet to fifty feet, then to twenty-five, then to ground-level. When the end of the line came into view, he reached above his head and released the trolley from the cable, silently dropping and rolling mere feet from a sentry standing near to a pool of soaking leaves carved out in the forest floor. He quickly placed his gloved hands on each side of the guard's head, turned it, and snapped his neck. A quick draw of his suppressed pistol fired on a soap maker when that sad sack emerged from the hut; a third unfortunate soul came from the trees on the opposite side of the coca mixture, but he put him down by gunshot.

He functioned on a maddening, adrenaline-fueled auto-pilot. With measured swiftness, he shoved the trolley in his field pack and removed an incendiary device, installing it within the open end of the hut—the one closest to the blue barrels of kerosene and sulfuric acid.

In the distance, he heard the echoing rumble of heavy trucks motoring along Death Road, which indicated that he had only minutes to get to his hide site.

Thanks to Bennet's satellite infrared signal directed to his watch, he had eagle eyes as he glanced down at the moving orange and red body heat of three more sentries: one at 18 meters to his left, another at 36 meters and the third on the edge of the coca bushes. It killed him to admit that he couldn't do this so seamlessly without his father-in-law's ingenuity, and silently thanked Charlie for the tipoff that Bennet had secured the previously inactive satellite.

A myriad of jungle creatures silenced his footfall while he crept on the dark forest bed, approaching the sentries flanking him. Unable to see through the thick fog, his eyes continued to switch back and forth to the hot targets displayed on his watch.

One after the other, they fell from his deadly accurate pistol shot; they never saw their enemy's approach.

For as long as he lived, he would never forget the perfection of Operation Samba's hide—and it was only five meters ahead of him. From that unique tree-within-a-tree he had taken out the Lord of the

Jungle, and it was even more perfect on this second visit, further concealed by overgrown vines barely touched by the rising sun. Above, in the dense leaves, he could just make out the coca zip line he'd employed to escape 19 months before, and as he drew closer, confirmation was made by the broken branch that had snapped under his weight when he catapulted off. This was the place that started it all. Yes, he'd come full circle.

With panther-like dexterity, he climbed the massive tree, settled into the deep hollow of the thick branch, and resumed the same position he previously laid. With unhurried precision, he positioned his rifle then locked in onto one of his targets: a second processing hut. He'd now wait for the burn-off to begin and for the appropriate time to blow both labs. Waiting ... tick tock ... with the inching ascent of the sun before the six dead cartel security forces would be discovered.

It wouldn't be long, and while his eye remained trained on the vast coca plantation covered in foggy mist before him, he thought of his wife and swallowed hard. Death-dealing at the business end of a rifle barrel as though she had never entered his crosshairs was something vowed to never revisit, but he reminded himself that this was all for her and their loved-ones' safety, all so that they could live worry-free in their future. He flexed and tightened his jaw. He could endure this! He must endure this! His anger and misery were nothing compared to that which she was most-likely suffering through right now.

Tedious minutes passed as he lowered his pulse and listened to the rainforest come alive. Stilled, he focused through his scope on the movements of the two cartel sentries at the far end of the coca field, talking to each other on the job.

His lungs filled with the heady scent of smoke and burning leaves. It had begun. Calculated patience slowed his breath and heart to barely beating. No thoughts other than his shot crossed his mind, no consideration or quarter was given to his enemy, and no conscience existed for the hell this shot would unleash. He waited on that branch, focused like a laser.

Fifteen minutes later, when the burn-off was fully underway, he fired five consecutive rounds: the two *sicarios*, the lab, and the three crops growing over 150 meters apart. The explosions shook the valley and the ignited field joined in the burn-off when flame and smoke married the early morning fog.

He quickly rose, slung his rifle, attached the trolley and hit his Bluetooth. AC/DC's "Shoot to Kill" at full blast filled his ear canal when he pushed off the already broken branch.

Like a ghost, he disappeared into the jungle concealed in the smoke and ash, flying overhead through the forest canopy. Able to hold his weight with one hand gripped to the trolley, he tapped his wrist and blew the second cocaine lab to smithereens as he sped by.

The thrill was real, pushing the blood through his veins with an intoxicating rush, but his heart felt hollow without her. "Soon, baby. Soon."

***

Virginia

As Thomas anticipated, at 10 in the morning, FedEx rang the doorbell and he bolted from his library before Frances could intercept the expected delivery from "John Thornton." As it was, they were both already on tenterhooks waiting for their daughters' arrival for lunch and the dreaded "confession" they vowed to each other was long overdue. Focused, he headed for the back door with the greenhouse in his sights and package in hand.

"Don't spend all morning out there, Tommy. I'll need you to set the table for me," his ex-wife called after him from the kitchen.

"I'll be just a minute. Don't worry, honeybun."

After closing the glass door, he pressed play on the old cassette player, filling the hothouse with Mozart's happy allegretto, "Flute Concerto No. 2 in D Major" and then closed the sun shades.

Inside the box was a singular item surrounded by bubble wrap: the modified burner phone, now, hopefully, successfully paired to Morales's lieutenant, number two man, Luis.

He plugged an earphone into the end and turned the unit on. Immediately, his head filled with a conversation happening at the moment between Luis and a Spaniard.

"Our local distributor is impatient in Cadiz, *señor*. We have assured them of the product's arrival, but they make threats to seek out El Negro for their supply."

Frustrated, Luis growled at the cartel's local middleman. "Ah! It has been difficult to ship our containers without inspection or paperwork. Security aboard the cargo vessels has tightened but be patient, my friend. We have an associate at the Venetian port who promises to be of assistance, allowing over a dozen of our armed *cruzadors* to accompany the transport set to arrive on September 6. I have been assured that future shipments will not be seized by authorities at Cadiz port."

"But what of El Negro we hear so much about?"

"They are meddling ... and destroying, so that they can gain a foothold on the worldwide distribution from their well-hidden crops somewhere in Central America. I am sure they are the ones alerting the authorities of our rat lines, in hope to fill the void with their own product ..."

The pairing worked! He knew he shouldn't be, but he was proud of himself. He felt liked Q from a James Bond movie, and Frances was his leading lady. Unassuming, studied, gentleman landowner by day— and spy gadget guru by night. One day, he'd write a book about it and make a fortune.

Knowing that the conversation was recording to the satellite's data gallery he'd programmed, he clicked off and turned his desktop computer on. Logging into the cloud database where the recorded previous conversations were stored, he chose a random one from two

IP addresses that showed frequent contact, assuming they could be both Morales's and his lieutenant given the date and hour.

Listening attentively to Luis's early morning telephone call to Morales after Darcy's explosive visit to Casa Luz, Bennet laughed. After an internet search of local sweet shops in Prague, he made the connection between Pilar's intel and the conversation between the two thugs.

He texted Darcy:

Pairing to #2 working; Intel incoming. You hit a nerve in Panama; Diablo on fire! Thinks El Negro came with an army. Well done! BTW where is this El Negro? Internet viral with articles but no location

Also, Macaroons = local shop Pâtisserie Saint Tropez, Wenceslas Square, Prague. Family compound is in Prague

He laughed again, the music filling his soul. He hated to admit it, given all the harsh words he had spoken to Darcy, but in truth, he was having the time of his life!

***

After a valium-induced good night's sleep and an even better cry, Liz felt renewed and she was back in leather, fully recovered (and alert) following her ridiculous breakdown the night before. The tight sheath felt good against her skin despite the dog days of summer heat, but it felt even better against the seat of a Harley, even if Dixon traveled behind her in the H2.

She'd considered purchasing another SuperLow so that she could give him Fitzwilliam's new motorcycle, as both a thank you and for the selfish reason of missing a riding partner. Riding partners didn't need to be great conversationalists, which Dixon was not. His companionship had grown to be more of a watchful older brother who dropped pearls of wisdom every now and again, but the security detail crap was getting tiresome. Besides, she didn't need a bodyguard any longer; she was technically safe now and he had a life somewhere to get back to. Anyway, there would be no need to purchase a bike for herself; she had a perfectly good one sitting back on Black Mountain, not far from the Tail of the Dragon. When she returned from her trip, she'd give him her husband's Harley, recalling that Fitzwilliam had once told her that the man used to ride.

Although the Softail had all the high-tech bells and whistles and it had been the last place her husband's fabulous thighs straddled, it was a monster to ride. Perfect for his tall physique, the cockpit was too roomy for her and she struggled slightly to accustom herself to the massive power of the V-twin engine and size of the bike as she navigated the winding George Washington Memorial Highway alongside the Potomac River. The murky waterway she loved so much symbolized her home. In many ways, this historic area would always be home, a piece of her that held both bright and muddied memories, as most childhood homes did.

While coming home felt off—like her skin was on the wrong body—this new day gave her fresh determination to face life ahead. She took a deep breath, gunned the throttle on the next stretch of two-lane highway, and felt no guilt for leaving Dixon in her dust as she passed cars over the dashed white markings on the pavement. After today, she'd leave for North Carolina before heading off to who knows where. All of Fitzwilliam's favorite tunes played from his playlist in her helmet on the ride from Washington to Longbourn, but the one playing was one of her own, which seemed to be on continuous loop for the last two weeks: Evanescence's "My Immortal." Like the lyrics bemoaned, he still lingered here, and she could hear him now cautioning her not to go so fast! She just chuckled to herself with a head shake, wishing to hear him admonish her through the head comms versus her imagination. Sadness overtook her spirit when she realized that, like almost all operas, their love affair had ended in tragedy. She hadn't listened to opera since that afternoon when Rick and Knightley showed up at the compound. Ironically, the duet from

Opera Lakmé that enamored him so, hence her nickname, had played in the background to their presence.

Twenty minutes flew by in her ruminations, and she found herself at the long, now-paved drive to Longbourn Plantation. Admittedly, she missed her dad and their close relationship. That too, had been muddied by his actions, but she understood him much better given her own depression. She stopped the bike, flipped her visor up, and waited for the H2 to appear behind her.

Within a few minutes, it arrived in a plume of dust. Visible through the tinted windshield, Dixon teased her with a shake to his head and a wag to his finger, but then smirked. God bless him; the dear man had been her solid shoulder when she had pushed everyone else away who wanted to be, even Jane. Since her arrival in DC, all of Obsidian had reached out to her, but each text and phone call had gone unanswered. Until her visit to see Rick, only Dixon had been allowed to stay close to her—and the man had been smart enough to not say a word at her short haircut.

She rode down the drive, passed the mighty Bennet Oak and the infamous gazebo, and a rush of tenderness washed over her heart when she spied her greenhouse near the garages at the back of the house.

Two cars were parked: one was Jane's restored Camaro, and the other, a rental evident by the sticker on the bumper, was unfamiliar to her and she parked the bike beside it.

"Great place to grow up," Dixon said getting out of the H2.

"Yeah. Jane and I had some good times. That's the greenhouse I told you about."

He simply nodded, and she stretched her back.

"Looks like your pop has visitors."

She removed her helmet then placed it on the seat of the Harley along with her leather jacket. "Jane is here."

"Oh. My. God!" her sister effused from behind the screen door. "Look at your hair!"

"Sure sounds like she is," he laughed.

The door swung open and Jane, looking adorable in a pink dress and ballet slippers, barreled down the steps. Her hair was a little shorter and wavy, just touching the top of the silver hoop earrings she wore. The welcoming hug was like none she'd ever received from her sister, and they stood there embracing for what felt like long minutes. Jane cried, and so did she. *Dammit, not again.* She knew why *she* was crying but why was Jane? Because she missed Fitzwilliam? Because she'd missed her?

"Let me look at you, sissy," Jane commanded, finally pulling back with a sniffle and wipe to her cheek. "You lost more weight, but I love this hair."

"It's all right, I guess. Jane, you remember Dixon right?"

"Yeah! Sure! Hi, Dixon. Boy, we haven't had this many people at Longbourn since your wedding to Bill. It's turning out to be a regular party," she said sarcastically.

"Oh? Is Charlie with you?"

"No. He wasn't invited."

"Is everything okay? Is he doing okay?"

Jane smiled wistfully. "I think he's depressed."

"About Fitzwilliam?"

"Yuppers. Anyway, you better ... well, c'mon in the house. I hope you have your big girl panties on under that leather."

"If it's all right with you, Mrs. D, I'm gonna stay out here. Such a fine day to soak up the sun."

He was such a liar; he hated the hot sun. *Soon, Dixon, soon, you can go back to your own life.*

Arm-in-arm, the sisters walked to the door and she could hear her father's voice above the cheerful music within the house. "Who is here?" she asked. "Is he talking to himself again?"

But Jane didn't reply.

"Jane?"

Literally tight lipped, her sister just shook her head.

The old house looked like and felt like a new house when she entered. Apart from central air conditioning, a tangible metamorphosis had taken place since last she'd visited. Was it the construction or something else? There was an aura of joy within like she remembered from long ago. On her great-grandmother's pier table, an antique vase held Virginia wildflowers and long sprigs of lavender, replacing the musty fragrance of dead generations with a calming, uplifting fragrance. Two colorful bouquets wrapped in plastic lay beside the arrangement.

"Is that ABBA playing? What's going on here?" she asked. *Disco? No classical?*

Still, Jane said nothing but her father came into the hallway with a spring to his step and a beaming smile. His ratty sweater was g.o.n.e! He'd even styled his hair with a little gel.

"Lizzy-bear!"

"Dad? Is that you? Are those blue jeans?"

"Lordy, can't your old man get with the times?" He kissed her cheek then put his arms around her. "How's my girl?"

There was that dreaded question—yet again! How did any of these people think she was? Like she'd suddenly exclaim, "I'm great! Couldn't be better. Let's party!"

"One day at a time," she said as cheerfully as possible, forcing a smile.

"Well, in due time, you'll be back to your old self. I have no doubt."

"I don't see how that's even remotely possible." Her hand immediately went to her necklace for comfort.

Something passed before his eyes, a sad expression—a secret. She recognized that look from his days of machinations with the repulsive lecher Henry Crawford. Was he reading *Crime and Punishment* again?

Jane just stood by, distracting herself by fixing her hair in the mirror behind the flower arrangement. Obviously, she knew something, too, which was even more evident when she began to hum along with the song in typical Jane Bennet-style deflection.

"You cut your hair, sweetheart. I like it."

"Thanks and thanks for fixing and sending the necklace to me."

"Of course. It was just a minor adjustment. Have you determined how it broke while *protected* in the safety deposit box?"

"Odd isn't it? I guess I'm just thankful it was there and not at Pemberley. We lost everything except what was in that panic room with me." She shrugged, then looked away. "At least I wasn't among the lost. Ya' know, being in the workout room and all."

"Right! That's my girl, always seeing the positive side of things. I must admit, I was quite surprised to find a microphone and transmitter within that tiny snake head. Your husband was quite ingenious."

She snorted, glad he brought the topic back to the necklace, and her hand toyed with the diamond-encrusted head. Thank God he didn't say "*late*-husband" or she would have burst into tears for the one-thousandth time. "He was always thinking of ways to keep me close to him. Unfortunately, this time I wouldn't mind his spying on me, but I'm too far out of his distance." If only he *were* listening; she'd give anything for him to be on the receiving end of the necklace's comms each time she'd spoken to him. Now, the only purpose it served was to remind her of their bond. "You didn't remove the transmitter did you?"

"I wouldn't dream of it." He smiled weirdly. Then again, he was dressed weirdly, was acting weirdly, and was listening to weird music, so she shrugged it off.

"Now, I have a very special surprise for you today," her father declared, sliding his hand into hers and led her toward the dining room as "Super Trouper" 70s music beat around her. The way he held her and kept looking over to her made her feel like she was being led to a slaughter while serenaded by Disco queens from 40 years ago. The abhorrent Disco was dead and, as far as she recalled, ABBA never played in Longbourn before. It all felt so surreal, like a bad movie or a time warp. What was next?—Olivia Newton John gliding across the living room on roller skates to *Xanadu*? A glance over her shoulder showed a now silent Jane wringing her hands as she trudged behind them with a furrowed brow and pursed lips. Okay, now she was officially worried. The woman looked ready to bolt, especially when she pensively glanced at the door over her own shoulder.

They entered the brightly lit and cheerfully painted dining room, revealing a beautiful table setting: more flowers, fine china, and assorted accoutrements.

… And her mother.

She gasped at the shock: nine years. For nine friggin' years, the woman had been gone from this house without a word.

The abandoner stood holding the back of the chair at the head of the table—a smile graced her face. "Hi, darling."

Cut and run! Liz gagged and bolted from the room for the bathroom, eliciting her father's immediate response of calling after her, his voice tinged with unwarranted and unrealistic frustration.

"Let her go, Tommy. We both knew how she'd react," she heard her mother's dispirited voice say before the vomit came, yet again.

"Oh, sissy. I know," Jane soothed, opening the bathroom door followed by a rub to her back as the dry heaves and spit continued to wrack her body. Her sister sighed. "I felt sick, too, when I saw her. It's going to be okay."

She rose and turned to Jane, blurred through the pooled tears and stressed eyeballs from upchucking food that wasn't there. "Why … what … how? I can't do this stuff all at once," she sobbed into her sister's welcoming embrace.

"Me either. I don't want to deal with this crap, but I can't *leave*, not now—not when you need me."

"Oh, why is she back?"

"She has lymphoma, and Dad wants to take care of her."

"Because he was sooooo good at taking care of *us* when we needed him! It was more like the other way around." Incredulously she spat her words, "She came home because she fucking wants to be taken care of? *I* needed to be taken care of when I broke my damned ankle my senior year! And she sure as hell didn't give a fuckety-fuck when you had that accident in Pot-Head Unibrow's truck! Where was her motherly concern and advice when I almost married that dick-wad Bill? For God's sake, I was trapped for seven fucking nightmarish hours down in the panic room! I didn't see her there when I emerged."

Jane bit her lip, probably because she hadn't heard her drop F-bombs like this since Caroline flew to Paris with intentions of seducing her husband! But she didn't give a crap about her salty language. She had zero tolerance and absolute bitchiness today—and she hated fucking Disco!

Now the tears rolled as furiously as her temper. "Un-fucking believable! My husband was just blown up and eaten by fucking sharks … and I have to feel pity for *her*? No fucking way! No fucking way!"

"I know. I know. You have every right to swear like a deranged sailor, sweetie. The world is upside down. It's been almost a decade of her not caring about anyone but herself."

With motherly tenderness, Jane wet a face cloth then wiped Liz's cheeks and mouth. "I'm sorry she made you sick, Liz."

"Everything makes me sick and that's why I need to get out of town. I thought I could find some peace back in Virginia, but I'm more convinced than ever that this *can't* be home any longer; there is no peace or home without Fitzwilliam. Only he mattered!"

"Is that why you didn't call me when you got into Washington? You're done with family?"

"No!"

"Well … um … I know you didn't mean to, but it hurt my feelings, blowing me off like that, even changing your phone number without telling me. I had planned such a great homecoming for you."

"I'm so sorry, Janie. I'm not myself these days. I'm—numb."

"It's okay. I really do understand." She smiled sympathetically. "Can I … um … ask you something else?"

"I guess," she huffed but immediately regretted it, not meaning for it to sound so pissy when the snarkiness came out.

"Had you come to see me at the houseboat, but then decided to get jiggy with Dave?"

She softly laughed understanding why—at this moment—Jane herself needed levity and she indulged her. The one person Jane had once admired most in this world had returned after abandoning her. "No! Of course I didn't sleep with him, but damn if he didn't look ready."

"I told you. That cowboy looks worth the wetness."

"It's strictly platonic, not romantic. And what about you? He's living with you on the houseboat. Don't tell me you're not tempted, even just a little to go all peeping Tom on that little shower."

And just like that, a shadow crossed Jane's smile ending their forced humor. "I'd never cheat on Charlie."

Dropping the subject along with the commode lid, Liz sat and rubbed her temple. "I'm so tired. I just don't have the strength to deal with this. Jane, what the heck are we gonna do about Mom?"

"I don't want conflict either. I have enough of it lately, and it's messing with my mojo. Whatever her motive or excuses, I do think we should hear her out—"

"I don't give a rat's ass what she has to say! It's over. It's done. I forgave her, and I don't need to rehash it." *It was much easier to forgive her when I thought she'd never return!*

"Right, but I guess we should just listen to what she has to say, just to say we did. Neither of us have the guts right now to fight the inevitable."

"What's the inevitable?"

"She's staying and Dad is happy and we don't have to like the reason why he's happy, but he is. He didn't like Darcy, but your husband made you happy and Dad had no choice but to deal with it."

"Two million dollars certainly made Fitzwilliam more likeable and Dad more accepting of our marriage. Besides, Fitzwilliam never broke my heart by disappearing then returning with flowers and some phony English accent after being M.I.A for nine years."

"The reality is that it doesn't matter what we think. All that matters is that she's here and Dad still loves her and is willing to forgive her for their remaining future together. It's his life, not ours—right?"

"He should be taking our side for all we did for him!" Liz argued.

"We're talking about Dad—that's never going to happen. Not like we want anyway. But maybe he's taking responsibility for running her off and is overjoyed at the opportunity to make it up to her."

"As always, you sound sympathetic to her, Jane."

"Believe me, I'm not. I'm waaay not, and I've been hiding my anger very well all these years, but it is what it is and we have to face our demons sometime."

She looked up at her big sister with a blank expression. The sound reasoning took her quite by surprise—as it usually did whenever the ditz cleared from Jane's brain. "I guess. Just before Fitzwilliam left for Bermuda he quoted something from a book he was reading. 'He who has felt the deepest grief is best able to experience supreme happiness.' I guess that's where Dad is now."

"Wowza, that's an awesome quote. It implies that you'll find happiness too."

"It's just a stupid quote from a stupid book. I'll never find happiness again."

"Sure you will. One night with Wentworth will put a smile on your face—and on your lady parts."

"What?!"

"I'm just kidding. See ... I got you smiling at just the thought of it. C'mon, let's go hear what she has to say. We owe it to ourselves to get the whole truth from her. What we choose to do with it rests solely on us without any guilt. If we want to forgive her—great! My mojo will be intact. If we want to tell her to go to hell—great! My mojo will have acted in good conscience."

"Who are you today?"

"I'm the sister who's not getting into my Camaro and driving away."

Whoa. She'd never called Jane out, and Jane had never admitted her failing so forthrightly. Smiling from her heart, she stood and hugged her. "Thanks, sis."

15
Mamma Mia

A s a unified force, the sisters walked down the hallway toward the dining room with clasped hands. Jane's hand was warm and soothing—strong, like an older sister's grasp should be when caring for her younger sibling. And make no mistake, she felt like the sixteen-year-old who'd woken to learn that her mother split in the middle of the night without a good-bye. Although she swore she forgave Frances last year, she was still in need of that rare sensible and protective Jane at this very moment. All her personal walls and the constructs of her life—as she knew it—were falling apart one by one. Pemberley, Fitzwilliam, her mother. How much more could she take?

She heard her parents talking and set her shoulders back, innately defiant, but holding onto that not-so-stupid quote from *The Count of Monte Cristo*. Admittedly, this was the ultimate happiness to her father's miserable life. He'd never stopped loving Frances or feeling guilty for her departure. Had she not herself dreamed of bailing on him many times under the strain of his needs? Had she not "abandoned" him after she moved to Pemberley last summer?

Silently, she prayed for Fitzwilliam's wisdom and assistance, and feeling him all around her, caressed the necklace as if channeling his strength through the love they'd shared.

When they crossed the threshold, the long dining table separated the two opposing forces. Her parents' hands lay piled one on top of the other at the corner of the table. They simultaneously looked up, and Liz's fingers tapped her thigh at the sight they presented: as united a force as their daughters. Her mother cried, her father comforted, and the "rest of their family" stood outside that private world of marital affection and reconciliation after years of self-serving deprivation. In a small measure, she could understand. Fitzwilliam was her life and their love was the only all-encompassing force in their private and secluded world. Their understanding of each other was not open for dissection or critique to outsiders. It was between them. The difference between them and her parents was that his "departure" from their world—his tragic death—was in the act of self-immolation in order to keep her safe. Unlike her mother, he wouldn't be returning, and further he assured that her future was safe. She was free from Diablo's retaliation. It was a heavy cross to bear, knowing that he gave his life for hers.

She tried to imagine how her father felt, having believed Frances dead (metaphorically)—and then her showing up on his doorstep. It must have shocked him for sure.

Frances abruptly stood, her gaze holding her daughters as she swallowed hard then cautiously walked around the table to them, taking a step with each sentence she expressed. "I know this is ... shocking, right? [step] "And I know how angry you must be even after all these years." [step] "My daughters ..." she stopped and more tears rolled down her ruddy face, then took another step closer. "I want you to know, I wanted you to come with me but ..." She glanced over her shoulder to their father whose fingers covered and slid down his eyes then cheeks.

"Your father decided it best if I just left."

"What!?" they exclaimed simultaneously.

Now Thomas stood and in barely a whisper he said, "It's true, girls. I knew she was going to leave beforehand."

Frances took her final step to them and reached out her hand but it dropped when neither of them accepted it. "I'm not asking for anything more than just the opportunity for your father and me to come clean on our selfish actions."

"Wait, Frances," he objected.

"Yes. Selfish, Tommy. We wronged them and they need to know the entire truth of what happened that week. Why I left them with you and didn't take them to England with me as I planned."

"Dad?" Jane asked, her voice cracking, but he just looked away in shame.

In an instant, Jane's rational, sympathetic consideration of her mother had disappeared.

"You didn't leave *me*, Mom. You left Lizzy with him. Do you even know what you did? How it affected her?"

Their mother bowed her head but said nothing.

And it was here that another veil lifted and Lizzy found her voice—the one that was no longer afraid to call out her sister's own selfish actions. If censure was going to go around today, everyone should take their share and frankly, she'd had as much as she can handle these past two months. "Jane, if we're all going to be honest. You can't really fault her for bolting and leaving me to shoulder the whole responsibility of Dad and Longbourn when you left me three days after she did."

She, too, dropped her chin to her chest.

"But I forgive you because I understand you and knew how hurt you were by her leaving. You and Mom had a special bond, one that I didn't."

Jane took her hand and squeezed it hard.

"Lizzy, Janie ... I'm so sorry." Frances squeezed her eyes shut and pursed her lips. "I know those words are meaningless, but I truly am, and I didn't come back to place any blame on anyone's shoulders other than my own. I should have done what I meant to do but there were dire issues to consider."

Liz finally sat at the end of the table and the other women followed suit, leaving Thomas standing alone and isolated at the opposite end. Oh, how apropos—how ironic. Silently, all three fidgeted as if it a familial trait, each one searching for words in the uncomfortable confrontation. Sure, she'd agreed with Jane about listening to the explanation, but did she really care at this point? Was there any minute measure of daughterly love remaining in her heart? And what *of* her heart? How many more broken pieces would fall from it until there was nothing left?

"I don't care," she finally sighed, breaking the tension. "I let it go and forgave you a year ago. Honestly, I have other hurts and pains to focus on now."

"I understand and I am so very sorry for your loss, darling—"

"Well, I care!" Jane yelled, startling them all. "Why did you listen to him? Why did you leave us to care for him?"

"Because ..."

"Franny!"

But she ignored his objections.

And, honestly, Liz was too shocked by her sister's outburst to pay attention to anything he had to say, but it surprised her when he interrupted.

"She didn't take you girls because I was hurt, infuriated with her. I felt betrayed ... and I threatened suicide if she took you both away from me."

"I knew he was telling the truth."

Where Jane's eyes grew wide, Liz's didn't. She believed this to be the absolute truth—and stark confirmation of her father's previous manipulative tendencies. She'd lived through them all, and where he used Longbourn and its familial history as his tool against her, he used his children as a tool against his separating wife, just so he could wound her as she'd wounded him. She couldn't help that rising feeling of resentment toward him after having put it to bed over the last year. Clenching her fist, she felt anger for what he denied his daughters. Their mother hadn't left in the night! She'd wanted to take them with her!

"For my own part, girls, I was too ashamed to say good-bye, too ashamed to face you both and tell you that I was leaving for another man."

"Is that true?" Jane asked. "You left us for some guy?"

Their mother's eyes pleaded for forgiveness. "Yes. I knew I made a terrible mistake both in abandoning you and in leaving your father. I always loved him, despite the challenges of being married to him. When I did telephone, your father said I was dead to all of you, but I kept writing. One month later, I received in the mail all the unopened cards and letters I wrote the two of you."

"You wrote?" she stammered, accusingly at her father who sat stone-faced, clearly shocked that it *all* was coming out. So many secrets!

"Don't blame him, girls. He was very sick—long before I left, and my own co-dependency and personal shortcomings kept me from getting him professional help."

A tiny measure of pity rose in Liz's heart for Frances. No, they could never get back those days when they were a family, but she understood pain, grief, mistakes, atonement ... and through Fitzwilliam's tragic upbringing—suicide. Was her father's illness at its worst back then? Had her mother acted in good conscience by believing that leaving her teenage daughters in the comfort of their home and school was the wisest choice? Had she thought it the best course of action in safeguarding their father's mental health? And had she returned or fought in the courts for custody of her minor daughter would it have made everything worse? The fighting, the misery, the gas-lighting? *Could they—and we—now forge a "new" family? I don't know ... but what else do I have?*

"Do you still love Dad?" was the only question she could handle at the moment.

"We love each other still—and we love you both with all our hearts. *That* had never changed."

"And did he tell you why he wears the ankle bracelet?"

"Yes, he did."

"All of it?"

"Tommy?"

"Yes, I told her all of it, Liz. We've been completely honest with each other and want to start over."

Oh dear. She took a deep breath and searched her soul for any sliver of absolution she could offer, considering that they had offered it to each other after what they'd been through. Finally looking to Jane seated at her left, she wondered how her sister's mojo was feeling. Those pursed hot pink lips were *not* a good sign. "Sissy, would you like to stay for lunch with me, Mom, and Dad?"

Jane looked at their mom's hopeful expression, and then to their father. "I just wanna know was he worth the cheating?"

"Who, darling?"

"The guy you left Dad for … Were those two months hell or bliss before you figured out what you lost, what you did to us?"

"Hmm … 'Conscience is a thousand swords,' " she quoted Shakespeare. "It began its assault on me as soon as the plane left Dulles."

"Did you love him?"

"No, but he did help me to discover who I had lost during twenty years of marriage: myself. Would I change that knowing what I know now? The cost of my decision? Change the past if I could? In a heartbeat, but hindsight and having experienced great loss is 20/20." She looked over her shoulder back at Thomas. "He wasn't your father and his type of love could never replace the two beautiful, strong, sensitive daughters I left back in Virginia."

***

Bolivia

As the getaway boat tripped at a 60 mph clip down the Amazon River, the adrenaline in Darcy's veins coursed from speed and exhilaration at the devastation he'd just wrought. His hair blew back and the chilled winter air stung his cheeks. Although at least 30 klicks from his targets, he could still smell the pungent smoke of the coca rising from the valley at his back. *Two down, four to go—for you, baby. I vow to you, this will be over soon—and you will remain safe!*

Distance and time were too powerful, making the pull to hear her voice irresistible, and he reached out for the satellite phone. He tapped in the code to access her necklace comms and Liz's stress came through loud and clear.

Obviously, Bennet came clean on yet another of his deceptions. She was in the thick of it with her mother and damn that he couldn't be there to comfort her. How much more could his girl take before she snapped? She'd come through the explosions just fine, right? She was the strongest woman he knew and she'd be able to compartmentalize it all—just as he had his entire life.

But fuck! For all his perfect planning, the absolute unexpected kept happening. First Wentworth (and that disturbing conversation), and now her mother's inopportune return to her life. Had he not considered his life experiences or the passage from *The Count of Monte Cristo?* *"Ah, but who can ever know what may happen, my dear fellow? Man proposes, God disposes ..."*

Ignoring Jane's encouragement to sleep with Wentworth, he focused on the real content of the conversation, and for a second he rejoiced that Dumas's quote about suffering and happiness had broken through Liz's psyche. Would she hold onto it when her dead husband reappeared in their life once Diablo was put down? Was this the beginning of her putting pieces together? No doubt, she'd been to the Darcy family lawyer by now. But maybe the trail and the pieces weren't enough. Surely, their conversation beside the waterfall must have broken through to her grief. He'd given her his word, and that wasn't something he did unless he could deliver.

"She's staying and Dad is happy and we don't have to like the reason why he's happy, but he is. He didn't like Darcy, but your husband made you happy and Dad had no choice but to deal with it."

"Two million dollars certainly made Fitzwilliam more likeable and Dad more accepting of our marriage. Besides, Fitzwilliam never broke my heart by leaving then returning with flowers and some phony English accent after being M.I.A for nine years."

"Just before Fitzwilliam left for Bermuda he quoted something from a book he was reading. 'He who has felt the deepest grief is best able to experience supreme happiness.' I guess that's where Dad is now."

"Wowza, that's an awesome quote. It implies that you'll find happiness too."

"It's just a stupid quote from a stupid book. I'll never find happiness again."

It killed him to admit that his father-in-law had been right. He disconnected and texted Bennet. *You were right. Shut down comms to the necklace.*

16

Revelations

Washington, DC

The sound of the ringing telephone filled Rick's ear as he impatiently waited for his friend to answer; it was time to call in a favor from one of his and Darcy's childhood buddies. Liz hadn't said anything, but he could see the disappointment in her eyes that his grief and inertia had kept him from following through on the information regarding the ass-wipe that destroyed Pemberley. She wanted answers, needed to scapegoat someone other than herself and Darcy for his death in Bermuda.

"Mason," the familiar voice on the other end greeted.

"Jimmy, it's me Rick Fitzwilliam."

"Ho! What the hell? It's gotta be like six years?"

"More like thirteen, but who's counting."

"You're making me feel like an old man. Where has the time gone?"

"Beats me. We're a little older, probably not much wiser, and I'm definitely a lot more cynical and regimented than that kid you knew. The military did that to both me—and Darcy."

"No doubt. I'm certainly a different guy, that's for sure. You grow up quickly on the job, not that the Leesburg Police Department is all homicide and burglaries, but it gets its share of Class A felonies mixed in with all those Rolls Royce traffic violations. So, what's up? Are you married with children, yet?"

"No, not yet—maybe soon. How about you?" he asked, going through the perfunctory niceties.

"I married Emma and we have two kids. We live up at Mason Chase, you know, my grandmother's old family estate. We're putting in a swimming pool, and just got a couple of horses for the girls."

"Good for you. Sounds like you're doing all right on the police force." *Or came into an inheritance.*

"One could say that."

"Listen, I know how close you were with Darcy and Wickham on the high school and UV polo teams, but … did you hear about what happened?"

"Yeah. Wickham is out on parole. I keep an eye on him from time to time. The breeder over at Mills Horse Farm told me that Darcy put in a good word for him, getting him a job as groomer. He's doing all right."

"I didn't know that, but that's not what I'm talking about."

"Then you're talking about Pemberley?"

"No … You didn't read the local paper?"

"Nah. I get first-hand accounts here at the station house."

"Darcy was killed in a diving accident in Bermuda."

Their childhood friend went silent and Rick thought he'd disconnected from the call. "Jimmy?"

"Jeez. I'm sorry to hear that. I only just spoke … Wow, I'm really sorry."

"You only just spoke what?"

"Nothing. Just ... um ... man ... he called me shortly after the explosions at Pemberley, inquired if I was interested in a couple of horses he had stabled. He asked about Wickham, you know ... the usual stuff. So, this must have happened recently then. How's his wife taking the news?"

"It was August 4th, and his wife is really struggling. That's sorta why I'm calling. I'm not gonna beat around the bush, but I need some information regarding the ballistics found at the estate following the explosions in July. The Department's forensic chief informed me that everything is gone, wiped clean from the server, evidence stolen and that the whole investigation has been shut down. I'm not buying it. I need answers and justice on behalf of Darcy's wife, you understand. The guy who did this shouldn't get away with attempted murder. In fact, this could be a real case for you to break—get you away from writing tickets."

Silence again.

"Can you help an old friend out, make some inquiries for me?"

The tone in his voice had changed, lowering and turning serious. "I already helped an old friend out."

"What do you mean?"

"This case. It's been taken care of out of state—closed up in Morgantown, West Virginia."

West Virginia! Holy fuck.

"Who closed the case?"

"Technically, a friend of our mutual old friend who recently died in a diving accident in Bermuda."

"Are you saying what I think you're saying?"

"Yes. Together, we made the problem go away. Tell Mrs. Darcy justice has been served."

Served? By her husband ... "Oh, shit. Did he smoke him?"

"No, just put him out of business. Call it a mercy for a wayward kid."

"Wayward, my ass. He was an assassin for one of the most notorious cartel kingpins. The ashes of Pemberley are *still* smoldering."

"I don't know anything about assassins or cartels. We only deal with small time drug busts around here."

"Hmm. Do you realize the trouble you can be in for this? How the fuck could my cousin ask you to do what you're implying?"

"He didn't. I offered. All he said was that he wasn't pressing charges, that he had no interest in the arsonist going to prison for the destruction of Pemberley and that he had other plans for him if only he could find him. This is Darcy we're talking about. I knew *exactly* what he was asking, without his actually asking. He's very persuasive in his silence."

"Let me guess, this was your payback for some ass-saving he did on your behalf."

"That's right. I owed him big time."

He sighed. "So you put your entire career at risk? Foolish, man … foolish."

"Not foolish. Loyal. And I also know that if shit fell on me, he'd have my six. Isn't that what you military guys say?"

"Yeah. You are right about him."

Damn. Who didn't owe Darcy something? For a man who hated snakes, he always managed to save them, charm them, and then … use their venom to his advantage at a later date. And if he couldn't use them—he'd destroy them under his boot.

"If you don't mind me asking—is that how you can afford two horses and the taxes on your grandparents' 150-acre estate on a detective's salary? Darcy paid you off to make the case go away."

"No comment."

Yeah … I'd say you've changed. Just goes to show that money talks, and that there was more to the story of the hows and whys Darcy moved it around. Had he paid the kid off in Morgantown to tap his resources? Why was the money *really* moved to Panama?

"Let it go, Rick."

Darcy had said the same words to him the night before they left for Bermuda. Unfortunately, having been too focused on laying out the op, he missed a very-telling reference that his cousin inadvertently revealed: "stupid kid." So *that's* how his cousin knew he was a kid? And what will said wayward "kid" owe Darcy in exchange for his clemency, for his life?

> *"Are you going after him?" Rick asked.*
>
> *"He's no longer worth Obsidian's focus."*
>
> *"I disagree. His mission for Morales may not be complete. After all, you are still alive."*
>
> *"I wasn't meant to be the target. Diablo's picking off all of you, one by one, to get my attention. Glancing over his shoulder, he, again, looked at the photograph of the assassin who tried to kill Liz. "I don't think we'll see him again."*
>
> *Rick bitterly laughed. "Iceman is so confident."*
>
> *"On this … yes I am. He's just a stupid kid who got charmed by the money that comes with the life of a hired gun. Let it go."*
>
> *He removed the image from the tack board and handed it to his cousin. "I already deep-sixed this, you should, too."*

"Thanks for telling me, Jimmy. Say, I'd like to keep in touch?"

"Sure, I'd like that, too. Don't be a stranger, old friend—and I'm real sorry about Darcy's death. He was one of the good guys."

"Yes he was. Take care." Rick hung up and that strategic military warrior Sun Tzu spoke in the back of his mind, unnerving, niggling words: *"It is essential to seek out enemy agents who have come to conduct espionage against you and to bribe them to serve you. Give them instructions and care for them. Thus, doubled agents are recruited and used."*

"All warfare is based on deception."

Deception. Could it be that *everything* had been a clever deception? Even Bermuda? He wouldn't put it past his cousin. He, himself, had stated there was nothing Darcy wouldn't do to protect Liz. Would he have gone so far to … to … fake his death?

As Sarah would say, "Absobloodylutely."

***

"Hey, boo. I'm home."

"Hey. Did you have a nice time?" Charlie robotically replied, his gaze fixed on his laptop screen. His eyes were tired and his mind raced, pulling him in a million emotional directions, from anger to understanding, to disappointment, and to absolute astonishment. Running his hand through his hair, he added "I'm in my cave," his eyes falling to the stack of seven—not eight—passports that Rick had given him this afternoon. The flight activity of number eight—a British one —was right there on his computer monitor facing him.

Above the head-banging music playing, he could hear cabinets opening and closing in their stateroom, and Jane said something about Wentworth. However, he couldn't focus on her right now, not that he didn't want to, but shock was gripping him by the balls.

"Hmm, right," he replied, not even sure if that was the correct answer.

"Are you listening to me?" she huffed, sliding back the pocket door to his Grateful Dead über-fan sanctuary.

Finally, he leaned back in his chair, mindfully shaking his annoyance away when she smiled at him. That feminine pink dress and the way her shining tresses fell around her cheeks as she looked down at him touched his heart, lightening his mood. Whenever Janie walked into a room, she brought rays of sunshine with her. She'd had that effect on him from the first time he saw her at the dance school 18 months ago.

"Is everything okay, Charlie?"

"Sure. I'm sorry; I'm just trying to get my shit together before Istanbul." He flipped over the legal-sized pad he had been jotting notes on and then turned off the music, giving her as much attention as he could muster.

"I forgot you were leaving tomorrow," she said dejectedly. She walked to him and bent down, depositing a soft kiss to his lips. "Damn, I needed that. I missed you."

"Did you?"

"I wouldn't have said it if I didn't mean it."

That little bit of snark from her tipped him off that either the visit to Longbourn for lunch hadn't gone well or it was something else—maybe him, maybe something happened with Wentworth—something he didn't even want to think about but he had to test the waters. "By the way, our houseguest cut-out this morning. He's headed back to Tennessee." He waited, examining her expression for any slight change.

But she just nodded, walking around the tight space, mindlessly touching things. Now that his anger over his project findings was temporarily checked, fear rose in its place. Was she upset with him? She was acting like a woman about to kick his ass to the curb, and yes, that did frighten him. They'd been "off" since Darcy's death, and she had been distracted by Wentworth's six pack abs, but that was nothing new. At the same time, she had been patient and understanding of his grief and guilt. The onus was solely on him; he needed to get back on his game both at home and at the dance school. He vowed that he would get their relationship on track when he returned from Operation Zeybek.

Forcing his unexpected research project to the back of his mind, he gave her all his attention, even if he didn't want to hear her say "I'm calling us quits."

"Why don't you cop a squat and we'll talk about what's gotten you so upset. I'll make us a couple of Long Island Ice Teas to get you through it."

"No booze."

"Okay, shoot. What's up?"

"She's back."

"Liz came home early?"

"Yes. She's home but that's not who I'm talking about." Standing over him, she put a hand on her hip and shook her head, then looked away from his confused expression. She ran her other hand down her face then looked back at him, holding his gaze, her blue eyes on fire. *Oh boy ... here it comes.* He braced himself for what was about to unleash on him when those pretty pouty pink lips of hers curled. Finally, after what felt like forever, she emitted a groan of absolute disdain, "My mother has returned."

He let out an audible sigh of relief. "Ho-ly crap. For reelz? Your mom?"

"Yyyup."

"Whoa."

She sat with a plop onto the sofa, looking about to cry. In truth, this announcement was much easier for him to hear, and while he felt bad for her, he was damned glad he wasn't the reason for their needed "talk" and breathed another sigh of relief. After today's discovery from those passports, he didn't think he could handle anything more.

"Remind me to never again take an unnecessary day off from the museum. Unless it's for Obsidian, I'm not doin it, nuh-uh. No one messes with my mojo there."

He rose, crossed the two feet separating them and sat beside her, sliding his arm around her shoulders. "I'm sorry, babe. Where was she?"

"England. She's a chef for some Michelin-rated restaurant in London."

"Did she say why she bailed on you?"

"Dad and some guy. She cheated and split."

Wow ...

Resting her head on his shoulder, she sighed. "I'm so confused. Until today, I didn't realize just how angry I've been at my mother for leaving. I mean, all along I knew I was blowing it off as not such a big deal, when it really was, trying not to upset Liz, but today I thought I'd be the forgiving one. Instead it seems to be my sister who's the forgiving one."

"Maybe it's because of what she's been going through. Maybe she needs her mother even after all these years."

"Or maybe she's just numb. I don't know. I realized over lunch that I'm not ready to let go of my mother's psychological beat-down of us even if she said she wanted to take us with her."

"Why didn't she?"

"Dad pulled his usual manipulative bull crap. Lied to us and her. Damn, I'm so over him. Anyway, I don't want to talk about it tonight. I'm sorta mentally burned out. Maybe tomorrow."

"Whatever you need, my shoulder's here even if it's over the phone from Turkey."

"Right, Obsidian business." Again, she sighed. "Liz is splitting on me tomorrow, too."

He ignored the "too" part. "What do you mean?"

"She's leaving in the morning for North Carolina, something about visiting all the places she and Fitzwilliam wanted to go."

"Is Dixon going with her?"

"No. She let him go."

"I'm sorry to hear that."

Should he tell her what he might have stumbled upon? Should he tell Rick? What the ever-loving fuck should he do? He squeezed her shoulders, pulling his girl in closer to him and kissed her head. "Can I make you some of that chamomile Zen tea you like so much?"

On his lap, her fingers wrapped around his and she sighed again. "No thanks. I'll deal with it. It's just, I don't know … everything is changing. I want it to go back to how it was after we came back from Operation Cancan. We were all so happy then."

"I hear ya'. Lately, I've been feeling the same way. Change is in the air, and Darcy's death ushered it in. I'm not sure about a lot of things now."

"Oh?"

"Not us—Obsidian."

"Thank goodness."

"And the sad part about it is that I'm also learning that not everything is as it appears, even *with* evidence. The devil is in the details we often miss, or maybe ignore."

"What do you mean?"

"Take your mother for example. You thought she didn't want you and Liz, but that was only your assumption because the evidence said so."

"My father's implication—and deeds—being the evidence provided to us."

"Exactly my point. Planted evidence. Under the cloud of mourning, it can hide a multitude of obvious hints to the truth. You and your sister were blind-sided and all your deductive reasoning fell to the wayside in shock. It's more common than you realize."

They sat there for a couple of minutes in silence, he toying with the hair at the side of her head and she snuggling beside him. No doubt she was searching her mind for all those moments she'd hidden away that had indicated her mother's love. For him, he was considering all the convenient evidence Darcy had left for them within Hungry Bay—without even a body to dispute or confirm them! That long walk he took the night they arrived in Bermuda ... had it been to plant the evidence? There was only one way to tell: revisit the cam footage from the night of the dive.

Jane broke their silence with an open clarity that came from nowhere and utterly shocked him. "I love you, Charlie."

Swallowing hard, he replied, "I love you, too Janie."

"I know you do, and I'm glad Dave is gone."

"Are you really?"

"Yeah. I really am."

"Then can I ask you something?"

She looked up, searching his face. "Sure."

"Are you gonna bolt for some other guy? Do I have to worry about every wet-worth who comes along?"

"Never. I'm not my mother. You're the only guy, Charlie … and truth be told, my days of splitting when things get complicated are over. Things'll work out for us. I know it."

A beaming smile broke out in his heart and on his face. With it, he put to bed—for the night—all thoughts of John Thornton (aka Fitzwilliam Darcy) currently landing in Bolivia after visiting Panama, Virginia, and having departed from Bermuda four days after his death (as confirmed by the UK Home Office's HM Passport Office and private and commercial flight manifests.) Thanks to said databases, he now knew that after Bolivia, Iceman was booked on a cargo flight to Peru.

Damn you, Darcy. Liz is gonna fry your ass after I get through with you.

He'd address this "non-dead issue" tomorrow on the long flight to Istanbul. Jane needed him tonight—all of him.

17
Dragon's Fire

September 2
North Carolina

L iz hated weepy good-byes. Having endured several of those with Fitzwilliam in the course of their relationship, it had been the reason she'd insisted they part ways on the motorcycles before he left for Operation Gombey. Yesterday's departure from Longbourn had been easy: not a tear in sight. Brought on by the knowledge that her mother had sent the Lady's Slipper orchid to her from England— and because she really liked the prized flower—she did sort of promise to return to see her mother (definitely not her father). The jury was still out on her decision to get to know her mother better—and search her heart for forgiveness—as she was still processing everything in the shock of it all. The extent of her father's unmitigated deception had knocked Jane and her for a loop. There had hardly been time to address it before Jane abruptly stood after eating, feigned a headache, and drove away in the Camaro. An awkward hour later under the guise of Dixon needing to leave, she also left her childhood home and all its memories. All that remained of their Disco party reunion were ghosts from the past and haunting truths of what *really* happened, not what their father had said happened nine years earlier. Grrr.

As painful as it all was, she felt a measure of pride that despite her fragile mental frame of mind, she'd handled it better than expected when she walked into the dining room. Fitzwilliam would have been proud of her. Was she ready to embrace her mother again? Only time and healing could tell. First, she had to survive the next 11 miles of deadly roadway winding through the Great Smokey Mountains—but was survival really the plan? The jury was still out on that, too.

As for sad good-byes, there was no getting around releasing Dixon from what he viewed as his obligation to have her back. It was time to cut the strings and attempt to go forward, and that she did so with tears in her eyes. Quick and to the point, she handed him the keys to the H2 and a check for $100,000 along with a hug at eight o'clock last night. The man argued and fought her tooth and nail to the decision, even tried to object to the money, but she wouldn't hear any of it. They'd been through too much together and he deserved the money and the Hummer, and deserved to get on with his life.

Although barely dawn and defiant of her husband's cautioning voice playing inside her mind, she straddled her new SuperLow, swapped out in the barn only two hours earlier under the cover of night—and Lennox's shotgun at the ready, in the parking lot of the Tail of the Dragon souvenir shop. Located at Deal's Gap Motorcycle Resort near the Tennessee and North Carolina state line, it seemed every adrenaline junkie and motorcycle group were ready for the brave or *brainless* challenge of 318 turns in 11 miles. To her right, a giant dragon sculpture attempted to intimidate, but she wasn't swayed and neither were the true disciples of this insane biking ritual.

She kicked the stand down then cut the engine, already feeling the kinetic energy in the air fuelled by the excitement of the unknown, and perhaps, known. Gazing up into that same lavender-infused morning sky under which she and Fitzwilliam parted, she closed her eyes and took several deep breaths, recalling her husband's riding acumen, which led to thoughts of his endearing smile, and then his laughter. She thought of the way his jaw flexed whenever he thought out challenges. She imagined his strong arms wrapped around her in a comforting embrace—boy did need that! Goose pimples formed on her arms below the leather jacket she wore. It was as if he was still here with her. This time, she didn't disregard that little voice way deep down in her when it repeated his words that emotional day at the shack. *"Look, babe, you're a strong rider, so don't give into the falsehood of fear. In fact, you're stronger than me in so many ways. Hell, what you've come through without even a complaint or a tear proves it."* In the nightmare of that day, she had been strong in the panic room, but she'd survived knowing that Fitzwilliam was safe, having left Pemberley for the District. Indirectly, his spirit had kept her company in her focus for survival.

And now, they'd face this ride together, he her silent navigator and riding companion. Her "mission" would begin the minute rubber met pavement in honor of him, and she desired absolute alone time to dwell in her mind and heart with only Fitzwilliam on her new motorcycle. Her next stop had yet to be determined but she knew for sure that it wouldn't include Dave Wentworth, having vowed to stay far away from that tempting shiny apple. She'd chucked his phone number into a gas station trash can 40 miles back. She was still married—always would be. There would never be another man to take her husband's place either in the bed or in her heart, and for her, one only came with the other. Meaningless hook-ups weren't her thing, and although he'd said it would be platonic, she recognized the look in his eyes—it was the same one Fitzwilliam had on that wild, fateful trip to save her father.

As for future destinations, maybe she'd head south toward Florida and eventually end up in the Keys to celebrate their wedding anniversary. There was no time limit to her wanderlust. With the sketchbook tucked in her saddlebag, she would go with the flow. When she had the guts get a new passport, she would head to Geneva and

Panama to investigate the nagging money issue. Right now, it wasn't going anywhere.

She removed her helmet and sat for a minute listening to the growl in her stomach. When was the last time she'd eaten? Was it that box of chocolate chip cookies she'd inhaled on a pit stop outside of Statesville? Eating would just make her sick with all this nervous energy coursing through her veins.

"Hey, is this your first ride on the Dragon?" some leather-clad, hard-looking guy wearing a skull and crossbones do-rag asked as he walked passed her. He appeared to be about Dixon's age.

"Is it that obvious?"

He chuckled. "Sure is. You're lookin' a little green in the gills."

"Don't let my looks fool ya', old man," she challenged, feeling churlish.

"Okay, okay, little lady, just you wait and see. That first corner at the .2 marker, Krudd Corner, will send you cryin' back to your daddy before you even get started."

"Oh, you think so?"

He stopped and turned to face her, eyeing her up and down and he couldn't help but to break a smile when she placed her hand on her hip. "You doin' this alone?"

"I am."

"You got armor under that gear?"

"Nope."

"Well, then you got bigger balls then me and I'm a one-percenter."

"No, that's not it. I just don't have anything left to lose. If I eat asphalt, so be it."

"Keep that attitude and you'll be just fine, just make sure you hold that wide line on Krudd Corner. It's a decreasing radius, and when you get to Gravity Cavity at 2.9 that damned right-drop and climb-out sneaks up on ya."

And with that he left her standing by her bike before she could thank him for the advice. She thought of Fitzwilliam. Life was probably a whole hell of a lot more daring and uncomplicated when he thought he had nothing left. She'd changed everything.

Pulling out the Blackberry phone (which Dixon insisted that she get) from her saddle bag, she looked up "decreasing radius," refreshing her mind with a tutorial on how to handle such a turn. "At only 30 mph, you can do this, Liz. It's now or never if you're gonna stand on your own two feet. No Fitzwilliam, no Dixon, no one from Obsidian, and certainly no one at Longbourn. It's just you. For the first time in your life, you don't have a safety net. You have to do this on your own."

Thirty minutes later, after yet another pee stop, she was back on the bike with the engine rumbling below her. Her helmet was back in place and she was ready to channel her inner Iceman. He was with her—he'd always be with her. Before riding out of the parking lot, she snapped a few pictures and texted them to Jane, just in case she wouldn't be on her game and if her mind froze to all of Fitzwilliam's tutoring.

Holy shit, I can't believe I'm going to do this! In case anything happens—I love you. You're the best sister in the world and you deserve every happiness in life. Stop selling yourself short on love. Make the commitment you want—live life filled with true, constant love. Don't run away—run to Charlie; he adores you just as Fitzwilliam adored me. And you are worthy of it!!!!! <3 <3

She gazed at the screensaver photograph on her phone for long seconds: their wedding portrait on the footbridge at Pemberley. He looked so incredible, so happy that day. Her heart filled with emotion as she secured the phone into the cradle on her dash. "We got this," she said then flipped her visor down before tugging on her riding gloves. Only one piece of music was suited for this ride and it filled her headset: "Scheherazade." Forty-two minutes of hers and her late-husband's story in *One Thousand and One Nights* reminiscent of that incredible night they shared in Marrakesh before he went off to rescue her father.

A tap to the GPS brought up an image of all those hairpin turns she'd have to get through; it triggered a thunderous pounding in her heart up to her ears and the cold prick of sweat on her neck before leaving the parking lot. Both might have deterred her when bikers passed by with roaring rumbles and the smell of gasoline filling the air, but she'd not let them rush her. Again, she heard Fitzwilliam's voice whispering one of his many SEAL mantras: "Slow is smooth, smooth is fast" and "crawl, walk, run." Today she finally understood what he had been telling her. Mentally she was ready for this, and she knew she had the controlled skills to do it in her time and her way. Recognizing that here and now, there was no need for speed and that born to be wild didn't have to mean "born to be carelessly stupid." She was comforted to know that the Dragon had plenty of paved pull offs on the shoulder to allow for passing. Perhaps death wasn't such a pleasant destiny after all? Not today; first she needed to finish the ride for Fitzwilliam.

Joining the line of motorcycles and cars riding past the metal dragon statue, she put her metaphoric big girl panties on and slowly turned the corner toward the Tennessee state line and the first turn: Krudd Corner. "I'm as ready as I'll ever be. It's time to do this for him and for you, Liz Darcy."

A biker posse wearing skull and crossbones patches on their leather jackets crossed the yellow line narrowly missing oncoming traffic and she noted her "old man" friend wearing a Kaiser helmet. He gave her a thumbs-up from his position at the back of the posse. While she appreciated the encouragement, crossing the center line was bad etiquette on the Dragon—even she knew that! She reconciled that there would be careless yahoos, so she'd be extra vigilant.

She refocused on the ride, loving the spectacular views that her peripheral vision captured, but was cautious not to sight see. The symphonic music playing in her head and the stirring vibration below her seat melded with twisting road; they were one as the blood rushed in her veins. Sunrise gave way to brilliant rays streaming through the flanking leafy trees along Route 129, and she felt a freshness that had been missing for a month. Why? Because he was with her.

Look where you want to go. Don't forget to countersteer. Controlling her fear, she checked for any unlikely passing yahoo and glanced over her left shoulder before the turn ahead. She let up on the throttle slightly, preparing herself and the bike. With a firm, relaxed grip and eyes up, she leaned the Harley into the sharp corner turn, putting her chin to the left mirror. The internal lie that the bike would wipe out when she slid her butt a little off the seat, knee out to transfer her center of gravity surfaced, but her determination beat it down. Fear was a deception—a bold-faced liar—just as Fitzwilliam had told her from the very beginning and it was now—in this moment—that she knew he was right. Together with Rimsky-Korsakov and, of course her husband's coaching she'd slay this Dragon and learn to master fear.

Even at only 30 mph on the straights, she was alive in this shell of a body, the adrenaline flowing after mastering the first, second, and third major switchbacks. Slow and steady was her credo on this ride of a lifetime, belying her belief that packing life in without her husband was the only direction her future would take.

Other riders weren't so lucky, and she ignored the two wrecks she passed. For her, the miles were flying by with each consecutive curve challenge. Krudd Corner? No Problem. Gravity Cavity? Stressful. Parsons Curve? Difficult. Good Lord, Guardrail Cliff nearly made her toss her cookies, but she was holding her own, her skill and focus carrying her forward with each wicked turn, and she was loving it!

The GPS on her phone indicated that the deadly series of pucker-factor twisties that had taken several lives was imminent and she braced herself, looking ahead at the bend in the road leading to Triple Apex Corner.

The nerves came back when an itchy driver in a sports car behind her appeared in her mirrors, headlights flashing. He was too close, too anxious for speed, and she didn't have a turn off available to move over so he could pass. Panic rose; her blood rushed to her temple. The voice in her head cautioned her but she ignored it, gassing the bike, creating distance between her and the car.

She leaned into the next downhill turn, a tight corner, but exited fine even if she was shaken. "Just pass me!" she shouted. He was right on her ass, playing with her. With him so close, letting off the throttle could be deadly, but breaking could be deadlier. There was no guardrail on this stretch, just a 200 foot steep drop off into the forest. Swallowing hard, she fought the rising bile of fear.

"Oh shit," she said aloud, terror gripped her to almost rigid disconnect and she clenched around the handgrips. Up ahead, gravel had kicked up from the side of the road, rocks lay on a section of line right in her pathway toward the corner. Avoiding—at all costs—the brake, she kept her eyes forward and dropped gear, bravely tightening her legs around the gas tank to keep her centered. A labored breath sent her riding straight through the gravel, but the wheel shimmied. She pushed the panic away, just like Fitzwilliam had instructed. Miraculously, a pull-off was up ahead and the bastard passed her when she moved to the right of the road at full speed. The long unoccupied shoulder gave her time to slow.

Hard breathing released the fear as she fought the pull to stop the bike and get off, but ahead, she could see the clearing for the touted overlook at mile marker 8.8.

"You got this, Liz," she bullied, getting back on the road. Thirty miles per hour tempered her anxiety and she loosened her white-knuckled grip on the handlebar. Seconds later, she slowed into the wide-open vista high above Calderwood Lake, and thanked God for surviving the close call. Her heart still thundered against her chest wall, but she tried to calm by absorbing the magnificent view around her.

On one side of the dangerous Route 129, cars parked, on the other, motorcycles—all needing a break from the concentration and dexterity needed to slay the Dragon. Once she cut the engine and removed the helmet, her hands nervously shook and she opened and closed her fingers, trying to restore circulation to them after clenching the hand grips for so long. Her legs felt wobbly from the intense ride—and almost wipeout—so she just sat there straddling her bike, feet planted on solid ground and taking deep breaths. The 1200 foot elevation, mountainous green vista before her was calming and her eyes drank in the breathtaking vision of the dancing shards of sunlight on the tributary, which led to the dam in the distance.

"How am I doin', baby? Did I do okay? That was so close; I almost bought it," she panted under her breath, still a little shook by the Apex but immediately felt embarrassed when another Harley, preceded by its distinct bellowing growl, pulled up in the neighboring space. She continued to gaze out at the dam in the distance and unzipped her leather jacket.

The bike shut down, but her thoughts were drifting … calming as she felt his presence beside her.

"Mr. D'd be proud of how far you've come. Near did me in," the rider said shocking the ever-loving-hell out of her!

"Dixon!"

He laughed and what a welcome laugh. "You didn't think I'd take your money then run, did ya'?" She couldn't dare be annoyed that he'd followed her, not after the guilt he suffered through regarding Pemberley.

She got off the bike, careful to hold on, ready for her legs to give out, but he got off his ride, too and was right there for her, holding out his arm.

"You big salty oaf!" she cried, falling into his firm chest for a bear hug. "I'm so glad to see you. I almost wiped out!"

"I saw, and you did real good. Sorry I lied to ya', Liz, but I made a promise to Mr. D to watch over you, and a Marine keeps his word even after he gets the heave-ho. I've been on your tail from the moment you left Washington."

"I'm sorry, but I had to do this alone."

"I get that, but it doesn't mean I like it. If you really insist then I'll leave you at the end of the ride, but I just had to be sure you finished safely. You understand that, don't ya'?"

"I do and I appreciate it and, somewhere, so does Fitzwilliam." Looking down, she recognized the painted grey flames on the gas tank. "This is his bike, Black Ice. So you even stopped up at the farmhouse?"

"Right after you left. Hope you don't mind. The Reynoldses were real hospitable, well apart from Gus almost blowin' off my head with that ole Winchester, but Mrs. R. tried to temp me into staying for breakfast, but I had to keep hot on your tail."

"You gave up Ellen's blueberry pancakes for me ... you're sweet."

"It sure was tempting, and I gotta be honest, it's real good living up here."

Laughing, she admitted, "I know it is. It's open to you whenever you want, and of course I don't mind you riding his bike. In fact, I was going to ship it to you when I got back, a gift from him for all you did for me."

They walked to the stone overlook and took in the magnificent view.

"How are you feeling?" he asked with a suspicious eye.

"Funny, I feel renewed—awakened from a slumber. I'm sure it's the adrenaline from biking on the edge. I guess, this is how Fitzwilliam had lived before I came into his life, and my ride is sort of a memorial to him, I guess." She looked out at the water. "In two days it'll be the one-month anniversary of his death."

"Any hardcore rider would appreciate such a fine gesture. So, are you gonna tell me what's next for you? Where will you go after this?"

"First, I'll be stopping at that cabin Fitzwilliam took me to before he left. Then ..." She shrugged. "Head toward the Florida Keys, I think. I was reading about this bungee jump in South Carolina and a crazy zip line in Georgia."

He raised an eyebrow.

"I'll be fine, worry wart. And where will *you* go next?"

"North to my son up in New Hampshire."

"You never said you had a child."

He shrugged. "I didn't know I had one until about three years ago."

"The woman who took your dog?"

"No. Like his dad, he's joining the Marines, and I'd like to be there before he goes off to boot camp. After that, I'm not sure where the wind will blow me."

She turned to face him and took his hand in hers. "Like I said, you're always welcome to live and fire up that forge at the farmhouse. You can finally make those throwing knives you promised me. Hey, now that you have the capital, maybe you can set up a business doing that."

"I appreciate the offer, and I'll keep it in mind." He looked down at her, his gaze holding fast to hers. "Seein' that we're at the end of the ride, and parting ways, I'd like to ask you something?"

"Sure."

He paused, dragging his long fingers over his chin as he considered his words. "Well, here it goes ... Mr. D was a SEAL."

"Yes. From what he told me, a damned good one, too, like they all are I suppose."

"I never asked you to explain what your friends said in the cabin that day they came, never asked you if it had to do with that Morales fellow who blew up Pemberley. It was none of my business if he was the drug trafficker your friends spoke about, but I figure what Mr. D was doing in Bermuda had something to do with retaliation for Pemberley."

"It did."

"So ... a damned good Frogman, expertly trained in underwater explosives, got killed in a covert diving accident while setting underwater explosives?"

"Yeah. I love irony, but not that kind."

"Ironic? I'm not sayin' this to upset you or drudge up the past but, something came to mind this morning when I stopped at the farmhouse. After we hid you away up there in Black Mountain, leading this Morales to think you died at Pemberley, Mr. D said to me, 'Dixon, the best defense is masked in the warrior's death thus concealing the greatest offense against his enemy. But when the phoenix rises from the ashes, he's the grim reaper.' I didn't think much of it at the time because he was about five whiskeys in."

A chill crept up her neck and she uncomfortably tapped her fingers against her thigh. "I don't know what you're implying, but Fitzwilliam was right in his plans. He did beat Diablo at his own game. I'm safe now. He meant that I'm the phoenix that rose from the ashes."

"You're right. I'm sure that's what he meant. Forget I said anything. Shall we continue the ride to its glorious finish?"

"Not so fast. I have a question for *you*."

"Okay."

"Does the town Morgansville, West Virginia mean anything to you?"

"Hmm ... sure, yeah."

Taken aback, she verbally jumped on him. "Yes?"

"Yeah. When we were up at the farmhouse, Higgins took a trip back to Leesburg and then onto West Virginia. Why do you ask?"

"Do you know who he met with?"

"Can't say I do, but he did say it was a productive trip and that there was one less snake out there to harm you."

"Geez ... what did he do?"

"That's all behind you now. We fellas did what we had to do, and you're not to think about it as you start a new life. Just promise me, as you would Mr. D, practice with those knives every day, and contact me if you need anything."

"Um, okay, I promise. I know I said it before, but I'm going to miss you, Dixon."

"I'm gonna miss you, too. It's been my honor to watch over you and be there for you through these dark times. Don't let them drown ya', kid. You gotta keep livin'. Mr. D would want you to."

Yeah, he would. She wasn't entirely confident that Dixon wasn't blowing smoke up her butt about leaving her to look after herself, but she wasn't going to worry about it any longer.

18

Dreams

September 2
Peru

D arcy lay on the bed, staring at the ceiling, expecting sleep to overtake him in his exhaustion, but it didn't. He had several hours yet before meeting his Peruvian National Police contact for an explosive night-time chopper ride over Morales's coca fields. The same ones he *should* have blown five months ago after rescuing Rick and Sarah.

Trying to focus on the hypnotizing sound of rain pelting the window of his hostel room in Tarapoto, it competed with the noises made by the sexed-up couple on the opposite side of the thin wall, and promptly tried to replace them with the stratagem for his next destination: a full-on attack to Diablo's transport convoy between Paraguay and Brazil.

The banging of the headboard in the neighboring room grew louder, faster and he hoped their romp would be coming to an end, but it made him groan and—truth be told—long for Liz. His anger at Morales and guilt for having not immediately sought retaliation after Moscow was always—*always*—at his surface. Revenge had become a genome in his DNA, yet … with meditation on his wife, a little of his glacial heart melted, only to re-freeze with focus on his mission, his resolve becoming harder than diamonds.

Putting aside thoughts of Paraguay and Diablo for the moment, he couldn't help where his mind wanted to go, and he tapped the Bluetooth always settled around his ear. He could hear Liz's caution about it "That thing'll give you brain cancer," but it would be a thing of the past in another week. For now, until go time, it was essential in delivering Otis Redding's soulful love songs, an evocative reminder of his and Liz's day spent at the cabin. "For Your Precious Love" dulled the razor edge of his soul, and he imagined rubbing Liz's feet and how he'd wanted more than loving massages on that glorious afternoon.

He reveled in the memory of his hand sliding upward from her toes, up her sensual shin bone, circling her knee before caressing her toned thigh. His fingers stroked her inner thigh, concealed by the oversized T-shirt she wore. The tingling sensation of how she'd felt against his palm remained engraved in his consciousness, and he opened his hand recalling her soft moan below his touch. His other hand rested on his chest, rising and falling with his breath. Man, he could still remember how soft her skin felt and how it was kissed with a fine layer of perspiration that made her ivory skin shimmer in the afternoon sunlight.

Longing to go back to that lazy, romantic afternoon—a respite from his worries—he smiled at the images before his mind's eye and recaptured the tranquilly he felt when observing her sleep on the sofa. She looked very delectable, lying there with disheveled hair and slightly parted lips.

His photographic memory recalled every sensual detail; he felt those same overwhelming emotions that had led to each of the three times they'd made love. Their intense intimacy had left them spent.

His index finger lightly trailed along the edge of her panties, until gently tucking below the silky fabric. He skimmed it along her soft flesh until meeting that small patch of dark hair that drove him mad. Although still fast asleep, a moan came from those perfect lips of hers, but the soft folds of her sex felt deliciously ready. What was she dreaming about? Him?

He watched her face for any changes in expression as he intimately stroked her. She must have been having one hell of a dream, and he licked his upper lip desiring to burrow his mouth against her wet heat, to taste her with his tongue. He needed the deeply erotic intimacy that came with the act.

That playful smile of hers slowly appeared and she opened her eyes, but she said nothing—just enticed him, welcoming him and clearly of like mind when she pushed her panties down.

His finger felt bereft sliding from her honey, but another yearning part of his body was about to be satisfied as he slid from the sofa, taking the silk and lace with him.

Rock hard, he fought the urge to shag her without foreplay, especially when she pulled the T-shirt over her head. Seductively, she laid there naked and gorgeous, eager for whatever his plans as demonstrated by a bend to her knee, opening herself up to him.

Everything about her called out to him: her glorious mound, her taut peaks, her succulent mouth. He was a man on fire—needing to feel every perfect part of her against and within his mouth, on and around his throbbing shaft.

But he tempered himself, wanting to take his wife to blinding heights without immediate intercourse. He grinned naughtily and kissed her toes, one at a time, dragging his tongue up her leg between kisses. Oh, how her inner thigh called to him when she bent her other leg, giving him room. The salty flavor of summer heat that clung to her soft flesh was a huge aphrodisiac and he relished each tickle he made to the skin leading to her slick entrance.

One kiss to her folds teased her; the first tongue swipe between them sent her hands to clutch his shoulders; and the second slow lick along her sex to her pearl caused her to rake and pull his hair. She guided his head into her with a needy moan commanding him to ravage her.

Oh yeah, that is what he planned to do! His lips met sweet heaven, coating him with an abundance of delicious nectar. With each suckle he delivered, she arched her back, spreading her legs wider. Soaring high in his ability to turn her on like this, he glanced up for a satisfied peek at the ecstasy written on her face. She was breathing heavily, and her hazel eyes were dilated with passion, watching him make love to her sex. This expression on her face would carry him through hell.

Then she closed her eyes and dipped her head back against the arm rest; the delicate tunnel of her throat and collar bone rose up and down with her heaving chest from each pant she made whenever his tongue touched her.

He flicked and licked, nuzzled into her, and she went wild. One of her hands slid down her chest, over a swollen nipple and she cried out. Oh, he would taste her there, too. He would taste all of her tonight. Inflamed by her arousal and his own passionate enjoyment, he needed to enter her, wanting to feel her when she climaxed. Gently, he slid his finger in beneath his tongue's ministrations. In the soft passage of her heat, he tickled that place—that magical place, which set her writhing below him. Her cries filled the cabin and her legs, covered with the wet sheen of perspiration, thrashed as he pleasured her to the point of no return. His finger worked in concert with his tongue and she called out his name, making him feel like the greatest lover ever. Above her head, her hands grasped the sofa arm and she arched her back, crying out in those delightful mews of building climax that he adored.

Another deep tickle and delving suckle sent her over the edge with stiffened legs until they trembled, wrapping around his neck to hold him to her. Silently filled with gratification and his own bursting need, he bathed in the rush of honey from her climax, and only when she moaned in absolute satisfaction and dropped her legs beside him, did he stop loving her with his mouth, just kisses—delectable, tender kisses.

His rock-hard arousal had grown from ready to near exploding, and he stood. Red hot and swollen with desire it breached to the top of his briefs. Their eyes locked onto each other's. Liz looked radiant from ecstasy, her cheeks were rosy, her chest flushed.

Taking his offered hand, he led her to the bed and she dropped his briefs. Gloriously sexy, she lay among the red roses scattered along the quilt, guiding him to lie beside her. Could he hope for reciprocal foreplay? God, it had been way too long since her talented mouth pleasured him.

She laid him down, kissing him and moaning at the lingering taste of herself on his lips—her tongue dragged over his mouth before sliding down to his chin, his neck, his chest.

"Oh, babe," he moaned when she nibbled his nipple.

Liz's hand cupped his tight sack, massaging him as her mouth blazed a path to his shaft.

He didn't mean to make so much noise when her lips covered his tip, but he cried out, about to burst in her mouth. His reward was a tug to his balls. Those lips, that tongue worked its magic, sucking and swirling, alternating with her teeth as they slowly teased upward against his throbbing veins.

Crazy mad in the best of ways, he ran his fingers through her hair, loving the feel of her head going up and down on him. But he couldn't take it any more!

He tugged her up and flipped her on her back, fighting the urge to explode—those pink nipples of hers called to him. They would be his undoing. Like a sweet berry, he surrounded one with his lips, causing her to arch her back and cry out. He suckled harder. "Yes! Yes! I can't take it. I need you inside of me."

He felt that way, too!

The plunge into her slick essence—and the feeling of being sheathed inside his woman sent him to the absolute edge. He thrust all nine aching inches deep to its hilt, reaching her core, delving hard and making her cry out with each pounding impale. Her tight tunnel felt fantastic surrounding him; his head felt light—euphoric from the frenzied coupling and how he'd made her feel, how she responded to his love making.

He could feel it, she was about to go over again, only different this time. It was more powerful, the most powerful they'd both felt in a long time. By God, he'd give her everything today—all of him and his essence, his undying love.

"I love you. I love you, Fitzwilliam!"

Her body shook and trembled below and clenched around his shaft like a full-bodied orgasm and he burst in white blinding ecstasy.

He fell onto her and she panted into his ear. "I will love you forever."

The recollection of those five powerful words gave him even more determination to finish this to the end.

***

North Carolina

Liz recalled the nervousness she'd felt exactly four weeks ago when last she rode the SuperLow down these mountain roads toward the cabin beside the reservoir. Although exhausted, after having survived the white-knuckle ride of The Dragon, this dirt passage was nothing. When her tire wobbled a little over the gravel, she naturally thought of how Fitzwilliam had coached her through it on their way to the love shack. But not now—now it was only her. She'd mastered 11 miles of the unthinkable and the pride she felt could not be measured. It felt unbelievable to her, and she knew unequivocally that he wouldn't chastise her for having taken the chance. No, he'd be beaming with pride if he were here because all it took was the spirit of him, his excellent training, and their love that had kept her focused on his memorial Dragon ride. But there was something more that she could not ignore: she was on her own for the very first time in her life and surviving. Perhaps overcoming being trapped in Pemberley's panic room had made her stronger; perhaps she had overcome those fears and memories in light of the scary road ahead—and the one she'd just mastered.

Her wheels slipped into the carved-out dirt and she recalled Fitzwilliam's stories of his SEAL days with such clarity that it made her bite her lip to keep from crying. He was the best of the best—and yet, he was dead. How *could* that be? It defied logic.

She gripped the handlebars when her thoughts traveled down the rabbit hole of Dixon's words at the edge of the overlook and his not-so-tactful implications. Marion—yes, Dixon's first name was Marion; he confirmed it at their final good-bye—was indirectly questioning the veracity of the claim! What the ever-loving hell? Of course he was dead!

She conceded that Marion was right about a highly-trained SEAL; Fitzwilliam would not have messed up or been reckless. They had been trained to be thorough and precise, and her husband, of all people, was fastidious about details and execution of everything.

And who the hell had Nick gone to see in West Virginia? Clearly Fitzwilliam had known about it. Then there was the issue of the money transfer there and to Panama. Ugh. Her head hurt thinking about all of it.

The sun reflected off the cabin's tin roof, creating a lighting-like flash of brilliance through the trees, like a homing beacon for her; she stopped the bike and walked it through the field.

Honestly, she never expected to come back here alone, but for a moment, she toyed with the idea of moving here. She climbed the stairs of the front porch, pulled her shoulders back, and removed the key from her jacket pocket, preparing for the onslaught of emotions she'd no doubt be hit with. Her stomach churned with nervous anxiety, a familiar feeling these days, like a bad tuna melt that wouldn't go away.

Silence and dank stillness met her when the door pushed open. The first thing she fixed on was the coffee can of wilted dead daisies in the center of the kitchen table spot lit by heavenly rays of afternoon sun streaming through the glass. Dried brown rose petals were scattered across the floor leading to the bed, carefully made before they departed. Sigh.

She removed her jacket then the sketchbook from her back pocket, placing it beside the flowers. Half-filled already, the book would memorialize these oxe-eyes later today.

> *"I'll not elaborate, but I hope you know that because of my love for you and my professional experiences, I may do things without explanation. You just need to trust me, no matter what. Right now, our life is not a normal one, but it will be after I set it right. I promise you. I ... just ask that you—as you always do—continue to use lateral thinking in all things."*

She recalled with crystal clarity his index finger sliding down her cheek. What had he meant? It seemed he was always doing something that got her panties unnecessarily in a wad: pulling back from her, not communicating, driving too fast, planning for things and their future without discussion, not sharing his past, e.g. Caroline, Lucy, contract-killing. Even his SEAL days were kept locked in the Iceman freezer unless prodded.

A tear pricked her eye as she lowered herself onto the bed and laid back. Lord, she felt guilty for all the crap she'd given him over the last year, especially knowing how, in most things, he'd held back for her benefit. Hindsight was rearing its ugly head; all of it was so irrelevant now that he was gone forever. Who cares about his former lovers? Who cares if he left his muddy stable boots in the foyer, and not in the mudroom at the back of the house? Who cares that he always balked at her driving the Ferrari?

Right now, our life is not a normal one, but it will be after I set it right. Those words nagged at her. For all the stupid things he didn't do—he did two things very well: loved her with all his heart and soul with powerful devotion, and fiercely protected her from preying family and foe. He was her lover, best friend, and brave champion!

So tired … she was so tired of fighting the pull of sleep and the push of bawling tears, but her mind and heart conjured the details of their lovemaking on this very bed.

She had been so ready for him that day; the mere caress of his hand was electricity against her skin. She'd never been so primed, so hot to have him inside her. Maybe because she believed that it would be the last time for awhile. Little had she known that he'd wake her a few hours later for a moonlit dance and tender, languid lovemaking under the stars.

A smile crossed her lips when she recalled how it started with his gentle caress up her leg then a tickling swipe of his finger under her panties while she slept on the sofa, or rather, pretended to sleep. It was all a test of course, to see what he'd do from his seated position. Otis Redding proved to be the most seductive music for a lazy day after being cooped up and celibate for so long.

> *His finger's tickle made her open her eyes, his tender insertion made her moan, until finally she couldn't take much more and slid her underpants down, delighting when he took them with him off the sofa. Heaven— absolute heaven, she thought when his tongue caressed up and between her legs. She heard a small moan from him when his mouth surrounded her pearl. He was enjoying himself as much as he was giving her pleasure. Oh, how she loved watching him go down on her. Horniness was too limited a term for the arousal he brought out. It was so erotically charged that she fought the urge to pull him up to her, demanding intercourse and immediate satisfaction, but she tempered—allowing and relishing in his ultimate expression of love. His talented tongue always took its time to bring her to climax before his own aching need was gratified.*

And then he gazed up at her with expressive eyes filled with so much more than passion. What was there behind them? An ache? A feeling of completeness with her? Such tender love lasted only a few seconds before his mouth consumed her again.

Tilting her head back, she focused on each lick and suckle and arched her back, bursting from the fire his tongue ignited. The palm of her hand swept over her taut nipple and the ecstasy shot right to her apex. She was so sensitive ... more so than usual.

Liz bolted up from the bed, tears streaming down her face, and ran to her Blackberry calendar. Had she been ovulating? No, that was two weeks before their stay at the cabin, the night before Pemberley blew—and man, they had been ravenous for each other that night, too. The wine they'd shared heightened everything to combustion level: her nipples, her wetness, his throbbing size, their orgasms.

Oh. My. God—could it be?

She counted back and forward days and weeks, recalling the times they had and hadn't had sex. Goodness! She was four weeks late.

Her period was never late.

Where the hell had her mind been? How had she not even thought about Aunt Flo?

Doing an internet search, she voraciously read: Six Weeks Pregnancy Symptoms: Nausea, fatigue, excessive urination, prone to crying, irritableness, breast tenderness.

Check, check, check, check, check, and check.

"Oh my, God! Baby, are we gonna have a baby?!"

"Babe, I will be back. You can count on it," he'd said to her that morning of good-bye.

"You never left me," she whispered with hand on tummy, at the dawning reality that they conceived at Pemberley before the explosions. He *had been* with her on the Dragon.

"The Dragon! Oh, my God! What did I do? I could have killed you," she lamented, looking down to where her hand still rested and then the tears came ... again.

19

Game Plan

Maryland

Now comfortably back in his home, Rick stood in the doorway to his master bedroom, apprehensive but determined after an evening of stalling. "I have something to say," he finally blurted. His heart felt full, swollen with emotions brought to the surface by the niggling reality that his cousin might have executed the unfathomable; the reasons why he'd gone to such extremes were understandable. Plain fact was he'd have done the same to protect Sarah.

With a quizzical brow, Sarah gazed up to him from her laptop and the paperwork spread out on the bed, and for the fourth or so time since dinner he was taken aback by her essence. She was more than a pretty face; she radiated poised elegance and a pure heart. Tongue-tied, he just stood there attempting to find the right words to that "something to say."

She raised an eyebrow. "Yes?"

Finally, he tugged the tie from around his neck and stepped into the room, walking toward her side of the bed.

Closing the laptop, she gave him all her attention. "You've been trying to say something all evening? Is everything okay?"

"Not really," he finally mumbled, sitting down beside her. This was harder than he thought it would be and not because he felt pressured to say it or because it lacked true feeling behind it. On the contrary! "The thing is, Sarah … I've made some decisions and in light of some intelligence I've recently uncovered, I think those decisions are sound, but … well, I hope they don't change our future—you and me."

"Whatever are you talking about?"

He looked down at the gold Corps ring he wore, and thoughtfully shook his head. "After November, I'm leaving Obsidian."

Glancing back up to look at her shocked expression, he added, "and I know that might mess with your plans since you seem to really like the work were doing together, but selfishly, I … want you to stay … with me, despite the work."

She took his hand, and when a smile spread across her lips he said, with relief, what had been on his mind since that telephone call to Leesburg. Swallowing down the knot, he finally admitted, "The simple fact is that I was wrong when I said no man loves a woman as much as my cousin loves Liz. Turns out—there is another man who loves his woman as passionately. Me. I love you like that. I'd die for you, Sarah."

Panic struck his heart when her smile receded and she bit her lip. The seconds of silence that passed between them felt like an eternity and he started to regret his honesty, especially when she furrowed her brow. How had he misread her? Had he now scared her all the way back to London?

"Rick, yes, I enjoy working with you, but that's not why I came to America—nor was it for that exclusive scoop I never got."

She took a deep breath. "Let me first say when you told me about Darcy's love for Liz, I was jealous. I knew you cared for me, but I didn't know how much." She smiled tenderly. "I know I gave you a difficult time in the hut … I admit, I didn't really think you were a nutter. In fact, truth is, I've been in love with you since the Amazon, and although I said I wanted to take it slow, it turns out *I* was wrong. I don't want to remain just partners, I want to marry you."

"You do?"

A slow nod accompanied her blush.

"Is that a proposal?"

"I don't have a ring for you but, yes, I suppose it is," she said with a grin that lit her eyes.

Threading his hand upward through the blonde waves framing her pretty face, he beamed. "Then my answer is an absolute yes."

Oh, her mouth caressing his burst his heart, and his arms slid around her waist, guiding her down onto the paper-strewn bed.

It was an amazing moment between them, one filled with relief and joy, yet as he kissed her he couldn't help but think of his cousin. Without his death, the introspection that brought about this revelation might never have happened. Sarah might have slipped through his fingers from his inability to express himself.

On his hip, his phone vibrated, but he ignored it, continuing to make love to Sarah's lips.

***

Sleeplessness wasn't something Jane ever struggled with, but she was still stressing about how to handle her mother's arrival on the scene. Damn that woman for screwing with her mojo!—and damn her father for messing with hers and Lizzy's life! For Christ sake, she could have lived with her mother and become a Londonista, but he'd denied her that choice. Everything could have ended up differently. She was normally a forgiving person, but this required some mack-daddy good will—more than she had. And … there was the fact that she had no choice now but to face the anger she'd hid all these years. Ugh.

She thought of her sister's texts from North Carolina. The first one before that crazy motorcycle ride was just what she needed to hear, and it proved to be true about Charlie's adoration and deserving love. It felt good running to him, not away from him or anything else for that matter.

Already feeling lonely and missing both Lizzy and Charlie, she sat in the dark in his Dead-head man-cave feeling as though she was trespassing into his inner sanctum since he had left for Turkey. Now, she was the one who felt depressed. Yuppers. It was as though she'd traded places with Charlie last night when he'd shocked the hell out of her with his attentiveness after she came home ready for a pity party. They'd just held each other in the dark, affirming their love and sharing their childhood experiences with each other. His comfort was way more than she expected from him, making Lizzy the wisest woman she knew.

But she wasn't surprised when he got up at three in the morning to continue working on the "unexpected cluster-fuck" project. Poor guy left for Istanbul feeling all discombobulated, half his brain still dissecting the scattered papers and stack of passports he decided to leave behind so that he could hopefully refocus on Operation Zeybek.

The passports still sat where she last saw them: on the edge of his workspace. *Why would he be so careless not to lock them up? It was unlike him to be sloppy with confidential intel or Obsidian business.*

Having become even more of a curious girl since joining Obsidian, she rose from the sofa and headed straight for the desk, turning the lava lamp on. Colorful circles and waves licked the walls and she smiled at the thought of her happy-go-lucky lover working in this room with his feet propped on the corner of his desk and heavy metal music playing. Her fingers deliberately displaced some of the paperwork, and she even knocked some off the desk onto the floor to pick up. With a casual glance, she scanned the top piece of paper. It was a copy of a receipt from Paget Fish and Tackle dated August 3, but she dismissed it. What was the harm in looking at the said cluster-fuck? She was after all, Obsidian, if only a part-time apprentice.

She turned her attention to the passports and examined them one at a time. They were from varying nations and the three belonging to her brother-in-law had a different alias that coincided with four female identities belonging to the same woman in the stack. She assumed it was former Obsidian assassin Lucy Steele who had a very similar look to her sister. Obviously, Darcy had a "type" of woman he was drawn to.

Placing them back on the desk, she slid out Charlie's chair with her other hand and took a seat.

Even his yellow, legal-sized pad was left where she'd last seen it; she turned it over. His kindergarten-like handwriting covered the page with random notes that made no sense to her. It appeared as though his hand was having a hard time keeping up with the rapid fire of his thoughts. The blue ink blots certainly didn't help matters. Short phrases making zero sense collided with doodles that had smeared from the wet ink. However, one underlined short word was very clear and the hair on her arms stood: chum.

Lizzy had once used that word to describe Darcy's gruesome end with the sharks … like he was bait. Bait. In slow motion, she picked up the previously disregarded receipt, reading it through. "Two containers chum: chopped pork and fish (with blood.)" No name of purchaser who paid cash, for delivery the day before the dive in Hungry Bay. It was a telephoned order.

Charlie had hastily crafted a disjointed timeline indicating events down to months, days, hours and minutes tracking the whereabouts and actions of someone named John Thornton. After several years of inactivity, his travels had resumed on August 8th.

Her eyes grew wide. She'd just read that name: Thornton!

Dropping the pad, she shuffled through the passports again until she found one of Steele's—a Margaret Thornton, the British passport that didn't have a matching Darcy one.

She quickly flipped to the next page trying to make out the words he'd scribbled.

"Confirmed travel plans of John Thornton British passport: From Bermuda (Operation Gombey)—to Panama (Morales compound, banking ?)—to Virginia (funeral?)—Back to Panama—to Bolivia (to re-visit Operation Samba)—to Peru (to re-visit Operation Macarena)—to Paraguay (coca cultivation ?)—to to Cadiz (rat line?)—Venice (rat line ?)—to Prague (Morales ?)—Geneva (banking ?)"

What the ever-loving hell? Is "John Thornton" Darcy? Why is the passport active? Who else would have had access to it?

Her mind worked in lighting speed, dissecting the gibberish and putting the puzzle pieces together, trying to discover the common denominator between this man and these locations and ops. Virginia, funeral!!

Her heart beat thunderously feeling like it was about to jump from her chest! Charlie's travelogue mess was the Rosetta Stone to this John Thornton ... could it be?

Could it be? Is the late-Fitzwilliam Darcy not late at all but traveling the world under an assumed identity?

"Ho…ly guacamole," she said, holding the pad next to the light so she could read the teeny tiny words Charlie had carefully (and clearly) printed in the corner. She whispered, "I think he's alive. This is your mission, Pussy Galore. Do what you think is best about your sister. I'll telephone when I land."

"Oh. My. God!" Panicked she bolted from the seat, pacing back and forth in front of the Shakedown Street zoot suit poster on the wall. "Alive? Did I just read *alive*? Oh my God!! How am I going to tell her? … I can't tell her! … I must tell her! … I'm *not* going to tell her! Rick'll tell her! Does he even know? *No one* should tell her. She needs to see him for herself to believe it."

She stopped abruptly, her gaze falling to the passports. "What have you done, Darcy? She's going to beat the hell out of you."

And then it came like a dam bursting forth. For the first time in nine years—she screamed at the top of her lungs then broke down in a guttural cry, falling onto the sofa. Every emotion came to the surface supplanting that easy, carefree spirit she hid behind for so long.

***

September 3 – Midnight Hour
Washington, DC

Charlie's eventual conversation with Rick from Turkey was cryptic at best, but alarming enough for Rick's decision to call an immediate videoconference back in the Freezer even though it was almost midnight.

That all-too brief romantic respite between him and Sarah ended with the third annoying phone call and thirty minutes later they were both out the door, headed back down to the District.

Now, with cups of steaming coffee, they sat side-by-side at the oversized desk in Obsidian's chilly headquarters.

The pocket door leading up to the dance studio slid open and Caroline entered from the dark into the light. As expected, she was flawlessly put together in a chocolate-brown designer suit as though ready to start the day, not finish it at twenty-three hundred hours.

"This better be good," she said. "I left a perfectly useable guy for this meeting."

"Trust me; it's worth your attention. Sarah put up a pot of coffee for us in the closet—you're gonna need it."

She plopped her cavernous Louis Vuitton onto the desk and flashed an annoying smile down at Sarah. "What a surprise … no Earl Grey tonight?"

To his astonishment Sarah flashed the same smile back, adding a two-finger salute.

"Yours is the mug that reads, Scrubber."

God, he loved this girl.

"Hmm." Caroline huffed, turning on her heel and heading for the coffee closet.

The door slid open again and this time it was a cosmetic-free Jane who entered, hair sticking up at her crown, bloodshot eyes, and a light blue sweat suit with the word "Juicy" sequined on her backside.

"Sorry I'm late," she groaned. "The Camaro wouldn't start."

"You're right on time, Jane. Thanks for coming at this ungodly hour," he replied, happy to see how Sarah and Jane hugged. As much as he'd like to announce their plans, tonight was not the night to do so.

Jane sat beside Sarah, and one of the fuzzy monitors went online. Knightley's crooked smile filled the screen until it zoomed out to his bald head.

"Hey ... ho, everyone," he said.

In unison, everyone said hello.

"Sorry to mess up your op, Knightley, but this is slightly more important than your Austrian diamond despot."

"No worries. I'm in a holding pattern for the next 48 hours until the International Diamond Conference gala. Then I'll be flying back home. Is there any word on Liz?"

"She's traveling," Jane said. "She went back to North Carolina for some hell-on-wheels mountain motorcycle ride."

"I mean, how is she mentally?"

"I think she's working it all out. We had a personal situation back home and it knocked us both for a loop, but she seems to have put it on the shelf for now. Darcy is taking up all the space in her brain."

"As expected. I'm sorry more crap was added to your plate."

"Thanks."

"I guess that's why she's been avoiding my calls. I had to go dark on this assignment and couldn't continue to check on her."

Holding a—wordless—cup, the ill-tempered ninja master sat on the opposite side of Rick, facing Charlie's frown when another monitor went live.

"Brother, you look like hell." she observed.

"It's been a rough 24 hours. Thanks everyone for coming. Jane, babe, did you find my notes?"

"Yuppers! And I hope you don't mind but I did a little confirmation on my own. It might be important news, I don't know, but there was a massive forest fire in the Yungas Valley, the location of Diablo's coca crops and two cocaine processing labs. Three soap maker bodies were found within the labs. Authorities are reporting that the annual burn-off of overgrowth got out of control. They're valuing the cartel's loss to at least $25 billion in lifetime street value, and their pretty happy about it."

"That's lovely to hear, but why should we care at this point? With Darcy's death, Operation Samba is long over." Caroline asked.

"Because John Thornton was there in Bolivia at the same time as this destruction," Charlie said, clearly pissed off.

"Impossible," she replied, but Rick wasn't surprised. He'd surmised this some twelve hours ago, only he didn't know the details.

"No, it's not impossible. Liz found Darcy's alias passports in their bank safety deposit box, and I handed them over to Charlie to clean them from international databases. Thornton's was missing from the pile."

"Wait … there's more," Jane eagerly continued like she was ready to burst. "There was something on Twitter about a huge, house explosion on Cerro Azul. Didn't you tell me that's where Morales has his compound in Panama?"

"Wow. You did great, Janie. Guys, I spent the better part of yesterday and on the plane today, tracking Thornton travel. I'm almost positive that these events point to Darcy. He's alive," Charlie said, his voice emotionless, his lips drawing into a thin line.

"Did anything show up on his current alias, the one I gave him before you left for Bermuda?" Rick asked.

"Edward Ferrars? Nothing."

"I'm sorry, Crash, but I can't believe this. I know what we saw," Knightley said. "He wouldn't. He couldn't do this, not to Liz, at least."

"Yes, he would. He did it *for* her. Three days before the Bermuda mission, he made arrangements over the phone with a local bait shop for a C.O.D delivery of chum a half mile up from Hungry Bay. Remember that late-night walk to clear his head? That was no long walk. He went for a dive."

A third screen turned on and the footage from Darcy's head cam during the dive appeared. Suddenly freeze-framing, Charlie said, "There, see them? The white containers, the soft cooler? I zoomed in on the logo; it's the bait shop. Everything else was optics left for us and Morales so that Iceman could go on his one-man killing mission."

"Without putting any of us—especially Liz—in jeopardy."

"Yup … as far as anyone knows, he's a dead man with a whole bunch of saps left behind to grieve his sorry ass. Unbeknownst to us, he'd been drawing the sharks in for 24 hours before his supposed death, making any kind of substantive investigation impossible."

"Man, in BUD/S, he finished first on that five and a half nautical-mile swim along the Pacific's Coronado coastline," John admitted. "Liz was right—the man was a fish."

"*Is* a fish," Charlie corrected.

"But you found his mangled re-breather," Caroline said, her face burning bright with anger.

"Who knew what he had in his dive pack? That portable oxygen unit I used for my recon dive would have gotten him far enough away in the aftermath of the explosion."

"But his wetsuit? You found a shredded leg."

"Again, we didn't find his leg *in* it."

"So, where the hell is he now?" Knightley asked.

"On his way to Peru, I guess to finish off Operation Samba in the same way he just hit Bolivia." The footage on the screen disappeared and a sloppy, handwritten travel itinerary took its place. "Before and after his funeral, he'd been hiding out in Panama, then flew to La Paz.

Fast forward 26 hours and he's on a flight to Tarapoto. Someone must be helping him because there is no way he'd know where and when to hit—or where to locate Morales for that matter. His last stop after Prague is Geneva. This is a timeline I put together directly from Thornton's flight reservations and manifests."

The faces on each Obsidian member were as cold as the freezer.

"Apart from La Paz, he's using small executive and cargo airports," Caroline observed.

"I picked that up immediately. He's avoiding bio-metric check-in scanning."

"Ch … Charlie? Do you think Dad is helping him?"

"Yeah. I do."

"What does he have on your father, Jane? Did he do a favor for him? Does your father owe him?" Rick asked in light of his conversation with Jimmy.

"Well, I don't know that he has anything blackmailable-like, but he did give him two-million dollars to restore Longbourn."

He laughed wryly and shook his head. "Clever man. Darcy's calling in his markers. He needs equipment and supplies in every one of these places and he's turned a lot of people into assets because they owe him." It all made sense and he went over in detail what he'd discovered from Jimmy about the Pemberley assassin and Liz about the money transfers.

"That bastard!" Caroline bellowed, slamming her hand on the desk. Gone was the cool composure of a *Kunoichi*. Perhaps her anger was more that he'd bested her critical thinking, taking advantage of all their distracting grief in order to hide under the radar.

"Actually," Sarah spoke up, "I think it's the most selfless, romantic thing I've ever heard. All of you may feel deceived because of the love you feel for him—and Liz—but he's willing to endure your censure and anger, and maybe lose his wife forever, just to keep you safe until he kills the enemy. He was gutted by the explosions at Pemberley that were focused on Liz. And then your safehouse was blown and

Knightley was almost killed. He knew the drug lord was going to pick you all off one by one to get under his skin and draw him out. Don't you see? There is no greater love, and Darcy has taken vengeance upon his shoulders. He's doing to Morales exactly what Morales had planned for him."

Caroline examined her fingernails. Jane nodded. Knightley wiped the sweat from his forehead, and Charlie smirked. As for him, he admired the placid expression on Sarah's face. Perhaps it was her outsider perspective or her technically-abandoned experience in the Amazon that caused her introspection. No one had come for her, had protected her, or sought payback for her captivity. Her own government turned tail. Further, his own love for her helped him to see how his cousin believed that this was *the only* recourse available to him. A dead man was the ultimate stealth weapon.

However, those in that room—and him—would still need time to process Sarah's wisdom and accept, let alone forgive Darcy's extreme decision. The guilt they had all felt for one reason or another was now being viewed as a betrayal of them.

"Okay, so … we need eyes on him for confirmation," Knightley stated.

"We already have it," Charlie said.

On the fourth monitor, he patched in two hacked security cameras at El Alto International Airport in La Paz. From two different angles, Darcy stood at the airport customs desk getting processed. The split-screen videos were very clear. Dressed in black, from ball cap to boots, to familiar gear bag, he looked like shit with a scraggly beard and long hair. The monitor zoomed in and froze on a close up of his face.

"Holy fuck. Well, there's no doubt it's him. And he's gonna need back up. Inevitably, something will not go as planned," Rick said, pushing his personal emotions down. Turning to Jane, he gave his first directive. "I think you get the hardest part, Jane. You have to talk to your father."

"What if he doesn't come clean with me?"

"He will. Use that charm we brought you into Obsidian to use."

"Well, I'm sorta mad at him right now."

"Get over it."

Knightley moved his face closer to his desk camera. "We're all overlooking something very important here: Liz. She needs to be told immediately."

"Does she? That goes against the whole reason he's doing this," Rick said.

"I'd want to know as soon as possible," Sarah spoke up. "I'd want to help him."

"The way I see it, we're damned either way. Not telling her makes this so much worse, and if we do tell her, she's just going to do things half-assed to get to him and end up screwing up his mission anyway. Maybe get them both killed," Charlie said.

"Um, excuse me? Screw it up? As I remember it, my awesome sister kicked ass in both Paris and Moscow, Charlie. She saved that damn mission and you all know it."

"She's right," Knightley agreed. "Even Caroline can't deny how she saved her ass."

"As much as it kills me to admit, it's true. She has certain skills."

"I don't know … I don't think my sister will believe anything we say. She'll need to see him for herself. Though I don't know how she would. Maybe we can show her the airport video?"

"Again, this hard part is going to fall on you, Jane. You know Liz better than any of us. I'm against showing the video, and against telling her, but I'm willing to defer to your measured, *sound* judgment on this. Right now, Darcy and Liz's safety, not to mention Obsidian's anonymity are tantamount in our next steps in light of this Intelligence." He hoped to God, she understood what he was implying.

"If … let's say, I think she needs to go to Europe, how can I get her a passport? She lost hers in Russia."

"*That* is out of the question," Rick said.

"What happened to deferring to my decision? I respect your personal and professional position, but this is *my* sister we're talking about—my impulsive, sometimes reckless, and love-sick sister. And frankly, her happiness is *my* mission."

He sighed, defeated by Charlie's agreeing head nod and Sarah's smile.

Caroline huffed, "Why doesn't she use *Mrs. Thornton's* passport." but she toned the snark down as soon as he gave her the evil eye. "Fine. I have a contact cobbler I used years ago with the Agency. He'll be able to amend the passport and get her a UK driver's license on the fly."

"Good. Thank you, Caroline," Rick said.

He smiled pensively and laid his palms down on the sleek desk, rising with a renewed purpose he hadn't felt in a month. "This is the only op on Obsidian's docket. Caroline, I want you on the first flight out of here to Paraguay. When Jane gets the intel and coordinates of Darcy's next hit from her father, we'll transmit everything to you. Be his back—anticipate his moves as though you are in his head.

"Mr. Clean, finish the job in Austria tomorrow night then fly directly to Cadiz.

"And, *I'll* go to Venice." He walked to the cork board filled with clippings and images and removed a data sheet pertaining to mobster Vito Cardillo upstairs in the Italian market. He wondered if the former regional head of Venice's Cazzatto Compagnia "society" had somehow become embroiled in Darcy's scheme? "You know, we're family, broken as we are, and coming together like this proves it. Sarah's right. He did this for us, now let's do this *with* him as quickly as possible so he and Liz can attempt to restore some normalcy to their life. If I know my cousin—he has a plan for that, too. Let's make it happen."

"I'm in," Knightley said. "How about you, Charlie?"

"I'll go to Prague. Let's do this."

20

Operation Liz Darcy

September 3
Virginia

Y ou've come back," Frances stated in wonderment when Jane walked through the back door of Longbourn at nine in the morning.

"Hi," she flippantly greeted. "Don't read into it. I'm still deciding whether to forgive either of you."

She couldn't help noting how sick her mom looked, and that tiny bit of concern defied her obstinacy. "Are you okay?"

"I'm fine. I started my chemo yesterday, and … I'm just getting a little sick."

That would explain the dark rings under her eyes, and yellow pallor—and the classical music. "Are you gonna lose your hair?"

"Oh, honey, I don't care about my hair. There are more important things that I must overcome than losing a few strands of dyed-blonde hair."

"Yeah."

"How … how is Liz?"

"Surviving on the edge. Look, is Dad around?"

"He's in the greenhouse. He'd been such a dear all night taking care of me that I sent him out to enjoy this glorious morning. No sense in both of us wasting it cooped up in this old house."

"Liz's greenhouse has that ability to cure everything—maybe you should spend time out there with him."

"He needs alone time with his projects."

And I know why.

Her mom's hand reached out and touched her bicep. "I … um … if you need for anything … to talk, or just someone to act as sounding board, I am here for you."

"Like you were all those years for Liz?"

"I know I deserve that, but I'm going to keep trying, Jane. My days of leaving are gone."

That statement made her uncomfortable. Was her absolute indignance toward her mother because she was looking in the mirror? She knew her own sins as they pertained to leaving those she loved the most when the chips were down or got too complicated—or bored for that matter.

A whiff of her mother's familiar perfume, long forgotten by the daughter who worshipped the ground the once "best mother in the whole wide world" walked on touched somewhere deep down, and she couldn't help it when the corner of her lip twitched upward. Undeniably, she couldn't slight the woman's resolve whether it because she was dying or because she had changed her ways.

"Thanks," she said. "I really have to see Dad now."

She walked to the door and placed her hand on the knob, then suddenly turned. "I have to leave town for a while with Liz, but when I get back … we can go to lunch."

Frances's face lit up. "I'll take you both to The Lucky Penny, just like old times when we girls would slip away on Saturdays!"

The Lucky Penny Café … she remembered. "Okay."

She left the house even more confused than before. Forgiveness. She would have to spend some time thinking exactly what the word meant and if she was truly ready for it.

As she trudged through the grass, nearing the hothouse, she heard that damn ABBA music again, and took a deep cleansing breath.

Putting on her Obsidian face and not the one Rick instructed her to use the night before, but the one she'd learned from Caroline, she spoke to his hunched back. "Dad?"

Before turning to her, he promptly closed one of the three open laptops facing him on the work table.

"Janie!" he greeted with a bright smile, obviously thinking she was there to forgive him, too. Because why else would she be at Longbourn?

"Are you emailing your son-in-law?"

"Well, that would be quite an email wouldn't it? Imagine if we could—it would put an end to séances, for sure!"

"Ha. Ha. You know what I'm talking about."

"I can't say I do." He slid from the bar stool, looking quite put-together and clear-eyed despite being called out for his usual duplicity.

"Darcy … you know, Liz's husband. He's in Peru now, not six feet under in some bogus grave in Leesburg."

"Janie, I assure you—"

"Just like you assured Liz and me that Mom just suddenly, clear outta the blue, abandoned her daughters? We know, Dad. We know that he's alive and going after Morales with your help."

He sighed then raked his hand through his hair before blowing out a long stream of air from his lungs. "He *made* me do it."

"I'm sure he did. Just like that creepy perv guy Crawford made you sell out America. Just like Mom made you lie to us. Look, I'm not here to rehash all your many past sins. This is Obsidian business, that's it, nothing more.

"I need all the info—everything you have on where he'll be and when and ..." she toyed with the hanging stem of an orchid above her shoulder. "And I need you to lie to him when he gets to Venice."

"You don't understand, Jane. This is serious, dangerous business with dangerous people he's involved with. One wrong move could cost his life."

"Whatever. One right move, will save his marriage. Priorities, Dad. He's technically dead anyway."

"His strikes are coordinated for maximum damage."

"Yeah, well, the strike to your daughter was a doozy. Give me all the intel on his field operations and we'll help him. We got this if you do the right thing just like you're doing with Mom. In Obsidian's hands everyone will have a happy ever after. You owe Lizzy this and I think it would destroy her to know that you'd been helping Darcy ... for how long?"

"Since the day before the funeral."

She shook her head in disgust. The man made her sick to her stomach.

Easily swayed by her guilting him, he nodded in agreement.

"So, she doesn't know yet?"

"No and I'm not gonna be the one to tell her he's alive. We're all backing away from that. You know how talented she is with knives."

"Have you talked to her? Where is she?"

She walked around the tight space, admiring the remnants of her sister's touch. "I spoke with her last night. She's still in North Carolina. You know, tomorrow's the crap-ola anniversary of Darcy's death."

"My Lizzy-bear ... I bet she's miserable. I must telephone her this evening."

"Don't bother, she's pissed to high-heaven at you and you'll just pee in her Cheerios, ruining whatever good feels she's finally having."

"Good feels? Has something happened?"

"Maybe. She went on some crazy-ass motorcycle ride in the mountains. I haven't heard her sound this happy since she got married. She giggled! Actually giggled."

Leaning against the worktable beside her father, she speculated more to herself than to him because, technically, she wasn't speaking to him ever again. "Something's up, and I hope it's not Wentworth. Three days ago, she was about to slit her wrists."

"Oh dear, that fella at the funeral? The one who had the eyes for her?"

"Yeah. Look, I have to get her to Venice, Italy and I need your help. Rick wants you to book two staterooms aboard that famous Orient Express train to Prague. You know ... the one from the movie?"

"You mean the Agatha Christie novel?"

"Who? Whatever. Google it. She'll be traveling under a Margaret Thornton British passport."

"And he's John Thornton."

"Yes and they'll be trapped together on the most luxurious, romantic train in the world, but book him a separate room under this name. She handed him a piece of paper with all the details. "We can't make their meeting look contrived. It has to be a coinky-dink—got it?"

He sighed. "I hope you know what you're doing, Janie."

"I hope so, too, but she deserves to know and like I said, I'm a chicken shit. I can't tell her; she'll shoot the messenger or thrust a knife in my chest, and she's all I have."

"I know how that feels. You're braver than I'll ever be and, well ... I know this may not mean much to you, but I am proud of you, Janie. Proud of the woman you've become."

Crappers. Now why did he have to go and pull the heart string? She swallowed hard, never having heard that from him before. "Thanks, but I'm still mad at you."

***

Jane's tears came naturally when she dialed Liz's new telephone number. She sat on the top deck of the houseboat with an afternoon cup of coffee feeling vulnerable as never before. All her true emotions were laid bare these last couple of days and she needed to put them aside and concentrate on her sister, just as she had done when visiting her father. Man, she was so proud of herself; she felt like Caroline delivering one of her ninja throwing stars to the man's jugular.

"Hi, Janie," Liz nearly sang into the phone.

"Hi, sissy. Are you okay? Where are you?"

"I'm getting ready to go up to the farmhouse and have dinner with the Reynoldses. I'm staying the night up there and then in the morning I'm leaving for Big Pine Key in Florida."

"Florida, huh? Um … that sounds like running water in the background."

"It is. I'm sitting in the sun, soaking up the gorgeous afternoon filled with incredible memories and good feels as I watch a waterfall behind a mountain cabin."

A mountain cabin? As in cowboy Dave feels? Is that why you're so happy? Have you gone for a ride?

"Oh, Janie! I have the most awesome news to tell you."

Fuckety, fuck, fuck. This was about Wentworth and she couldn't bear to hear it. This was her doing! Oh, damn. Her tears came full force, more out of guilt for even *suggesting* an uncomplicated hook-up in the first place and for the lie she was about to tell, than for her own pity-party emotions.

"Lizzy. I need you to come home."

"Why? What's the matter?"

"I'm leaving Charlie."

She could hear the air go out of Liz's lungs. Like a "here we go again" moment. Jane is bolting, yet again.

"Oh, I'm so sorry, honey. What happened?"

"We're just not happy anymore."

"Don't you want to work it out? He's worth it, Jane. He's a keeper, not like any of the other guys you've dumped."

"No …" this is the part that killed her but she just had to lie and throw Charlie under the bus. "He's having an affair."

"Are you sure? I know he's been distant but it's because he's still hurting from Fitzwilliam's death, I'm sure. It's his one month anniversary tomorrow, and Charlie's not thinking straight."

"We are all still grieving, but … I have to go … and … and we bought these tickets for a romantic trip to Venice and Prague and I just don't give a damn anymore. I'm going anyway, without him! Come with me. It'll be good for you." She let out a big nose blow, then came a rush of blubbering tears, because, in truth, she'd be devastated if Charlie had been cheating. They'd gone that road of suspecting the other last year, and she was very upset.

"Europe? I can't go, Jane. I have plans and they're important for me to see through to the end."

"But I need you, and I know I'm a shit for asking and for bailing on you when you needed me all those years ago, but I can't do this alone. I need my sister."

Liz grew silent. Ten seconds (and she counted them) seemed like forever until her sister finally spoke. "You were there when I needed you most and that's what matters."

"You're amazing. How could you forgive me so easily?"

"Because I love you and in the end love and family is what's most important in life."

"I love you, too."

"Even if I wanted to, I can't go to Europe; I don't have a passport."

"Just come home and I'll take care of the rest. I'm a full-fledged Obsidian girl now. I can make just about anything happen. I have contacts, you know." She nodded proudly.

"Can I get back to you? I'm not sure. It's not that I don't want to be there for you, but I'm not through with my memorial bike ride. This is really, really important to me for a million reasons."

"I understand, really, but please, please, please consider it. I leave the day after tomorrow outta Dulles."

"Ugh. The last time I was at Dulles was when I left for Paris. If it wasn't for you then my marriage might have gone to shit before it really went to shit."

What's that word Lizzy uses? Ironic? Yeah.

***

Europe? Venice?

Clicking off the call to her sister, Liz's heart tugged as she sat cross legged beside the waterfall and pond then reflectively returned to sketching the ducks. Birdsong filled the air, and the sweet scent of honeysuckle filled her lungs. Her joyful news would have to wait until it was confirmed with a pee test. Not that she needed confirmation—she knew, but she'd wait until her sister's situation was ironed out before announcing her pregnancy.

Sighing, she considered if she could be a party to Jane's bailing out on Charlie and the people she loved most? Did he really deserve this kind of dumping? Not that cheating deserved any absolution, but was he *really* cheating or was it a convenient, maybe imaginative, excuse for her sister to leave? Hadn't she done the same with Uni-brow when he proposed? And thank goodness for that! But still, Jane had been afraid of commitment and Pothead had loved her fiercely. Maybe it all stemmed from their mother.

Closing the near-full sketchbook on two pencils, she looked out at the waterfall. "Should I go, babe?" she asked believing Fitzwilliam sat beside her. "And if I do, will you be there? Oh, that we could have done this together. See Venice … kiss under the Bridge of Sighs."

Her gaze settled on the cascading fall and her mind traveled, once again, for the umpteenth time, to the money. "I could stop in Geneva and go to the bank using my birth certificate as identification, but I really *should* be going to Panama or England instead . All that money you moved … why?"

Following Operation Macarena, they had spent a few days relaxing and recuperating in Santorini. She recalled a special conversation they had had on their last night and now the memory of it was like a cloud dissipating from her mind. It seemed so long ago, yet only a few months had passed. At times, memories of their adventures came back with clarity, but other things, like conversations in the dreamy afterglow of lovemaking, were forgotten. But at the mention of Panama, his words came rushing back:

"Liz, humor me for a minute," Fitzwilliam lazily propositioned. They'd just made passionate love, so sure they were going to conceive the night before they left for home. His fingers caressed down her arm in gentle strokes.

"Okay, shoot …"

"What would you say if I said, run away with me? Let's leave everything behind, change our names, and disappear to some exotic island before our baby is born? Or we could come back here after Georgiana's wedding, find ourselves a small Greek island and live among the locals. I can become a fisherman or something."

"You're being silly. We can't do that. We have responsibilities: the horses, Pemberley, our friends at Obsidian. And my sister would never survive without me," she laughed.

"Sure we can. I'll set up a couple of offshore accounts with enough money to last ten lifetimes and the world will think we disappeared in some deep-sea boating accident or Jet Ski crash." He snuggled into her, pulling her closer to his nude body and kissed her neck, murmuring, "We'll become nudists and make babies all day."

She laughed. "Ew, nudist on an island? Won't sand and flies be an issue?"

"Not on our island. We'll try the nudist lifestyle when we get to Big Pine Key in October."

"Walk around naked all day?" She snorted. "Iceman goes nudist? Yeah, right. And why would we want to fake our death? And what would we tell Rick and your sister?"

"Eventually, we'll let our family visit us—just not my aunt—and definitely with clothes on."

"Very funny."

"I'm serious. Think about it. The threat of criminals like Morales will disappear and you and our children will be safe."

"Safe, but nude … and you'd have nowhere to carry your Baretta."

"I wouldn't need one, and you'd have an island full of orchids and a great tan."

They laughed and the jokes continued about riding horses literally bareback on the white sand beach, and birthing their babies in a hut.

"You know, they'll always try to find us, but not if we're dead. Consider it, Liz," he said, the tone in his voice changed, but she was sure he was still playing with her.

"If I thought for a second that you were serious—and since I'm feeling so euphoric at the moment—I would be a little more disagreeable over the idea, but since you're toying with me, I'll just state that I'd much rather be naked in Pemberley than anywhere else in the world. Pemberley is our heart. It's where I feel the most at peace and happy with you beside me. And I'll birth my babies in a hospital—thankyouverymuch."

But, Pemberley was now gone. Technically, if he was alive, they'd have to start over anyway. Like a lightning rod to her memory, Dixon's face and words shocked her straight:

"So … a damned good Frogman, expertly trained in underwater explosives, got killed in a covert diving accident while setting underwater explosives?"

"Yeah. I love irony, but not that kind."

"Ironic? I'm not sayin' this to upset you or drudge up the past but, something came to mind this morning when I stopped at the farmhouse. After we hid you away up there in Black Mountain, leading this Morales to think you died at Pemberley, Mr. D said to me, 'Dixon, the best defense is masked in the warrior's death thus concealing the greatest offense against his enemy. But when the phoenix rises from the ashes, he's the grim reaper.

Her stomach roiled and she broke into a cold sweat. But this was different than pregnancy nausea, this was something else. This was her gut talking. What if it wasn't a what-if? The 'hero of the bride' has always felt-duty bound to protect you, but would he be that insane to do what you're thinking?

"Oh, stop being delusional, Liz. It's just wishful thinking. There's an empty grave to prove he's dead." *An empty grave.*

"Besides, there is no way he'd leave you open to attack for any amount of time." But you weren't left unprotected, were you? Dixon. Did he know for certain?

Her hand caressed her tummy. "But if the Iceman did fake his death, there's only one of two reasons he would. You said it yourself: to ensure our future, to protect me … or to go live that exciting life he loved so much with someone else."

Ugh. Why was she feeling so insecure about his love? Why would she even consider that he left her in such a crazy way? Was this hormonal or, like Dave had said, the effect of mourning? There was only one way to find out what was fact or fiction.

She fumbled for the phone and with trembling fingers, nervously tapped in her sister's number. The ringing felt like forever and her heart slammed against her chest wall.

"Hey. Can we stop in Geneva when we go?"

"Um … yeah. I guess. Why?"

"Because I need to see a banker about some wire transfers to England, Panama, and West Virginia."

"Why?"

"Because."

"Does this have to do with Fitzwilliam?"

"Yup."

"Okie Dokie."

She'd explain everything on the long flight over, even her insane paranoia, feeling further queasy at the thought of it. *Paranoia is the height of awareness.* She recalled everyone saying that as though it confirmation of either her craziness or … or was it something else? Then the sour tuna melt started to rumble in her stomach followed by a tiny bit of burning acid reflux rising up her esophagus. "I gotta go. Talk to you later."

At breakneck speed, she bolted through the woods and just made it to the nasty outhouse.

This was morning—in the afternoon—sickness.

21

Ninja Lifeline

Paraguay

Camouflaged in the dense landscape between the San Rafael and the Cordillera mountain ranges near Caazapá in Eastern Paraguay, Darcy lay masked by the ghillie suit left for him by yet another asset. Hale had proved an accurate weatherman judging by the storm front from Patagonia pummeling his back and the water-slogged forest bed covered with rotted oranges and mud. The wind whipped around his hide site, but this wasn't his first rodeo of uncomfortable environs. At dusk this time of year, the temperature was dropping to extremes, but that was also expected. Such had been the nature of sniping and the SEALs had trained him well to adapt to all conditions. The only thing unfamiliar to him was the supplied weapon: an armor-piercing Russian Dragonov incendiary tracer, sniper rifle. The gun enthusiast in him couldn't help but delight in the opportunity to employ this fine semi-automatic, but, as he often lamented since starting this mission, employing his *own* rifle would have been best (but a hassle to travel with), having formed a bond of intimate understanding to its workings. Such was the nature of sniping, ballistics, and weaponry. He also knew well enough that to execute this op on so many moving targets—through hundreds of swaying trees— with this type of wind velocity coming from the south west, *while* using an unfamiliar weapon—lost seconds between shots wouldn't be his friend. There were too many obstacles in his way to successfully leaving this hide alive. He'd be skating on the edge of both discovery and retaliatory gunfire before he could re-position, lock in on his targets, and dial in for wind and distance before getting off another round. Here was the ideal situation for the need of a second man: a spotter to help with overwatch. Namely, Charlie—the best of the best.

From the helicopter in Peru's Huallaga River Valley only seven hours earlier, the minute details of accurate firing hadn't mattered. They weren't sexy shots but damn it was a blast. The firepower from just one rocket propelled grenade (RPG) launcher managed to take out a small airfield used for trafficking, two cargo transport planes, and three La Muerta Mundial illicit coca crops. Now *that* weapon delivered uncomplicated justice for Rick's kidnapping and probably cost Morales close to $12 billion. All delivered in perfect accompaniment to AC/DC's "Black Ice." He even got a free ride to Paraguay from the Peruvian National Police asset flying the chopper.

An incoming call from Bennet caused his hand to slowly ascend to his ear and he listened carefully to his father-in-law's instructions following a tap to the Bluetooth.

"I'm patching in coordinates of the caravan to your GPS. The satellite reveals six, two and half-ton army trucks and three commercial vehicles, two leading the caravan the other at the rear. They are eight miles to your west and coming over the ridge onto the mountain pass. Oh, and we have a change of travel plans between Venice and Prague, nothing to worry about but airport security is on heightened alert. I've booked train travel under your 2nd alias: Edward Ferrars. Contact me when you're in the clear."

Damn. The last train he'd been on was with Liz from Monte Carlo to Seville. Yeah, he could get lost in that daydream of what she did to him in the lavatory. Those luscious lips—that tongue—and how she left him with blue balls. He wanted to laugh, maybe even indulge his drifting thoughts but his targets were only 12 klicks out from his position. *Focus man and pray this rifle doesn't jam—one second off and an unanticipated wind band and you're fucked. Then you'll never get home to those lips.* He gave his word to her, dammit, and would not even consider the untenable position of failure in this mission.

What was Liz doing now? Was she with *him*, shacking up with cowboy in a run-down double-wide in Tennessee? He felt the anger burn under his skin at the thought and groaned, missing her as much. His blood boiled in revenge toward Morales and jealousy over Wentworth. His hate had grown exponentially over the last week.

Although his father-in-law had assured him of her well-being, he still couldn't stop worrying about her, but he knew that no matter what, she'd remain in Dixon's sights, no matter where or with whom she was with. There was no doubt in his mind that of all his security team, that man would see through the fog of deception and know he was alive.

"Get ready, Diablo, because I'm coming for you. I'm going to destroy everything you hold dear," he said under his breath.

In the steadily increasing darkness of the storm and dusk, he patiently passed nine minutes by controlling his breathing, willing his heart rate to lower, and relaxing his diaphragm. Again, he checked the wind, which had increased and, no doubt, was fiercer on the open dirt bypass 200 yards away as it whipped through the forest clearing. He watched through his scope's magnification how the torrential rain beat up the road, muddying the thick earth and pooling in its many uneven depressions.

Below him—even at his distance from the target—he could feel the swampy ground rumble from the weight of 15 tons of steel loaded with their precious cargo on their way through the barely-wide-enough mountain pass leading to the Parana River and then Brazil. They weren't counting on him and the firepower of his new Russian pal, Dragonov.

Within the rifle scope's peripheral, he could see a black SUV, which most likely held the protection detail, known as *sombrillas,* crest the hill with ominous clouds at its back, but a zipper-like noise—loud enough to pierce through the beat of the rain—competed with the heavy drone of the deuce and a halfs. Out of nowhere, a dirt bike burst from the forest, barreling down beside the commercial vehicles at full throttle, kicking up sprays of mud and water from the tires in its effort to get ahead of the convoy.

The rider, perhaps one of their falcons, crouched low when he cut in front of the first vehicle. The old military trucks were now all lined in a nice neat row ready for him to pick off one at a time as they came into his crosshair, but the 65 mph gusts directed the freezing rain sideways. For the fourth time, he had to adjust his mil-dot calculations. Lost seconds, yet again, as they continued to drive faster through the downpour.

If the SUV pressed the horn, he couldn't hear it, but the dirt bike pushed on until its unexpected spin-out in a blaze of circling mud around it. The jackass was riding too fast for both the weather and roadway conditions. The wheels slid out from under the rider and toppled the motorcycle right in his crosshair in the middle of the narrow road some 50 yards ahead of the convoy.

This was an interesting and fortuitous situation. Yes, a definite open window when the two SUVs leading the caravan abruptly stopped, hence, trapping the fleet of drug-laden trucks that slammed their brakes behind their security escorts.

The rider lay inert under the bike.

The driver and passenger from the front vehicle exited into the rain to check on—or most likely—move the bike and body now impinging their progress. Cautiously, they approached with rifles ready to mow the biker down just in case.

The driver and passenger from the second SUV followed suit and walking behind their comrades, they readied their AK-47s as back-up.

A crack of lightning lit the sky followed by an immediate boom of thunder that he felt in his veins.

It all happened in a millisecond; through his scope, he watched the biker effortlessly shove the motorcycle from atop her and rise with the grace of a firebird ready for destruction. Leggy and slender, she wore red and black leather. She, because no man would have a figure like that, was fearless against La Muerta Mundial and, with the rain attacking her, she bent clutching her side with one gloved hand; perhaps she's wounded.

In an instant, she withdrew two shuriken stars from her belt and flung them simultaneously with both hands into the first two thugs' chests. They fell dead without having had a chance to fire a shot at her.

Rat-a-tat-tat AK-47 machine gun fire rang out from the two remaining *sombrillas*, but she ducked, twisted, and flipped narrowly missing bullet contact. As she did so, she released two more stars from her hands, flinging them in an impressive take down.

Four dead bodies lay on their back staring up at the pummeling sky. With the convoy now halted behind the immobile SUVs, the lethal woman had given him the perfect set-up. It all happened so fast— within only a fraction of a second—that he barely had time to hold his breath to take his shots before the truckers could respond with directed gunfire.

One after the other, three SUVs and six deuces, each carrying tons of narcotics, exploded in under five and a half seconds.

The woman ran to the bike and throttled full tilt, disappearing down the mountain-pass in the heavy rain. She was gone before he could assess the situation or speculate who she was, but she had skills—Caroline–type of skills.

He rose, muddied and cold, leaving the rifle and ghillie where he found them, then bolted through the trees, warming to the five-mile run south in the rain where his own motorbike awaited to take him to safety. "Next … stop … Cadiz," he panted.

***

It took every ounce of restraint not to give Iceman the middle finger before getting back on the dirt bike. Oh, yes, he would have seen it through his riflescope. If she hadn't promised everyone else to keep her identity secret, she certainly would have made sure that ass knew exactly who she was. Affronted by his deceit—not to mention that she hated ops in the rain—Caroline cursed him with every four-letter word she could think of as she barreled through the torrential weather. Lightning and thunder were nothing compared to the anger boiling below her surface, devastating her equilibrium. If it weren't for the circumstances, she might have otherwise enjoyed this mission. The thrill of staring down and defeating four locked and loaded AK-47s should be making her feel invincible not vulnerable. Further, she couldn't deny that—on this particular mission—she would have given her life, gladly. And *that* pissed her off.

There was no doubt he was alive, and during the massive fire power reigning down upon the truck convoy, she screamed, "He's fucking alive!" She sped like hell through the mud, splattering it upward onto her helmet. "You fooled everyone!"

But how could she not admire the ultimate chess move made to his enemy—a man who tried to kill Iceman's wife? How could she not admire his single-handedness in bringing down such a villain as Juan Sanchez-Morales? She'd always known he was the best, the most tenacious, and someone not to be trifled with. But she'd never known him to pursue vengeance on this grand scale—and that broke her heart.

A surge of emotions supplanted her anger, coming strong like a tidal wave, so much so that she couldn't continue onward. Slowing the bike, she rode it into a break in the trees for shelter.

Here, alone in the middle of nowhere where not a soul was in distance of the fearsome *Kunoichi* warrior, she stopped and removed her helmet. Cutting the engine she sat straddling the bike, giving in to the massive weight of repressed feelings.

Lightning cracked overhead followed by its angry partner in a thunderous boom.

Lifting her face to the canopy, she let the rain pummel her hair and flesh, and finally released the dammed-up fat tears she'd held in for so long. Concealed by and comingling with the rain, they rolled down her cheeks, unfettered, unrestrained. Tears that should have been shed years ago when Iceman broke it off between them, suppressed tears that kept her bitterness toward him alive, tears that would have helped her move on from loving him.

Yes. After many endeavors to purge him from her blood, she still loved him. Loved him as much as he loved his wife.

Sobbing forward onto the handlebars, she asked "Why?" Why she was *this* irate over his duplicity and the answer came resoundingly clear with her scream. "Because he died for her! Not you!"

She knew that the bond he had with the little woman was a rare, unbreakable and unshakeable thing, and she'd never have it—not with him, at least. No matter how hard she had lied to herself about moving on, she never was able to, was never able to admit to herself that she didn't have "it," whatever that "it" was to make him love her as violently as he loved Liz.

Weeping, she conceded to her emotions; she was finally, ready to release him from her heart—for good this time.

22

She Devil,
He Devil

September 5
Venice

The last time Liz had flown without her husband was on the flight to Paris from Dulles to save him from the clutches of Caroline's home-wrecking, manipulative hands. Although her persona had been severely altered, she'd at least traveled as Elizabeth Bennet, sporting a blonde wig and a cheesy, fake southern accent. She'd worn skinny blue jeans and a T-shirt that read "I Have Mad Ninja Skills." No, she hadn't had Caroline-like ninja skills, but she could throw a few knives with dead-on accuracy.

Now standing in the ornate, ancient lobby of the Hotel Danieli on St. Mark's Basin in Venice, waiting for her sister to wrap up check-in, she wore short hair and an equally short skirt supplied by her sister. Also borrowed from Jane, her T-shirt read "Fight Like a Girl." She felt out of place in such opulence and her accent was barely-British, try as she might to mimic Sarah. Further, her name was Margaret Thornton. And, while not angry, she was getting there with each passing minute;

everything was ticking her off. Four weeks and one day had passed and here she was in the romantic city of Venice in a six-hundred year old building that her husband would have absolutely adored.

The interminable nine-hour flight obsessing over everything Fitzwilliam had said and done before his departure to Bermuda and the horrific circumstances of his death, left her even more sullen than before. *If he … if there was even … if my suspicions are correct … death would most definitely come to Fitzwilliam Darcy! But it can't be true …*

Oh, and the bumpy flight, the claustrophobia!—the sickness — made her outright belligerent. Simply put, she felt like a she-devil and Jane astutely was keeping her cautious distance, whether because she didn't want to be at the receiving end or because she was keeping a secret. Her sister's laissez faire reply, "Lizzy, it's been a long day for you. You're just tired," felt like the supreme blow-off. A master at deflection, Jane had employed almost every tactic on the plane: incessantly talking about Charlie's supposed affair, (which she wasn't buying); her parents' reunion, (which she'd not dwelled on in 48 hours); and the latest lecture series at the Spy Museum, (which she could give a crap about) so that she couldn't get a word in edgewise. And dammit, her sister may have even faked sleep—and tears!—just to not discuss this wife's paranoia over the remote possibility that everyone was wrong, even her, regarding Fitzwilliam's death. Or maybe it was all just a delusion of wishful thinking now that she suspected that she was pregnant. But still, it deserved at least a conversation. Well, at least her sister left her stupid jokes at the boarding gate in Dulles.

Surrounded by stunning marble and opulent Venetian gothic architecture, she dispelled her grumpiness with a long sigh, feeling a little more lighthearted when her thoughts clung to the word: Pregnant.

Amid a myriad of foreigners in the lobby, she recalled that time in Monaco when waiting for her luggage with Knightley eyeing her up at her back behind cool shades. Goodness, Iceman was soooo jealous. She couldn't help but to chuckle aloud at the recollection of his stone-cold expression. He was an untouchable, god-like enigma to her with that brooding scowl and bad boy persona, which had turned debonair in a heartbeat and a red Ferrari. My how he had changed after they arrived in Seville and he sat in the hotel bar staring and flirting with her over the phone. It must have been that lavatory tryst that broke him.

She flexed her hand—open, close.

The thing is ... we were made for each other, and no matter what this trip reveals—be it another family or a faked death, or both—he'll always own my heart no matter how broken it is. I'll always be his, always love him, understand him, forgive him, sacrifice for him, and fight for him, again and again and again—after I beat the shit out of him if he's alive, of course. But, if my trip to the bank in Geneva reveals nothing at all beyond the fact that I'm a crazy, paranoid bitch with whacked out hormones, then I'll go on with my life with our child, a manifestation of our intense love. His memory will give me strength.

The week before he left, he'd shared a line from the book he was reading: *"Pure love and suspicion cannot dwell together: at the door where the latter enters, the former makes its exit."* Was this his way of saying when the time comes, her heart would decide?

At the reception counter, Jane glanced over her shoulder, obviously checking to see if her attitude had improved. Her sister's glossy pink lips spread in a gleeful smile and then she held up two fingers, followed by a fist pump, meaning they got two rooms instead of just the one Charlie had reserved for their intended romantic getaway. Yes, her sister needed her on this trip, and she'd do her very best to focus on *her* happiness as she secretly sought her own answers. Jane was her priority. And sleep. And peeing on a stick. She smiled back and waved.

Venice ... the floating city known for romance; any normal person would be excited about it especially after the water taxi and seeing all those gondolas, but her arrival felt empty, just as she knew it would. Her gaze panned the old-world lobby and the concierge desk, settling on the framed tourism advertisements; one in particular drew her toward it: The gala premiere of *Madama Butterfly* at the renowned Gran Teatro La Fenice di Venezia opera house.

"See something you'd like to do?" Jane inquired coming beside her with their shared wheeled suitcase.

She simply sighed. "Fitzwilliam and I loved opera. In fact, this particular one had significant meaning for me last year when he left for Peru to rescue Rick. Like Bermuda ... I was so afraid he wouldn't return, and he didn't. Of course, our marriage and his intentions weren't a sham and a scam like the Naval Officer's in the opera."

"Hmmm," her sisterly sarcastically replied.

Testily she snapped. "What? You don't think going to save his cousin in the Amazon was noble?"

"No! I didn't mean that. I don't know what I meant!"

"I admit my life does feel like I'm living in an opera ... and almost all of them end badly."

"Do any end good?"

"*Turandot.* Fitzwilliam's favorite."

"Well there you go! Do you want to check it out?"

"*Madama Butterfly*? This is your trip, Jane. You don't like this kind of music."

"It's your trip, too. I think, after all you've been through, a special night out might help to get your mojo back. You'd certainly look better, maybe finally get around to tweezing your eyebrows. You have to admit, you sort of let yourself go a little."

"What?"

"I'm joking. Look, it's cool. I'll try the opera for you. I mean, it's not Taylor Swift but maybe I'll like it."

How wonderful it would be for their baby to experience Puccini as it grows, and for her to dress up in something Fitzwilliam would have liked. She toyed with the necklace that hadn't left her collar bone since after the funeral. "I doubt we can get tickets so late."

"Don't be so negative."

"I have nothing to wear," she offered as another excuse.

"Whatever, moneybags. We *can* go shopping, you know—and maybe you can get a better bra because, baby girl, that one you've got on is making all these Italian dudes go ga-ga."

At least I didn't pay for mine. Okay that was too mean. Stop it, Liz!

Her sister leaned in and whispered behind her hand. "You'd think since you lost so much weight your boobs would be smaller. Isn't your back hurting?"

She rolled her eyes. *If you only knew why my boobs are killing me.* "I suppose I could shop, but I don't think on such short notice—"

"Hey … I got you the passport, didn't I? Trust me. I'm an Obsidian girl; there's nothing I can't get done, especially for my sister. I may not be Caroline, but I have my own skills."

"Yes you do, and I love every one of them," she hugged her sister, passive aggressively adding, "And so does Charlie."

"Pfft. I meant I know how to schmooze an Italian concierge. We're in Venice now, so to hell with Charlie. I want to party, party, party!"

"You mean you want to find his replacement, *Pussy Galore.*"

Behind tinted sunglasses, her sister's eyes narrowed. "Ha, ha. That wasn't very nice. I'm wounded that you think me so shallow. I'll have you know, I'm grieving. Sex with a Venetian is not a priority on this trip, even if I've never had one before."

Grieving? Not very convincingly.

She gazed out the window then scanned the lobby. It still seemed so unreal to be here in Italy without Fitzwilliam. The next ten days were going to be very interesting. "I'm sorry, Janie. I'm just bitchy and tired and I have to pee. And … I can't help the feeling that we're being watched."

"Don't you worry about a thing. I'm an Obsidian girl—I'll protect you if trouble comes."

"So you keep saying, but who's going to protect you?"

"You, silly!"

***

Prague

Morales couldn't control the rage when it came to the surface. His world was literally burning around him—and most of his money had disappeared into thin air from his accounts. The cool persona that came with the confidence of being a very dangerous and powerful man had snapped under the weight of his enemy's winning. El Negro should be called El Fantasma. Every falcon, *sicario*, *los capos*, and *soldados*; every *regionales barrone*, *narcotraficantes*, and—AND—the *Junta Directiva* themselves (the group of various worldwide drug kingpins!) had heard of and feared this El Negro *supposedly* based out of Argentina, yet none had met its *jefe*.

The second-story of the Sanchez-Morales family townhouse overlooked the Vltava River, but he was oblivious to the beauty before him. He stared out a window and swore aloud, uncaring if the children heard. His hands balled into tight fists, digging the tips of his fingers into his palm in frustration. Every tense nerve had snapped in his ability to retaliate for his losses: property, men (including the disappearance of Claudia), and now his finances beginning with the hacking of all his legitimate (laundering) enterprises bank accounts. Even his *comercializador* located in London was found murdered, floating in Bristol's River Frome with his neck sliced open.

Feeling utterly helpless to control the bleeding destruction of his late-father's empire, swear words flew from his mouth. La Muerta Mundial's operations in Bermuda, Panama, Peru, Bolivia, London, and Paraguay had been destroyed by a nameless, faceless enemy who wanted absolute control of the business.

"Argghh!!" he yelled, violently running his hands through his hair, almost pulling at the roots.

"*Juan*, your language influences the children!" Maria foolishly disciplined from the doorway.

"To hell!" he barked.

"Can you please—"

He picked up the vase closest to him beside the window and threw it against the wall directly behind her, narrowly missing her head. Crystal shattered into tiny pieces in a cascade of ice. "Do not tell me what to do!" he screamed at the top of his lungs, charging to her.

She backed against the wall, terrified of him, but that was nothing new.

Pinning her there with his grip against her shoulders, he yelled again and she tightly shut her eyes.

"If you dare, question me again …" He raised his hand to her then slapped hard. "There will be more of this!"

***

September 6 – Early Morning
Cádiz

Unlike Darcy's many well-placed assets along his warpath, Knightley only had one: the second richest man in the world, his former employer. Far from honest, closer to dirty, the Arab owned a share in just about everything, except drugs, weapons, and human trafficking. Ruthless and shrewd as he was, he drew hard lines on running operations in those three. Further, he was a generous man by repaying loyalty, which ensured continued loyalty. He also owned three of the six shipping lines into Reina Sofia Quay at the Port of Cádiz Bay, one of which La Muerta Mundial chartered. That was what made him dirty *by proxy.*

As Operation Vienna Waltz's diamond despot grew colder, having died by brass constipation on the toilet with a bullet to the chest, Knightley had grabbed a taxi to the airport and was on the first plane out of Austria.

Five hours later, having ditched his tuxedo following the murderous International Diamond Conference gala, he leaned against an inert crane blending into the blackness of inactivity on the pre-dawn dock. It would be another two hours before the port's labor union (the one supplied by Morales's Cadiz connection) went to work on unloading the uninspected 23 containers.

Behind the Ray-Ban night vision sunglasses Bennet customized for him, he made out Morales's thugs along the ship's perimeter, Uzi's draped over their shoulders, trails of green-tinted cigarette smoke rising into the midnight sky. Security was tight; he should know. He was acting sentry for the port, one sent by his former employer, the owner of the Transmediterranea Shipping line. At this hour, no one else was allowed on the quay. No Uzi for him, just a suppressed Glock 9mm, work clothes, which included a black wool hat, an identification badge, and the shipping manifest—all had been left for him at the Inspection Station. Of course, all of it was on the off-chance he got made, which he had no intention.

Iceman was expected to emerge from the water to join the kill-fest *after*-party at 03:30 and, following his departure, the Spanish National Police (not the local) would respond to Bennet's anonymous tip around 04:00. A follow up call to the police by his former employer would confirm weapon and drug trafficking aboard one of his vessels. Imagine Iceman's surprise that someone beat him to the killing. He'd done enough of it to last a lifetime the past few days.

With a gloved hand, he scratched his chin and toyed with the idea of hanging around for his friend's arrival. The anger he fought against needed release. Sure, he understood Darcy's solo Operation Black Ice, but that didn't mean he liked it, and he had a right hook waiting for him to tell him what he thought. If there was one thing—and only one—that had kept him alive after his son's death, it was the brotherhood.

No. He was not happy. They were an effin' team and Iceman broke protocol. Going it alone to this degree—no matter how noble—was unacceptable.

He breathed in the salty air mixed with heavy fuel oil. From his position, he could see the dim light coming from the Dock Manager's office surveying the entire quay. No worries, it'll be over before he knows what went down.

With that thought, he left his position and walked between several containers and stacked pallets toward the small feeder cargo ship. For security reasons, the gangway was missing, but the wire rope tethers hung inertly down the side of the vessel.

Cake.

Grabbing hold of the rope, he effortlessly climbed up the port side. When his feet touched the deck, he melded into the shadows supplied by the stacked containers. A single light shined in the pilot house, but most likely the captain and crew were asleep. They were not his target, nor would they want to be involved. Perhaps they may even have been alerted by his former employer to stand down and lay low.

Slowly, he withdrew the Glock from its holster and crept between the four-high cargo containers; he felt that anticipatory high he got when about to go all Dirty Harry. He followed the stench of burning tobacco until the mumbling voices of his targets came into range. Grinning, he stepped out from the shadow, surprising them. "Hello, boys," he said, firing before they could get off shots.

Stepping over one of the dead, he continued—one after the other fell as he took sixteen men in total down.

From the corner of his eye, he caught movement at the starboard railing, panther-like black crawling onto the deck. His pulse increased when he glanced at his watch. Is Darcy early?

Quickly he pressed his back against the forecastle, blending into the shadow made by the containers and peered around the corner. Naturally hidden by untrained or unaided vision, wet dive boot prints were made visible by his night vision glasses. Darcy had arrived early; the man had huge feet.

Fuck!

Trapped between the cargo and the forecastle and a good 25 yards from the gangway tether cables, he had no recourse but to go overboard. Holstering his pistol, he ducked low, making his way to the bow. An effortless climb over the bulwark put him awkwardly onto one of the three mooring lines connecting the ship to the dock.

Man, he was going to have some serious rope burn tomorrow.

23

Ciao, Bella

September 6
Venice

Surprisingly, Janie had come through. They were at the opera in all its bravura splendor and, no doubt, somewhere was a satisfied concierge.

With Fitzwilliam in mind, Liz felt as beautiful as her psyche would allow; perhaps acceptance and hope for the future was the last stage of grief.

The black heels and striking black lace cocktail dress delivered to her room this afternoon brought her back to happier times, but she had arranged it that way in honor of him and their upcoming wedding anniversary. The garment box, tied with a red bow, held not only the dress, but chandelier ruby and diamond earrings to complement her snake necklace. He would have purchased them for her eventually, since the ones made exclusively for the set had perished at Pemberley. With each exciting trip they'd taken, he'd always indulged her with a special dress and jewelry; he'd never spared expense when it came to spoiling her. This visit to Venice and a gala premiere at the magnificent Teatro La Fenice opera house shouldn't be any different. A lover of Puccini *and* designer apparel draping her body, her husband (late or not) would heartily approve of her choice of performance and ensemble.

At intermission between the emotional second and third acts of *Madama Butterfly*, she stood in the lavatory, staring at herself in the mirror after refreshing her lipstick. Stall doors opened and closed behind her and the confining air was filled with the fetid aroma of mixing perfumes. Her stomach turned, yet her thoughts did not sway from her daydream as her fingers toyed with the necklace. Elegant, jeweled women came and went beside her to wash their hands—another noxious whiff accompanied the surge and resistance to vomit. Still, her fingers continued to mindlessly rub the snake's head resting on the hollow of her neck. *We're having a baby* she said to herself, thinking that the Cio-Cio-San (Madama Butterfly) felt the same euphoria only to be heartbroken.

Yes, her life *was* a melodrama, only unlike Butterfly and her husband's little son, their child would remain with her. And unlike her own mother, she'd be there for every happy and sad moment in her child's life. In that instant, the melancholy she felt had been supplanted by an inner joy that came from that plastic stick thingy's blue confirmation that she and Fitzwilliam had conceived in the Darcy home. He'd be soooooo over the moon.

Are you alive, somewhere out there, babe? Will you be coming back to me?

The lights turned off then on indicating it was time to take her seat for the last and final act and she snapped out of her meditation, unnecessarily fixing her short locks with a brush of her fingers. For sure, he'd hate her hair, but it suited her now and would most likely prove a smart decision when her life began as a single mom.

Exiting into the crowded foyer, she spotted Jane standing below the grand chandelier between the two staircases while attempting to admire herself in the floor-to-ceiling mirror hanging on one side. Dressed to hip-hop nines wearing a red sequined sheath, her bare legs had no problem going from ballet shoes to spiked sandals. She blended right in with all the cosmopolitan Venetians who found La Fenice's contemporary production of Puccini's most famous opera a welcome diversion. Alas, her trendy sister could not appreciate the bel canto, nor had she made an effort to. At five hundred dollars for a seat in a central box, one would think she could have at least tried to respect the magnificence of the diva's soprano range!

"Here? Tonight?" She overheard Jane say into her mobile phone as she slowly navigated through the assemblage. Finally, she broke through and tapped her sister's shoulder.

"We have to go back to our seats, Jane."

"You go ahead. I've about had it. I'm sorry, but I did try, sissy."

"Who are you talking to?"

"Um, Charlie."

"So you made up?"

"Maybe," and just like that she went back to talking, pushing through the crowd toward one of the open doors of a salon.

I thought she was grieving.

It was just as well that she quit on Act III. Her sister lacked the finesse and manners to stop huffing or to pull the ear buds from her head. The best Jane could do was to empathize by holding her hand at the close of Act II when Butterfly, dressed in her wedding gown watched the darkening harbor for her lover to come back to her. She nearly lost it when as background music (*The Humming Chorus*) set to the vigil's hopeful anticipation Cio-Cio-San felt, filled her heart with a rush of emotions that she had to bite her lip to keep from crying. Surely, Jane's fingers felt all the loneliness, all the uncertainty and misery channeled through her grip.

Amidst the crushing herd-like legion shuffling in the small lobby, she took the stairs leading up to their box located at stage right, careful not to teeter in the increasingly uncomfortable four-inch heels. The last time she'd wore pumps was at the funeral and burned them with the little black dress in the forge back in North Carolina.

Holding tightly to the banister, she felt a million eyes on her, but was sure it was just her insecurity about everything prickling her skin.

***

Punctuality is one characteristic of military life—and hence, has always been one of Darcy's many credos: On time is fifteen minutes early. No if, ands or buts … especially when meeting with the underboss of a prominent Mafia "society," but in this case tardiness couldn't be helped. His first flight from Cadiz into Venice had been cancelled and then there was the matter of getting appropriately cleaned up once he arrived. One does not simply accept the invitation, made by the "boss of bosses" of one of the most dangerous organizations in Italy without showing respect when discussing business. Old school esteem and reverence were expected no matter how vile the enterprise or subject matter was. And by respect it meant presenting himself as a worldly, educated man unworthy to be in their presence but worthy enough to have been asked. To not do so would cast aspersions on the veracity of his proposition and put his new Mafia friend Vito Cardillo, back in the Italian deli, in bad light. Insult was not taken lightly by these pernicious crime bosses. Favors given, even if paid for, were rare and always came with a payback. He knew that first hand in his own acquisition of sleeper assets around the world, just in case the day ever came. And it had.

Physically exhausted as he was, he forced himself to stay awake on the flight to Italy from Spain, going over what went down by—or rather not—his hand in Cadiz. Twice now his ops had been usurped by outsiders. Further, he felt uneasy going into this conversation with his next asset given that Bennet couldn't be reached for any update on chatter from the paired Luis and burner phones. Given the time difference, perhaps, he was at the cancer doctor with Frances. Still, he couldn't be too angry with him. His father-in-law had come through with the details necessary to make this meeting happen. Not that Traitor Tom was completely off the hook; if he had anything to say about it, Tom never would be. He would never forgive his lies to and emotional abuse of Liz. However, in a small measure (very small) he was making it up to her by keeping them both alive.

The opera, he thought shaking his head as he crossed the marble courtyard leading to the columned entrance.

There was no denying that irony sure loved dealing blows to his guilty—as good as it may be—conscience. If he were a man without a conscience, he'd miss the poignant significance of *Madama Butterfly*: Specifically, his deceit at leaving her alone—but only he knew that he'd be returning, and not after three years of longing as in Butterfly's case.

He rushed through the entrance doors, and was met by a cacophony of chatter of the well-dressed attendees and the flashing lights overhead, thankful he'd arrived during intermission so that he could join his hosts in their box (and selfishly enjoy the closing act.) Hastily, he handed over the ticket left for him with the hotel concierge and he joined the shifting crowd with a polite "thank you," spoken in proper Queen's English. Taller than most, his trained gaze spanned the heads, settling on the red-carpeted staircases, now filled with opera-goers headed back to their seats.

His feet stopped dead.

His heart seized.

He narrowed his eyes.

That shapely bottom, those long legs and their well-defined calf muscles, the way the woman's hand grasped the railing. With each step up, every nuance of the rising beauty spellbound him into thoughts of Liz, so similar she was to his wife.

You're imagining things, man. Everyone has a doppelganger. She has short hair and she's a good 10 pounds thinner.

Then he recalled Paris, and how similar that exotic stripper was to his wife ... and she was. Part of him couldn't help but want this woman to be her—here and now—with him. The ache he'd suppressed these many days, deliberately smothered by his gelid focus, bubbled to the surface at the sight of that lace encased swaying backside. And that neck … he'd kissed one just like it a thousand times.

The crowd continued to push around him but he remained inert. *Could it be her? Nah. Why would she be here in Venice? She doesn't have a passport any longer.*

A sea of people separated him from the object of his attention and from afar he gaped at her deliberate steps with his heart racing. His subconscious mind formed words that expelled under his breath with steely persuasion.

"Look back at me," he willed. *Just a glimpse … is it you?*

He waited.

"Look back at me," he repeated; his heart hammered against his chest wall, his breath captured in anticipation, his mind hoped it was her.

Crestfallen, he swallowed hard when she didn't turn, and he watched as she disappeared in the assembly once she reached the staircase zenith.

He *would* find her when the meeting and opera were over—if only just to satisfy his curiosity, and later tell Liz that a woman in Venice could be her physical twin.

***

Darcy placed the vision of the woman deep down into the recesses of his cold heart and stony demeanor as the bodyguard outside the private box owned by Cazzatto Compagnia Mafia's don, patted him down and took his mobile phone. Of course, the box just happened to be situated beside the Royal Box.

He passed through the narrow door and was greeted by a good-looking older man, suave and graying. His smile was pleasant and welcoming, keeping the appearance that the "society" was clean and respectable, which they prided themselves on.

"*Signore* Thornton, I presume. Welcome to *Venezia*."

To further ingratiate himself, he continued the conversation in Italian, holding out his hand for a shake. "Thank you for meeting me *Signore* Perini. Please forgive my tardiness. My business in Cadiz did not go as expected."

"*Si*, I understand and it is this business in which you requested our meeting?"

"Yes. I'm honored by the opportunity."

"The boss has sent me as his emissary at the benevolent request of our respected associate in Washington. While you do not play Scopa, it is a great thing that Vito Cardillo has asked. He was impressed by you." He chuckled, his mustache spreading wide above his smile.

"Thank you again, sir."

"Come, please, sit. As a dead man, you are no doubt in need of socialization. Tell me, are you a lover of opera, *Signore*?"

"Yes, very much so. Since I was a child, and it's something my wife and I share."

"Ah, *Signora* Thornton. She is always on your mind, yes?"

"Always."

"And this is why you come to us. She is the reason for your *business*?"

"She is."

"You seek a vendetta for her honor."

He simply nodded, feeling as though he was acting out a scene from *The Godfather*.

"This I understand. A man must protect his family."

"And how do you know this? I did not mention this to Mr. Cardillo."

"*Signore*, our society knows everything. We know that you wish to destroy La Muerta Mundial for the destruction of your family home, the attempted assassination of your wife, and the kidnapping of your cousin."

"Yes. But, I wish to *specifically* destroy Morales and all that he has his finger on."

"And that includes the cargo containers that transport his drugs into and his weapons out of Venice."

"That is correct, *Signore*. With your help of course, as I understand that Cazzatto Compagnia controls loading and unloading at the Port of Venice."

The lights flicked for a third time and the crowd below them grew silent. Perini leaned closer to him and whispered, "The don has but one question before we enjoy *Madama Butterfly*. Do you know this El Negro? Be truthful with me because Cazzatto needs to fully understand the situation. *Faida* or *conflitto* with our friend Sanchez-Morales is not something we would like to involve ourselves in unless, of course, it is beneficial to us. You understand that when I say that La Muerta Mundial is our friend, it is a euphemism for an enemy whom we politely allow to exist because we profit from our business arrangement on the quays."

"I understand, and yes, I do know El Negro."

"*Sì?*"

He opened and closed his fist resting on his knee; his jaw flexed. "They are Morales's sworn enemy."

"And that is all?"

Now he chuckled. "All? No. Similar to your society's relationship with Morales, and now me … the enemy of my enemy is my friend … Isn't that how the saying goes, *Signore* Perini? I have no quarrel with El Negro. In fact, they have advanced my cause greatly by providing me with the perfect scapegoat to my wrath."

"And quite a wrath I have heard. You have been very effective. Diablo is quite infuriated."

"There is much at stake. My wife's safety and happiness depend on my success."

Damn. He hoped he wasn't making of mess of this. He was a trigger man, for God's sake! Rick was the negotiator and the diplomat. His cousin made both seem effortless with that shit-eating grin of his. Alas, he chose to do this on his own. Any mucking up was on him alone, and that's the way he wanted it.

"We do not know this El Negro, but we have ears. Okay ... we discuss shipping business *after* the opera." He handed him a pair of leather and brass opera binoculars and the Italian smiled before sipping his champagne.

The lights dimmed to black and the only glow came from the orchestra pit as the curtain opened on a lone Butterfly waiting for her lover's return in the dark night—her hopefulness slowly draining as dawn drew near without his arrival.

The orchestra's intermezzo filled his heart. Yes. He was choked up. *I will come home, Liz.*

Birdsong on stage signified a new day, springtime as the light grew like sun on the stage. He lifted the glasses to his eyes, scanning the front two seats of each curved central box flanking him in five tiers above, beside, and below him.

Breathlessly waiting for Butterfly's first words, attentive, nameless opera devotees passed before his "scope," as the binoculars slowly panned one side of the theatre, then the other. Ever aware of his surroundings, he observed the expectant expressions on each face until ...

One face changed his world, taking his breath away. Literally, he stopped breathing.

What the hell?

There in the magnification of the lenses, so close he could almost touch her, he spied the profile of the most beautiful woman he'd ever laid eyes on. Her delicate left hand grasped the gallery edge before her, displaying her gold wedding band's shine in the darkness. Her short locks gave highlight to the sparkling ruby earrings dangling against her elegant neck. Ah, that neck … surrounded by the gemstone snake. She looked stunning.

It *was* her: His Lakmé.

With a small measure of panic, he instinctively leaned back into his seat away from the edge of the box. If he could see her—she could see him. *Damn!*

Torn between panic and delight, reason and logic commanded "Do not go to her!" But his heart prodded otherwise. Her captivating presence—and the pull it had on him—was dangerous for her, him, and this entire mission.

One hand drew to her luscious lips where her fingers rested as she waited for Butterfly's pronouncement.

Cio-Cio-San finally sung: "He'll come. He'll come, you'll see."

Yes, he will come to her but first he had business to complete and a face-to-face meeting with Diablo in Prague.

***

A pair of mother of pearl opera glasses switched back and forth from the stunning Elizabeth Darcy … er, Margaret Thornton … to her jackass husband.

At least you cleaned yourself up. Idiot. What are you going to do when she sees you?

Concealed by the shadow in the third seat of a lateral theatre box Rick Fitzwilliam sighed. *I love you but you messed up, cousin. Going all Rambo was foolish and dangerous, and your wife is going to beat the ever-loving crap out of you.*

***

In a fourth box sat another man, and he was damned pleased that he had been able to scalp a ticket on the water taxi on the way to the theatre. For the sixth time during the performance (not that he watched it much or always stayed in his seat) he tugged at the tie knotted at his neck. He hadn't worn a suit since, well … his military years. And, as for opera, he'd grown accustomed to it over the last six months of employment.

Italy. He never had any desire to visit Europe and sure as hell would have ever guessed that his security detail would take him here, let alone that his charge would go off half-cocked with her ditsy sister. Well, he needed to lose a few pounds and keeping up with her and out of sight was certainly doing that. Of course, given how much he cared about her, he didn't feel bad lying. It was done with the best of conscience. Although she had been insistent that she didn't need him as a bodyguard, he wasn't about to argue with her and definitely not leave her unprotected. Not after he confronted that girl outside the dance school. What was a few white lies between friends when he said he was headed back up to New Hampshire when, in fact, he stayed on her tail to and from that hunter's cabin in the mountains.

He'd let Mrs. D down in July when Pemberley blew, and Mr. D had entrusted her care to him. Nope. He'd not let either of them down again.

His small military monocular fixed on her. She sure did look pretty tonight. Good for her! She fit right in with all this hoity-toity international set and was maybe gonna start living again.

Through his optic lens, he zoomed in on the boxes flanking the outlandish gold gilt Royal box and … and …

Holy Fuck! Is that … is that Mr. D … watching Mrs. D? Holy … mother. You gotta be shittin' me. I was right; he is alive!

***

Watching his wife cry was heart-wrenching, and Darcy silently cursed himself for causing the grief that seized her heart. Liz's tears weren't shed for Cio-Cio-San; they were spent for him and the promised future that died with him four and half weeks ago. He'd make every minute lost up to her in their new home waiting for them. Her idyllic life will be restored and, above all, she will be safe. Oh, his brave, strong wife.

He sat back in the shadow, ignored the opera, and fixed his gaze on her every move, every tear—and the empty seat beside her. Evident of ownership over the ticket, her program lay upon the red velvet. Who had she come to Venice with? He tightened the fist on his knee. That Wentworth snake? Probably not; the guy didn't have a cultured bone in his body. And certainly her sister wouldn't attend with her. Perhaps her mother? If only he hadn't broken comms with the necklace.

Did you sleep with him? he silently asked her. His heart sank at the thought of it, then began beating a mile a minute as he vacillated between emotions.

Why did she cut her hair? She never wore that lipstick color before. She's so skinny. Is she not eating? Why are you here, babe? Of all operas to see, what were you thinking?

"*Signore*," Perini whispered and he lowered the opera glasses, hating to tear his gaze from his wife.

"You stay and share a glass of Barbaresco with me after the curtain closes. We celebrate."

"And what shall we celebrate?" Admittedly he sounded too annoyed for a man such as the underboss, but dammit, the Italian was drawing his attention from Liz.

"That our business is complete."

"Is it? We haven't discussed anything."

"It is taken care of. All that remains is the payment of the two million in crypto and we are settled."

Suddenly, from the corner of his eye, he saw Liz abruptly rise from her seat and leave her box … in tears. He gripped the arm rest, fighting the urge to cut and run after her. Just one more city—Just. One. More. City.

"I beg your pardon, but what exactly have you taken care of?"

"A friend of our friend has come to see me this morning. At his proposal, we have already taken control of La Muerta Mundial's business in Italy. The local banks have transferred Morales's holdings to us and we now control *all* shipments in and out of the port of Venice. It is done," he explained waving it off. "You see, Cazzatto Compagnia's relationship with Diablo is only one we inherited from the Lord of the Jungle, his father whom we had fostered a respected partnership with. And *he* is dead."

By my rifle shot. Darcy shook his head. "I don't understand … did this *friend* have a name? Not El Negro?" Of *that* he was sure!

"Not one I will share, but someone who made a very compelling case for you, *Signore* Thornton. I believe he called you a love-sick, foolish jackass for seeking revenge on your own."

Stunned, he sat back, feeling the blood drain from his face. Only Rick would say something like that. Dumbfounded, his hand dragged across his mouth in anxious thought. His cousin knew. Had Bennet talked? Oh, shit! Is that why Liz is here!?

Perini chuckled as the red curtain closed on a dead Butterfly to thunderous applause.

"So you've been toying with me all along?"

"*Si.* You are a very lucky man, and he is a faithful friend. Do yourself a favor, *mio Amico,* do not be angry with him. Go, sleep easy tonight; dark rings shroud your face and your eyes show that you need help. There is no need for you to physically destroy Morales's product in Venice; it is now ours! The last blow to your enemy requires a good night sleep. This is our gift to you … to Vito for the Padrone's life service to the society."

He glanced back over at the empty box Liz had vacated. Did she know? "Thank you, *Signore* Perini. I think I need that drink now," he said morosely.

"I thought you would." He snapped his fingers and his bodyguard poured two glasses. "Stay for a while and we will talk of Vito, and then you will meet my niece to congratulate her on her performance as Butterfly."

No urge had ever been stronger to run after Liz, but respect and appreciation to the society had to take precedence—otherwise all bets (favors) were off. Yes, he did need a good night sleep. He'd been running back to Liz, balls to the wall for seven unholy days.

24

20/20 Eyesight

September 7
Venice

Traveling in a gondola through narrow waterways, under romantic bridges, and arriving at the station via the Grand Canal felt like an electrified crescendo to their departure from Venice. The activity of the Santa Lucia Train Station bustled all around Liz as she and Jane walked side-by-side down the platform reading the carriage numbers on each car. It all seemed so mysterious, like the history of the train itself. Perhaps it was the fact that her sister had kept this next leg of the trip a tightly kept secret, springing it on her last night following the opera.

Admittedly, her emotions were all over the place, but still, something stirred deep within her soul about this rail journey—or it just could have been post-breakfast morning sickness. Jane had insisted that she eat, unsure of when they'd get to eat again and insisting that she was too thin for her height. When questioned about the oddness of the statement of not having lunch provided—because, let's face it, this was the Venice-Simplon Orient Express—not a thing would be spared or detail omitted, her sister blew her off her questions. Anyway … she still hadn't told Jane the reason for the vomiting, the tears, the huge boobs, and the loss of appetite or repulsion for coffee and chocolate. Two addictions Liz Bennet Darcy would never ever forsake, even upon pain of death. How does one explain not indulging in either when in Italy?

Good Lord, declining wine—in Italy no less—was tough to explain especially when all her sister wanted to do was "party, party, party."

While the passengers boarded the legendary train, she felt the need to pinch herself. Boy, Charlie had outdone himself in planning to romance Jane. She gave her sister a long, sideways glance; she seriously doubted her sister's story of his infidelity. Nope. Not buying it.

"It's hard to imagine … us … going on the train Agatha Christie immortalized," she remarked. "We're a long way from Longbourn."

"Was she the director of the movie?"

"More like the first screenwriter." Sigh. Maybe one day her sister would pick up a book.

They made their way through would-be passengers toward the restored century-old famed train awaiting their boarding. Jane was nearly hyperventilating from the sexy-sounding international announcements overhead and the beefy Italian railway workers.

"Damn, girl, even the blue train is a turn-on. Well, *Ciao bellos*! Would you get a hold of those hunky Venetian stewards and that hottie chef in the groovy hat," Jane cooed as they neared. "I never did it on a train! Have you?"

No, but I did blow Fitzwilliam's—ahem—mind. "Would you have said that aloud if Charlie was beside you instead of me?" she joked.

Jane stopped in her tracks, her jubilant expression growing serious. "Of course I would have! He knows that's just me being me. I may love men, but I'm devoted to Charlie, Lizzy."

"Gee, that was quick. Not that you hold grudges, but on the plane over you said you'd like to make his testicles into a Manriki ball bola."

Jane giggled and shrugged both shoulders.

"I think you're hanging around Caroline too much."

"I didn't mean that, not really. Look, you said it yourself. Love and family are the most important things in life. I know that now," Jane admitted.

"Then do you forgive Mom and Dad, too? Or do you still want to try out your new Ninja throwing spikes on them as you also stated on the plane?"

"Ha. Ha." She chuckled wryly. "One thing at a time, and I don't see you forgiving her."

"I'm working on it. Right now I'm juggling more emotions than any one person can handle at once. And I'm still trying to forgive my husband for dying." *Or not.* She gazed at the train, thinking the last one she had traveled on had cemented their romance. "Jane … There's something you should know before we leave Venice. I haven't been entirely truthful with you."

"Okay."

"I keep getting sick because I'm … um, pregnant. I took a test when we arrived at the hotel."

"Holy shit! Preggers?" Jane yelled out, turning heads. She grabbed her, bouncing them both up and down. "That is so awesome! You a mom, me an aunt, a little handsome Iceman or Lizzy mini-me!"

"Stop. Stop. Oh, my God, stop. You're gonna make me throw up."

"Sorry. This is so great; I'm so excited! A baby, Lizzy. A real, friggin' baby!"

"Yeah. I know. I can't believe it myself. We tried and tried and it finally happened."

Jane's smile softened to something so tender, so … unusual for her. She'd only seen it once before when they were in the hotel in

Marrakesh when they shared their hearts to each other about the men they'd fallen in love with.

"I guess now would be a good time for me to come clean, too."

"Oh?" *I knew it!*

"First, we're not going to Geneva. The train ends in Prague."

"But we have to go to Geneva. I have an appointment at the bank, and I specifically asked you—"

"And second, not we—you. I'm not going with you on the train."

"What?"

"You're going alone. Charlie and I didn't really split up."

"I knew it!"

"And, he didn't cheat on me … and we didn't plan this trip for us. We arranged it for you so you could get outta dodge—far away from the Mom bullcrap and Wentworth's lasso—"

"But nothing happened between him and me."

"It doesn't matter. We just figured this trip would do you good while you figure out your next move. Charlie said that Prague is magical; anything can happen there." She snorted, pointing to the platform sign above their head that read: "Venezia. S. Lucia." "You know, Catholics say that Saint Lucy is the Patron Saint of eyesight. I suppose it's a coinky-dink or one of those irony things you talk about, but maybe you'll see something that'll take your breath away on this train trip."

"Jane! I can't go by myself and I have to get to Geneva."

"Go to the bank after Prague. It's not like you can't afford it or have anything or any place to get back to." Jane hugged her again. "And you don't need me to hold your hand. You're an independent woman, Lizzy. Damn, you're going to be a mother."

A push to her back propelled her forward. Grrr. "As pissed as I am with you, I can easily forgive you given that you got tickets to the opera last night." She paused, then added, "You're a hot mess, Jane Bennet, but I love you."

"And I love you, sissy. Above all things in this crazy-ass world, I want you to be happy. You can do this. Just promise me one eensy-weensy, teeny-tiny thing."

"I'll try."

"Whatever decisions you make on this journey, I want you to promise me that you'll listen to your heart over head and just go with the flow. Oh … and and don't be mad at me."

She took a step away and glanced back over her shoulder at her sister's wave. "That all depends on what happens. The only magic I'd hope to happen is far from reality. It would take a miracle."

"Don't be so sure. I bet Saint Lucy is known for those, too, and if Charlie says that the road to Prague is magical, well then it is."

"At this point I'll just wish that train travel doesn't have me hugging the toilet during the whole trip. Where will you go?"

"Home or maybe kick around here for a few days. I hear Venice has some awesome gay nightclubs."

She raised an eyebrow.

"Hey, hot gay Venetians who love to dance? It's the safest place for me."

Laughing, she turned and headed toward the end of the length of the train where her designated carriage awaited. Her heart thundered, and she suddenly was gripped by apprehension. The electricity she'd felt before was replaced by fear. Was she turning chicken? What happened to "born to be wild?"—her proud motto acquired last year? Goodness!—she had survived the Pemberley fire weeks ago, and conquered The Tail of the Dragon only three days ago. Surely she could take a luxury adventure without companionship. Four and a half weeks had passed since Fitzwilliam's death; she had been challenged and pushed beyond limits she never knew she had. Yet she had proven to herself that she not only could, but also wanted to live beyond the limits, fly solo using her own wings—especially now that she had something to live for. The memory of his love and the hoped-for child they'd conceived was the wind on which she soared. From day one of falling under Iceman's spell, he had encouraged her, instilling in her a confidence and worth she lacked. Each day they'd spent together had been preparation for this time without him. Had he known what he was doing? Had he always known there would come a time when he would leave her?

With each step taken toward the marine-blue uniformed steward standing two cars up from the locomotive, she considered Fitzwilliam's words on that dangerous night they had dined at Turandot Palace in Moscow.

You're Liz Darcy, but you are no more defined by that name than you are by referring to yourself as Lizzy of Longbourn.

Her hand rested upon her tummy. *But now, I will happily be defined as mother, and for that role I will need to call upon all those attributes he said he loved about me. This trip is just another step to survival in the future, another rite of passage to self-reliance, Liz.*

"Welcome, *signora*," the man greeted.

Softly smiling, she handed him her paperwork and straightened her shoulders. "Mrs. Margaret Thornton."

Checking the forged documents to the notepad he held, his face lit up. "Ah! You are staying in one of the finest cabins aboard: The Venice Grand Suite. Very good! I am your cabin steward."

Whoa, Jane!

"You are traveling alone?"

"Yes."

He frowned slightly and made a notation on his notepad. Motioning for her to follow him he said with a refreshed smile. "Very well, follow me and I will take care of everything, *Signora* Thornton. One is never truly alone on the Orient Express. You will make many new friends on your way to the Czech Republic."

"You are my first then. What's your name?"

"Salvatore."

"Thank you, Salvatore. I'm a bit nervous."

"It is expected, but there is nothing to fear. Train travel is very safe even when traveling through Brenner Pass."

From the corner of her eye, she thought she saw someone gawking at her, and abruptly glanced over her shoulder before following Salvatore onto the train. Maybe it was Jane lingering to make sure she got on or it just could have been another passenger waiting for the arrival of their train on the neighboring track. She could literally feel eyes burning at her back, just like the night before at the opera and it made her uneasy.

Old world design reminiscent of train travel in its heyday and Art Nouveau elements amazed her when she stepped aboard. Following the porter and the overhead trail of small light bulbs down the carriage corridor, she admired the polished wood and all the small details that welcomed her to unparalleled traveling.

Fitzwilliam would love this! How could she remain annoyed at Jane's deception? Her sister had done so with the best of intentions knowing full-well how she would balk at the thought of traveling in Europe alone. This was top of the line, a once-in-a-lifetime opportunity to be treated like royalty and it must have set them back a mint. They did this for her—to help her heal from the hell of the last six weeks and look ahead to the future.

Salvatore stopped at a closed stateroom door and turned to face her with a grin. "Are you ready?"

"Yes." Her fingers tapped her thigh.

He opened the shiny wood door, revealing a 1920s opulence she'd only read about; her eyes widened and a huge smile crossed her face. Two compartments combined made up the grand suite in colors of gold and rich marine. Under a frosted, domed ceiling accented by brass, a double-bed filled one section of the stateroom; the other was an intimate lounge and dining area. Mirrors and art-deco fixtures married jeweled brocade fabrics and inlaid geometric-designed wood panels, all transporting her back in time.

Salvatore entered the cabin and immediately filled one of the two champagne flutes set out beside fresh-cut flowers. Handing it to her with a smile, he said. "To your exciting journey."

She did not drink, but pretended to when she held the crystal to her lips so as not to be rude. The celebratory bubbling draught, by its very presence, was bittersweet. She was standing in the most romantic boudoir (outside of Pemberley's master suite) without the man she loved. Her heart crashed into her stomach.

"You have luncheon reservations in the Cote d'Azur restaurant at 2:00 and dinner will be in the L'Oriental dining car at 9:00. If you would like, tea will be in your cabin or you can take in the sights of Northern Italy from the Lalique Car."

"When does the train depart Venice?"

He glanced at his wristwatch. "You have time to settle in and rest before departure at 4:30 this afternoon. Now, I would be obliged to give you a tour of the Grand Suite, *signora*."

***

Dixon's heart sank into his gut as he watched the luxury train pull away. He'd been following her and her batty sister all morning and even now, although she'd been settled on the train (which he could not get a ticket on) for the last five hours, he'd been lurking on the platform and examining every passenger getting on for anyone who looked suspicious or out of place. Why was Mrs. D going this leg of the trip by herself? She was heading to Prague without him at her back for the first time since that terrible day on July 22nd, but there was only one consolation: he'd watched the not-so-late Mr. D make a last-minute mad dash to board just before final departure.

Now he could rest easy. She was in good hands—the best actually—and more than likely the passengers aboard the Orient Express would be witness to either murder or never see the two until its arrival in the Mother of Cities.

Chuckling to himself, he considered it would be the latter after she gave him a tongue lashing he'd never forget. Those two could never keep their hands off each other for very long.

***

Dead to the world on the best mattress ever, Liz had barely felt the train depart the station. She had been that exhausted following tea in her cabin and fully clothed curled into a ball. Seconds later she was out like a light.

At her request, Salvatore's gentle knock on her door had reminded her to get ready for dinner in case she overslept, and boy had she. Darnnit. She would have liked to remain awake to see Northern Italy and the Dolomites at sunset! Unfortunately, she was still fatigued and perhaps not quite recovered from the jet lag followed by the late night at the opera.

Making her way down the never-ending corridors from carriage to carriage toward the bar car, she occasionally stopped at the windows to her right to admire the passing city lights blurred in the dark as the northbound train bulleted through Italy—or had they entered Austria by now? Her nose tickled at the heavenly floral scent wafting in the air. Strangely, it didn't repulse her. In fact, she had yet to visit the commode even though the train had been rocking along the rails for three hours.

Her stomach growled and that, too, was a good sign. At least she would enjoy dinner in the L'Oriental restaurant and was able to wear the black lace dress again.

She felt as glamorous as she had the night before, like starring in a movie, jet-setting just as she had beside Fitzwilliam in Greece, Monte Carlo, Seville, Marrakesh, Paris, and Moscow. He'd rescued her from Longbourn and shown her the world. Heck, he gave her the world exposing her to her to private planes and priceless jewels, danger and excitement—and hot sex on steroids with a man who trusted her with his heart. Yet, here she was aboard the Orient Express with only her memories. What good was all her money and freedom to enjoy life if not beside him?

Holding to the railing as she followed the lights and the piano music floating from the bar lounge, she held her head high determined to allow the enchantment of the venue to sweep away the sadness and uncertainty for her future ... at least for an evening. Tonight, she would mingle and have a good time meeting strangers. Tonight she'd assume the pretend role of Mrs. Margaret Thornton, the divorcee—not Mrs. Elizabeth Darcy, the widow.

"Good evening," a handsome older man dressed in a tuxedo greeted as she neared the decorative door of the bar. His warm smile was reassuring and she returned it, feeling a little more confident.

"Good evening," she replied, continuing on her path to the bar, even if for just a soda water.

The silver and black door slid open to the susurrations of passengers enjoying the novelty of luxury. The mystery in the air was palpable and sensual. Clinking glass combined with the tinkle of ivory added to the already charged evening. She stood at the edge of the private party, very much a newcomer to friendships formed while she had slept and those previously made from London and Paris during the two previous stops. In the ambient light, she admired the pianist closest to her, and the debonair men and elegant women seated in the sofas beside him, enjoying the jazzy rendition of Gershwin's "Embraceable You."

The sound of liquid and ice swishing in stainless, mixing with the music swirled around her, calling her attention to the far end of the car.

It all seemed like slow motion, when her gaze through the narrow lounge was blocked by a woman sashaying toward her. Capturing Liz's attention, the fellow passenger's ice blue cocktail dress shimmered like water kissed by sunlight, until sitting in a glittering pool beside the baby grand. Liz gazed up and through the long carriage, her eyes falling to the bar area where several more passengers sat watching the mixologist shake martinis over his shoulder.

She froze. Her breath caught with a gasp.

Wide-eyed, her gape fixed at the back of a man leaning against the bar. Oh, the cut of the fine, black suit he wore and how it complemented his height and broad shoulders. The subtle bend to his waist and identifying cock to his head seized her heart.

Seated beside his towering physique, a gorgeous blonde held his attention as she chatted with him.

A ragged breath escaped Liz when he slightly turned his head to raise a rocks glass to his mouth. That unmistakable Romanesque nose and sensual quirk to his lips, that proud chin! Oh, God, that strong hand had burned her flesh a thousand times.

She gasped again, punched in the stomach with the full-fisted strength of shock.

Fitzwilliam.

In the instant, her body broke into a cold sweat and every emotion collided in her mind: shock, relief, disbelief, anger, and unmitigated joy.

Her heart thundered into her mouth, ready to cry out his name, but her lip trembled. She bit it and held onto the wall beside her, bracing herself from the same spinning she felt when learning of his death.

And then he glanced over his shoulder, whiskey still in hand and looked straight at her.

Her husband's dark eyes met hers and he furrowed his brow.

He is alive. Good God! He's alive! And with another woman!

Darkness closed in on her. The voices of those around her faded. Her knees buckled, sending her down onto the floor in a well-dressed heap.

25 Murder on the Orient Express?

D arcy's heart shattered along with the glass in his hand when it dropped to the bar. "Liz!"

Bolting from the bar, he pushed through the crowd as astonished cries rang out and the piano stopped when his wife fell to the floor from the shock of seeing him.

He was beside her in a flash, raising her into his arms. *How is she here? Why is she here?*

"C'mon, baby. Wake up," he pleaded, caressing her face. "Can someone get some water," he asked a little too anxiously.

One hand smoothed over and down her forehead and soft cheek while his other cradled her shoulders.

Filled with concern, the crowd stood around them—interlopers to the unexpected reunion. He felt all eyes upon him except for the ones he so desired to look into. After endless seconds, Liz's long lashes fluttered open. Her expressive hazel eyes locked with his—half awake, half asleep, definitely believing him a ghost.

"Is it ... you?" she asked dreamily. "Fitzwilliam? ... is that ... you?"

"It is, baby. I'm right here, holding you tight. You're not dreaming."

Her eyes fluttered, fighting the pull to close in the tense silence between them.

Her hand tugged from his. Her eyes now wide open and on fire.

Whack!

Palm and fingers slammed against his cheek with all her reserved strength.

He winced, closing an eye from the hard sting.

She passed out again.

His wife sure packed a wallop, but it was small potatoes compared to what was to come. He knew that the sting of her hand was nothing compared to her sharp tongue's biting words. They were going to tear him to shreds.

He heard someone laugh. Embarrassment had been his primary emotion just moments before, but now he was angered. Yes, he was embarrassed that his wife's slap actually stung, but he knew he deserved that and so much more from her. That idiot in the background had no idea what she had been through.

Lifting her into his arms, he ignored all the onlookers and the outstretched hand bearing a water glass, then carried her from the carriage. It was not even ten seconds before strains of "Isn't it Romantic," floated down the hall behind his determined feet.

The train rocked uneasily over the rails through the mountains, going as full-tilt as his adrenaline.

But, oh, how the feel of her lying in his arms was heaven. Holding her against his beating heart and breathing in her distinct strawberry scent that only a lover would recognize filled him with a sense of peace despite the burn to his cheek. He was home, doing exactly what he loved the most in this world: sharing one space and every second with her.

Having lost so much weight, she felt light as a feather in his arms, and she stirred when he carried her into the next carriage, but he'd not wake her until they were safe and soundproof in his Pullman compartment.

In the silent, hurried aftermath of what just happened, he readied himself for the blow-out to come. After seeing her at the opera last night, he'd finally faced the intrusive thoughts that had tormented his conscience over the last four weeks: how the hell was he going to reappear into her life? In fact, he was thinking that very thing when tuning out the overtly interested blonde to his left. But then ... Liz entered the car and he felt her electricity carry in the air straight to his soul.

"There are two ways of seeing: with the body and with the soul. The body's sight can sometimes forget, but the soul remembers forever." Dumas had written.

His heart nearly burst from his chest when their eyes met across the length of the carriage.

She'd never looked more captivating at that moment than any other for the simple fact that his soul had been living in a frozen abyss of death and revenge. All he'd seen around him was darkness and the face of evil. Her radiance tonight, lit his soul, calling him from his focused mission of facing Morales in two days, and calling him into the light and purity of the love she had for him.

Ahead, his cabin steward opened the compartment door and winked. If only the evening would end the way the man thought it would, but he knew better!

Under the soft diffuse of a reading lamp beside the pull-down bed, he laid her down and the porter closed the door behind them.

His heart thundered. She was here—with him—and it was only for the next 24 hours on this train that she'd be safe. *Why was she here and who was she with? Did Rick have anything to do with this? Had Traitor Tom betrayed him? This is too dangerous!*

Staring down at her peaceful countenance, he felt like he had that night in Monte Carlo when he walked away from the feelings he had for her. He'd watched her while she slept, his heart breaking, his spirit separating itself from hers in order to protect her, yet all he wanted to do was to make love to her and proclaim his undying devotion. Just like now.

He ran his hand through his hair and paced the narrow strip of carpet alongside the bed, then abruptly stopped, turning to squat beside her.

"Liz," he whispered in her ear. "Lakmé, wake up."

Bending over her, he closed his eyes, kissing her plump burgundy lips, lingering on them as his hand brushed down the side of her face.

Oh yes, she came to life, but not as he hoped. Like a wild animal, she thrashed under him with a fight, arms flailing and pushing at him.

"Stop, stop, Liz. Calm down."

Her breath was ragged as she tried to make sense of the nonsensical. Was he alive, a dream, or a ghost?

"It's me Fitzwilliam—in the flesh."

He waited for her to say something but nothing came even when she opened her mouth to speak. He reached out but she pulled away.

"I couldn't tell you my plans."

Sitting up, she pushed at him to get away from her when he tried to assist her in her confusion and grogginess.

"Get away from me!" she snapped, folding her arms across her chest. He could feel the tension rolling off her body, filling the cabin with a coldness that even the Iceman couldn't withstand. Such was the power and strength she possessed and had over him.

"I know you're angry; I knew you would be, but I had no choice."

He said nothing further when she didn't look up at him or reply. She just turned her head to the window, and he waited, listening to the train's steady hum and click over the rails and the undeniable pulse throbbing in his ears: one minute passed, two minutes, five very long incommunicado minutes with the same unbreachable posture.

His hand flexed open, close to keep from reaching out to her only feet from him.

Finally, she abruptly stood, nostrils flaring like a bull charging as she powered toward him in two steps. The set to her mouth was unmistakable and he braced himself for her wrath.

And it came, hard and swift like a cobra strike—a fisted right hook to his chin that knocked him back against the cabin door.

Whoa. Regaining his footing, he rubbed and reset his jaw, cocking his head with a wince and an "Ow!"

"That's for lying!"

She made to punch him again, but this time he caught her right wrist. Instead, she blindsided him with a southpaw punch to the left side of his jaw. "That's for dying!"

And then it came ... all the raw emotion within her erupted into a cascade of tears. He let go of her arm and she fell into his chest, arms squeezing him, touching him everywhere in disbelief. "Oh my God. You *are* alive," she wept. "Alive!"

"Yes."

She sobbed from her core. "I love ... you ... so much! I couldn't do it without you. Why did you go?" Her uncontrollable weeping wracked her body against his chest and then her fists angrily pounded against him.

"You left meee ... all alone without warning or a word!"

He took her wrists in his hands, holding them aloft when he locked his eyes to hers. "What did I say to you by the waterfall? Tell me?"

"That I ... should trust you, no matter what."

"And what did I promise when we parted ways?"

"That ... that I could count on you ... coming back, but you didn't, Fitzwilliam! You died. I ... wanted to ... die," she finally choked and then the weeping came stronger than before in short anguished breaths. "I begged ... that you'd come back!"

He sighed, wrapped his arms around her, and pulled her against him. His heart broke for the pain he inflicted on her, and his tears mirrored hers when they slid down his cheeks.

They stayed like this, leaning against the door for sweet and sorrowful minutes until she finally whispered. "You … kept your promise. You're here. You're … really here. Tell me I'm not … dreaming."

The man he'd been for the last four weeks was beaten and broken, melting onto his wife as the tears tracked from his own eyes. It took her love to pull him from the abyss and overcome, his knees went weak. Together they lowered to the floor. "I've missed you so much, baby. I have been dead, but seeing you … "

Holding her face in his trembling hands he softly smiled, "brought me back to life. We're not dreaming now, but I have dreamed of holding you every minute of every day since I left you in North Carolina."

"Where … where have you been?"

"Everywhere."

She draped her arms around his neck, and buried her face under his chin, her tears pouring out in sobs against him.

"Oh God! Kiss me, Fitzwilliam, just kiss me!"

His soft gaze held hers as he lovingly wiped the tear streaks from her cheek with his thumb. Slowly, his lips sought hers in a tender, blissful caress. Her soft trembling lips took his breath away and he pulled her tightly to him. Their embrace nearly suffocated the other as their hunger grew to consuming, mouths claiming and hands reaffirming that they were once again together.

But her unstable emotions turned on a dime when her head caught up with her heart. Abruptly, she pulled back from him, eyes burning into his. "Who is she?"

"Who?"

"The other woman. Do I know her?"

"Is that what you think? That I faked my death to be with another woman?" Of all the things she would assume he hadn't expected that!

"I don't know what to think!" She stood then angrily wiped the wetness from her face. "All the money you transferred … the mysterious person in West Virginia … and now you're on this luxurious train … dressed like Mr. GQ without your wedding ring! Who is she? The blonde you were with at the bar? Or is there someone waiting for you in Prague?"

He stood to his full height, finally able to convey his own disappointment in Wentworth but crestfallen that after everything they went through in Paris, she still didn't trust the depth of his love. "There is no 'she'. That woman was another passenger."

"Hitting on you or the deed was already done?"

"Stop this. You know why I did this, Liz. And do you really want to go there? What about you? You didn't wait even a month to mourn me before you hooked up with Wentworth—and here *you* are on the most romantic train in the world! And who were you with at the opera last night? Believe me, I understand the loneliness you felt, but c'mon … Wentworth and his slick cowboy moves? You could do better; you deserve better! A guy like that is after only two things—sex and money! For Christ's sake, he tried to seduce you at my funeral!"

"You were at the opera? At the funeral?"

"Of course I was at the funeral. Obviously Morales's assassins weren't the only ones deciding to hit on you!"

"But how did—"

"Not a week went by and you and he were cozying up! Is that how you honored my memory by renewing your fascination with the cowboy? I would have better accepted you spending time with a good friend and brother like Knightley than that eager Army dick. At least John's comfort would have been genuine and he would have taken care of you!"

"What the hell are you talking about? And how do you know about Dave?" She gasped at the sudden realization and her hand flew to her necklace. "You rat! You snake!"

He raised an eyebrow. "How else was I going to be sure that you were okay? How else do you think I could keep from going crazy from missing you?"

"For your information, nothing happened between us, not last year and not now! He's not my type. *You* are my type, you dumb ass! My only type and it would seem that *you* don't trust *me* either!"

He took a step to her with his arm outstretched, which she promptly swatted away. Softening his voice he said, "Babe, I have and always will trust you, but you can't fault me for jealousy, just as I can't fault you. Even still, if you *had* slept with him, I admit ..." he looked down at the floor and put his hands in his trouser pockets. "I did it to myself. You believed I was dead. As for me, you know there will never be anyone else. It's just you and always will be. I swam out of Bermuda to *protect* you, not cheat on you. Damn, don't you know my heart and the depth of my love by now? The extremes that I'd go to ensure our forever? I died for you—for us—for our future together."

"Love me? Protect me? Your death destroyed me. The pain never goes away," she wailed. Tears rolled down her burning cheeks filled with red anger. "When I did start to consider that you might be alive, what else was I to conclude since you hid in the Iceman vault whatever operation you'd concocted? What happened to our undivided, un-conquerable strength when together—not apart?"

"It was for your own safety, and I expected you to trust me when you did see through the ruse. I near laid it out at the edge of the wading pool. After all, you insist that I'm so transparent."

She snapped, "Gee, I'm sorry I missed the clues when your friends told me you were devoured by sharks! What should I have done, demanded a forensic analysis of your mangled re-breather in my critical thinking?"

He chuckled sardonically, "Yeah. Maybe. C'mon ... do you really think I'd allow for sharks to take me down, Liz? I'm a SEAL—we're taught how to deal with situations like that."

"What the hell do I know about big bad SEALs and sharks? You kept that in your Icebox, too! I don't know anything anymore beyond the fact that you lied and I haven't stopped crying since that day. You should have told me what your plans were! I would have kept it in the icebox, too."

"No. I should *not* have told you. And what if they grabbed you—tortured you for information about me. You think they would have stopped at torture? Huh?"

"I never would have said. I would have taken it to the grave!"

"And you would have! These people would have killed you after they did God knows what to you. And I was not about to take that chance, ever!"

He took another step to her, but she stopped him with her hand.

"Does anyone else know that you're alive?"

He looked away and tugged at his necktie, loosening it.

"Tell me! Have I been played a fool by Obsidian?"

"It was strictly on a need to know, but only one knew the details: your father."

"My? My father?"

"Yes. He's been helping me. Without him, I couldn't have pulled this off as seamlessly as I have."

"MY FATHER!"

"Don't be angry with him. I didn't give him a choice."

"You fucking strong-armed my father to lie to me!?"

"It wasn't like that." *It was more like black-mail.*

She stormed past him then pushed the cabin door open. Saying nothing further, she ran down the hall, needing separation and time to think … and to talk herself out of murdering him!

"This is not going well … at all, *jackass*," he said before bolting from the room, hot on her heels.

***

"Stop. Let's go back to the cabin," Fitzwilliam said from three feet behind her, but Liz ignored him.

With each furious step she took toward her stateroom on the other side of the quarter–mile long train, she ruminated to herself: *He lied to me! He broke my heart. He didn't want my help! He listened in to my conversations. He didn't trust me with his plan or my constancy! He enlisted my father! Who also lied to me! Oh, but Fitzwilliam is alive! He's not cheating. He ended Diablo's focus. He looks so tired. He's going to be a daddy.*

Her emotions were all over the place, barreling through her brain with the same ferocity as the train raced through the snow-covered mountain pass beside her. In her haste to beat a path far from her husband and the unsteady rocking of the carriage, she stumbled in those damn heels that pinched her feet and fell against the window. Of course, he was right there catching her waist in his firm grasp and then her tears came again.

"Liz, where's your cabin?" he defeatedly asked.

"At the rear of the train."

With a swift motion, she was in his strong arms again. She said nothing but buried her head into his neck, taking in his soothing scent. She was back where nothing and everything made sense, except for the one fact that made her feel whole: she was home and *that* made perfect sense.

He kissed her forehead and said, "Please don't fight me until we get to your cabin, okay?"

"Fine," she replied, then kissed his neck, reconnecting to him.

"You look beautiful tonight, but your hair may take some getting used to."

She snorted at how easily they slipped back into their comfortable repartee.

"And you look like you've been through hell, but ... hot as ever." Her fingers ran down his necktie. "Italian silk; nice choice."

He chortled.

She pointed to her door and he opened it and gently set her on her feet. Her eyes fell to the turned-down bed and fresh bottle of champagne; Salvatore had left her a snack of chocolate-covered strawberries for when she returned later tonight.

"You still didn't answer my question," he innocuously stated, gaping over the grand suite elegance when he let go of her waist.

"What question?"

"Who are you travelling with in such luxury? It's very unlike you to spend *this* kind of money on accommodations. Is someone sharing this stateroom with you?"

"No one. It's just me. Jane and Charlie gave me this trip so that I could visit the damn bank in Geneva and get away from my parents."

"Because of your mom?"

She threw up her arms and walked away from him.

"In my defense, I didn't know she was back until the day before the funeral when I showed up at Longbourn to elicit your father's help. Had I known before I left for Bermuda, I might have maybe … done things differently, considered another way."

"Why?"

"Because you had to go through that alone."

Again she snapped unable to control the bite laced in her tone. "She was only one of a long list of painful things I had to work through—alone—thanks to you."

"I'm not sorry for how I chose to keep you safe, Liz."

"You should be."

Mentally and emotionally exhausted, not to mention still in shock at his very presence, she was ill-prepared for this argument. She plopped down on the edge of the bed, ignoring her stomach's growl and the enticing pull of the strawberries, which would only make her vomit anyway.

Glancing up at him, her gaze softened. He looked so tired, so beat down. "What are we doing, Fitzwilliam?" She let out a deep breath. "None of it matters, does it? All that matters is that you're here—with me now—back from the dead."

He crossed the room and knelt before her; his strong hands pushed her skirt up over her thighs and hips. He shifted to move his muscular form between her spread legs and caressed her skin with gentle thumb strokes. Damn, it felt so good to feel his touch again. The imprint of his physical touch made long ago, tickled with renewed life. She quietly moaned at his tender ministrations and, allowing her heart to dictate her actions, rested her forehead against his.

"I want to hate you for what you did and remain angry with you for not including me or trusting me, but I love you so much I can only try to forgive you, because you're *here*." Her right hand trembled as her fingers tucked below his suit jacket and rested upon his firm pec and beating heart. Life coursed through his body; he wasn't dead. And she had to move past her anger—had to listen to her heart not her head, just as her sister had advised.

"I'm sorry for all the pain I caused you, and … and I'm sorry you ever got involved with me," he said with a distressed mien.

"Please don't say that. You're the best thing that ever happened in my life and I'd do it all over again."

His index finger lifted her chin and he softly kissed her lips.

"What now?" she whispered when the connection broke.

"Now, I kiss every inch of my wife and we don't leave this cabin until Prague."

He deposited kisses to her chin, cheek, and then the hand that had just pressed against his chest.

"And what happens in Prague?"

"It's my last stop in revenge. I'm going to face Morales head on."

"Good. Because …"

She took his hand in hers then rested it firmly against her tummy. "You need to kill him. We have to protect our baby and its future, Fitzwilliam."

"Baby?" His large hand cupped and squeezed her belly, connecting mentally with the life growing in her womb. "Oh, babe. Really?"

Nodding, her grin spread as wide as his. "Yes, Daddy, I'm about six or seven weeks pregnant."

Leaning back on the bed, propped up by her elbows, her heart swelled when he rested his head on her belly, kissing it in loving pecks.

"I promise you both, our future will be safe … and happy … and far, far away from Obsidian's reach."

Her stomach growled in his ear and she laughed.

"You need to eat; you've lost too much weight. Call the porter."

In the breaking and mending heartbeats of reunion, he was back to dictating and calling the shots. And you know what, she didn't care, not one iota! He was alive and so was she! And they were together!

***

"Mrs. Thornton?" Salvatore asked through the door, having responded to the press of the call button beside her bed.

Fitzwilliam looked surprised and was clearly ready to say something but she didn't wait, instead she opened the cabin door.

Bearing a tray of covered dishes, the porter entered. "Oh! I am sorry, I did not know that you had company."

With a smirk, her husband stood. "I'm Mr. Thornton."

"Very good, *signore*! You have surprised your wife after all. When she informed me that you would not be travelling with her, it was nothing to cross your name off my carriage passenger list, but it was not so easy to remove the sadness from her eyes."

Fitzwilliam turned his head to look at her and their eyes met; something tender and wonderful passed between them for a second until he asked Salvatore, "Are you saying this reservation had been made for Mr. and Mrs. John Thornton?"

"*Si.*"

The steward went about his business and, again, Fitzwilliam looked to her this time with a quizzical brow. He pulled the tie from his neck then sat on the bed in deep thought.

She walked to him and stood with her back to the porter, barely hearing the door click behind him after he laid their meal out on the table.

"What is it?"

"You're traveling with one of the passports from the safety deposit box, aren't you?"

"I guess. I don't know. Before giving the stack to Rick, I only glanced at the first one in the pile before becoming annoyed at Lucy Steele's face. Maybe Jane gave me a passport and a forged British Driver's License from the pile."

"She did. And you said that your sister made this reservation?"

"Yeah."

"Well, I'm pretty certain that Rick may have been involved in my business dealings in Venice, and someone took care of my business in Cadiz, and in Paraguay a woman on a dirt bike showed up with a couple of throwing stars."

"Boy … you *have* been everywhere. What are you saying?"

"I'm saying they know. Obsidian knows and they've been helping me for the last 3 days, and the fact that your father put me on the exact train as you means he's betrayed my confidence to your sister and reneged on the deal we made."

"Good! Then he is my friggin' hero! Coming clean by his own guilty conscience."

He smiled thoughtfully. What a turn of the key. Traitor to country and to his son-in-law, yet redeemed father in a matter of minutes.

"But, really, I don't think Obsidian knows. In fact, I met with Rick last week. He didn't know and even told me how he and Charlie feel guilty over what happened the night of the dive," she said.

"No. They know," he confidently stated and looked down at his hands clasped between his legs. She could see the wheels turning and burning in his mind just as they were in hers.

"If they know, then it would appear that my sister is the only one with big enough balls to put me in your path!" She was trying to hold her temper at bay, too tired to mentally fight with each chicken-shit member of Obsidian. "It would seem that everyone has had their piece of fun at Liz Darcy's expense. Is that what people you care about do in this business—lie? Your own cousin!"

He sighed. "I know it seems that way, but they're not playing with you. They love you, and I doubt they knew what to say … 'Um, sorry, Liz. We were wrong. He dicked us all and he's been running around South America blowing up shit.' Even your sister couldn't come right out with it. She had to send you on a five-star vacation so you could see me with your own eyes."

"True. They're going to kill you, you know."

He finally gazed up at her with a chuckle on his lips and a head shake. "I didn't expect anything less. What a mess."

"*Your* mess."

Gliding his arms around her hips he pulled her into him and down onto the bed. "Mrs. Darcy Thornton …" he murmured. "Will you ever forgive me? Please?" He kissed her earlobe in a delicious suckle.

"I don't know, Mr. Darcy Thornton. You have a *ton* of making up to do."

"Starting now. For the next 24 hours there are only two things I care to think about or discuss: you and me and how to redeem myself."

"Three things: you and me and our baby, and then when we arrive in Prague, I want to know every *other* thing, like where and what you've been up to for the last four weeks. I want that Iceman vault opened and aired out. *Then*, I'll consider forgiving you."

"Fine, and I want to hear everything that happened between you and your mother."

"It was awful and weird, and Dad lied … yet again. Oh, how I wish you had been there."

"I wish so, too. Babe, I will never leave you again—not like that. You have my word."

"Prove it."

"That'll have to take forever to prove."

"I'll hold you to it," she said breathlessly.

Rolling on top of her he kissed her with searing, truthful lips that told her that *after* Prague the future was theirs where happiness and peace awaited. No tears, no fears, and no Obsidian.

"Is it safe? You know ... to make love?"

"During pregnancy?"

"Yeah."

"Yes, Big Daddy, it is."

***

Back in her embrace was a start, back in her best graces would be a long process, and back to living was just on the horizon, he thought as her mouth loved his. She's carrying our child ... they were going to have the family they dreamed of. How did he deserve such a woman, such a life, and future on the horizon? Perhaps Dumas's view was a compliment to his mind. The author had written that lesser men would view happiness through a darker, narrower lens: *"It is the way of weakened minds to see everything through a black cloud. The soul forms its own horizons; your soul is darkened, and consequently the sky of the future appears stormy and unpromising."*

As dark as it had been these last six weeks, he had never lost hope in the joy that would follow them once his attritional warfare was complete and she was back in his arms. He'd always known that *if* she forgave him, their future would be blissful—the stuff of dreams.

Only one more city to go and it would be in their grasp. Tomorrow, he'd have to figure out how to keep her safe once they arrive.

26

Whispers in the Moonlight

September 8
Somewhere in Austria

Her husband was sleeping so soundly that she hesitated to move, but her fingers longed to slowly trace the planes of his rock-hard physique, to trace the tattoo circling his bicep and inked on the arm resting across his abdomen. Curled beside his nude body, Liz clung to him for dear life, listening to the strong, steady cadence of his heartbeat in her ear and reveling in the feel of the rise and fall of his chest below her head. She never imagined in her wildest dreams these were two things she'd experience ever again.

After having grieved so deeply and having shed so many tears, this moment felt surreal to her. Here he was in her arms—not as the ghost of her valium-induced nights, but in the flesh. Ever so lightly, she smoothed her fingers up through his chest hair and closed her eyes, her sense of touch reconnecting to each unique impression. Hard body, soft flesh, downy curls, taut nipple. He and this moment were complete perfection.

The train continued to rock a lullaby to him hours after their emotionally charged love-making. It had been only minutes afterward that he tightly held her and passed out with the moon trespassing across their spent bodies and rumbled bed linen. She couldn't slight him for that—he'd obviously had little sleep since Bermuda.

Opening her eyes, she shifted her head to gaze at his handsome profile in the moonlight. Hours ago, she considered that what he'd done was unforgiveable, irreprehensible, but her joy displaced her anger. The "hero of the bride" had once again sacrificed himself to protect her and those he loved. She came to see that his intentions had been honorable and good and he'd have kept his promise had Jane and her father not interceded before his planned resurrection from the dead. Admittedly he was correct; she never would have been able to fake absolute grief had he told her beforehand.

"I love you," she whispered, but he didn't stir.

Her hand caressed the red welt to his chin. Boy, she didn't know she had it in her but surmised that all that training in the bunker had paid off. Yes, he deserved it for lying to her, but she still felt bad.

His hand rose to hers and he closed his fingers around it before kissing it.

"I'm so sorry," she said. "Does it hurt?"

He lightly laughed. "I always said that you had skills."

Moaning, he stretched then turned to his side to face her; their eyes locking on the others. "I haven't slept this good since … I don't know … Pemberley."

"And I didn't need valium—just you."

They lay their gazing at each other in silent disbelief until his hand reached up to her hair. "Why did you cut it, babe?" he asked in a hush tone.

"Because I was angry with you for dying and you loved my long waves."

The thoughtful expression on his brow and the brush of his thumb against her cheek said how sorry he was.

She whispered. "Fitzwilliam ... how long had you been planning this?"

His jaw flexed as he considered what to tell her. *Could he be about to open the icebox?*

"Since the day we arrived in Santorini."

"But I wasn't interested in starting a new life, when you jokingly proposed running away was I?"

"No you weren't."

"And then Pemberley was destroyed."

"Yes. There's a quote in *The Count of Monte Cristo* that enticed me to expand on the plans I began to form when in Greece even if it meant that in doing so, I'd lose you. '*Oh, certainly, death, sudden and violent, was a good way to foil his implacable enemies, who seemed to be pursuing him with some incomprehensible desire for vengeance. Yes, but that meant dying!*' But my anger isn't about the estate. I could care less. It was always about you ... and Gigi ... and everyone around me. After the close call in July, I couldn't bear the thought of losing you twice in a lifetime cut short by some madman."

Her hand cupped his cheek where she slapped him. "My great protector, now I understand why you were so tormented that night in the stables and why you made our last day together so memorable. You meant it to carry me through the darkness without you."

"To carry *both* of us. Liz ... you're all that matters to me. Doing this ... this way ... was the hardest decision and I hated myself for the grief you'd experience."

"Because you felt it when you thought I was killed in Pemberley."

"It gutted me both then and when I got on that plane to Bermuda."

"Then I'm glad that I didn't tell you the truth about my experience at Pemberley. Your decision would have been that much harder to make."

"Oh?"

This was the tough part, but since they were baring their souls, she needed to tell him the truth. "You're not the only one who kept secrets. You thought the explosions didn't affect me and that I emerged unscathed, as some mighty phoenix unaffected by the flames, but that's not the truth. I just chose not to burden you with what really happened because of how you were suffering, and I didn't want you to go half-cocked after Morales and get yourself killed."

"Tell me," he said gravely.

She expelled a deep breath. "It was the most horrific thing I have ever experienced. When (swallow) I couldn't open the airshaft to crawl from the panic room, I had a full-blown anxiety attack in my fear of being trapped and surrounded by flames. I was terrified of burning to death. Since then, I've suffered nightmares and even cold sweats at the recollection of what happened in the bunker. The only thing that kept me from snapping was the comfort of knowing that you had been out with Rick and nowhere near the estate."

His hand caressed the side of her face. "My brave wife ... you've borne so much for me. You should have said something. I could have helped you through it."

"It's okay now. I talked it out with Rick and feel better about it. Nothing could be worse than having been eaten alive by sharks," she teased, making light of it but he still held onto her, petting her waist in long caresses.

Silence in the moonlight and the passing landscape outside their stateroom hushed between them again until she reached up to his concerned brow, tracing her index finger over the crinkles on his forehead. "Can I tell you something else without you getting mad at me?"

He nodded. "I can never be mad at you."

"I worked through my demons and ... conquered the Tail of the Dragon."

His face lit and he threw his head back in a laugh against the pillow. "You're kidding!"

"I really did it, and it turned out to be so exciting. The adrenaline was fantastic and I could see how you love the challenge. In the back of my mind I heard your instruction and listened to 'Scheherazade' the whole ride. I couldn't have done it if we weren't taking those twisties together on that ride."

The grin on his face took her breath away.

"You did it *all* on your own, not because I was in your head, but because there's nothing you can't accomplish when you put your fears aside. I am *so* proud of you. But what on earth made you do *that* of all things?"

"It was a memorial bike ride for your anniversary … and," she bit her lip.

"And?"

"A death wish."

"Oh, babe," he groaned, his lips growing taut with the furrow to his brow, and before either of them got too emotional about it, she broke the intensity of her declaration with a snort. "I wouldn't have gotten very far at offing myself. Dixon followed me even though I fired him."

"I knew that man was just who you needed to have your six. He was the right choice to entrust your safety."

"I'm glad you feel that way; I gave him your new motorcycle."

He blinked.

"And the Hummer."

His lips twitched.

"And a hundred grand," she whispered.

"His protection of you was worth every penny and then some," he said, running his index finger down her cheek. "Just not my Ferrari."

"Tease! Anyway, it was that night when I realized I was pregnant. I was at our secret cabin and thinking of the magical night we shared and then a light bulb went off in my mind."

With a wicked smile, he tightened the arm draped around her waist and slid her against him. "I know when it happened," he whispered in her ear.

"You do?"

"At Pemberley, on our last night there. Don't you recall?"

"Oh, I remember. Your *Chironius carinatus* snake charm was extremely talented that evening."

"It would seem so," he laughed. "That night, Liz was … unforgettable, and I think that vintage of Cabernet we drank had something to do with it."

"Ha! You credit the wine, not the fact that my body harmoniously coordinated and cooperated with your talent?" she laughed.

His smiling lips met hers when he rolled her onto her back.

"Again, Mr. Thornton?" she joked, feeling the hardness of said snake pressed against her thigh.

"I have a lot of making up to do, Lakmé. Let's *coordinate* again. I can think of no better way to tell you how much I adore you …" (kiss to her chin) "worship you …" (kiss to the hollow of her neck) "need you" (kiss between her breasts.)

Her husband's mouth surrounded her berried peak with a kiss and suckle and for the second time tonight, she shot through the cosmos.

She moaned, tilting her head back against the pillow as he loved her body with his lips. "Oh, Fitzwilliam … this cannot be a dream." She gasped in absolute delight by his thrust into her. This was no dream. He was alive and loving her in the flesh. Yes, she was still seething below the surface but, by God, his touch could make her forget all the angst leading up to this very moment.

***

Wenceslas Square, Prague

The knob looked—and felt—ready to fall from the door when Jane turned it. Using just her fingertips, she was careful to not contaminate her entire hand. *Yuck. Sticky!* With one last glance down the hall of the sleazy by-the-hour motel, she gaped at the brown stain in the carpet. Reviled, she animatedly grimaced. It looked like dried blood or vomit and she fought the urge to gag, but gagging would mean breathing and that had proven difficult from the minute she entered the establishment not far from the Vltava River and New Town in Prague.

Jane considered this place rock bottom, having come from the opulent and tres chic Hotel Danieli in Venice, and she wondered why Charlie would have chosen such a dump. Man, they didn't even have a complimentary coffee bar! At this wee-morning hour, her waltzing in and asking for a key to his room hadn't even garnered an eye-bat—not that the clerk really understood what she said, but he handed the key over quickly enough. Sheesh, either she looked like a prostitute or he was half asleep.

Well, who cared, really? She was about to see her guy, and that was what was important. Now that they were back on track, with the assuredness of no detours and total commitment, she had an itch that just needed to be scratched.

She slowly opened the suite's door into a dark abyss and, before she could whisper his name, she felt the press of a cold pistol barrel against her temple.

She froze, fingers unfortunately stuck to the doorknob.

"Dammit, Jane. I told you to text me when you were on your way up to the room."

Charlie lowered the handgun and pulled her in. It smelled only slightly better than the hallway and when he flipped the light switch, her heart sank; it looked worse!

"Hey, teddy bear," she greeted when he pulled her into his arms before she could even drop her purse on the gear-covered table in the center of the room. He smelled like coconut oil and for that she was extremely thankful.

"I missed you," he moaned into her neck, holding her tight until his lips finally met hers in a searing kiss.

Turns out this hotel did have something going for it after all.

"How was your flight?"

"Lonely, but good. I did a lot of thinking once Lizzy got off—probably more ways than one—on the train. Oh! Do you remember when I texted you that I thought we were being followed at Dulles and then in Venice?"

He sat on the nasty-looking sofa and pulled her down onto his lap. "Yeah."

"Turns out, it was her bodyguard Dixon. I saw him watching her board the train."

"Righteous! I knew I liked that dude! He's had your back this entire time?"

"I guess, but he didn't get on the train."

"Did Darcy?"

"Just like we planned. Dad came through on his promise and Mr. Edward Ferrars checked-in at the last minute. Holy moly, I would have loved to have been there when they saw each other. She's probably still screwing his brains out."

"Or using him as a punching bag."

Glancing around the room, her eyes fell on the rumpled bed linen. "You know, speaking of screwing, this dump you chose for our reunion has one thing going for it. It's kinda kinky—like role-play kinky."

"Only if you're gonna play a hooker in this place."

She waggled her eyebrows, and ran her fingernail up his thigh. "You're my faaavorite john, teddy bear. I make you holla for fifty-dolla."

He just chuckled and grabbed her hand in his.

Shucks. "It would alleviate … stress," she teased, toying with his shirt collar.

"It would but we have too much to go over before day after tomorrow's op. There's too much at stake."

"Hmm … are you okay with what you're going to do from the Basilica?"

"I'm just overwatch and back-up at the park. As always, which he seems to have forgotten, Iceman needs a scout to make sure it gets done if something goes tits-up. If this isn't finished tomorrow, then all his plans have been for shit and this nightmare will never end."

"Like … like tits-up if he gets killed?"

"You got it. Liz's future is our focus. Let's hope she listens to him and stays put in her hotel room."

"And if she doesn't?"

"Then you'll have eyes on her. Where Dixon has left off, you are now her bodyguard—only prettier." He winked with a smile.

"I'll blend in; she won't even know I'm there."

Charlie shifted her off his lap then rose. He walked to the table where all his weapons and gear were neatly laid out. Lifting a small caliber pistol, he pulled the slide back and handed it to her. "This is yours. Only fire it if you absolutely have to. They don't take any shit here in Prague so don't go brandishing it or anything."

She handed it back to him with a mischievous smirk. "I don't need it; I have the lipstick gun."

"Damn, you didn't return it to the museum like I told you to?"

"No, silly. I thought it could come in handy."

"You're killin' me, Janie. Killin' me."

"I know," she giggled. "But I won't disappoint you, Charlie. I promise, I won't mess this up. There's a lot more at stake here then just protecting Liz and helping Darcy. She's gonna have a baby."

"Holy shit! For reelz?"

"Yeah. How about that? We're gonna be an aunt and uncle."

"Well, you'll be an aunt. I'll be an honorary uncle."

"Not if you marry me."

He cocked an eyebrow in disbelief and examined her expression. Slowly, his lips spread into a smile. "Sounds good to me."

***

New Town, Prague

Maria Sanchez-Morales's tears of joy—and fear—continued to flow down her cheeks as she silently slipped out the servants' entrance of her husband's townhome in the dead of night. Her five-year-old son whimpered at her side and she bent to his chubby face, soothing him with a tender cup to his cheek. "Shhh, *mi carino*. For mamma, shhh."

Her ten year old daughter, still half asleep, barely questioned why they were going for a drive at this ungodly hour. Perhaps because the child had witnessed one too many beatings by her father and had always tried to intercede. Children could see evil much more readily than adults—especially women blinded by safety and comfort, particularly women who once fancied themselves in love with an older man since the age of 16. For ten years, she had been Juan's property. (The first year was nice, romantic even.) But the last nine saw her endure the back of his hand while he took many lovers, some as young as she had once been. She knew about most of his women, and she was oddly grateful for them. In the end, he had always come back to Prague—to her and the children, oftentimes too exhausted to touch her.

A decade ago she found herself cast out of her father's home, pregnant from Juan's flattering seduction (the son of the Lord of the Jungle!). She had chosen wealth over poverty; immature infatuation over love; evil over piety—and she had paid for those choices every day no thanks to Juan's father's insistence that the son take her as his wife for his foolish dalliance.

Tonight she was leaving with the only two prizes of their loveless union, and enough Euro to help them disappear into thin air. While her husband had given her the former, El Negro, her husband's sworn nemesis, had provided her with the latter. Terror and glee dwelled in her heart.

The wrought iron gate surrounding their compound squeaked slightly when the child's nanny opened it, but not one security guard stopped them from leaving. They knew. How could they not? She'd been ostensibly locked in this townhome with them for years. Several were more loyal to her than to her husband. So much so that three *sombrillas* would be transporting them to the airport under protection. Her kindness and prayers offered for them and their families were much appreciated and gained their devotion. Those who travelled and guarded her husband were devoid of any moral clarity or godliness, but some, here in Prague were a different lot.

The tears were not so much for the decision to leave or to separate the children from their father as they were for the contents of an overnight letter that had been delivered the day before. Juan had just left for urgent business in Venice, and she was all alone (yet again—and thankfully because he had been at his worst) when the delivery came.

Her finger stroked her name printed on the shipping label. She'd never before received correspondence here, and considered it a mistake. Nevertheless, she walked through the marble foyer, pulling the tab to the cardboard envelope.

Handwritten in Spanish, it read:

Dear Señora Sanchez-Morales,

It is with a heavy heart and the grace of all that is holy that I send this package to you. Enclosed you will find the details of your husband's nefarious activities, which consist of much more than the cultivation and trafficking of coca on three continents, which I am sure you are aware of as they have added to your comfort as his wife and mother of his children. However, I am sure that you are not aware that his other activities, which keep you living in grandeur, are crimes against humanity. I have been instructed to forward this letter to you by the organization which has been responsible for your husband's downfall: El Negro.

I have agreed to do this because I cannot stress enough how evil Juan Sanchez-Morales is and I feel that it is my sacred duty to inform you of his trading drugs for men and women to human traffickers, as well as weapons running, which brings despair to nations and furthers La Muerta Mundial's cartel goals of "death to the world." According to the man responsible for my safe passage to another country, your husband is also involved in the cultivation of various nerve and psychological agents to help destroy his enemies and perpetrate his crimes. These will inevitably—I am sure—fall into the hands of our youth one day. Do you wish that to happen? Maybe your own children will find them in your home?

Listed below are the fake corporations he has established to launder money through. However, you will later learn that all his fortune has already been seized and transferred to non-governmental organizations to help rebuild the lives of those he has ruined. Your husband's days are numbered and you will not want your name associated with his when everything comes to light.

Here is the part that will hurt your heart. He rapes, beats, and uses women all over the world. I was one, but I got away thanks to a very good man. I now have a new future ahead of me—and this letter to you releases me from all debt I have to him for my new life. I had been trapped by Juan's power and thought myself in love because of his sexual attentions. How foolish I was! Oh, how I lost my way! He paid handsomely for me to please him in sick fashion, but I was able to care for my mamma. As evident by the enclosed photographs and I caution you they are not for the faint of heart, his dark, sexual pleasures are sinister. I call upon your sensibilities as a mother to protect yourself and your children from him.

Leave at once! For tonight is the open window to your new life where El Negro has established finances and travel to New York City for you and your children. You can never go home, but you can create a new one where your wounds and heart can heal, just as I am learning to do. I am sure that after Diablo's murder, you, my friend, will not want what remains of your finery for they have been purchased by the blood of innocents. The attached piece of paper details your course of action (if you choose to take this opportunity) before your husband's return on September 9 to Prague.

With respect,

Pilar Montegro

Soon she would be free from him and forever grateful to El Negro for destroying him.

27

Back to Black

September 9
Somewhere in the Czech Republic

The Orient Express was three hours away from pulling into Prague's main railway station, and Darcy sat drinking tea (because the smell of coffee turned Liz's stomach) in the lounge of her luxury cabin. His eyes had hardly left her as she readied for the adventure ahead, and that unnerved him. In no uncertain terms, there would be no adventure on her part!

He glanced to his left at her packed luggage, ready for her porter's conveyance, and internally he shook his head. This brief but incredible respite in her arms was a gift and he owed Jane and his father-in-law. It gave his angry, tired soul the determination to fulfill Operation Black Ice to its glorious finish without worry over her absolution of him. Only, with that, new worries surfaced. Whereas before he only had himself to think of during the op's execution, he now had her safety to consider. Would she listen to his warnings and do everything he instructed? Or would she be as headstrong as she was in every other operation they became embroiled in?

That luscious mouth, he thought admiring the way she applied lipstick. Occasionally, she'd glance up at him through the mirror as if to reassure herself that last night had actually happened and that he wasn't an apparition.

"I'm still here," he said, bringing the cup to his smiling lips. The spill of her heaving cleavage in the reflection stirred him … yet again, but his worry over her superseded his carnal desire.

"And you're a sight for sore eyes, my husband."

"How do you feel?"

"Better, not as nauseous as before."

He placed the cup back in the saucer then rose, coming behind her and thankful that he was with her when she got sick. To hold her head and rub her back felt so insignificant given all the tumult he'd caused, but he was grateful that he could be part of all the nuances of their growing baby and be there to help her through every joy and challenge. Her slender waist felt wonderful below his sliding hands and he imagined with delight how it would feel expanded by their child.

Pressing himself against her back, his fingers clasped over her belly.

"You look beautiful this morning."

"Thank you. It must be because I'm so happy." She dipped her head back to rest on his shoulder. Their eyes met within the reflection of the glass. "Oh, Fitzwilliam. I never want to be without you again. To feel you inside me, loving me with all your emotion and tenderness brought me to life again."

Too choked up to speak, he placed a lingering kiss on her temple.

Lost in the moment, a quiet calm settled around them and she closed her eyes, feeling the security of his arms as the train rocked them both. She laid a hand over his upon her womb. He'd been so devoid of anything for the last few weeks that for him, too, this felt unreal. Time had halted just for them.

"We have to talk," he said breaking the spell before depositing a kiss to the curve of her ear.

"I thought we were talking."

"We have to discuss Prague."

"I guess we do."

Liz turned in his arms to face him and he held her tightly against him, unwilling in body and spirit to move from this moment, but they had no choice. "I have to get my gear from my cabin and then I'll be back. Once we step off this train, everything will change, Liz."

"I know that."

"*I'll* change."

"I know, but I understand."

After depositing a quick peck to her lips, he said, "I'll meet you in the Cote d'Azur dining car—please eat something."

"Yes, darling."

***

Liz had entirely missed the touted dining experience on board the train. Needless to say, she was excited to be sitting in the nearly empty restaurant carriage at a table for two. Each table had been set with the finest china and fresh flowers. And although the view beyond the window showed cloudiness and a heavy mist hovering between mountain and river, it was still breathtaking. Funny, how she'd been aboard this train for 24 hours and she'd not even admired the scenic journey, which was the reason for the trip for so many. Was this and last night real? Maybe it was all a dream. Perhaps, she'd wake up tomorrow realizing that her husband's presence and lovemaking had been nothing more than a figment of her desperate imagination.

She ran her hand up her arm, mimicking his manner of caress and she smiled. *It wasn't a mirage.* Only Fitzwilliam would have gone through such insane measures to keep her safe. A dark, suffocating cloud had lifted from her head and heart, and her spirit rejoiced for her and their baby's future. Although not a praying person, she whispered under her breath. "Thank you, God and whoever you are, Saint Lucy." It didn't matter whether magical or miracle, just that he'd risen from the dead like Lazarus.

Above the clinking dishware and quiet conversations, his throat clearing rose above the din, and she looked up at his severe expression.

"Is everything okay?" he asked with a crinkled brow.

"Perfect. I was just thinking of last night."

He bent and peeking out the window remarked, "I'm sorry the weather isn't better. This part of the Czech Republic's countryside is exceptional."

She could sense the change in him by the mundane topic of the weather. His chilly severity rolled off his black jeans and long-sleeved gray Henley and she secretly wished that if he was going to speak of the weather it would be something more along the lines of how the earth quaked from their tornadic intimacy the night before.

"I don't mind the weather. I'm just glad we're together. These clouds … and others … will drift away."

"Yes they will."

"Although it is suddenly cold *in here*," she couldn't help stating.

He said nothing, just sat, eyes not leaving her face when she raised the tea cup to her lips.

"I ordered you coffee," she nervously stated as she lowered the cup with a sharp clink (perhaps done with definitively more emphasis.)

He just nodded a wordless thank you then forced a smile. It was clear that Iceman had banished Fitzwilliam back to their stateroom. But it wasn't like he hadn't warned her.

"What did you think of the opera the other night?" he asked.

"Oh! Incredible. You didn't tell me why you were there."

"Business."

Soooo tense. Where had Fitzwilliam gone in the span of thirty minutes? She no longer cared much for Iceman.

"Okaaay. Then what did *you* think of the opera?"

"I wasn't watching it. I was watching you. Why did you put yourself through the agony of *Madama Butterfly*?"

"I know. What can I say? I guess I'm a glutton for punishment, salt in a gaping wound and all that." She laughed lightly and looked down, toying with the handle of the tea cup. "Still, I guess I owe my sister big time, huh?"

"*I* owe her along with an apology for underestimating her for far too long. She rose to the occasion and didn't bolt when you needed her, and she pulled off getting you to Venice. That accounts for something."

"Are you feeling guilty?"

"About my opinion of Jane this last year?"

"No. Guilty about leaving me?"

"Yes—and no. No, for the simple fact that the grave in Leesburg is not yours, and yes, for the obvious reasons of making you go through what you did and my missing you."

"Were you successful in your *business*?"

"Yes." He averted his gaze to the couple at the table beside them.

"What have you done?"

"I became him. I've stripped him of everything, just as he almost did to me and he's been on defense ever since." He glanced at his watch. "The final blow he is about to discover when he returns to Prague."

The waiter came to the table bearing a small coffee carafe and spoke to them about the lunch. Pleasant chit-chat with the Hungarian server was welcome because she got a final glimpse of the husband she knew and loved—the one summarily banished at the return to his cabin. But the chill descended again the moment the waiter departed.

Minutes passed in silence. Iceman watching her and enjoying his coffee and, she, staring out the window feeling his intense gaze. Finally, she said what needed to be said. "You should know, Fitzwilliam ... I haven't quite forgiven you yet, but at least I understand where your mind was."

He grunted. "I didn't expect you would immediately do so even after the incredible night we had together." Pausing, he then added. "It was … amazing, Liz."

Victory!

"It was and we'll have others."

Nodding, he gazed out the window, unable to meet her smile.

"Tell me about the money."

"I guess we're getting down to brass tacks now. I had every intention of sharing the details with you, but in private after this ends." He glanced over his shoulder to be sure that no one sat directly behind them. "The money is spread out all over the place to pay for assets and to set up our future. I couldn't have done the things I've done without the cash or the cryptocurrency to pull it off. Money solidifies the markers I've called in."

"And the wire transfer to West Virginia?"

"It was payment to one last vital asset." He half-smiled and shook his head. "*Not* a woman."

"I don't feel entirely bad about accusing you of that; you always say 'paranoia is the height of awareness'," she teased.

"True, or in my case it's just plain jealousy. I'm sorry I thought you succumbed to the cowboy's slick moves."

"I must admit, you weren't too far off from his true intentions, but your assumption was entirely wrong, babe. No matter how lonely or in need of comfort you believed me to be, it would never happen." She laughed wryly because he should have known this by now. "I was born to find you and love you and only you and that means that even after your death, I was still yours not just mentally but my body, too. You know that for me, sex … is making love."

She reached her hand out to him across the table and he took it. His gold wedding band was back in place on his finger, clasped against hers and her heart soared. That small yet powerful symbol shined like a beacon on the man hidden beneath the cold warrior exterior seated before her.

"And now you understand the depth of *my* feelings for you. Why I did what I did. Why I must finish this mission tomorrow."

"Yes, but promise me when it ends there is only a new beginning ahead."

"I promised you that the morning Pemberley blew, then in the stable at the farmhouse, then beside the waterfall. Oh, and when we parted ways on the interstate." He gave her a pointed look. "I keep my word."

Sighing, she admitted. "You always have with me, and I'm sorry I gave into the doubt. At first, I didn't believe that you were killed but the guys assured me."

"It's okay; we're together now. But you have to understand that a new beginning means a new life for us in every way. We can't go back but I assure you, I will never be this person you see before you, again."

With a reflective smile, she spoke softly. "You know, I admit that I fell in love with the enigmatic Iceman in Monte Carlo, but after I discovered Fitzwilliam Darcy buried below the surface, Iceman pales significantly to the man I married. My husband is an amazing man, a devoted husband, an accomplished horseman and dancer, a fabulous lover. He's an intelligent businessman and my best friend. He's the hot but sensible biker, the man who loves life and romance, who's loyal to his family and friends and he makes me laugh."

"Is that all?" he joked.

He joked!

"Hardly. The man I adore won't watch horror movies and never complains about my watching chick flicks. He's an avid reader, a music aficionado, and a wine connoisseur. And yes, he's the hero of the bride, too—my bad-ass former Navy SEAL protector who looks so damn sexy when playing with knives. And in eight months he'll be a gentle and loving father, a real role model of what is good and honorable to our child."

She watched his jaw flex and how he swallowed hard fighting the two personas that dwelled within the once broken and healed man before her. "Fitzwilliam is my perfect match in every way. But Iceman on the other hand only knows one thing …"

"Two," he choked out.

"What's the other?"

He squeezed her fingers. "That above all those things, he treasures and worships you, and that's what drives the one thing Iceman does best."

Le sigh. How could she not forgive him?

She thought of how her father and mother forgave each other; how her father was willing to relinquish the absolute malice he held onto toward Frances and to commit to caring for her because deep down he knew that she was the only person to fill the void in his heart and soul. And Frances knew that in her final years, there was no one that she'd rather spend it with than the man who still held all her affection—if not love—despite his keeping her from her daughters. Could it be that their forgiveness of each other and nine years of separation and lies could become an example to her? Perhaps.

Yes. Hers and Fitzwilliam's trials were unique to them, but their love was steadfast in the gale forces that blew their way. She could absolve him. "I forgive you," she said followed by a bite to her lip.

Lifting her hand, he bent toward their clasped fingers, and then kissed her wedding ring. "Thank you."

"But please don't leave me again. I proved to myself that I could go on without you if I had to but I don't want to have to."

"I will have to leave you one last time when we get off this train."

"And what about me?"

"As Mrs. John Thornton, you'll be staying at the place I arranged."

"And where will you be?" was met with silence and a gaze out the window. His hand withdrew from hers.

"So is that it going forward? We'll no longer be Mr. and Mrs. Fitzwilliam Darcy to the world?"

"Correct."

"Then I should have chosen a better name than Margaret."

"Aliases don't matter, babe. You'll always be Lakmé to me."

***

Prague

"She is not in the garden with the children, *Jefe*," Luis said entering into the master suite. Based on the state of the room, he didn't need for anyone to read aloud the letter he held in his hands for Diablo. Standing in the middle of the room, his employer's stiff posture and angry profile confirmed what they both surmised.

Strewn clothing and empty hangers littered the bed and floor. The bed was unmade and dresser drawers were left partially open attesting to the fact that Maria took only what she needed. On his way to the master suite, Luis had noted the same tornado in the children's bedrooms. Those remaining on her residential protection squad were going to hang for this.

"She is gone," Morales morosely said turning to face him. The man's dark scowl cautioned him to approach with trepidation and the man's hooded eyes seemed to glow blood red like Satan himself. There was not much more *el jefe* could take before snapping in an unstoppable murderous rage.

It was good that she'd left as he'd personally seen the bruises she'd received by *el jefe's* hands. Hers was a gentle nature, and Diablo's penchant for bondage and submission in the bedroom was a violation to her sensibilities labeling her defiant and uncooperative. When she produced an heir, her husband had left her alone.

Luis was not a timid man by nature—in fact, he prided himself on being ruthless when necessary, but couldn't help but to internally shiver when he held out the letter left for his employer. "This was left for you on the dining room table from the *señora*."

He examined Diablo's expression turn scarlet with fury not embarrassment as he read the contents.

"And there is this," Luis added, sliding the already opened 8x11 envelope out from under his arm.

Diablo dropped the letter from his wife to the floor, dismissing it when he swiped the overnight express from his hand.

"You have read this?"

"No, *señor.* I only test the paper for chemical sabotage for your protection." It was a short missive—and to the point. He knew because he had read it.

> *It is time to meet face to face to discuss the end of La Muerta Mundial. Unarmed and alone. 7:00 a.m. tomorrow—Vysehrad, overlooking the Vltava River outside the gallery.*
> *Know this, I have anticipated your every move, tomorrow will be no different. —El Negro*

Luis braced himself when Diablo ran his hand through his hair. "I want our best *sicario*! This ends tomorrow morning with El Negro's death! The dog will be destroyed once and for all!" he commanded with the false bravado of a broken man who knew full-well that he'd already been defeated.

"There is none, *señor,* even our finest *cruzadors* have been murdered by El Negro. Jorge was killed with the narcosub in Bermuda. Benito was blown in Paraguay escorting the caravan. Dmitri was found dead on the docks in Cadiz, and both our CIA contract killer and the girl you sent to Washington are still missing. There are only a few loyal soldiers left. Many of our *sombrillas* have departed with *Señora* Maria and the children."

Luis stepped back, but not fast enough. Diablo withdrew his knife and, in less than two seconds, it was pricking the notch of his throat. Oh, it would be so easy to take it from his boss and, turn it on *his* throat sliding it into his neck … slowly. Oh, to hear that gurgle sound of defeat come from *Jefe de Jefes* when the steel blade took his last breath.

"Find someone!" Diablo shouted.

Damn loyalty, he thought as his boss's foul breath invaded his space. He could not bring himself to do it, just as he could not kill Pilar before her escape. There was a big difference between calculated ruthlessness and pure evil.

With a measured calmness, he lowered the man's arm and locked his eyes with Diablo's. "*Sí, señor*," he placated before removing the mobile phone from his pocket. He knew of a few contract killers ... but none who would work for free now that the money was gone.

"Perhaps, you will consider enacting your own revenge with your own hands on this El Negro."

Juan stepped back. Knitting his brow, he ran his hand through his hair. "If I must, then I will. I want the park filled with every soldier you can find. It is time to call Carlos back from Moscow. He enjoys torture."

28
Macaroons

Prague looked to be a city worth exploration in Liz's brief estimation. Unfortunately, the extent of that opinion was based on a taxi ride from the railway station to the decrepit flat she now sat in. What a difference a few hours made in going from top-shelf luxury to a metal bed with a layer of dust and kitchen faucet running rust-colored water. This once Czech national police, anti-drug surveillance apartment clearly hadn't been used in at least a decade if the musty smell and the dated calendar on the wall was any indication. Still, she couldn't help but to be impressed by her husband's connections and itched to grill him on every facet and asset of Operation Black Ice, but he was too far gone to the dark side right now. Cold and impenetrable, even more so than on the last leg of the train trip into the Mother of all Cities, he squatted at the bedroom's curtained window with a military-grade night vision binocular pressed to his face for the last six hours.

She understood his hyper-vigilance. The third-floor, railroad-apartment was situated two hundred feet behind the Sanchez-Morales townhome and that was the target of his surveillance. He hadn't expected her to be with him but she agreed, for the sake of their baby, that she couldn't go with him and would stay in the most inside room, farthest from the windows. Everything was different now.

Within the living room, she sat cross-legged wearing Fitzwilliam's T-shirt and gym shorts, fighting the pull of her eyes closing on the remaining time they had together. She heard him zip his gear bag closed and her heart sank.

The wooden floor boards creaked when he walked through the kitchen and dining room, entering the living room; his commanding presence and dark aura filled the doorway. Black as usual, down to his leather jacket and wool cap. "You'll be okay, just … sleep. You need to sleep," he repeated.

"I'm afraid to."

"You're safe in here. Diablo's compound just went dark. And dammit, Liz, don't go out and don't make any unnecessary noise until it's time to leave. Get dressed and be at the ready for anything."

From his back waistband, he removed a pistol and chambered a round. "If you have to use this, leave everything except our ID and travel documents and meet me back at the railway station at 1:30 this afternoon. Find a coffee shop or bookstore until then and just blend in. Do *not* call anyone."

"Okay."

"In fact, just keep the passports and money in the neck wallet in case you need to make a quick getaway."

"Then maybe I should be going with you."

"Absolutely not."

He placed the gun on the table near the archway connecting the living room to the hallway that ran alongside all the rooms, a little smile escaping as he walked to her. "I would never put you in harm's way. If you have to get to the train, remember that Mr. and Mrs. Thornton will be finishing our trip to London in the same stateroom as before. I made arrangements before we arrived yesterday afternoon."

"And what if you're not there?"

"Trust me; I'll be there."

Rising from the armchair, she smiled back, even if her heart felt like jelly convulsing inside her chest. She would trust him this time.

The rippled frown lines across his forehead indicated how he straddled two worlds, struggling to maintain control of Iceman when he stated, "Damn, I should have sent you ahead."

"But you didn't because you knew that I would have objected. If this does end badly at least I'm here with you—and it ends for both of us."

"Not an option," he added and she knew why.

"Did you get in touch with Dad?"

"Yes, everything is in place. He'll have satellite visual on the park and I'll have my receiver in my ear."

"But no gun."

His lip twitched. "I don't need a gun." The telltale sign of his affection attempted to put her at ease when he ran his finger down her cheek then forced another smile. "Don't worry so much, beautiful. I have to go now."

His kiss felt non-emotive, but she understood. This was not her husband. The expressive, romantic Fitzwilliam was safely protected below the tundra for both their emotional protection.

Sliding her hand into his, she walked with him to the door.

"Stay away from the window," he directed for the third time this morning before letting go of her and turning toward the darkened staircase.

As in days of old, the last she saw of her husband was his back as he descended the stairwell.

After closing the door, she ran to the bedroom window, ignoring his caution for just a minute—just to see him leave her one last time. Peeking between sash and curtain, she spied him exit out into the night. But, he suddenly stopped in front of the abandoned jewelry shop then glanced up to the apartment as if he'd forgotten something. Abruptly turning, he took two determined strides back into the building.

Her breath caught and she could hear his creaking footfall up the steps, most likely two at a time, and she held her breath, waiting … wondering.

When the door opened, his gear bag dropped to the floor.

"Liz!"

She bolted from the bedroom, exiting into the foyer hallway. The chasm separating them across the long, near-empty space seemed so great when their eyes locked with wordless, breathless anticipation. The look in his eyes spoke volumes and she ran into his arms, jumping onto him with her legs wrapping around his waist.

"I love you, baby," he said with a passionate pant before his lips slammed against hers.

She kissed him hungrily, consuming him and relishing his response, ignoring the hard Kevlar vest under his shirt.

He kicked the door shut behind them then strode to the center table; his searing lips never left hers. A powerful swipe of his arm cleared the table as his other cradled her backside.

His kisses grew fast and frenzied, hungrily devouring her when he sat her on the table and her hands did what they did best, unzipped his jeans and immediately released him into her palm. Long and stiff with every emotion, his manhood felt hot to the touch, throbbing in pent up words needing cathartic expression.

He tore the baggy shorts from her body then slid her to the edge of the table. Lying back against the wood, she was more than ready for him.

Looking down at her, black-clad Iceman stood between her spread legs, the expression on his face nearly exploding her heart. His dark eyes looked onyx with passion-filled dilated pupils. Naughty and sexy, dark and dangerous, he was that fearless rebel on the motorcycle. His torrid ferocity was a hot turn-on, overtaking her with an intense fervor unlike she'd experienced before.

Engorged with desire, his tip rubbed against her slick heat, scorching her throbbing pearl. "Now. Please," she begged needing all of her bad boy biker—hard, fast, and deep.

But even in his haste to be one with her for what might be the last time, he took occasion to tease her.

His tip's dilatory touch made her writhe with each tormenting dip followed by its taunting removal until it became too much for either of them to bear.

Her body was on fire. Her womanhood trembled and clenched in absolute hunger for satiation and he knew it.

The joining, unhurried slide of his thick nine inches shot her through the roof in quivering spasms.

Sheathed in her womanhood, he stilled and gazed down at her with a seductive smirk as if asking "are you ready?"

Oh yes, she was.

"Ohhhh…" he moaned with a releasing breath when he seated to its hilt. His strong hands grasped her hips to keep her from sliding across the table.

In piston precision, each powerful thrust reached that place of white light and electricity. She cried out in rapture, but his index finger touched her mouth, and it took every ounce of willpower to silence her ardor with a bite to her lip as her orgasm ignited again and again.

Faster, faster, building like a crescendo of stifled moans and table legs banging, he made love to her soul—pounding her, their flesh slapping, their hearts pulsating until he pulled her flush against his hips and spilled into her all his love.

Their eyes never left the other's—an unspoken promise that they would be reunited on the train to their future home.

***

The creeping sunrise was hidden behind the dreary clouds as Jane's hiking boots beat the cobblestoned, mosaic sidewalk. Focused, she remained vigilant to her surroundings especially since all hell was to break loose in Vyšehrad Park in a couple of hours. Burrowing into Charlie's camo jacket, she wished she'd worn her slouchy wool hat and gloves given the cool temperature, but was thankful she was only a block away from her destination, at least that's what her mobile phone's GPS indicated.

Externally and internally, she shivered thinking of the big day ahead and the role Charlie would play in it. Gone by the time she woke at five, he left her feeling confident of their plan for both their days, covered back and forth over the last 24 hours since her arrival to the motel shithole. By now, he was carefully positioned in the bell tower of St. Peter and Paul's Basilica overlooking the gallery and the river and she was on her way to see her sister.

In the end, she and Crash had determined that there was no way she could pull off covert tailing of Liz and it was best to face her head on. She'd have to eventually have her day of reckoning anyway. It's not like she was blameless in the ruse to get her to Europe.

She glanced over her shoulder—just to make sure she wasn't being followed—and then scanned the windows of the passing tram. Man, she felt like she was in some *Mission Impossible* movie, or better yet *Lara Croft!*

This "old" section of Prague was way cool with its ancient vibe and very mysterious passages of trendy stores and cafés. She wondered how the night life was and considered that when things settled down maybe she and her *fiancée* could come back. Yeah, fiancée.

Even that was cool and she had no regrets blurting out her proposal the other night. On the flight from Venice, she'd read Liz's text before her death ride for what seemed like the one hundredth time: *Stop selling yourself short on love. Make the commitment you want—live life filled with true, constant love. Don't run away—run to Charlie; he adores you just as Fitzwilliam adored me. And you are worthy of it!* And when her heart skipped when she saw him, and she noticed how tired he looked and how he held her so tightly against him, she knew then that she wanted to be with Charles Bingley forever! She couldn't help blurting out her pseudo-proposal.

She glanced over her shoulder again.

Yeah, there was a definite change in Crash, like he had finally gotten over his depression and anger at Darcy. Sure, he did say that he'd like to have a go at him on the mats, but that was guy talk and expected. Her brother-in-law had played everyone but, unlike the others, she wasn't angry. Apart from her concern over the nightmare Liz had lived through this last month, she got it. In fact, she admired the man for taking the ultimate risk to protect her sister. Sarah was spot on in her assessment: what girl wouldn't dream of their lover going balls out for them? Charlie would do that for her, no doubt, and perhaps that realization is what snapped him out of his guilt-ridden, crappy attitude. He'd go all Iceman for her; she was sure of it. After all, these big bad military, Black Ops assassins thought they could conquer the world without their chick screwing it up beside them. *Pfft.*

She stopped at the entrance of Lucerna Passage in New Town when she caught a heavenly whiff of strong coffee and the sight of sugary sweets displayed in a café window.

Upon pushing the door open, an exiting guy barreled into her as she passed through the threshold. He did not even hold the door for her, but instead tried to pass her. In his hand he held a cup of coffee.

"Ooff!" she said, pushed to the side of the glass door that her body held open.

"I'm sorry," he apologized glancing up with a frown. Wide-eyed, he gaped at her as if he'd never seen a blonde before. Or maybe one as cute. She'd always considered this pink shade of lipstick her favorite and smiled in response.

"Boy, you must really need that coffee this morning," she replied. "I know exactly how you feel."

The corner of his mouth lifted and his body relaxed. "Do I know you?"

"No. It's my first time to Prague."

"You are American?"

"Yuppers! I'm from Virginia. Have you ever been?"

His silent reply was a full crooked smile before turning on his heel. Through the window, he glanced back at her as she watched his departure. Yeah. It was the cool camo jacket and lipstick.

The glass display cases were filled with every goody that her sweet-tooth yearned for and after ordering a cup of tea for Lizzy and a cup of coffee for herself, as well as a box of pastel-colored French macaroons, she, too was beating a path out the door. There was no possible way her sister could be mad at her now.

With the most vital task completed, she stood at the curb, waiting for another tram to pass then crossed the double lane to the building across from her. She considered it a lucky break that someone was coming out the narrow door beside the closed jewelry shop, and she ran to it before it locked.

The hallway was eerie and the staircase looked dangerous, but she ascended all the same—three flights of a creaking and groaning staircase. It sounded like it was going to collapse under her weight. She stopped on the second landing before ascending to the third floor, and placed the coffee carrier at her feet. Pressing speed dial on her phone, she didn't have to wait long for her sister's quick answer.

"Jane?"

"Hey, sissy."

Liz whispered, "You're in big trouble."

"Am I?"

"Kinda. Maybe not. I'm not sure yet if I should thank you or beat you."

Leaning against the wall, she propped the sole of her boot against the decrepit plaster wall and teased. "Was the sex at least mind blowing?"

"Best. Ever. Look, I can't talk on the phone right now."

"Okay, then open the door and I'll come in. You can fill me in on all the naughty details of your train ride."

"What? Where are you?"

"I told you, silly. I'm in Prague, downstairs, looking up at your apartment door. I brought you tea."

Her sister hung up and then she heard the deadbolt slide.

Quickly, she grabbed the coffee, ran up the last flight, and slipped into the apartment. Before even a hello, the cup of tea slid from the caddie and Liz was making a sip hole on the edge of the cover.

"God, you're a lifesaver. I so needed this," she whispered.

"And hi to you, too."

"Sorry. What the heck are you doing here and how did you find me?"

Glancing around the long hallway, littered with papers and a smashed vase surrounding a round table, she couldn't help but to remark. "Boy, this place is almost as big a dump as I just came from. You think Darcy would have put you up in better digs, huh?"

"There's a reason we're holed up here," she replied leading the way to the living room. Plopping down on the sofa Liz prodded for an explanation just as she expected she would. "Jane?"

"Okay, so … like … um … don't be mad. I'm here with Charlie."

"Charlie? So Fitzwilliam was right; Obsidian knows."

"Yes. But it's a good thing. You don't have to worry about Darcy's meeting with Diablo in the park. Crash has his back. He's there now, rifle ready to take that a-hole down."

Her sister sighed in relief and sat back on the pillows. "How did you find out that he was alive? Dad?"

"At first Charlie discovered activity on one of the passports missing from the stack that you turned over to Rick and then Dad came clean on Operation Black Ice. I'm not really sure how I feel about his involvement—and lies—but, whatever, I'll think about it when I get home; I need my mojo intact to protect you. How are *you* feeling, mommy?"

Liz raised her eyebrows. "How do you think I'm feeling? I'm a nervous wreck and feel absolutely helpless to help him. If you could have seen him, Jane; I hardly recognize him as the man I married. He was so cold when he left ..." Her voice trailed and her gaze fell to the archway leading to the foyer as if lost in a daydream. "But then ... he came back. It was the gazebo in Seville all over again. So intense ..." Liz licked her upper lip. "So desperate ..."

"Gazebo? What happened in Seville?"

"Um ... nothing." She snapped from her vision and shook her head with a small smile playing on her lips.

"Ohhhh. A *shag* in Seville."

"Neveryoumind."

Liz glanced over to the coffee table at the carrier. "What's in the box?"

"Macaroons!"

"Gimme," she begged.

"So, you forgive me for bullshitting you?"

"Sure ... I'll just add you to the list of everyone else who has done me wrong. I don't care anymore. My one and only wish was granted—the rest is insignificant. I'll leave it at that, but you should have told me."

"I was afraid to."

Her sister said nothing further on the subject, just bit into a macaroon and looked in the direction of the hallway again.

Just like that, the air had cleared. Liz didn't take her to further task about hiding what she knew about Darcy, or the train, or the role their father played. She didn't ask what the other members of Obsidian had done to help him either. The details didn't matter—all that mattered was her husband's success and safety when facing Diablo and the fact that he was alive.

The alarm on her sister's phone beeped and she put the half-eaten sweet back in the box. "He'll be meeting face-to-face with him in sixty minutes. Tell me again that Charlie has his back."

"Don't worry." She reached out and took Liz's hand in hers. "I promise you, everything will be hunky-dory. Iceman is totally bad ass and Charlie has his back if anything goes tits up."

"This isn't a movie, Jane. This is real life; *everything* goes tits up."

Jane rose from the sofa, ignoring her sister's crankiness and vacated the living room toward one of the three front rooms. "I *know* it's not a Bond flick, but it sure is exciting."

"Tell that to the three guys we buried because of Pemberley. I don't think they thought it was exciting."

***

Oh, yes, he knew the blonde-bubble-head *señorita* in the café. Carlos recognized her almost immediately. How could he not? After following Fitzwilliam and the British reporter from Peru to America, he watched her come and go in her muscle car to the apartment on U-Street in Washington. If it weren't for that blonde, he might not ever have found where Iceman and his woman lived out in rich suburbia. She'd led him right to their horse farm in Virginia.

About to leave for the park to execute whoever this El Negro was, he considered what she was doing here and Prague—in a building a street over from *Jefe de Jefes'* compound.

At the street corner parallel to the building she went into, he leaned his elbow on the roof of one of Morales's black Mercedes, pressed speed dial and said, "You'll never guess who is here in Prague. I think you have been set up, *Jefe*. It's the sister of Iceman's woman— the one who led me to them."

He continued to monitor the building and grinned from ear to ear when the third floor front room's curtain pulled to the side. "Yes. I am sure. I'm looking right at her." The girl glanced over her shoulder and the curtain closed.

"Is she alone?"

"I don't think so, but I have a few minutes to spare before I get to the park. I'll go take a look if you want."

"Yes. I think that is wise."

"It seems coincidental, doesn't it?"

"There are no such things as coincidences." Diablo paused. "Bring her with you. I am sure I will find some use for her."

"Are you thinking what I'm thinking?"

"Yes."

Knocking against the roof, the driver cut the engine and the two men escorting him to the park emerged.

Carlos was three feet ahead of them, his long black coat billowing in the wind behind him as he crossed the cobblestone street toward the third floor apartment above the jewelry shop.

29

Hero

"Jane! Get away from the window." Liz admonished from the doorway connecting the dining room to the bedroom.

"Sorry, I just wanted to check out the view from here. You could see the river, you know."

"And people can see *you*! That stone building is the back of Morales's townhouse! Fitzwilliam watched all the happenings over there, all night."

"Holy moly! You know—"

"Sush!" Liz whispered harshly, ears suddenly perked to the creaking stairs heavily laden with more than one body.

She rushed toward the pistol on the table in the living room where Fitzwilliam had left it, but it was too late.

The door kicked in, slamming against the wall with a resounding whack, and the doorframe splintered.

Both Jane and she froze, pressing their backs against the walls. She in the kitchen, two rooms away from the gun and Jane, in the bedroom—defenseless. Her heart thundered against her rib cage and all she could think or react to was the memory of being back in the panic room as though she was back there—frozen in silent terror as the wave crashed over her here-and-now reality. A cold sweat instantaneously erupted on her skin; her eyes were wide as she struggled against the tide. Horror immobilized her and she could hear her pulse throb in her ears only to be supplanted by the sonic-sounding blast of Pemberley's demise. Before her, her mind's eye she saw the burst of flame come at the bunker door only a second before she had slammed it closed.

"I know you are here, *señorita*," the voice called. "Come out and we will not kill you."

"Fuck off, ass-wipe!" Jane yelled, slipping into the kitchen and crouching low beside the refrigerator.

Liz turned her head toward her sister in what felt like slow motion. Had she had any wherewithal, she would have grimaced and silently admonished Jane at the outburst but when she withdrew a gold tube from her pants pocket Liz simply furrowed her brow and tilted her neck in wonderment. *Now is not the time for lipstick!*

The old wood floor creaked underneath the heavy boots that stood at both ends of the hallway; only a lathe wall and rooms each end of them separated them from whomever.

"It is time," he said, "that you come to meet Diablo."

Liz gasped and quickly covered her mouth.

"Fuck you and that fucker," Jane yelled out with foolish hubris. "He's got bigger problems then us two girls to worry about!"

"Oh! So there are two of you?"

"Shut up!" Liz mouthed to her sister, her mind finally emerging from the bunker with startling clarity. She was tougher than the woman trapped in the panic room. She was Iceman's woman. She conquered the Dragon. She had a child to protect. Her hand finally reacted, moving to her favorite belt buckle. If only she could get to the pistol.

Suddenly a tall, fat thug appeared in the archway connecting the bedroom and kitchen. His girth filled the threshold; his nasty smirk twisted his face and his mocking laughter rang out when he sized her up. And then he charged her, but her sister's—probably "borrowed"—lipstick fired into his chest.

But the brute kept coming—now at Jane—despite the bullet wound!

Cornered, Jane tossed the empty, one-shot weapon at him then readied her stance for a fight.

Liz withdrew one of two concealed knives encased within the buckle and rushed at him from behind, screaming, "Get away from her!"

With all her strength, she swung her arm wide around his thick back and stabbed the fisted, small blade into his carotid artery at the side of his neck, tugging it upward to his ear—just like Fitzwilliam had taught her to do.

He fell only inches from Jane's feet, blood pumping from his sliced tree-trunk neck as he gurgled and struggled to stop the bleeding. He'd be dead in under a minute and she didn't have time to consider that she'd just taken a life.

Grabbing her sister's shaking hand, she tugged her over the dying blob and they ran toward the dining room—and the pistol in the living room. She could feel her sister trembling from shoulder to fingers and she held onto her tightly. Reality bites and the first sight of blood must have shaken Pussy Galore's mojo to her core.

"Don't be in such a hurry, *señoritas,*" the apparent leader said with an expression of surprise then recognition when he stopped them in their tracks before getting to the living room. "Or should I say *Señora* Darcy?"

Her free hand wasn't quick enough to grab the other knife from the buckle. He'd already grabbed both her wrists just as the third massive soldier wrapped his arms around Jane's willowy body, pinning her against him to keep her from thrashing, which was moot because Jane was shell shocked. All her sister could manage was a breathless, stumbling, "Y …y … ou?"

"Once again you have led me to Iceman's woman," he replied. "Now, would you like to see me kill your husband, *Señora* Darcy?"

"My husband is already dead, dickhead," she spat.

"I think—*not*. You are a clever couple. We thought *you* had been killed. Yet you miraculously survived in Virginia."

"Oh, he's dead I assure you. Shark bait at the bottom of Hungry Bay after he blew your boss's mansion to shit!"

He rotated his hands inward causing a painful burn and twist to her wrists but she did not wince. She refused to give him that satisfaction.

"Let us go and see for ourselves, and if you are right, if he is already dead, then Diablo will have other uses for you both."

He sneered when his eyes dropped to her breasts and her eyes darted to the gun calling to her only six feet away. She calculated the odds of success if she struggled to break free and thought of her sister's immobilized fear. Narrowing her eyes, she stared him down, confident that Fitzwilliam would kill them all.

"Yes. Let's go see if—," she challenged but did not complete her sentence before the unexpected auto injector needle stab into her neck.

***

A miserable, drizzling rain fell as Darcy strode through the grassy field toward the brick wall located at the perimeter of the Vyšehrad national park overlooking the river. Shrouded by the ominous mist, the revered basilica loomed at his back and the ancient castle fortress hugged the rocky promontory to his left.

At this time of the year, this section of the 10th Century site wasn't scheduled to open until later and it also provided the cleanest route following the kill shot to Diablo—just in case something went wrong. He stopped at the very position where only three hours earlier he'd prepared for his getaway.

Stone-faced and emotionless, he lifted his chin to the cold breeze, meeting it head on and stood with his hands tucked in the pockets of his black leather jacket. Gazing out across the river and the dark dreariness encapsulating the city he thought how sweet revenge tasted. Diablo had crossed the point of no return when he targeted Liz. Oh, the satisfaction he would get at seeing the evil bastard's expression when he put two and two together.

"Diablo has just arrived," Bennet said into the comms. "I count at least six of his men already in position, the closest of which is behind the art gallery 50 feet to your left. He has a machine gun, I think."

"Does Morales approach alone?"

"Yes."

"And will I have unexpected back-up support this time, *Dad?*"

"I'm not at liberty to say, *Son*, but … my Janie is in Prague if that is any indication."

"For Christ's sake!" The hair stood on the back of his neck. Just because he appreciated his sister-in-law's efforts in getting Liz to Venice, didn't mean he trusted her not to screw things up. This wasn't a friggin' movie! The fucking women in his wife's life had caused nothing but problems!

"So you're saying Charlie is in Prague as well?"

"Affirmative."

Humored, he shook his head pondering whether Bennet was getting into his role. Admittedly, he felt better about this meeting, knowing that somewhere—unseen by any human eye—Charlie was strategically positioned with a rifle. That would make two shooters who had his back, and before Diablo or his henchmen knew what hit them, he'd be gone and they'd be dead in under five mikes.

Glancing at his wristwatch, he noted the precise time: zero seven hundred hours. He thrived on punctuality and felt oddly at ease with the imminent meeting.

Through the swaying tree branches reaching over the walkway like tentacles of death, he could make out Diablo's approach at the far end of the path. He wore an opened black trench coat, which revealed a dark suit. Sunglasses, even in the rain, shielded his eyes, and as he drew nearer, he could make out just how much his hair had turned grey in the last four months of creeping sabotage to La Muerta Mundial cartel operations. The set to his mouth gave Darcy a chuckle.

"That's far enough," he said when Morales was about three meters from him. Close enough for the fucker to get a good look at him.

Recognition crossed Morales's face, then a smirk and head shake. He lightly laughed in the revelation that he'd been bested by a dead man—or was it something else? Surprise had not crossed his countenance.

"Darcy, a solider is approaching from around the supply building to your right," Bennet said into his ear. "And there are now only two of Diablo's men remaining in the trees. Charlie has been a busy fellow."

A removal of Diablo's sunglasses preceded his cavalier posture, "I hope you do not mind, but I brought my *secretario* and he would like to divest you of any weapon you may be hiding."

"I am the weapon." He readied his hands. Oh, how he'd love to snap Luis's neck for Pilar, but he held back.

"We shall see."

Luis patted him down from chest to legs, to back. "Apart from a vest, he is clean, *Jefe*." Then held out his hand. "But I will take that receiver in your ear, *señor*."

Complying with a sly grin, Darcy placed the small earpiece in the center of Luis's open palm. "How is Pilar, Luis? Did you tell your boss that she got away with the help of *El Negro*, just like *Señora* Morales?"

"What is this?" Diablo asked with a head twist, his face burning bright red, and not from the chill in the air.

"Tsk, tsk, tsk. You failed to tell *Jefe de Jefes* that you did not kill her as instructed? Such betrayal and disloyalty from a trusted lieutenant," Darcy added

"You lied to me, Luis?"

"No ... I—"

Morales removed the pistol from under his coat and shot Luis in the back. Just like that: no warning, no words, just an irrational, unglued reaction at having lost everything including the loyalty of his most trusted man. Oh yes, revenge has no bounds; he'd even managed to strip allegiance to Diablo. And now he knew that the bastard carried a weapon.

Morales pointed the barrel straight at him.

"How do you know this about the woman in Panama?"

"Because *I* am El Negro, otherwise known as Iceman, and I have been systematically ruining you since Moscow. *I* am the phantom of your nightmares; *I* am the ghost who destroyed your empire—first by rumor, then by fire, and finally by financial ruin. Your death in the same manner in which I killed the Lord of the Jungle, your father will be my final revenge."

Red with rage, Diablo demanded, "Say it—you're real name. You are Darcy."

Narrowing his eyes, he spoke gravely. "Alive and in the flesh—a calculating, ruthless, and focused enemy who doesn't like when someone fucks with his family."

"How did you do this?"

Smirking, he quoted the *Count of Monte Cristo*. "How did I escape the blast in Bermuda? With difficulty. How did I plan this moment? With absolute pleasure. You wanted this, Morales. You begged for it when you went after my wife in my ancestral home."

"Impressive, but you will finally meet your demise today."

"I don't think so. You should have listened to me when I said come alone. You have five men less than when you arrived, you lack leverage and you are devoid of a skilled shooter to take me out. You've already lost, Morales." He watched as the sniper red dot emitted from high up on the castle roof appeared on Morales's forehead.

"Oh, but I do have leverage!" Morales proclaimed with renewed cockiness.

"A 9mm is not leverage and will not stop me. Right now there are two semi-automatic sniper rifles dialed in on the center of your forehead."

"Ah … but I have something infinitely more valuable to you than witnessing my death."

From the forest, two soldiers assisted and pushed two shuffling, lithe women to the pathway. Their heads were covered; their wrists bound together at their abdomen. They ambled as though drugged. Darcy knew that shapely body and motorcycle riding boots. *Fuck!*

His heart dropped to his stomach. *No! No! No!* His fist tightened at his side, opening and closing as his mind worked.

"I should like to kill you all at once and be done with it, but I would very much enjoy watching you squirm, *El Negro*. Carlos is very talented at gutting dogs."

"You—and he—will not leave this park alive, Morales; you can count on that."

"Perhaps not, but I will depart this world with the satisfaction of having destroyed you in the end."

Ten feet from him and his enemy, the soldiers stopped and pulled the black hoods from their captives' heads.

Immediately, Liz's sedated, sleepy eyes met his and he was proud to see defiance and strength in them despite whatever drug had incapacitated her struggle. Her sister, however, was a zombie—devoid of fight or flight. There was fear in her eyes.

"So now you see …" Morales said, walking to Liz, "I have what you want." He held the pistol to her temple. "Who shall you choose to die first? Your beloved or her sister?" His hand grabbed Liz's breast. "Maybe I will take her right here in front of you."

The rain began in a steady fall, matching the pounding pulse in Darcy's temple. His pumping blood raged inside like a wild animal ready to shred his prey's flesh, but he held his cool on the outside. His eyes had not once left Liz's. "I wouldn't do that if I were you, Diablo," he said menacingly, his head twisting, his fist clenching to the point of white-knuckled fury.

Morales lowered his hand and the pistol, but it was replaced by Liz's captor's jagged-edged knife pressed against her throat. The greasy-looking goon must be Carlos. He remembered the name as Julia Bertram's kidnapper and via a phone call Luis made yesterday through the paired cell.

Liz's wide-eyed gaze, now tinged with fear, held to his.

With a confident swagger Morales walked to Jane, promptly placing the barrel to her temple, then dragging it down her cheek. Jane whimpered. "Perhaps *she* will die first and I will take *Señora* Darcy with me in place of Maria, Nadya, Pilar, and my father's empire."

Any second, Charlie's bullet would no doubt take out her captor. He must be going ballistic out there, watching this through his rifle scope.

With palms up, Darcy held out his arms, taking several measured steps closer to Morales. "Let them go and do what you will with me."

His hands were primed for destruction … his body about to rush at Morales. He just needed to grab and twist the pistol, break his hand and then snap his neck.

"Stop there and instruct your men to lower their rifles."

Offering momentary appeasement, he raised his right arm high and the one red dot disappeared. *Don't fail me now, kid.*

A quick glance and nod to Liz precipitated her surreptitious wink and, before he knew her plan, her bound, fisted hands had somehow fingered the blade from her buckle. She thrust it upward over her shoulder into her captive's eye.

At the same time, a damn impressive shot from the basilica took out the back of Jane's captor's head, dropping him in a heap and pulling her down with him. The poor girl was covered with matter, but the rain washed it from her in red streams.

Liz barely took two running steps to him before Morales turned the pistol on her.

Darcy dove straight into the gunshot between his wife and the bullet, taking it in the left shoulder at close range.

Fuck! Three inches to the right and it would have hit the vest!

The red dot reappeared from the castle and, a second later, Diablo fell dead with a single shot to the center of his forehead, delivered by a hired gun in Iceman's signature glory. The evil son had met the same fate as the father, only Iceman hadn't pulled the trigger. It was the best two million dollars he'd ever spent. The not-so stupid kid from West Virginia had come through.

"Fitzwilliam! Oh my God!" Liz cried, cutting her restraints. Tears rolled down her cheeks as she fell to her knees, cradling his head on her lap. Unsure of what to do about his shoulder, her hand trembled over his saturated shirt. There was blood everywhere around her, filling concrete potholes with red in the rain.

"What should I do? You're shot!"

"Forget about me. Did they hurt you?" Did they hurt you!" he demanded, capturing her hand in his, heart breaking at the bruises on her wrists.

"No. I'm okay. I'm fine; I promise."

He grimaced as his hand pressed hard to his wound but he forcefully instructed Liz. "Focus, babe. I'm all right, but we have to get out of here. Get the ear comms from that guy near the wall." He wasn't all right but he'd worry about that after they got to safety. Thank God it didn't hit an artery and the bullet had gone clean through. The last thing he wanted to do was to dig a slug out from what might be a shattered shoulder.

"Liz!" Jane cried.

"It's okay, Jane. Everything is going to be okay," she called out after her.

Liz's wobbly legs ran across the walkway to the wall and Darcy got up from the ground.

At his feet, Diablo's lifeless eyes stared at him. Darcy's lip curled, and then he spit on him.

"Jane. Are you hurt?" he asked, his eyes still focused on his enemy.

"No," she replied in a daze.

He turned to face her and through the downpour, he could see Crash behind her running full speed darting between trees. "Stay right here; Charlie is on his way. Do exactly as he tells you."

And with that, he ran to Liz—his sole focus—took the receiver from her fingers, and plugged her ear with it. Grabbing her hand, he tugged her along the length of the wall to the very end closest to the castle ruins.

"Do you trust me?" he asked with a forced smile, but damn his shoulder was killing him.

"Always."

A tug to the black strap of his gear bag pulled it from the thick bramble beside them and he diagonally draped it across his back.

"We're going over the wall but I need your help." He removed his tactical gloves from his pockets and handed one to her. "Put this on."

She helped him over the perimeter and together they grabbed the rope he'd already secured—he with his right arm and she with her left—taking the weight of his wounded side onto her as she wrapped her right arm around his waist. They half-walked and half-slid down to the top of a tunnel hulled out in the rock then continued their descent to the street running between hill and river.

As soon as their feet touched concrete he grabbed her hand again, leading her into the tunnel where a motorcycle, thankfully, still awaited their getaway. He removed the gear bag from his back, then his jacket, followed by the agonizing removal of his shirt over his head, and standing before her in the bullet proof vest, he noted her changing expression. She was about to cry when she saw the bloody gunshot wound only inches away from his bullet protection.

"Shit happens. I'll be okay, Liz," he assured before removing the military clotting syringe from his bag, tore the sterile sealed pack open and handed it to her. "After I get out of this vest, quickly insert the plunger into the tube, take off the blue tip, and insert the applicator into my wound."

"What? What is this?"

"Hemostatic granules that will clot the blood and eventually stop it."

She moved to his back and gasped at how large the hole was compared to the front.

"Exit wound," he simply said, trying not to groan when she inserted the applicator.

"O ... kay, now what?" she asked handing him the emptied tube over his shoulder.

"Press this antibacterial gauze to the wound and hold tight to stop the bleeding."

He could tell she was nervous, afraid to mess up when she stated, "I'm sorry, I'm just not any good at this."

"Sure you are. Come over here," he softly ordered, taking her hand to bring her in front of him. With a kiss to her forehead, he murmured, "I'm going to be fine."

"Of course you are ... it's just ... I only just found you, again."

She helped him dress and he straddled the bike, tossing the Kevlar vest on the ground. "You ride," he finally commanded.

"Just like Moscow?"

"Just like Moscow, only don't let up on the throttle until you get to the railway station." He tapped the receiver and said, "Your dad will tell you how to get there."

Smiling from his heart, he brushed her cheek with his finger. Expediency was suddenly halted by his intake of breath as their gaze held the other's steadfast. She was an incredibly brave woman and he'd die a thousand times just to keep her safe. "You were awesome back there."

"So were you, my hero."

Her two hands cupped his cheeks and she kissed him languidly causing his lips to tingle.

Seconds later, she straddled the bike and shoved the helmet over her head. He squeezed his thighs around her backside to anchor himself and leaned against her back for support, bracing himself for a crazy ride through Prague. His good hand continued to apply pressure to the dressing, but it did nothing to stop his slowly ebbing strength or the pain. He silently prayed that he wouldn't pass out.

Like the bad ass rider he knew she had become, she effortlessly kicked the motorcycle to life and promptly burned rubber, leaving a skid mark, smoke, and the remnants of Mr. and Mrs. Fitzwilliam Darcy, Iceman, and Obsidian behind them.

30

Pack Clouds Away

Prague Main Train Station

The hustle and bustle of train travelers gave Liz and Fitzwilliam cover as they made their way under the dome and stained glass windows through the crowds. Overhead announcements competed with the sound of her thundering heart, which had not resumed any semblance of a normal cadence since getting off the motorcycle in what was literally a ride for their life—specifically Fitzwilliam's. They needed to clean the wound and re-apply the dressings. With gear bag now slung over *her* shoulder, she listened intently to her redeemed father as he viewed a map of the station, hurriedly directing her: "turn right at the café, make a left near the elevator" until they found the "family" restroom.

She looked up at her husband's wane face before turning the knob and entering.

Little had she known that he carried a medic field kit within the bag. "Like I said, shit happens. I like to be prepared," he groaned, emptying a bottle of pills into his palm then shoved them into his mouth.

"Please, honey, we need to go to the hospital," she begged, helping him to remove his clothing once again.

"Not a good idea. We need to get on that train."

Gingerly, she removed the gauze from his torn flesh and was surprised to see that very little blood seeped from the wound.

Each item that he handed her from the bag came with his explicit instructions as though he'd done this a thousand times but, again, this was part of his mysterious SEAL world that had been locked away in the Icebox for so many years. Who knew they taught those warriors combat trauma medicine? She didn't.

She cleaned the outside of the bigger hole at his back and then watched—mouth agape and grimacing for him—as he stitched the entry hole closed without even a grunt. A fresh set of anti-bacterial gauze temporarily patched him up. Finally, the last item he removed from the bag was a gray polo shirt, but before she helped him into it, she kissed his shoulder. "To help you heal."

Fitzwilliam smiled softly and slid his arm around her waist. "That's all I need." He raised his right hand to her hair, toying with the short, messy strands. "I was so scared back there … when I saw you approach with that hood on."

"You? Scared?"

"Yes. Me, scared."

"It was Jane – she led them to me in Pemberley and at the apartment."

"I had a feeling. She wasn't aware of it."

"I know, but still … anyway, you saved me back there, and now look at you!"

"And *you* saved *me* on June 24th at 11:05 in the morning. Yes, now look at me. I might be shot, but I'm damn happy."

She furrowed her brow. "June 24?"

"Operation Virginia Reel—the first time I saw your beautiful face," he whispered, lowering his lips to hers.

***

This Orient Express train boarding was entirely different than when Liz departed Venice only two days ago. Sure, the carriage and Salvatore's cheerful smile greeting passengers were the same, the excitement of embarking travelers and the platform announcements in a foreign language were similar. Even the weather was reminiscent of that fateful afternoon when she stepped on board alone believing herself a widow. While she'd waited for boarding in the Prague station beside her resurrected husband, the rain had stopped, giving way to what promised to be a glorious departure, and she wouldn't miss a single moment by sleeping it away, no matter how exhausted she was.

But what was entirely different was that in the short span of 48 hours her life had changed, yet again. She squeezed Fitzwilliam's hand and looked up at him with a smile as they walked toward their Pullman car. Everything was different now, especially her.

Gorgeous white rays streamed through the remaining few clouds, eliciting her happy goose pimples. "It appears that the clouds have packed away just in time for our travel," she said.

"I'll feel better when the train leaves the station and we're headed home."

"And I'll feel entirely better when you get to a doctor."

"Don't worry; we'll be in England in 24 hours."

"Tell me again what it's called."

"Helstone Manor in Northern Derbyshire."

"Is there a greenhouse?"

"Not yet, but there will be … and a nursery."

Her grin matched his, reaching her eyes. Yes, she considered that the sudden sunshine signified a brilliant new beginning for John and Margaret Thornton's new life. She might even learn to like the name or settle on a nickname. Maggie? Meg? Margie? Peggy? Only one fit: Lakmé.

"It's a shame I had to leave my sketchbook back in that apartment."

"Good-bye and good riddance, I say. The next one I buy for you, you can fill with happy things, unlike the last."

"The last few pages before I left for Venice were very happy. They were sketched at the cabin when I realized we were going to have a baby."

He gazed down at her, smiling wistfully. "One day, we'll go back there with our child; I promise."

"I hope—hey …, is that who I think it is at the end of the platform?" she asked, gaze narrowing to make out a familiar couple waiting beside the row of train porters: Rick and Sarah.

Some 40 feet away Sarah's golden blonde hair shone in the sunlight and, spotting their approach, gave a wide wave. She wore a fashionable, maroon sheath dress and a stunning smile to match. Although sour-faced, Rick looked as sharp as always wearing a navy suit.

"That jackass," Fitzwilliam said with a chuckle and a head shake.

"I love him," she replied with a definitive laugh. "And you have no right to complain. Remember this is *your* mess."

He grunted then laughed.

They walked in humored silence toward the couple and with each glance up she noted the relief on her husband's face. He was ready for the fallout from his actions, but he'd get it over and done with before arriving to their new home.

"Heard you ran into a bit of a cluster fuck," Rick greeted with a smile. "Good thing this *particular* Marine with medical know-how was already on his way to the train station."

"Hey, my attentive nurse and Special Ops kit did just fine. I don't need any stinkin' Marine to patch me together."

"It's better than an Army dude," Rick laughed. "But if you ask me—it would serve you right." He cocked an eyebrow. That admonishment followed an immediate hug—not a punch, not a set down—and not a mention made of lying, dying, or rising from the dead.

"Good to see you, man," Fitzwilliam said, clearly choked up.

"Yeah. Why don't we get on board and I'll take a look at Liz's nursing skills. You look like crap, Mr. Thornton."

"My back needs a few stitches. How good are you with a suture?"

"For you? Terrible!" Rick laughed.

He hugged Liz hello, and goodness it felt warm and strong, and completely reassuring that reinforcements had arrived.

"Hi, Sarah," Fitzwilliam greeted and she laughed. "I want you to know that I gave them all bloody hell when they were crucifying you."

"That's because you're a romantic," Liz replied with a hug.

"How are you, Liz?"

"Better now that he's alive!" She laughed, feeling suddenly giddy. "I'm pregnant."

"Oh! How wonderful! Congratulations!"

Of course, her husband looked like a proud peacock especially when Rick slapped him on the back with a hearty laugh. Fitzwilliam winced from the shot of pain. "Fucking Marine," he said under his breath.

Arm-in-arm, the girls walked toward Salvatore, chatting about their news, which included Sarah's own announcement of proposing to Rick. Ha! Liz knew they were in love!

But the cousins held back, needing their own moment to reconnect—and to clear the air. Through the crowded platform, she could feel Fitzwilliam's eyes burning into her back and turned to look at him over her shoulder.

He winked.

***

"I missed you, Darce," Rick admitted, like the sap Darcy always knew him to be. The man's voice trembled slightly as they watched their partners.

"I missed you all. How is Georgiana?"

"A wreck. I haven't told her yet."

"I'll be the one to tell her. It's my responsibility. I owe her at least that."

Shifting his weight, Darcy averted his gaze to the Pullman car beside them. Gratitude and apologies always came hardest. "Thanks for helping Liz through her trauma … and for what you did in Venice. Thanks for calling the team together to help me in the field."

"You're welcome. Look, I'm not mad, just disappointed, but I *do* understand."

"Do you? Sometimes, even I can't comprehend the depth of my love for her, the ends I'd go to keep her safe and make her happy every day that we're together."

"I can. That kind of love is an amazing thing … rare, I think … I mean … when you are willing to die for the one you love it's an overwhelming feeling."

Now he raised an eyebrow. "Yes it is."

"I'm leaving Obsidian and … Sarah and I are getting married."

Darcy felt released from guilt at that pronouncement. In the awareness of the safe passage he'd cleared for all their futures, the pain in his shoulder and his conscience was negligible.

"Would you die for her, Rick?"

"Yes, a thousand times, yes."

Again, his tender gaze fell to his wife's laughing countenance, his heart bursting with emotion. "Is your heart and mind so filled with her that she's all you think of? That the only place you ever want to be is by her side?"

"I never thought it could be so … but, yes."

"Then you *do* know *exactly* how I feel. Congratulations, cousin, just like I have, you've finally found your true and final mission in life."

Epilogue

June 16
Derbyshire, England

No bride could have asked for a more perfect day for her nuptials. What girl didn't dream of a romantic country wedding in the magnificent Peaks District of Northern England? In fact, to this no-longer newlywed's eye, its beauty resembled the location of her own wedding day, right down to the horses grazing in the west field and the lily-pad strewn pond.

One day, she'd sit with the gardener and design the landscaping and footbridge and fill that pond with Koi, but right now it was delegated to her to-do list along with the greenhouse. She currently had something much more pleasing in which to attend: her bundle of absolute love: Richard Darcy Thornton born ten weeks ago, at a monstrous 9 pounds, 6 ounces and 22 inches.

On this fine summer morning, Liz stood on the master suite balcony overlooking the lush landscape surrounding Helstone Manor, feeling as though she were admiring Leesburg, Virginia with its splash of bluebells at the height of their season and the splendor of Pemberley's wooded perimeter. From the hilly verdant eminence on which the manor majestically stood, she reflected on how she had always considered that there had never been such a place where nature had done more, or where natural beauty had not been altered by modern tastes than at Pemberley, but she was wrong. So similar were the two estates that she felt entirely at home. Her husband had planned it that way when he purchased Helstone for half of the 22 million he transferred to England before his departure for Bermuda.

She took a deep breath, closing her eyes for a few seconds, infusing her lungs with the sweet-scented air. A contented smile emerged from deep in her soul at the absolute euphoria she felt not just at this moment, or because there was a wedding about to take place, but because she felt safe and content and, admittedly a bit emotional—a result of adjusting hormones. Never had she felt so at peace, or so in love with life and with both of her fellas. Dumas—and her husband—were right: *"He who has felt the deepest grief is best able to experience supreme happiness."* Serenity had finally come to both their souls.

Her hand grasped the railing and she admired the huge, sparkling emerald ring hugging her simple—yet profoundly symbolic—gold wedding band, a gift from Fitzwilliam along with a new sketchbook when their son was born two months ago. *Fitzwilliam* ... he may have been John Thornton to 99% of the people in their circle, but he was still Fitzwilliam to her, but never Iceman ever again.

Bird song and chatter commingled with Mozart's "Piano Concerto No 21 (Elvira Madigan)" coming from the nursery behind her. Mallika and Kalendar Prince chased one another below her and she could see, in the distance, the colorful gardens and birdcage gazebo surrounded by white banners tickled by the breeze. The party planners were hard at work placing the final swags and floral touches on the two dozen chairs facing the gazebo—the place where another couple's forever journey would begin.

On the path below her window, Dixon walked beside a hedge of yellow roses toward the carriage-house-turned-apartment/security headquarters. The debonair-dressed man had cut his hair and was whistling a happy tune, and she smiled. Boy, his crustiness had sloughed off significantly since moving to the English countryside. Rumor had it (from her husband) that Dixon was seeing a woman in the village over.

"Howdy, Mrs. D," he said with a look up to her and a raise to his arm as he ambled by.

"Good morning, Marion!" she teased. "It's a beautiful day for a wedding, isn't it?"

"Sure is."

"You look very handsome today."

"Aw, go on with ya'. It's just a suit."

"It wasn't necessary to dress up. We're all family."

He stopped and shielded his eyes from the sun behind her when he gazed up to the balcony. "Yes we are, but keep calling me Marion and you'll be off my Christmas card list."

"Liar. Uncle Dixon would never leave the little man without his security detail."

"You got me there," he said, grinned then continued on his mission with a spring in his step and whistle on his lips.

"Babe, who are you talking to?" her husband asked, coming through the open French doors to join her.

"Dixon. He's in a great mood today."

"We all are."

Her breath caught when she turned, gazing at the picture Fitzwilliam presented: dancing dark eyes and a smile that swelled her heart. Looking so dashing, he wore a gray suit and pink tie and the most endearing accessory: the baby blue layette blanket draped over his shoulder. But it was the image of what he held that caused her wide grin. Their chubby boy—their pride and joy lay spread out on his father's right arm, happily sucking on his bottle without a fuss as Fitzwilliam held it to his mouth.

Her husband had the magic touch in keeping their son calm, cool, and collected. Fatherhood, like motherhood, seemed to come naturally to them, but her husband's protective concern allowed her to get some much needed rest in Richard's every two hour feeding demands.

"The caterer is asking for you," he said.

"Are you sure they need me? Maybe Gigi can handle it? I mean … I would like to hold my son for at least *five* minutes this morning before the barrage of aunts, uncles, and grandparents wake up and get a hold of him. I am Richard's mother after all, darling." She teased, cocking an eyebrow, which he understood very well. "Between you, our sisters, and Dixon, he probably won't recognize me after this week!"

A sigh of pretended disappointment left his lips. "I *suppose* you can hold him," he teased back. Bending down over their son's head, his lips met hers, lingering with a moan. Oh, she knew that particular moan. It's been a looong twelve weeks of abstinence for them.

"No," she lied in response to his moan, having every intention of seducing him tonight after the wedding.

He waggled his eyes and whispered, "When?"

"When you least expect it, sexy."

He waggled his eyes again. "Tonight? When there is romance in the air?"

"Perhaps. Although … I don't think the timing is ideal. Unless, of course, you want to build the muscles in *both* arms in another nine months—just when your shoulder is feeling good, now you want another chubbster draped over it!

"We won't get pregnant so soon."

"Yes we will. I'm not breast-feeding, and it's not like we use birth control."

She loved teasing and goading him and thoroughly enjoyed his frustrated grunt. Fitzwilliam removed the bottle from the baby's mouth and she bent, kissing the little one's head with a brush to his dark hair. "My precious sweetness; I don't think you're ready to share Daddy's attentive hogging with a sibling, are you?"

"Hey, I have no problem with a repeat performance. In fact, there's a case of 2008 Spottswoode Cabernet on the tables down there."

"Ha. Ha! Again with the wine. It *wasn't* the wine, Fitzwilliam, and might I remind you of the 23 hours of labor in which I swore to kill you at least a half a dozen and divorce you at least 48 times?"

"The thought of getting pregnant so soon … or shot … or death … or divorce … will not keep me away from you—not even your knives or lethal tongue, savage woman. Not in the past, not now, not ever." He kissed her again then seductively whispered into her ear with longing in his voice. "I miss you, Lizzy," before turning from her—with the baby *still* in his arms.

The butterflies in her stomach fluttered at how he breathed "Lizzy." Yeah, she was going to love him passionately—maybe even on this very balcony after their guests retired for the night. Although, she did expect the partying to continue into the wee-hours of the morning. Maybe she'd even have wine.

Stopping at the crib, he turned to her with an unmistakable grin. "Tonight, Lakmé, when there's romance in the air and after I ply you with copious amounts of that Spottswoode—"

"And a foot massage," she interrupted.

"*And* a foot massage … expect me to seduce you."

"Baby, I don't need all that enticement. I just need the promise of your extremely talented *Chironius carinatus.*"

He laughed. "*That's* what gave us Ricky!"

She chortled, fully in agreement and open to the idea of expanding their family but, of course, she wouldn't tell him that! "Please stop calling him Ricky."

"We'll see what his uncle has to say about it."

"Ha! I'd say that today of all days, Rick'll be quite agreeable to anything you say."

***

There were times in Fitzwilliam Darcy's life when he had considered a bullet to his own head was the only recourse in finding peace. The demons had chased him from the day he learned that his mother betrayed her family with his best friend, directing him toward a path of vengeance and death until he met her ... Elizabeth Bennet.

Those dark days were gone—banished forever—never to return. She'd been his salvation when he was too focused on revenge to even realize that he needed saving. She was his life and breath and because of that he'd always go to extremes to ensure her happiness and safety, but he'd never be lulled into a false sense of security even if Operation Black Ice ended with him the victor. Here at Helstone, he'd taken the same security measures as they had in Pemberley because, frankly, the world was filled with assholes doing dangerous things and his family's safety was paramount. But he was confident that Iceman's past was dead and buried. No one would come calling. No one would find them. Liz Darcy had disappeared before leaving for Europe, never to be seen again. And when they'd stepped off their final train in Victoria Station, the Thorntons had emerged hand-in-hand, blending in with every other Briton heading toward their home. Although he'd been worse for the wear and in need of medical care beyond a temporary combat fix, they'd strode to the limousine waiting for them with Nick Higgins installed in the driver's seat.

Just as he had promised, a new dawn ... a new day.

The swell of pride filled his heart as he stood as best man beside Rick and Sarah in the 19th Century birdcage gazebo adorned with yellow roses and ivy.

He'd never seen his cousin look so fulfilled. The man's ruddy complexion beamed with joy and his relaxed body language indicated that he was comfortable in his decision to marry, and freed from a future of death-dealing, instead uniting to one of life-giving. Marriage to this woman—someone who adored him and cared for him above all things—would suit him well. Their relationship, born in the worst of circumstances, had proven serendipitous, just as it had for Liz and him.

"Best man?" he and Rick had joked with still a little sting in his cousin's voice about his deceit. Hardly the "best", but Liz and Ricky thought so and that's what mattered. It had been a long few months of making up to the men in his life, especially the military men; the women were more forgiving of his solo mission—even Caroline. Two days ago they had arrived at Helstone for the wedding, and an immediate no-holds-barred fight was called; the guys took it to the mats where he got a proper beat down by all of them. Sure, they were sympathetic to his rehabbed shoulder, but not enough to cut slack to the rest of his body. He still hurt from Charlie's roundhouse kick to his ribs and Justin's guillotine wrestling move. Still, it was in good fun and he fully understood—and expecting nothing less.

His gaze settled on the wedding couple's clasped hands and he listened to Rick's prideful recitation of his vows, loud and clear for all to hear. The future in-laws looked on with joy at the former Marine who saved their daughter from death, the Amazon … or worse at the hands of Diablo's butchers. Sarah's sister, the maid-of-honor, cried in equal measure as Georgiana, seated beside Liz in the first row. Maybe his sister's tears were pregnancy tears. He was familiar with how that worked, and both he and Liz were happy for her and Justin's news. But man, his sister's beat down of him for "dying" was just as ugly as Charlie's, only she went for a verbal lashing guilt trip prior to her absolution—followed by more tears.

Wearing a strapless gown and a delicate floral tiara, Sarah looked every inch the classic English Rose. Today two dozen guests were witness to something akin to his and Liz's nuptials. Private and meaningful, the day was about the vows and the power of commitment to another until the end of time, not the party afterward—even if Liz had outdone herself in the planning of both weddings.

As the bride professed her vows with a tremble in her voice, he looked out to Liz cradling their son in her arms. Their eyes met. *So beautiful; so absolutely breathtaking.* She was stunning because her serenity and bliss came from inside her. She was happy and didn't have a care in the world beyond doting on Ricky—and him—and doing everything that brought her enjoyment. Unconsciously, his chest swelled with pride. He did that. He'd made her happy. She told him so. This life they now led was what they'd always dreamed of.

A little wink preceded the slow movement of her luscious lips as she mouthed "Tonight. Sex" and he bit back his laugh. How could he deserve this halcyon life after all his many sins, no matter how noble the intent or at ease his conscience felt at his end of the rifle?

Prayers for the couple offered by the pastor floated out to the guests and up to the heavens. He lifted his own prayers asking for blessings upon his cousin's marriage and adding some of his own intentions. Not that he was a religious man, but what better time to give thanks. He continued to hold Liz's gaze, recalling the last time he'd prayed they were in that hillside chapel in Santorini. Made in the silence of their hearts before the cliff jump, their petitions had mirrored the other's: to create life from their love.

Thank you, God for bringing Liz and me together. Thank you for the many second chances you've blessed my family with. Thank you for the most incredible wife and son and a family of true friends. Thank you for this new beginning. Please help me to be the absolute best husband and father I can be and help me to always keep them safe.

He wondered if Bennet had asked the same given the smile on his face, seated beside his ex-wife. Ah, forgiveness was a tricky thing—the man had attained absolution from him for his assistance—but it meant wiping the slate clean for his past offenses to Liz. If she could entirely move on and forgive both her parents, then so must he. She put it all in a box when her father guided her through Prague with reassurances and calmness. In the light of a new day, she'd considered that Operation Black Ice had protected their baby's future—and that was more than enough. Grudges were a thing of the past now and, just as he had with Wickham, he needed to put it *all* behind him to maintain peace. Living in the moment was his and Liz's credo.

One row behind Liz and the baby, the redheaded viper sat beside Higgins, and based on their roaming hands at last night's not-so-bachelor party the two were a hot and heavy item this morning. In fact, Caroline looked clingy and in awe of the take-no-shit-from-anyone guy. Perhaps she had finally moved on from her lust for Iceman. It had always been Iceman she wanted—never Fitzwilliam. Only one woman succeeded in breaking through to the man he'd pushed so far down below and she wanted him, redeemed him with her love and trust before it was too late.

Among the onlookers to this auspicious event, Knightley sat beside Charlie and Jane. Only two of the three remained in the employment of the newly reformed "Obsidian," renamed "Benzaiten" under Caroline's direction. Darcy had laughed aloud when he heard the name, and while his two friends thought it was some funky ore like obsidian, he wouldn't be the one to tell them that it was a Japanese water snake goddess. He still hated snakes!

As for his sister-in-law, she wanted nothing to do with her former employer and had now taken up the charge to get Charlie to pack it in before their wedding at Christmas. As Liz repeatedly stated, "reality is a bitch; it's a real life, friggin' opera" and Pussy Galore had a frightening taste of it.

In the romance department, everyone came up a winner, even Knightley. Iceman's death inspired him to jump feet first into a relationship with Fanny the receptionist. Unfortunately, she could not be invited to the wedding. The Thorntons lived out in the open and she knew them as the now-dead Darcys—one at the bottom of Hungry Bay and the other in a motorcycle accident in Europe.

The only ones outside of immediate family and Obsidian that were let in on the Thorntons' not-so-little-secret were the Reynoldses, Dixon, and Higgins because they were family, too, and would take it to the grave.

He smiled at the pastor's pronouncement of husband and wife and then kiss—what a kiss! His cousin was off to a perfect start.

***

"Who knew that you were such a good dancer," Liz admired as Knightley spun her around the floor at the intimate reception. The baby was safe in his grandmother's arms and there was laughter in the air. A feeling of palpable happiness filled Helstone's magnificent ballroom as the band played, and the 19th Century mirrored panels reflected their smiling faces.

"Hey, I do work for a dance school, and my days in Monte Carlo were spent … among other things … charming the ladies. Can't have two left feet in that town."

"Gosh, we've missed you."

"Yeah. It just ain't right without you and—ahem—Thornton around. Do you like it here?"

"We love it. It's sort of liberating to leave all our baggage on another continent and start fresh."

He turned her under his arm and said, "Wish I could do that but I'm working on it."

"So I hear. She's a lovely girl."

"I think so. She's honest about herself and her opinions; she's kind to me. It's refreshing."

"It certainly is. But, will you consider staying with us another week and not rush back to her? I have to admit I'm feeling a little jealous. I mean, I don't know when we'll see you again."

"Can't do. Crash's plane is scheduled to drop me off in Paris for a quadrille lesson."

Another turn and she could feel Fitzwilliam's eyes burning her skin. She nonchalantly glanced over her shoulder and spied him standing at the edge of the dance floor like he was ready to pounce on Knightley. But she laughed to herself, ignoring him so she could finish the dance.

"Charlie did a great thing by flying everyone here in the middle of the night to avoid the airports, not to mention providing and creating aliases and documents. He has an amazing talent as a cobbler," she said.

"Your sister is trying to get him to do it full-time and pull him out of the field."

"I hate to say it to you, but I agree with her! Maybe you should think about it, too."

"Nah. I like offing assholes."

"Liar!"

They danced in silence for a minute until she cleared her throat. "You know, John, I never properly thanked you for everything you did for me in those dark days."

"It was my honor to be there for you, and I knew you needed to work everything out in your own time. The last thing you needed was me hanging around 24/7."

"Strange how life works, huh?"

"Strange that big oaf staring us down is a father now."

"And great at it, too. Mark my words, Richard will be his little Mini-Me."

"I'm real happy for you both. You deserve it all." The song ended with another turn under his arm and then a dip—and just to get a rise out of Fitzwilliam, he kissed her. "That should piss him off good."

Sure enough, her husband stood over them in the middle of the dance floor, with a smirk on his lips and humor in his voice. "If this wasn't a wedding I'd beat you to a pulp, Mr. Clean."

"One kiss from your stunning wife was all the payment I needed for saving your ass in Cadiz."

"One kiss from her is worth a hell of a lot more than that."

Fitzwilliam signaled the band and they began a familiar song from that incredible night under the stars: Van Morrison's "Someone Like You."

She laughed, "You're such a mush, Fitzwilliam."

"No. I'm just trying to get into your pants."

"No … you're just a romantic."

The guests and the bride and groom gathered around them, giving them the floor in a spotlight dance that was so much more than a dance between husband and wife. All but Sarah's family, whom they'd only just met, knew what they'd gone through and how important dancing in his arms was to her. Several guests knew that it had been a tango dance lesson that changed their lives, but only she and Fitzwilliam knew of their moonlit dance before he "died." She would never forget that night for as long as she lived.

He took her in his arms and when his hand clasped hers, an electric current traveled through her. They swayed at first, her body moving in perfect unison with every step and motion he made as though brushing through the blades of grass and oxe-eye daisies. He said nothing, just gazed at her with the most endearing smile. His dark eyes spoke volumes to her, and she could see every emotion displayed in them like the stars that had filled the sky that magical night.

"No tango?" she whispered.

"Not today, Lakmé."

His feet glided across the floor, leading her—as he had these last two years since finding each other. But he didn't really need to lead anymore … she anticipated each step he made. Connected, they danced in coordinated bliss. Never had she felt such absolute completeness and unfathomable intimacy before.

"Why no tango today?" she asked as he turned her under his arm. When she came back into his embrace, he lowered his lips and pulled her against his body. Her feet stepped beside his as if one body in one space.

"Because the spirit and passion of the tango is meant to heal strangers ... or lovers ... through conflict and mistrust. I think we're beyond that now. You transformed me into a better man."

Smiling, she playfully replied, "I see. So the tango is reserved for when we argue?"

"Can you think of a more satisfying, passionate way to make-up after one of our disagreements?"

"Oh yes I can, lover," she laughed.

He stopped dancing and kissed her in a delicious tingle that traveled straight to her womanhood. Their family cheered with cat calls and claps and the song swirled around them like a cocoon.

"Let's skip the argument," she breathed, when their lips parted. "Grab a bottle of Cabernet and I'll meet you upstairs."

Have you enjoyed **The Conscience Series**? If you have, please stop on by the Facebook Page and give a like!
www.facebook.com/DenialofConscience

Or share your positive reading experience with others in book review on your favorite platform.

Thank you for taking the ride!

Glossary

Agency - Central Intelligence Agency (CIA)

Bang and Burn - Demolition and sabotage operation

Bel Canto - Italian: beautiful singing

Conflitto - Italian: conflict

Cariño - darling, honey

Comercializador - arranges meetings between two or more cartel members that don't do business together directly

Cruzador - assassin sent to another country for hit

Deuce and a half - military nickname for 2 ½ ton truck

E and E - Escape and evade

El Fantasma - The ghost

Faida - Italian: feud

Five Eyes - The Five Eyes, often abbreviated as FVEY, is an intelligence alliance comprising Australia, Canada, New Zealand, the United Kingdom, and the United States.

Foxes - Cartel member in police department

Goombahs - Italian slang: friend, comrade

HAHO - High Altitude High Opening military parachuting

Inferno - Hell

Jefe - Boss

Jefe de Jefes - Boss of Bosses

Klicks - .62 miles in military lingo

Mikes - Minutes

Mil-dot - Within rifle scope, helps to calculate distance to target

Overwatch - Provides cover for the unit

Railroad Apartment – 4 or 5 room train car layout, a hallway runs alongside

Ring out - Signals quitting SEAL training during Hell Week by ringing bell

SCIF - Sensitive Compartmented Information Facility

Scopa - Italian card game

Soap makers - cocaine manufacturer

Sock puppet - Online identity for deception

Sombrillas - Umbrellas, cover protection

TOR - The Onion Router

Music References

"Shake it Off," Taylor Swift

"Back in Black," AC/DC

"Enter Sandman," Metallica

"Black Ice," AC/DC

"I Stand Alone," Godsmack

"Concerto No. 2 in G Minor (Summer)" *The Four Seasons*, Antonio Vivaldi

"Make a Memory," Bon Jovi

"These Arms of Mine," Otis Redding

"Someone Like You," Van Morrison

"My Immortal," Evanescence

"Scheherazade," by Nikolai Rimsky-Korsakov

"For Your Precious Love," Otis Redding

"Serenata D957, Ständchen," Franz Shubert

"Trumpet Concerto Allegro," Joseph Haydn

"The Flower Duet," Opera Lakmé by Léo Delibes

"Shoot to Thrill," AC/DC

"Flute Concerto No. 2 in D Major," Amadeus Mozart

"The Humming Chorus," Opera *Madama Butterfly* by Giacomo Puccini

"Un bel dì," Opera *Madama Butterfly*, Giacomo Puccini

"Piano Concerto No 21 (Elvira Madigan)" Amadeus Mozart

"Embraceable You," George Gershwin

"Isn't it Romantic," Richard Rogers

Note: List is inspirational and is not meant to convey or imply musician's endorsement of novel

Acknowledgements

When I introduced Iceman to his destiny in *Denial of Conscience*, I had never intended on a series, but I fell in love with our protective alpha-male and how he fell in love with his Lakmé. They are two characters who wrote themselves in each of the three and half books, and I oddly feel they deserve thanks for taking me along on their international, dangerous escapades to places that I only dreamed of going. These three years, I have lived vicariously through Liz and am so utterly happy they have found a place of serenity now. And, of course, I have to thank Jane Austen for inspiring me through the wonderful characters in her books.

Thank you to all the readers who have joined me in these fantastic adventures and to those in Iceman's fan club (you know who you are!) I value every one of you and feel immense gratitude for your support and enthusiasm.

My heartfelt appreciation goes to my editor and friend Kristi, who is always at the ready to get to work on our latest project. Thank you for striving to keep "my voice," and for attempting to teach me (even though I'm slow to wrap my head around modifiers, semi-colons, and comma usage.) You, my dear, have helped to publish the best book we can to readers through your dedication and professionalism! *Smooch*

Thank you Debbie and Gail for the generous time you took to beta IGC's raw manuscript, offering invaluable insight and excitement while patiently awaiting updates as I researched and attended to other spinning plates. *Hug*

And of course, I could never have finished this series if not for my personal cheerleaders: Mom, Dad, Pamela, and Sheryl. Thank you for believing in me when I didn't believe in myself!

And to my own Mr. Darcy, Bill: 25 years of coordination and bliss I love you!

About the Author

Cat Gardiner loves romance and happy endings, history, comedy, and Jane Austen. A member of the National League of American Pen Women and a PAN member of Romance Writers of America, she enjoys writing across the spectrum of Pride and Prejudice inspired romance novels. From the comedic Christmas, Chick Lits Lucky 13 and Villa Fortuna, to the sultry Conscience Series bad boy biker Darcy, these contemporary novels will appeal to many Mr. Darcy lovers.

Cat's love of 20th Century Historical fiction merges in her first Pride & Prejudice "alternate era," set in a 1952 Noir, Undercover. Her greatest love is writing Historical Fiction, WWII–era Romance and it is in Memories of Old Antique Shop Series where she has merged her two loves: WWII and P&P with time-travel in three novelettes. The fourth is on its way!

Historical fiction devotees will thoroughly enjoy Cat's debut WWII epic novel, A Moment Forever, a 2017 Next Generation Indie Book Award Romance Finalist. She is currently working on her second novel in the Liberty Victory Collection.

Connect with Cat
facebook.com/cat.t.gardiner
vanityandpridepress.com / twitter.com/VPPressNovels
cgardiner1940s.com / twitter.com/40sexperience

Vanity & Pride Press

AUSTEN-INSPIRED ROMANCE BY CAT GARDINER

The Conscience Series
Contemporary, Romantic Adventure
Denial of Conscience, Book 1
Guilty Conscience, Bonus Vignettes
Without a Conscience, Book 2
In Good Conscience, Book 3

Conscience Rising – E-book Boxset Bundle
The Conscience Series – Books 1-3

Time & Again Antique Shop Series
Contemporary, WWII-era, Time-travel Novelettes
Vintage Valentine
Vintage Victory
Vintage Halloween
Vintage Beginning
Seasons in Time: e-book & Paperback Bundle
Books 1-4

Undercover – An Austen Noir
Mid-20th Century, Steamy romance, Mystery

Villa Fortuna – Pride, Prejudice, & a Haircut
Contemporary romantic comedy, Holiday
* Honorable Mention, 2016 Hollywood Book Festival

Lucky 13 – Matchmaking & Misunderstandings
Contemporary romantic comedy, Holiday

HISTORICAL FICTION ROMANCE BY CAT GARDINER

A Moment Forever
An unforgettable WWII Historical Fiction Epic Romance
* Romance Finalist, 2017 Next Generation Indie Book Awards

AUSTEN-INSPIRED HISTORICAL ROMANCE BY PAMELA LYNNE

Dearest Friends
A heartwarming Regency Romance
* Bronze Medalist, 2016 IPPY Award in Romance

Family Portraits
Romantic Regency, a Dearest Friends continuation

Sketching Character
A compelling Regency Romance